Midnight
Confessions II

Midnight Confessions II

BONNIE EDWARDS

APHRODISIA

KENSINGTON BOOKS

http://www.kensingtonbooks.com

APHRODISIA BOOKS are published by

Kensington Publishing Corp.
850 Third Avenue
New York, NY 10022

ISBN-13: 978-0-7582-1421-8
ISBN-10: 0-7582-1421-9

First Kensington Trade Paperback Printing: June 2007

10 9 8 7 6 5 4 3 2 1

Printed in the United States of America

1

Faye Grantham placed her cheek next to the smooth pine planking of the wall and peered through a peephole set at eye level. The angle of the hole gave her a perfect view of the bed in the next room. Odd how she already knew it would look like this. The walls were in shadow, with the bed spotlighted.

All she could see was the bed and a couple standing beside it. Their faces were obscured. The woman wore her long blond hair in a fall of cascading white and cream. Faye couldn't make out her face behind the curtain of lustrous hair.

She fingered her own shoulder-length waves. Hers were shorter, but the color was similar.

The man's upper face was in shadow. His jaw, strong and lightly bristled, glowed from the odd lighting. His mouth, mobile and hard, dipped in and out of the light so Faye couldn't see it clearly. A mystery couple about to do unmysterious things.

The man untied the laces at the bodice of the woman's nightgown to let it drift and skim down her body to her feet. White, cotton, chaste, the nightgown gave no clue to what era they were in.

The man wore trousers, but his chest was bare. Suspenders dangled at his hips. His erection strained for freedom until the woman guided it to peek out the top of his waistband.

Yum. Great chest, slim hips, hard belly, and a wide head on his cock. Faye responded as if she were the one cupping his balls and feeling his hot thumbs swirl across her nipples.

Odd, but pleasurable, the sensation of his callused hands aroused her.

Hot! She was suddenly aroused beyond tolerance by the seductively slow foreplay she witnessed through the peephole. She slid her hand to her crotch and pressed a fingertip to her clit through her thin silk nightie. She was wet and needy and the finger pressure made it better, but she still couldn't ease her need. She pressed harder, rubbed.

The narrow passageway she stood in closed in around her as she caught her breath. The man, naked now and gloriously hard, pressed the woman's shoulders down. She sank to her knees and took him into her mouth. Drew him in deep.

Faye's mouth worked in conjunction as she watched the woman suck him deep into her throat. Faye tasted hot manflesh and swirled her tongue around her mouth, feeling him.

Slowly, carefully, the man pumped into her mouth while the woman continued to lick. He was big and she had to adjust, but eventually, she took most of his full length.

The man's face was still in shadow and he hadn't spoken. Silent but for the sound of mouth work, lit from a spotlight, the two performed while Faye watched through the bullet-sized hole. The man pumped harder; the woman's head bobbed more quickly. Tension rose around the silent couple, while Faye's arousal deepened.

Faye closed her eyes in passion while she worked to bring herself closer to climax. Next time she could focus, the couple had climbed onto the bed and were writhing together, with deep kisses and rough and ready hands. Still, no more sounds came to Faye. No bedsprings, no sighs or moans torn from the amorous pair.

The woman's pale calves flashed in the dim light from the bedside lamps, as she raised them to offer herself to her lover. Was this *her* room? Was she watching herself with Liam?

The long, slick invasion stretched her wide and she felt the man enter her, knew what the woman knew. The man's heated scent, the feel of his weight on her chest, the incredible stretch of his cock as he pressed her deep into the mattress.

Faye rolled her hips in acceptance and began the dance of need.

Vaguely, she understood she was dreaming. In Perdition House, anything could happen, and often did. She lived with ghosts who saw nothing wrong with siphoning off her orgasms, inciting her to sex with strangers, and causing wild, insatiable desires to bubble under her skin.

Pleasure rose under her hand as she played voyeur and rubbed at her pussy. Suddenly, her nightie slid off her shoulders and drifted away on a breeze that caressed her heated flesh as she watched the lovers, moaned along with them, and felt every sensation they did.

She fought the rising tide, trying to see whose room they were in. As she focused her eyes away from the couple, the details of the room came clearer. Past the bed, light shone on a wallpaper design decades old.

With no French doors, no staircase to a widow's walk on the roof, it wasn't her room. Hers was larger, airier, prettier.

Comforted, she settled in to watch, unable to tear her eyes away even though the couple deserved their privacy. After all, the man had paid for it.

The light in the room dimmed, but still the wall danced with the lovers' shadows, grotesquely erotic. A woman prone, her legs raised, the man's head at her crotch. Finally, she heard sucking and licking sounds as the man pleasured the woman.

The lover's lips and tongue slid harder against her tender flesh, wilder and wilder until the woman crested and moaned, eyes closed, in a low, deep, delicious orgasm that pulsed out in waves from her lowest reaches. Faye rode out the come, closed her eyes, and melted and shook along with the lovers.

A sudden scream rent the air, ripping into Faye. The piercing wail came through the wall, clear as a chime and full of terror.

Faye opened her eyes and tried to see what had happened, who had screamed, but the light in the room was suddenly bright as a cloudless day and hurt her eyes. She could see nothing, and all sound faded.

She rolled over and woke, fading pulses the only proof that she'd dreamed again.

A nap—it had all happened during a nap. Groggy and sated from the still-pulsing orgasm, she rose to her elbow to look at the bedside clock. She had two hours. Lots of time.

She stretched, still shaken by what she'd heard. This dream was different from her usually pleasant unfolding stories. She could hardly make sense of it.

The narrow, secret passageway ran between two bedrooms on the second floor. She'd been in there once. The peepholes were installed by the original madam who built the house. She and a troupe of intrepid women had come to Seattle from Butte, Montana. They'd operated an exclusive men's retreat that catered only to the very wealthy and powerful.

Retreat being a polite word for the country's most expensive whorehouse of the last century. Completed in 1911, Perdition House was now hers, left to her by her great-aunt, Mae Grantham, who in turn had inherited it from the original madam, Belle Grantham.

Faye had decided to sell and cash in on her inheritance.

The only obstacle to that decision—Belle still lived here, as did the original four prostitutes. Salacious spirits, the five of them wreaked havoc on Faye's libido.

Not that she minded all that much. What red-blooded woman wouldn't want three or four orgasms a day, she reasoned.

Faye had moved into the mansion and discovered Perdition House was a place of sin, sex, and secrets.

Faye loved every minute of living here.

Logic dictated that the screamer in this dream was one of the women who'd worked here. She hadn't recognized the woman, though, except that the color of her hair was so similar to Faye's.

She couldn't trust anything she'd seen in a dream anyway. Her great-aunt Belle would have done anything to keep Perdition House going when she was alive. Now that she was dead, she was even more determined. Belle manipulated everyone who came here with sexual need and sleight-of-hand.

"Are you sure what you heard was a frightened scream? It might have just been a rapturous climax." Belle, her dead-for-decades great-great aunt, suggested.

For the moment, the beautiful spirit was perched on the staircase to the widow's walk, one of her favorite spots to sit.

"I don't know," Faye said, no longer fazed by speaking with a long-dead madam. "Maybe it was just a lusty come. Why not tell me what happened? Why the secrecy?"

Stupid question. The keeping of secrets was the backbone of Perdition House. Its whole structure was propped up by secrets.

"Oh, Faye, if I told you everything at once, we'd never have any fun." Her aunt's serene smile said it all. The woman enjoyed sending Faye dreams of tantalizing bits and pieces of the lives lived in Perdition. They unfolded like story lines out of a confession magazine: "How I Found Myself Working in a Whorehouse and Loving It."

Belle had reasons for everything she did, and if she wanted to keep the story behind the screaming woman to herself for a while, so be it. Her aunt didn't have an impulsive bone in her long-dead body. All Faye had to do was wait. Eventually, Belle would tire of playing with her and the truth would come out.

"Smart girl," Belle said with a slight lift to her lips.

Faye blew her a raspberry and threw off the covers. She padded through to the adjoining bathroom to get ready for her date with the deliciously sexy and accommodating Mark.

She hadn't meant to nap, but when the spirits insisted, she couldn't refuse. The dreams had turned her into a prurient hedonist with two lovers; Mark, a down-and-dirty businessman from Denver, and Liam, a lawyer in her auntie's law firm.

Two lovers was down from three, but her repressed, boring ex-fiancé, Colin, hardly counted in the sexual satisfaction department. It still bothered her that he'd been boffing his slut of a receptionist while she'd been convinced their ho-hum sex life was her fault.

She set those thoughts aside. No point dwelling on her disappointments. Not when life had taken such an interesting turn. "Still," she said, "living with a bunch of horny spirits is a pain." She spoke to the empty bathroom.

At least she assumed it was empty. There hadn't been any cold drafts or shadowy movement behind her yet and Belle hadn't followed her. "But I love you all," she amended, meaning it.

She showered quickly, mentally picking out her outfit for her date with Mark, the first man with whom she'd released her inner sex imp.

She'd found him in a hotel bar on a night she'd planned as a one-night stand with a stranger to discover whether her sexual inadequacies were actually hers. Turns out, they weren't.

Mark had taught her to enjoy her sexuality, to revel in wild abandon and have fun with the act. Colin the pencil-dick had nearly convinced her she was a sexual dud. Mark's attentions had cleared the path for a rebirth inside Faye. The new woman she was owed him a lot.

She was afraid their one-night stand would turn into more.

Which would be fabulous, if she wasn't already sleeping with Liam Watson, of Watson, Watson and Sloane, the law firm that had handled Auntie Mae's estate. Watson the Elder had been her aunt's lawyer, while Liam had been electrically hot at first sight.

She filled her toothbrush with paste and hit the button. Around the vibrating buzz, she considered her options. Sex with Mark was incredibly intense and liberating. He'd taught her more in one night than she'd ever known.

He was supposed to be back home in Denver, fading into a luscious memory while she enjoyed herself with Liam.

But in the farce she was now calling her life, he'd decided to go into retail outlets with his wholesale business—starting with Seattle. Which had brought him straight back into her life.

His expression when he looked at her was warm and affectionate. She liked Mark, admired his business acumen, and loved his sexual prowess.

She hit the shower and washed her hair in record time, then couldn't decide what to wear. With an entire vintage clothing store to pick among, she most often dressed in Hollywood castoffs. Clothes that had once belonged to the blond bombshells of the 50s and 60s suited her fair hair and heavy breasts best, but there were times she liked to play with a retro-hippie look.

Sunset-orange light beamed in through the lacy white curtains as she combed out her damp hair. She wanted long, straight hair tonight, parted in the middle. Straight bangs, too.

Belle appeared, preening prettily in the mirror Faye used. She frowned and peered closely at Faye from the mirror. "Straight hair? That's unusual."

Faye stuck out her tongue. "Yes, as long as it doesn't rain or get damp, it'll be straight."

"This is Seattle, honey, it won't be straight for long. What will Mark think?" Belle asked with a teasing glint in her eye.

"I have no idea. He loves it when I go with a fifties look, and I do so enjoy playing the sex kitten." She pouted her lips into a kiss. "Mohair sweaters and cantilevered bras, platform sling-backs and tight knee-length skirts make me feel sexy and available. But this mini-skirt makes me feel young and hot." She smoothed the wide white belt at her waist.

"Young, hot, and ready." Belle's smile turned sultry.

Faye was ready all the time these days.

Ready. Willing. Available.

Faye cleared her throat. "Thanks to you and the others, I'm a far cry from the repressed woman I was before I moved into the mansion. But that doesn't give you the right to keep pushing my libido into overdrive."

Rather than invite Mark here, she preferred to see him at his hotel. Except for Belle, who could tap into Faye no matter where she was, the spirits' influence decreased the farther away she was from the mansion.

"So," Belle chimed in, "what's on for tonight? Dancing? Dinner?"

"Dinner and then, with any luck he'll love this style so much he won't be able to keep his hands off me."

The madam enjoyed a spicy orgasm through Faye once in a while. All the spirits did. "I hope the outfit works, too," Belle murmured.

"The sex-kitten look is sultry, but I wanted to go for fun tonight. It's good to keep a man guessing." Especially Mark, who'd shocked the hell out of her by calling out of the blue.

She finished straightening her hair and slicked on a heavy black eyeliner, making sure to give it an upward lift at the outer corner of each eyelid. Catty.

Belle gave her a final inspection. "I like it."

"Great, now would you mind getting out of the mirror? I can't see to check my eyebrows. It's disconcerting to lean in close to the glass and have you looking back at me." She shooed at the mirror. "I need to check my brows, not yours."

Belle obliged by floating beside her instead.

"Thanks."

"You're welcome."

Faye continued to prepare for Mark, thinking of his hands, his lips, his teeth scraping lightly over her nipples. He so loved her breasts. She softened between her legs and felt the telltale slide of moisture that came with thoughts of him.

Their brief affair should have faded into a pleasant memory, but it looked as if it was off to a roaring start.

"I never thought Mark would fade away," said Belle, responding to Faye's inner dialogue. A habit that proved living with horny spirits was a pain. "He likes you too much."

"Maybe it would have been better if he'd decided against expanding his business and moving to Seattle. I wouldn't have to choose between him and Watson the Younger."

"Liam Watson's a lovely man: well-built, well-hung, and isn't afraid to show his kind heart. I'm impressed that he takes on hard-luck cases."

"This comment from a woman who prefers bad boys?" she asked, with a smirk at her dead lookalike.

For a lawyer, Liam Watson was a kind, compassionate man. A man Faye could fall for.

"You don't need to choose between them, Faye. A woman's entitled to take her time and more than entitled to take a second lover if one man isn't enough."

"If I wasn't providing all of you with your orgasms, one man would be enough!" Perhaps Belle was right. There was no reason to rush to a decision.

She wasn't committed to either man. Neither had they made

any commitment to her. Mark had slept with her knowing she was engaged. Besides, she was having fun with each of them.

Liam, soft-hearted and more open to fun sex and maybe even to the spirits, was a great guy.

But something dark in Mark appealed to her too. He was more intense, harder, brisker, and she admired his business sense and sharp intelligence. In truth, she didn't know enough about either man to make a choice.

She decided to keep things light. That way, no one would get hurt. If things got serious with either Mark or Liam, she'd tread carefully.

"I'm just out of a five-year relationship," she said to Belle. "I'm not ready for commitment." Not to anything more than opening a new store to help pay for the repairs to the mansion.

That had to be her priority.

Belle smirked. Faye glared back and slicked on a pale pink lip gloss. She pouted into the mirror to see if it caught the light and made her lips more kissable.

Belle didn't need an explanation—she could read Faye's thoughts—but still, Faye needed to vent. "Liam's a sweetie. And I like that he already has a sense that you're here. He responded very well when he heard Lizzie laughing out in the trees by the gazebo. I think he might even come to accept you're all here some day."

"But you're not sure about Mark's reaction?"

"Exactly. Sooner or later he's going to want to see the house. I don't know how to handle that unless you promise to leave him alone."

Belle rolled her eyes. "I can only speak for myself."

"Yeah, right."

She never knew when one of the spirits would act up or get cute. They loved men and loved sex. And Lizzie, in particular, enjoyed turning up the heat.

"How much does Liam know?" Belle asked.

"He's intrigued by the house, by what he senses here. He liked it when Lizzie got us hot and bothered out in the gazebo."

"We all liked that. It took, what, all of thirty seconds to have you writhing on the floor? I must say Liam's size was quite a shock."

She and Liam had been so hot for each other they'd barely had time for hello. Since then, their friendship had developed. She'd visited him in his office for another round, then he'd stayed with her in the mansion overnight. The man was a bull in the manly endowments department. Her mouth watered just thinking about him.

Faye turned and leaned against the sink and crossed her arms. "He heard Lizzie giggling but didn't care that we might have an audience. Then, the next day in his office he told me he has sex whenever and wherever the need strikes." A pearl of desire slid low in her body. "I've been thinking of testing that statement."

The room chilled as more of the spirits joined Faye and Belle. They could ice up a room in no time. Faye had taken to keeping sweaters all over the house, in spite of the warm spring they were having.

Felicity, pretty in green velvet with her lustrous brown hair swept into a Gibson Girl hairdo, drifted into the bathroom from the adjoining bedroom. At least she arrived through doorways. Annie, a tomboy at heart, sometimes jumped down from the ceiling, scaring the hell out of Faye.

And Hope, the most tenderhearted of the troupe, often smelled of cinnamon, cloves, and apples. All she'd ever wanted was to be a wife and mother. She filled her time with household chores like baking and doing laundry. Not in the real world, but on the spirit plane.

Felicity grinned and perched on the side of the claw-footed tub.

"I always loved sex outside," she said, picking up on the conversation. "We'd dance in the gazebo, then I'd take my man out to the swing Annie built for me in the trees. I had this hole in the seat, you see, and my man would sit just so in front of the swing." She laughed and clasped her cheeks. "I did love my contraptions!"

Faye cocked an eyebrow. "Did you? Am I going to see these contraptions?"

Felicity laughed. "Of course! In due time."

More dreams. "I'll look forward to it." The dreams made her hot and needy. Most times she woke with her hand on her pussy and had to take the edge off. The way things were, she did need two lovers.

"Of course you need both men, Faye. Just like you need another store. Two's always better than one."

"A second location will help, but only time will tell if two stores will be enough to keep this place going." She'd given up millions of dollars to stay here and keep the girls in the house.

None of them, Faye included, wanted to see the beautiful grounds plowed under for multi-family housing. But the pressure would only increase. The house, north of Seattle, overlooked lovely Shilshole Bay and Bainbridge Island. Oceanfront acres would always be under the watchful eye of developers. If she ran into financial trouble, the vultures would circle.

Faye held their fates in her hand. She took the responsibility seriously, as had Auntie Mae Grantham.

Sometimes she thought Belle had tweaked her thoughts to go in that direction. Other times, she thought her need to keep the house going came from inside herself. A need for family? Her own was distant and cool. Her parents' volatile marriage, while passionate, left little room for grown children.

"There are a lot of neglected areas around the house and I don't want to settle for scraping by," she said, returning to the conversation. "I want to prosper. Now that my marriage is off, I have to rethink my future."

"Spoken like a true Grantham woman. And that marriage was no loss, honey," Belle drawled.

"I know. It's just that I haven't had to worry overmuch about profits in the store for the last few months. Now, I've got to gear up again."

"Your staff will help?" Felicity asked.

"Of course. Kim and Willa are great. That reminds me, Belle, I want to check out the attic to see if there are any clothes or shoes up there. I saw some photos from the 1940s in your trunk. I love the open-toed slingbacks from that era."

Hope glided in, bringing in the delicious homey smell of apple pies baking. "What in the world are you wearing?" she asked at her first sight of Faye.

Faye smoothed the mini-skirt and felt a rush of desire trill a need deep inside. "Like it?" She lifted her skirt a half inch to show she'd neglected to put on panties.

"Very sexy," agreed Hope.

Belle chuckled. "That's our Faye." To Faye, she said, "We'll see the attic tomorrow."

Felicity nodded. "You'll need inventory if you open a second location and the attic's stuffed full. You'll see." She beamed a smile. Felicity's assurance made Faye feel more hope that things would work out. She'd been the house's finance manager and had a good head for accounting.

"Give us a twirl, Faye," Felicity begged. "I haven't dressed for a man in so long, I've forgotten what it's like."

Faye obliged and pirouetted. Felicity laughed and clapped her hands. "Gorgeous! What era?"

"Sixties." The clothes had been worn by a hip young TV actress. "The mini-skirt, wide white belt, and go-go boots are a dead giveaway."

"Maybe to you, but that's after our time."

* * *

"A go-go girl?" Mark grinned. His hazel eyes glowed with heat at Faye's appearance. "That's hot. Love the boots." He opened his arms and Faye walked straight into them, ignoring the bustling hum and buzz of the hotel lobby.

"You smell so good," she said. The sizzle of arousal skipped along her muscles and ligaments as he gathered her to his chest. Her heart picked up speed, and her blood rushed to her deepest core, warming as it moved through her body.

Bellmen pushed luggage carts every which way, cell phones rang incessantly, and the elevator arrival bells chimed a steady beat. Business people came and went and lined up for check-in. Welcome signs for a conference sat on easels all over the lobby.

None of the hustle around them interfered with the deep sexual need simmering under her skin. The need she read in Mark's eyes. She lightly rubbed her softer skin along his hard, bristly jaw line. She wanted him and needed to know this came from her, not the girls' influence.

His hands dropped to her ass and he clasped both cheeks as he pulled her tight into his hips.

"Food? Or dessert?" he asked, letting her know what he wanted first.

"I'm hoping dessert has nothing to do with food."

He growled into her ear. "Damn straight." He glanced up. "Shit, let's get out of here. There's an old friend I don't want to share you with just yet." He took her hand and stepped toward the exit.

She held back. "Share me with?" Fanciful thoughts skipped through her mind. Thoughts that wouldn't normally be hers. Damn that Belle!

"I don't want—damn—he's seen us. Man's a bloodhound when it comes to beautiful women." His eyes turned wary as he looked over her shoulder.

She turned. The man who approached with an appraising

eye must be the friend. Handsome in an angular way, taller than Mark but thinner. She saw a bit of tall, thin Adrian Brody in his shoulders and long limbs.

"Grant Johnson, Faye Grantham. Sorry, we're out of here."

"Whoa, you sure about that, buddy? I mean, Faye here wouldn't want a man to eat a lonely bowl of soup in a hotel café, now, would she?" He stuck out his hand to Faye.

She clasped it. He pulled her close and kissed her cheek. Then he lifted her hand and kissed her palm for good measure. She felt the tingle to her toes. Very warm. Hot even.

She smiled, enjoying the sensation.

2

Faye laughed at the heated response from Mark's friend. "Nice to meet you, Grant."

Beside her, Mark straightened. Frowned. He didn't like that she'd smiled so warmly at Grant. She leaned in close to Mark's side, pressing the side of her breast to his arm. Her other hand patted his butt gently under his suit jacket.

"But we do have to leave," she said smoothly. "Mark and I were in the middle of something and we like to finish what we start. I'm sure you understand." She took Mark's hand again.

There was no mistaking the signal she gave.

"Another time, then, Faye."

She suspected the hot look Grant gave her was as much to rile Mark as it was to catch her interest.

Mark turned her toward the exit. "Asshole," he muttered.

She squeezed his hand. "You have to be good friends for Grant to try something like that. It was all in fun, I'm sure."

He slanted her an amused glance. "Have I told you yet today how much I like you?"

"No, but you'll show me soon enough."

They stepped outside and a misty rain floated around them. Seattle's rain might keep a girl's skin moist, but it was hell on straightened hair. Waves and soft curls sprang to life all over her head.

Mark tugged her to his side. "Listen, we haven't been anywhere but in the hotel room yet. Any chance we'll run into your fiancé?"

"No. No chance." Mark didn't know about her broken engagement, and with Liam in the picture she wasn't sure how she should proceed. "Yes, about that—"

"I promised not to get between you and your fiancé," Mark said, holding up his hand so she couldn't interrupt. "We agreed we shouldn't let the most incredible sex I've ever had ruin your life, but, Faye"—he held her closer—"now that I'm staying in Seattle, I'm not sure I can stick to our agreement."

The scent of his skin, the sex-need in his eyes, her own response to both combined to make her want to turn around and go straight to his room.

A cab pulled up and the doorman opened the door for them. She sighed and allowed Mark to hand her into the backseat.

Mark slid in next to her.

As soon as he closed the door, he gathered her into his lap and slipped his hand up her skirt.

She sighed, and decided to let him find out for himself that the only panties she had with her were the ones in her purse for the morning.

Mark rested his hand on the silken flesh of Faye's knee. "I love that you look so different every time I see you. The tight white boots with the chunky heels are a real turn-on." He ran his hand up her long, silky thighs. She had the smoothest skin that heated immediately. "I even like the huge flowers on your blouse."

"This look was very stylish for a short time." Her smile lifted the corners of her eyes, emphasizing her fuck-me eyeliner.

He lifted the neckline away from her chest and peered down her top. There they were, her breasts, as white and full and luscious as he remembered. Her warm body-scent drove him wild as he trailed his tongue from the tip of her collarbone to the back of her ear.

She purred and let him lick the lobe of her ear. Blood rushed to his cock. Faye was the most pliant, eager woman he'd ever had. Nothing turned him on faster than a ready woman.

He stretched a finger higher up her thigh. No barrier so far, but her skirt had ridden up so high that if he moved his hand any closer to the honey that waited for him, she'd be completely exposed.

The cabbie's hot gaze in the rearview stopped him. But Faye noticed and slid his hand higher up her leg.

She was the hottest woman he'd ever met. Slowly, he traced her hemline from the outside of her thigh to the inside. She bit her bottom lip, but didn't move, not so much as a flexed muscle.

He traced the hemline back again, careful not to raise her skirt any higher. She still showed no reaction. Game, that was Faye. Always ready to play.

She might not react yet, or to this light touch, but she would.

Mindful of the cabbie, he slid his flat palm up the backside of her skirt, cupping the cheek of her ass. Her firm, high ass. No material to skim, just smooth soft flesh.

He felt the slightest quiver under his palm. Her cheek warmed and she tilted her mouth to his. He took the kiss she offered. Her tongue slid into his mouth to coax and taste while his hand squeezed and weighed the soft mound of her cheek.

Faye was all woman, ready and willing to let him do whatever he wanted, whenever he wanted. He could learn to love a woman like this.

This thing with Faye had started with a wild one-night stand where she'd had the audacity to beg for sex lessons. She rarely came with her fiancé, but with him, she'd been a firecracker, exploding constantly. Hot as barbecue coals, she was ready to flare up at the lightest touch, the silkiest kiss. He figured to teach her how to get off and let her move on with her life.

He'd been surprised as hell when she called out of the blue the next day, and he'd had her all over again. She'd done a private striptease, then made him ache with her tantalizing lips.

At the end, she'd made him promise not to call her. He'd given his word, but there was something about her that made him hungry.

"I tried not to call," he said. "Even got close to fucking some girl I met in the hotel bar, but in the end, I wanted to see you again." He had no idea why he made the confession. It was probably a terrible tactical error, but it was out now, in the air between them.

She tilted her head back. Looked serious. "Mark, I have to tell you something. But you can't go making assumptions about us because of it."

"What?" His heart slammed.

"I'm not engaged anymore."

Hallefuckinlujah. "What happened?"

"I went to see him at his office. Found him facedown in his receptionist's lap. He's been fucking her for a long time, while I was busy with the wedding arrangements and worrying about our sex life."

"I don't know what to say." And he sure as hell didn't know what to think. "But I won't say I'm sorry. It must have been rough, but I'm glad he's gone. Now—"

Her hand across his mouth cut him off. "See, this is where you need to stop talking. We, you and me, this thing we're doing, having, whatever, is just beginning. No promises—I can't make any." Her eyes clouded, her thoughts turned inward.

Whatever she had to deal with she wanted to work it out on her own.

"Okay, you're right. We'll take things slow. I'm caught up in a lot of work anyway. And you're busy with this house you've got to sell. We'll keep it light." He kissed her hard, needing to claim some part of her.

He wasn't a guy to let a woman like this loose on the world. He might not want exclusive rights yet, but to find a woman like Faye was rare. So, yeah, for a time, he'd play it easy.

She sighed, wiggled her fine ass more deeply into his straining lap. "I'm a hungry woman. When are you going to feed me?" She pulled his lower lip into her mouth and sucked it, driving food right out of his head.

Faye slid off Mark's lap, grabbed her purse off the seat, and followed him out of the cab. The rain had formed heavier drops, chased by a new wind. The sting of it lashed her bare thighs as she dashed into the covered doorway of the steakhouse.

She waited while Mark saw to the cab fare. Belle's reminder about a woman taking two lovers rang through her head. She agreed, determined not to ruin two good things in her life by allowing the old Faye's repressed attitudes to call the shots. The old Faye would never play the field, would never enjoy the attention of two wildly different men.

But this new, improved Faye accepted the truth. She was now a highly sexed woman, spirits or no spirits.

She didn't want to give up Mark's lessons in bed. She was making terrific progress, but he had more to teach her and she wanted to learn everything he could teach her.

But that didn't mean she had to give up Liam.

Mark paid the cab fare and they entered the restaurant, which was cozy, quiet, and smelled of fresh garlic and other spices. The restaurant also had a piano tucked into a corner.

Mark had reserved a private booth in the back, screened for privacy by schefflera and some delicate ferns. "Very pretty," she said, "I've never been here before."

"Good, we start fresh."

"Yes, let's. We'll make this our first date."

"As long as you put out on first dates, we're good to go."

She laughed. "Mr. McLeod, do I look like that kind of girl?"

He chuckled and set his hand on her back, scorching her spine and making her melt.

Conversation stayed suitable for public consumption and she managed to keep her hands to herself, but the glow of sexual need built rapidly. A speculative gleam in his eye heated her.

"Ask," she said, "I can tell you want to."

"You walked in and caught him in the act?"

"Yes." She rimmed her wineglass with one fingertip. A dry Italian white was delicious and loosened her up just enough to find some humor in the end of her marriage plans. "His face was between her legs."

"Where was she? On a desk?"

"Why?" She hadn't considered the fun to be had in describing what she'd walked in on. "Do you want a full description?"

"Might as well hear all the dirty details."

She slid closer along the banquette. Her thigh touched his, but she kept both hands on top of the table. She interlaced her fingers primly.

"She was in his dental chair. Her uniform was shoved up to her waist. I wondered why she insisted on wearing one, especially when tunics and slacks are more practical."

"She wore a sexy nurse's uniform?" The gleam in his eye glittered harder.

"Sort of. But she was overweight and usually her front buttons were gaping open. Her ass looked huge—the material stretched across it so tightly that it rose in the back."

"Know the type."

"Definitely. Odd how I never noticed before. She wore cheap perfume and cheaper jewelry, too. I can't believe Colin thought she was hot."

"Some men love cheap. Like to think they're one of many men who've been there."

Buttered buns. The thought came from Belle, she was sure of it.

Faye tipped her wineglass and drained it. "Anyway, I stood at the doorway and heard her moaning and asking for it. Colin's pencil dick was in his hand while he licked her pussy."

"Pencil dick?"

"Really skinny."

He suppressed a chuckle. "Go on."

"She looked up and smiled right at me. Nasty." She sighed. "Her knees were draped over the arms of the chair so she was spread really wide. When she realized I wasn't going to say anything right away, she started to buck against his mouth and moan louder. Colin thought she was into it, I guess, because he stood up and slid his cock in to the hilt. Bitch screamed and pretended to come. Colin did his usual two limp pumps and spewed across her belly."

"Why didn't you say anything?"

"All I could think of was *Now I'm free. Truly free.* I didn't even feel angry that he'd had me convinced I was lousy in bed."

She patted his thigh, felt it bunch and harden under her palm. "Thanks to you, I already knew better."

"My pleasure."

She gave his crotch a skim just to tease.

"Then what happened?"

"He followed me out of his office, more worried about what his mother would say about the canceled wedding than about losing me."

"Asshole."

"I put five years into that relationship, listened to all his complaints about our sex life. So, obviously, I'm not interested in settling down any time soon." Besides, her mind had wandered into completely different territory.

"Smart girl." He held up the empty wine bottle. "Another?"

"Yes." She felt deliciously wicked behind the screen of plants and surreptitiously slid the zipper down the side of her right boot. She smiled at Mark, content to wait a moment longer while the server took away their empty dinner plates and wine bottle. He was so understanding and hot hot hot.

"Dessert, sir?"

"Bring the tray, we'll have a look. And more wine."

"Certainly." The man gave a bow of brisk efficiency and left them.

She leaned toward Mark. "You look pleased with yourself tonight. Are you that happy with your plans to expand?"

"Yes. I'll have to work my ass off in the next few months, but the payoff will be worth it."

She scooted to the far side of the table and slid her boot off.

Raising her toes to his knee, she began a slow, tantalizing slide up his inner thigh.

He raised his eyebrows, then blinked when she found his readying package. Soft on the underside and hardening on the top side, his organs moved gently under her questing toes.

"I take it you're ready to leave?" he asked.

"Not yet."

"Ah, payback for the cab?"

"A little."

He opened his legs. With more room to maneuver, Faye slid her toes to the top of his erection, watching each change of expression on his face. Surprise changed to amusement, turned to desire, changed into full arousal. His cock rose and hardened between her big toe and the next. The sensitive pad of her big toe traced each ripple up his cock, then stroked the rim around the head. His breath caught for a second as she pressed against the tip of his penis.

Sliding back down his shaft, she wiggled her toes against his sac with a feathery light touch. He closed his eyes against the onslaught of sensation. Oh, this was fun.

The waiter returned, with the wine and another server with a full array of desserts on a tray. They were expected to make a choice, to think and talk.

Mark straightened in his seat. Sharp disappointment speared her as he removed her foot from his lap.

"I think we'll pass on dessert after all. We have some pressing matters to attend to," he said, reaching across the table to gather her hands into his. Gallantly, he raised her fingertips to his lips and seductively pulled first her index finger then her middle finger into his mouth.

She melted.

The waiter cleared his throat. "Perhaps the lady and gentleman would prefer to decline the second bottle of wine?"

"Good suggestion," Mark said, with his eyes focused on hers. "Let's move along, the night's wasting."

It took all of thirty seconds for Mark to shut and lock the hotel suite door, step out of his slacks, and let her straddle him on the bed. Faye shivered with pent-up desire as she slid her fingers around his stiff cock.

She slid the tip along her slit from back to front, coating him with her juices. When the rounded head tipped her clit she rotated it around and around, in exquisite pleasure.

First the hot feel of his hand on her ass in the cab and then the decadence of sliding her bare foot along his package had readied her. Moisture, slick and heavy, eased the slide of his cock into her channel.

3

Sensation rose as Faye's inner walls contracted. Impaled on Mark's cock, she rocked and rolled, grasping at every slide of skin on skin. Her pubis rubbed his, and her clit, sticky from her juices, tapped against the springy hair at the base of his cock. Back and forth, she rode him until in a rush of tension she fractured into shards of heated, wild release.

Just as her own shudders faded away, his began. She held still as Mark strained up into her and geysered against her delicate, sensitive flesh.

She fell to the bed, mini-skirt hiked to her waist, laughing. "Oh! It was wonderful to come with you without a guilty conscience. Free! I'm free!" Deep pulses in her belly faded.

"Sex is too much fun to feel guilty about. If you want it, you should have it." He rolled onto his front and rose to his elbows.

"You're right. This is the best thing I've done in months. Years!"

He reached for her belt buckle and slipped the catch. "I want you out of these clothes. But leave the boots on."

* * *

Three hours later, Faye settled in Mark's arms. Sore and sated, she rolled over to let him spoon her. He murmured in her ear, but the pull of sleep insisted she hurry.

But no one hurried to sleep, she thought, unless one of the girls had a story to tell. She smiled and let sleep claim her. The dream came gently and without fanfare as she slid beneath consciousness.

Hope Teague's sense of urgency fluttered near her heart. The shopkeeper's hand—strong, lean, gentle, with a stiff sprinkling of hair above each knuckle—brushed against hers as she slid her purchase toward him across the counter. Even through her glove, heat spiked up her fingers from the slight touch. Without looking at her, he took the bolt of cloth, checked the tag. Those large, well-shaped hands settled on each side of her bolt of yellow gingham.

Then he set his tea-colored eyes to hers. "New curtains, Miss?" His voice, sandpaper on velvet, stroked her ears and trailed down her neck to her lower spine, where it settled, raspy and soft.

Hope shivered inside at the sensation of being stroked by nothing more than a voice.

"Yes," she said. The urge to look deep into his eyes was terrible and wrong, so she looked past him to the cans of peaches and apricots over his left shoulder. His broad, muscled left shoulder. Heaven help her.

But Heaven had abandoned her two years ago. Left her alone. Left her scared. Finally, desperation had led her to a life of shame in Perdition House. The likes of her shouldn't look at a man the likes of him. Not when he looked so kindly on her.

"This'll make fine curtains. A kitchen window?" His long fingers splayed out, stark white against the heavy-grained oak of the store's counter.

Hope nodded, held out her dollar, making certain to hand the bills over long-ways. She didn't want another accidental brushing of fingers. Couldn't take it again.

She had to stop coming into this store. His store.

But she knew she wouldn't. She was drawn here like filings to a magnet. Stupid, torturing herself this way.

He was married! With four children. Beautiful children, each and every one.

For a while she'd told herself it was their happy laughter that drew her back time and again. To hear laughter and squabbles and little-girl giggles coming from the upstairs rooms was exquisite torture.

Once, she'd seen a girl. A blond sprite about four years old in a dress covered in flour had peeked out from behind the door. Wide-open eyes the color of her father's, ringed with thick black lashes, had caught and snagged on Hope's.

The shopkeeper had seen Hope's delighted expression. With a waggle of fingers he'd sent the child back upstairs with a kiss on the forehead that had torn Hope's heart out. The sweetness of the gesture leaked into her thoughts for weeks afterward. Since then, she'd found every excuse she could to come into the store.

She blinked away the smile that threatened to expose her secret yearning and slid her change off the counter and into her hand. He wrapped her cloth in brown paper and tied it with string. As she watched his deft hands maneuver the wrapping and string, she saw that she'd been lying to herself.

As sweet as the children were, it was the man she came here to see. It was his gesture of sweet caring that she wished for herself.

It shamed her, this yearning to have him notice her. If she ever saw his wife, she'd die of guilt.

She bobbed her head once when he passed the package to

her, then scurried like a lovesick girl out the front door, promising this was the last time. It was a lecture she gave herself every day on the way back to Perdition House.

Once outside, in the fresh sea-scented air, she breathed deeply, got her bearings. She rubbed at a spot on her rib cage, but the ache she felt remained.

She gasped in fright when the storekeeper stepped up behind her. "Miss?"

Rigid with fear, she caught her breath. He knew! He knew she was drawn here. Her pining had become an embarrassment to him. "I'm sorry!" She straightened her hat, smoothed her hair, studied the planks in the sidewalk. "I won't—"

"No, I'm the one who's sorry," he interrupted. "I overcharged you. That bolt of cloth's been here for months and I reduced the price last week. I should have changed the price on the tag."

"Oh! That's, I see, well, I . . ." she trailed off, confused by his confession.

"I'd like to make it up to you, if I could. Maybe buy you lunch? My clerk will be here soon. We could go on down the block to the café."

"I—" she looked up and down the street, wanting to run as far and as fast as she could. Away! She needed to get away! She palmed the ache in her chest again, certain her pounding heart would burst through any moment.

"Are you all right?" he asked and clasped her elbow gently.

The tingle of his touch ran straight to her chest, and her lungs failed. She gasped and he steadied her. "I'm sorry, I didn't mean to offend you with the invitation."

Finally she looked into his face, saw his warm concern and confusion.

He straightened and she noticed a red flush start by his collar and rise to the tips of his ears. "We haven't been introduced. I'm Jed Devine. This is my store."

"Hello, Jed Devine. I'm Hope. Hope Teague. And yes, I'll have lunch with you." *And burn in hell while I'm at it.*

"A widower?"

"Yes." Hope slid the freshly ironed curtain along the rod and spaced the gathers evenly. Belle stood behind her, ready to catch her if she fell. Belle had a ridiculous fear of falling. Even someone else's falls.

Hope hitched her knee onto the kitchen counter and pulled herself up. "Stop hovering, Belle. I'm only sticking a rod on two brackets four feet off the ground. If I slip it'll only be into the sink."

Belle shuffled backward. "Don't change the subject. This man's a widower with four children?"

"Yes. And I don't want to talk about it. We only had lunch." But she kept her face turned to the task at hand and out of Belle's view. She was far too discerning.

"Widowers don't 'only have lunch,' especially when they're on the lookout for mama number two."

Hope's belly dropped. "Don't be silly. He doesn't see me that way."

"Well honey, there's only two ways a man sees a woman. Either she's the beddin' kind or the weddin' kind. Which do you think you are?"

The curtains, rod and all, clattered into the sink.

Jed Devine tucked his youngest into bed, kissed her good night, and picked up her empty milk glass from her bedside table. She was still young enough to think he didn't know she only asked for a drink to forestall bedtime. He turned off her lamp, then left her to sleep and dream her sweetest dreams.

For the first time in months, he expected some sweet dreams of his own. Hope Teague! He'd watched her come into his store for weeks now. Shy and proper, she seemed gentle-hearted and kind.

Hope's manners at lunch had been impeccable, her behavior befitting a lady. She dressed demurely, but there was a warmth in her gaze that hit him below the belt.

He'd taken a chance asking her to lunch. Nice women waited to be introduced to gentlemen, but she'd always come into the store alone. Because he hadn't lived in Fremont long, they had no mutual acquaintances, so an introduction would not happen by chance.

She intrigued him more tonight than ever before. Even though they'd spent a pleasant hour sharing a meal and interesting conversation, he didn't know any more about Hope than the few things he'd figured out himself.

She'd even avoided telling him where she lived. He'd never known a woman so unwilling to talk about herself. All he could go on was his first impression. Warm, gentle-hearted, kind—and as much as he wanted to make his thoughts stop there, he couldn't.

Something about her called to his baser instincts. His needs, set aside since his wife's death, had been rising since the first time Hope had come into his shop.

He was rarely able to step around his counter now. He got hard at the first waft of her perfume, the tilt of her head, the way she smiled gently when the little ones caused a ruckus overhead. Everything about Hope made his pulse pound and his blood rush.

Once, he'd fantasized about locking the door and pulling the shades. In his daydream, she had run into his arms and kissed him passionately. They'd made wild love on the stacks of new work pants and she'd let him do unspeakable things to her. Dirty, animal things that no decent wife would contemplate. The daydream had shamed him for weeks, but he hadn't been able to let it go. As time had gone on he'd begun having it everywhere, any time of the day or night.

Decent men didn't think of those things, not with a lady, and he was afraid he might lose control if he didn't do something to ease himself soon.

It was worse now because he knew she was single, very pleasant to spend time with, and kind-hearted. Her conversation was well rounded, she read the newspapers and was up on all the latest news. She liked children. She never seemed put out by the girlish squabbles, nor thudding feet overhead in the store.

Hope wasn't at all like Miss Spencer, the schoolteacher who came into the store with a pinched mouth and sharp eyes. She'd taken to calling him by his first name, but she never found joy in anything that had happened in her classroom. What he considered normal childhood antics caused her face to close in disapproval.

He hated to admit it, and felt disrespectful thinking it, but Miss Spencer was just the kind of woman his wife would pick to raise their daughters.

As he readied himself for bed, he wondered what it would be like to have a woman Eloise wouldn't approve of.

A woman more inclined to pleasure. He'd loved his wife as a husband should. But, she'd done her duty and nothing more. Eloise had given him beautiful children, but he'd always been aware of a distance between them. By the time of her death, their marriage bed had grown cold.

He slid between the sheets and thought of Hope. Her scent, light and flowery, the skin of her fingers, soft and delicate, the gentle rise and fall of her ample breasts. He stretched out, cradled the back of his head in his hands, his head braced against the iron bedstead. Pictures of Hope flickered through his mind's eye, the prelude to his fantasy scene with her.

She laughed with a warmth he rarely heard in other women's twitters. She listened with intent patience to his awkward questions, apparently aware that he was going against his nature to be so forward.

He'd tried hard not to look, but he'd been all too aware of the size of Hope's bosom, the slimness of her waist, the glorious fall of her hair. He thought of that hair draped across his naked chest, the silky feel of it, the warmth of her skin. The scent of her arousal and his. The remembered muskiness of sex.

He closed his eyes, the steadiness of his own breathing taking him into a dream. . . .

Hope, in the store. The shades are drawn, the shop quiet and still. They're alone.

She turns, smiles, and walks toward him. Her dress falls open and her breasts break free of restraint, but instead of being ashamed, as Eloise would have been, Hope lifts them so he can touch. He hefts the weight of each breast, and watches her eyes close in anticipation. He bends and takes first one nipple, then the other into his mouth. They bead as he suckles.

Unbelievably, she croons encouragement, and shifts in urgency. Heat rises between them and suddenly his clothes are gone. His cock, harder, larger than it's ever been, juts toward her naked belly. Soft, soft, her flesh is soft and pillowy as she takes his cock in hand. She presses his hard shaft into the softness of her belly, while reaching to cup his sac. His balls contract with need and he pushes against her.

She climbs to the top of the stack of jeans and parts her legs so he can see her deepest secrets. It's a mystery, dark and wet. But he wants to know everything, wants to see . . . everything.

Wants to taste . . . everything.

But he doesn't know how.

Hope, with a warmth and humor he's never experienced, guides his hand into her wet, dark slit and welcomes him.

She lets him touch first, explore her deepest secrets. She

blesses him with a kiss while he slides his finger along a sodden, welcoming trench. Centered where he couldn't see, he finds her inner channel. At his first slight touch it opens and he sends his finger in up to the first knuckle. Hot, wet flesh closes around him and he plunges farther inside, up to the hilt.

She moans and accepts the exploration, encourages more. Encourages anything he wants to do.

Dirty things. Wanton things.

He groans at the slick feel of her, the soft, hot walls of her cunny. She moans again and again as he looks at her. Her flesh gleams wetly. Her scent goes to his head, making him shudder with a need to take.

In, he needs to get in.

Hope gathers him close, wraps her legs around his waist and urges him to plunge into her soft wetness.

"Unhhhh."

He came before he wanted to, driven by a need to possess, to own. He'd do better next time. Take her places Eloise never went. . . .

Hope. His Hope. His woman, pure and sweet and ready to learn all he could teach her. It wasn't proper to think these thoughts, not about a woman he could get serious about, but he couldn't help himself.

In the morning, he woke to sticky sheets and a need to ease himself he couldn't deny. It wouldn't do to court a woman like Hope while these wild needs raged through him. He might be tempted to overwhelm her with eagerness.

He might ruin things before they got a chance to blossom. She'd promised to come back to see him on Saturday afternoon. They planned to have dinner and take a stroll in the twilight.

He was already planning to buy flowers and pick out her favorite candy. She liked lemon drops best.

But first things first. He needed to take the edge off his rapacious thoughts. For the first time, he considered a visit to a house of prostitution. It was common enough among single loggers and sailors down by the docks, but for a decent man looking for a decent woman, things were different.

He'd heard rumors of a house. Not a bawdy, raucous whorehouse, but an elegant home with fine ladies, fine food and wine. If he went to visit one of the women there, he'd be better able to court Hope without ravishing her. He could treat her like the lady she was if he didn't suffer such need.

Already his rod was stiff at the merest thought of Hope.

The house expected patrons to reserve in advance. He decided to see to it today. The sooner the better. And once Hope showed her interest in courting, easing himself with another woman would be the only way to control himself.

Men had needs, he reasoned, something Eloise had coolly ignored. He wouldn't press Hope for more than she was prepared to give—he was too much a gentleman for that. Hope was warm and lovely but was certainly not the kind of lady who would encourage behavior unbecoming a gentleman.

He wouldn't have to visit the house for long, because with some luck, Hope would be exactly the kind of woman he could take to wife.

Belle answered the telephone in her melodious, welcoming voice while Felicity waited at a tea table set in a comfortable alcove. Felicity had invited Hope to join them for tea in the hope she and Belle could talk some sense into her. Of course, Felicity hadn't actually made the tea. She'd expected Hope to take care of it.

"Why, yes," Belle was saying, "there's an opening this weekend. We provide hostesses of quality for several gentlemen of character each week. Of course, we expect all our guests to behave like the gentlemen they claim to be."

Felicity listened and grinned, happy for the moment to regroup. Hope needed to let go of this dream of hers. It was hurting her to pine for a man two years gone.

She listened and grinned as Belle explained the facts of life at Perdition. Belle was intimidating when a gentleman called for the first time. She made it clear Perdition House was no ordinary cathouse. Wild, drunken revelry was not tolerated. Not by Belle, nor by the other gentlemen.

There were measures taken to insure both the safety of the women employed here and the quality of the experience each gentleman enjoyed.

Hope came in with a full tea tray and quietly set it on the hexagonal occasional table beside Felicity. She smoothed her hair, then took a seat across from her while they waited for Belle to finish with the call.

"Sounds like a new client," Felicity said softly while she poured tea for herself and Hope. "You look tired," she commented as her opening salvo.

"Do I?" Hope added a lump of sugar to her tea, stirred, then subsided into silence.

She missed her dead husband too much. Grieved for the life she wouldn't live now he was gone. As sweet and loving as Hope was, she was deeply disappointed that life had brought her here. She needed to let go of her girlhood dreams the way Felicity had. Pining for what would never be would cause nothing but more heartache.

"Is it so hard for you to live here?" she asked.

Hope looked at her sadly. "You seem to enjoy it." She sipped delicately then put down her cup to fuss with her brooch.

Belle continued to lay out the rules, discussed terms, then picked up her pen to write in a reservation.

"I do enjoy it," said Felicity, "like most of the other girls. I love the money, independence, and fun of the place. I'll never dance as much as I dance here. Never laugh as much, never enjoy the pleasures of the flesh as much. This is a wondrous time to be alive and a woman, Hope. I wish you could see that."

Hope's gaze glided around the room, a favorite tactic of hers to avoid unpleasant discussion.

Belle's call ended and she hung up the receiver. "Tea! Just what I need. It's been a busy morning." She rose and walked around her desk to join them at the occasional table.

"Why so pensive, Hope?"

"I'm berating her again," Felicity responded. "She's pining and I don't think it's good for her."

"Pining? I think not," Belle said, giving Hope an appraisal. "It's a man."

"Belle! I expected you to have more sense than to—"

"A man?" Felicity cut her off. This was more like it. A heated *crush* with one of the gentlemen was just the thing to get her to move along with her life. "One of our gentlemen?"

Hope flashed her an angry glance. "No!"

Sometimes men made fevered promises in the first flush of acquaintance, especially the younger ones, but that kind of thing came with the territory. Most times, the girls took such declarations of love in stride. Things only became painful if a girl took them to heart.

"Worse." Belle looked serious. "He's an upright man."

This time it was Felicity's turn to exclaim. "No! Oh, Heaven save us from upright men. They're the worst. Oh, Hope, tell me you're not that foolish."

"Stop," said Hope, breathlessly. "I'm under no illusions."

But dreams die hard and Hope lived up to her name. Time and again, she'd been the one to cheer on the troupe when things looked dark. Moving halfway across the country with a fugitive and a runaway, building a house from nothing, starting from scratch, had been a fearful adventure for the five original women. Sometimes the only one who kept them going was

Hope, talking cheerfully about what a grand time they'd have once the house was built.

"I think you do suffer illusions," said Belle.

Felicity moved around the table, knelt in front of Hope. Taking her hands, she held them and squeezed tightly. "This is dangerous, Hope. Protect your heart. Please, let this go."

"There's nothing to let go of. He would never forgive my situation here. He's a family man, a widower with four adorable children. We had lunch, but, truly, I've already decided I can't see him again. I'm canceling our Saturday evening dinner plans."

"Good." Belle's tone was brisk as she poured herself more tea.

Felicity's mind reeled that Hope had even entertained the notion of dining with the man. To pretend she was something she wasn't went against the grain for Felicity. As flighty, as experimental as she knew she was about sex, she also knew she had an inner core of directness and ruthless honesty.

"Besides, it's hard enough to be trapped in this hellish existence," Hope went on, patently oblivious to Belle's outraged expression. "I don't need to pretend I'll ever have my dreams come true. It hurts too much when they fall apart."

"Hellish existence?" Belle's brow arched and her voice went icehouse chilly.

Felicity ignored her and focused on Hope's unblinking gaze. She hugged her friend tight. "Good girl." She patted her cheek. "You have us, Hope. Are we so bad?"

Hope sniffed. "Only when you're being a pain in the neck."

Felicity straightened and went back to her seat, pleased to have this crisis averted. "Most of us consider Perdition House heaven on earth. Someday maybe you will, too."

"I didn't meant to judge any of us. Oh!" Her eyes filled and she flapped her hand in front of her face in distress. "What a mess I've made of everything. I love you like sisters, I do."

"Oh, calm down, both of you," snapped Belle. "It's obvious to everyone you're pining for something and hate the idea of working here. But Perdition provides good food, nice men, great wine, and the ability to make a lot of money in a very short time. Most of the women here cherish their independence, Hope."

Hope reached across the table to both women, hands outstretched in a plea. "I cherish *you*. I'm at home here with you, my friends, my champions. Without you I'd be lost, adrift. But independence is not what I crave."

Unlike the others, Hope wanted a man of her own, children, a home. She put on a good front most days, but Felicity still worried because no matter what Hope said, a broken heart never did any woman any good.

"Was that a new client who called, Belle?" Hope's pathetic attempt to deflect the conversation was obvious.

Felicity felt some progress had been made and she and Belle exchanged relieved glances.

"Yes, it was a new client," Belle responded. "A fellow named Jed Devine."

4

Hope's face paled to bone white and her teacup rattled in her saucer. She put both down gently. "No, it can't be."

"What's wrong?" Felicity asked. When Hope didn't reply, she looked to Belle.

"He's a shopkeeper in Fremont. A dry goods store, he said." Belle's voice slowed with each word. "He's your shopkeeper, Hope?"

"He knows, and he's coming to mock me." She rose, still shaking. "He hates me, wants to shame me." She twisted her hands.

Felicity stood too, and hugged her tight. "No, he's doing no such thing. If he's the kind, upright man you say he is—"

"Nonsense," Belle said sharply. "He's coming here for the same reason every man does. He's got no idea where you live. No idea that you work here. He didn't ask for you—he didn't ask for anyone by name. He hesitated to even confirm."

Hope's eyes lit. "You mean he might cancel?"

"I doubt it. But when he comes, you won't be anywhere in sight. He can't shame you if he doesn't know you're here."

"Call back and tell him not to come. Tell him we're full up! Tell him anything," Hope pleaded.

"He used a public phone." Belle gave a derisive snort. "Like most of our gentlemen, he didn't want it known he was calling us. Telephone operators love to spread gossip."

Felicity nodded. "Don't worry. He'll never get near you, Hope. We'll see to that!"

Time dragged until Friday afternoon, then suddenly went fast as a blink. Hope finished setting the table for dinner and it was suddenly five minutes to seven. She'd dallied long enough.

It was far past time she went to her room. Dinner was served promptly at seven and most of the gentlemen were already here, with everyone else in the parlor.

She'd considered leaving the place settings to the kitchen staff, but she loved to set a fine table and Belle had come to rely on her. Besides, fussing with the table kept her mind occupied and off the looming disaster of discovery.

She used the back stairs to avoid the front hall. Her dinner waited on a tray and she settled into a chair by the window to watch the front drive. Men had been arriving since four, jovial, happy men, looking forward to a pleasant weekend full of wonderful diversions.

Business was booming, in spite of the price Belle charged. There were some things well-to-do men were willing to pay extra for. One of them was exclusivity and complete privacy. Perdition House was more country club than passion palace. More retreat than harem. More genteel than a lot of homes.

Some of the business tycoons who came here regularly came to do business as much as anything else. Away from the pressures of the world, they relaxed, fortified themselves with the gracious company of the women Belle housed here.

Several women had already made enough to move out and on with their lives. Some had moved back East, some had moved out as kept women, their men so enamored as to want exclusive rights.

But the core group remained. Belle, of course, Felicity, Annie, Lizzie, and Hope. These friends had been together since the start, traveling out from Butte, Montana, together. They'd even built their own secret passageways after the workmen had left.

Annie's plans had been devilishly simple and the placement of the peepholes into a couple of the bedrooms downright sly. No one would ever notice the holes.

More than once, the women had used the holes for their own protection. Some might call it blackmail, but to the women, it was simple insurance.

These women were all the family Hope would ever have, and she would do well to remember it. Having children with a husband who loved her had been her dream once, and it had been within reach until Jonathan had been caught cheating at cards. Beaten to a pulp, he died without waking. She'd never said good-bye, except to her dreams.

She'd been with Belle ever since. She expected to be here a good long time. Maybe even live out her life here. She was needed. She was loved. She had great friends who had become the family she'd never had.

Her dinner had grown cold by the time the light faded.

The dinner downstairs would be over by now. Still no Jed.

Perhaps he'd changed his mind. Maybe he'd decided not to come here to denounce her after all. Maybe he thought to do it tomorrow in a public place in town.

Something about the thought didn't sit right. She would swear the Jed she'd come to know would never be that cruel.

And then she saw him. Jed Devine. He pulled his automobile up to the front portico and climbed out.

Hope's heart broke at the sight of him. Tall and gentlemanly, Jed had treated her like a lady during their time together. He'd asked so many questions at lunch that day, it seemed as if he wanted to know everything about her. She'd felt guilty avoiding his questions, but she'd had no choice.

The remaining sunlight touched a fire to the dark red in his hair when he took off his driving cap. He gallantly tipped the young valet they had—a boy Lizzie had found on the street in Seattle.

How could a man so kind, so gallant, be so cruel as to humiliate her? It didn't make sense.

Belle and Felicity thought she should hide away up here, not let Jed see her. If she did, she could continue to go into his shop, maybe meet his children someday. But, oh! The deceit there would kill her, if God didn't strike her dead first.

But how could she stand it if he'd been with someone else in the house? The thought was beyond bearing.

A man like Jed would be horrified to learn he'd exposed his dear little ones to a woman like Hope.

That must be why he was here, to warn her away. If that was the case, the conversation would be short. If she hurried, it could also be private.

She ran to Belle's room and found her putting the finishing touches to her hair. She dressed elegantly for dinner, then retired unless she had a business meeting in her office.

"Send Jed to my room," she said, when Belle looked up. "When we talk, it'll be on my terms, in private. If he's here to humiliate me, I won't let him. If he's here to hurt me, that part's been done."

Belle bit her lip. Her eyes blurred with kindness. "You're sure?"

"Positive."

"Best to get it over with, I suppose," Belle said softly with a pat on her hand. "I'll send him straight up."

"Thank you." Her belly did a flip and she flattened her palm against it to hold herself together. Then she straightened her spine and strode briskly back to her room.

To wait.

Mercifully the wait was short. There was a sudden tap at her door and she went to open it, her breath held.

Jed's eyes widened at first sight of her. Then his face went red. "Hope?"

He stepped back, a look of horror on his face.

"Jed, come in." The flutters in her stomach increased in tempo and gathered strength. She waved him in.

He walked in like a man who had no idea where he was. He glanced around the room, but seemed to register nothing of his surroundings. His Adam's apple rose and fell as his gaze swept back to hers.

"What are *you* doing here?" he asked, his face reddening. "Are you the housekeeper?"

An out. She could lie, let him think . . .

"No, not the housekeeper." She stepped close to his chest, drank in the wonderful scent of him. Clean clothes, fresh starch in his collar, the heat from his skin. Desire and deep need washed over her. Oh, to feel this way about a man again.

Her belly got heavy with need. Her heated places melted for want of him.

"I . . . work here, Jed. I'm a . . ." The word failed her. She couldn't say it, not to him.

"No. You can't be. Not here, not like this." The truth of the situation dawning in his gaze made her feel ugly, unclean, but she wouldn't bow her head. She wouldn't.

With shaking fingers, she raised her hands to her blouse. She undid the top button; his eyes followed her fingers. With the second button, his gaze got dark, angry. The next button revealed the shadowed cleavage of her breasts.

Was it possible he really had had no idea?

Then slowly, ever so slowly, his fingers stilled hers.

And continued down her blouse, revealing more and more of her chest. He brushed the back of his hands against the top slope of her breasts, achingly slowly.

Hope shivered under his gentle touch. Shivered and melted and prayed he'd be pleased. She wanted him in the most elemental way a woman could want a man, because that was the only part of himself he would ever give her.

She could fool herself no longer. Belle had been right. Jed was here because he was a man, like any other.

He scooped her breasts free and they hung, heavy and firm and pebbled for his mouth.

His eyes glazed with desire as his thumbs brushed slowly against her nipples. Two at once, rubbing and brushing the peaks while she stood quietly and let him look his fill.

"I'm dreaming," he said.

She didn't speak for fear of breaking the wonder in his expression. The full impact of her situation hadn't sunk in yet, she thought. All he saw was her offering, all he needed was to take, the way any man would take what was offered.

But Hope could offer more. Maybe even enough that Jed would come back again.

Her own body cried out for his as she slowly sank to her knees in front of him.

"What? What are you doing?"

"Shh," she gentled. "Let me."

She opened the buttons on his trousers. Jed was long and heavy and clean. She caught a whiff of soap as he sprang free of his pants.

She looked up at his face, watched his eyes widen as she tipped out her tongue. One long slide from root to tip and he saw no more. His eyes closed on a groan and she took him full into her mouth.

His flexes began immediately and she recognized the signs of an overdue man.

She released him. "Do you want me to finish you now?"

"I want . . . I want you."

"To lie with me?"

"Yes."

She rose, his long, hot cock still clasped in her hand. She led him to the bed and motioned him to sit.

She settled beside him, keeping one hand sliding up and down in tantalizing touches.

"Are you all right, Jed?" Her voice cracked under the weight of her sorrow. This was all she would ever have of him and once the haze of desire cleared from his mind, he'd see her for what she was.

He'd walk out of her life forever.

But until then, she'd do whatever she could to keep him here for a little while. These memories would have to last a lifetime. These stolen moments and one too-short hour in a café were all she'd ever have of Jed Devine.

He shook his head, reached for the back of her head to bring her lips to his. She went into his arms and kissed his soft, giving lips for all she was worth. His tongue danced with hers and they fell back onto the cool, crisp sheets of Hope's bed.

He rolled to cover her, kissing her neck, her jaw line, the softly scented skin behind her ear. She moaned with need and heat, a woman crazy with need. With love.

Oh, God, she loved him. This was her hell. Her punishment for the life she'd chosen. Her heart broke, shattered by her acceptance of her fate.

She lifted her hem and opened for him. Jed reared back so he could look at her.

She bit her lip and turned her face to the side. Tentative touches to her slick heat inflamed her and she melted onto his

fingers as he smoothed through her curls. He found her opening and rimmed her outer lips, spreading them. She raised her
hips in a woman's invitation and heard him groan.

Speared by two fingers, Hope moved and took them in,
shuddering with each push and pull, but still she couldn't
watch his face.

Finally after a long moment of play, Jed covered her. She
welcomed the warmth of his body and felt the nudge of his
cock at her entrance.

Jed pushed. Hope accepted.

His breath fanned the hair next to her ear and he held still
for a moment while she drank in the scent of him. Man and
soap and heat and aroused yearning.

He moved in a silky inner caress so sweet that for the first
time since the last time with her husband, Hope's body craved
release.

She pressed up while Jed plunged in deeper. She felt the
press of his pubis against hers, his strong arms wrapped tightly
around her, while his bristly chest hair tantalized her nipples.

And his kisses!

Deep, heavy yearning kisses that made her want to cry and
fuse him to her forever. This was hello and good-bye to all the
life they might have lived together.

Hope sobbed as her tension built, as she felt Jed's flex of release.

"No, no, don't cry," he said, kissing her temple sweetly.
"I'm sorry, I have to—" He groaned as his spew filled her.

Shuddering, Hope's heart shattered with orgasm as they
came together.

The world righted itself, and Jed raised his head to look at
her. She saw realization dawn as he pulled away.

"No," she whispered, wanting to say more, wanting to deny
what she was, how she lived. Wanting to take back the last two
years of her life.

Jed rose, pulled on his pants. Stood with his back to her for a long moment. She reached out a hand, but he was too far away to touch. Too far away to reach with her heart.

He'd taken what he wanted. And now he'd go back to his quiet life, his beautiful children and think no more about her.

Without looking at Hope again, Jed picked up his hat, placed it carefully on his head, and walked from the room with his jacket draped over his arm.

She would not cry.

She would not.

Hope cried for two days, until even Belle was worried. She rearranged the flowers Hope had just dumped into a vase in the front hall. "A few days ago, Hope would have fussed for twenty minutes making these look just right," Belle commented.

"Her seeing that man was a mistake. She's been weepy and out of sorts ever since. I've never seen her like this," Felicity commented, "not even when we first met her and she was so recently widowed."

"By the time she came to me she was mostly cried out," Belle said. "And she was beginning to feel the stirrings of anger that her man would do something foolish enough to get himself killed over."

Felicity heard an automobile come up the drive and stepped to the front door to peer through the beveled glass. "Someone's coming."

"Captain Jackson, I expect. He called a couple hours ago. The *Nancy Belle* docked this morning." She removed an already overblown rose from the vase with a *tsk*. "Hope would never have put this in here before. She's half out of her mind, I think."

Felicity took the rose and twirled the stem absentmindedly. "She needs time. How bad was she when you met?"

"I very nearly didn't bring her along, she was so sad and withdrawn. But I had a talk with her and she pulled herself together admirably during our trip out here. Remember? She took awhile to warm up to the rest of you."

"But once she did, she kept reminding us about our bright future. There were some dark days when we worried about Lizzie's husband catching up to us. Either him, mad as hell, or the law. Hope kept us on an even keel."

Belle considered. "Hope's a private woman. We'll give her a couple more days before we go sticking our noses in."

"Fine." But Felicity had already moved into the parlor and sidled up to the front bow window.

"Felicity, stop ogling Captain Jackson. It's unbecoming," Belle snapped.

"What? I'm not! Why would I ogle the insufferable man? He's a hard-nosed bastard." But she put her back to the wall and peered out through the side of the parlor window, lifting the drape just enough to see.

Belle rolled her eyes. "Not every man who comes to Perdition House comes to see you," Belle said kindly. "Let it go."

"Hmpf." Felicity dropped the curtain, and walked into the front hall as if she hadn't a care in the world.

The front door opened and Captain Jackson strode in, full of life and vigor as usual. "Ah, Belle!"

He opened his arms and Belle stepped up close for the peck on the cheek he always gave her. They were old friends from childhood.

They embraced and put their heads together to whisper their welcome. Then he reached into his pocket and pulled out a wrapped package tied with twine.

"Thank you, Jackson. I knew I could count on you!" Belle said and slipped the brown-papered packet into her housedress pocket.

They completely ignored Felicity. Not that Felicity cared. Not that Jackson would even notice if she did.

"Belle, I'll just go on out to the swing, make sure it's ready for later," she said, pointedly ignoring the Captain. She tossed her head and strode away, jaunty as could be.

Three days later Jed came out of his shock. Hope lived in that house. Lived and worked there. His beautiful Hope.

A lusty Hope. A woman he hadn't expected to meet.

And God help him, he burned for her.

5

Another week went by while Jed dreamed of Hope every night. The burn he felt for her never eased. It settled near his heart every morning and caused him no end of discomfort.

But at night! The burning heat moved south of his chest and set his dreams on fire. Hope was so much more than he expected. He couldn't get the vision of her sitting across from him in the café out of his mind. But he also couldn't make it blend with the sight of her on the bed, legs splayed, with the slit between them glistening.

To think of her as a dinner companion in public and a bed companion who would go on her knees to take him in the mouth made his head spin.

He'd been taught and had lived by the idea that there were two kinds of women: those you marry and those you don't.

But Hope's expression when he'd slid into her, the way she'd turned her face away, haunted him.

Afterward, with the door shut behind him, he'd taken a moment to put on his jacket and smooth his hair. He'd been weak in the legs and needed the time to gather his beleaguered wits.

Behind the closed door, he heard Hope sob. A gut-wrenching, lonesome sound that wounded him.

He'd wanted to turn the knob and go back in to comfort her, but he felt too ashamed and confused by what had happened.

His fingers tapped out a rhythm on the counter while he waited for Mrs. Johanson to finish with her shopping. She always took her time, determined to get the most for her money.

It was a hard place to live, this limbo. Wanting Hope in a way that couldn't be eased with another woman. Even so, he needed the woman he married to be pure of heart, and to be the kind of woman he wanted to raise his children.

No man would be able to help him sort out what he felt, and no woman should be exposed to this situation.

He had nothing but his conscience to guide him.

Mrs. Johanson finally picked out the thread she wanted and brought the spools to the counter. His heart burned in his chest as he pondered his constant problem, halfheartedly passing a comment on the weather.

"Mr. Devine, seems to me you've got a load on your mind. You've rung up my thread twice."

He rubbed his palm across his chest. "Oh, I'm sorry. Don't know where my mind is today."

"You feeling all right? You been rubbin' your chest since I got in here. My pa did that just before he dropped dead."

He lifted his hand as if it caught fire. "No, I—just got a lot to think about."

"If it's a matter of the heart, you better see to it, because that kind of trouble stays with a man." She patted his hand and took her package of thread out the door. The raucous clatter of the bell over the door echoed his jangled thoughts.

He'd taken to Hope's visits in the store and he missed them. Missed seeing her shy smile, her quiet grin when the girls upstairs made a ruckus. She thought he didn't see how much she liked to listen when they squabbled and giggled, but she never failed to stop what she was doing to smile along with the noise.

She glowed with interest, as if hearing the sounds of family was strange and exotic.

That was what had drawn him to her in the first place. She didn't push her nose into his business, didn't ask a load of personal questions, didn't fawn when he'd finally told her over lunch that Eloise had passed on.

His chest burned again and he knew his loins would too. She'd been so sweetly loving when he'd fallen on her like a rabid dog.

But the scene in her bedroom had played out so much like his dreams that he'd been confused and wild with lust. Her breasts had sprung free and he'd gorged himself. Her wet, luscious slit had called to him and all he could think of was filling it.

She accepted him fully and with passion of her own.

Eloise had never been so slick, so welcoming.

Hope was a woman who pleased a man.

Eloise would never approve.

Suddenly, he no longer cared what Eloise would think.

Hope pulled her thoughts together enough to remember to take her pie out of the oven. There was never a shortage of ingredients at Perdition House. With Jonathan, at the end, his gambling had forced her to stretch her larder thin to the point of failed meals. Pride had stopped her from going begging at the neighbors for a pinch of salt or a cup of flour, but pride couldn't keep a body going for long.

She sighed and put those thoughts away. That was an old pain and she'd sucked the life out of it long ago.

Now she had new pain. A new loss. She missed going to Jed's store, missed hearing his children's feet thudding overhead.

Missed Jed's kind expression, his gentle hand.

It had been three days since his visit here. Now she was convinced he hadn't known that he'd find her at Perdition House.

He'd been shocked when she'd opened the door to her room. Shocked even more by what had happened when she'd closed that door.

Perhaps she should have explained about Jonathan. Maybe Jed would understand that coming to Perdition House had been a matter of life or death. She could have gone elsewhere, into a different house, but all the talk had been about Belle's new venture and Hope had wanted a fresh start in a new place.

She had no idea what Jed thought of her now, after what they'd done together. Well, she had some idea, but she couldn't think of that.

What she wanted to think of was the time they'd spent together before he'd come to Perdition.

She slid the pie to the counter to cool, then dived back in to pull out the rice pudding.

Captain Jackson loved her rice pudding. And what the clients wanted, the clients got. Belle made sure of it.

"Hmm, smells wonderful!" a man's voice declared.

Hope turned to see Felicity and one of her regulars enter the kitchen through the dining-room door.

Tall and brunette, Felicity was a favorite because of her adventurous spirit. She loved trying new things and a lot of the men went right along with her in a spirited search for the best sex they could find.

"Off to your new toy?" Hope asked.

"I want to show Hiram what fun it is," Felicity said with a coy smile.

Hiram ate it up.

"And when we're done, we'll be back for a piece of that pie, Miz Hope, so make sure you save me a slice," he said.

"I certainly will," she promised.

Hiram held the door for Felicity and she trailed her fingers across the bulge in his trousers as she led him out the kitchen door to the side yard.

Somewhere in the trees, Felicity had had Annie design a swing for sex. Hope hadn't ventured out there, so she wasn't sure how it worked. But the men were happy as cats with a bowlful of cream when they returned from a walk outside with Felicity.

Of course, they were always happy with Felicity anyway.

Lizzie came in to filch a dish of pudding. She grabbed a bowl from the dish rack and took a spoon from a drawer.

"How is it you always know when the baking's done?"

"I open the dumbwaiter upstairs and sniff." She scooped out a spoonful. "This is too hot. I'll get the milk and some pudding for you too. You're not eating, Hope."

Hope made a racket by filling the kettle and putting it on to boil.

"Hope?" Lizzie touched her forearm gently. "What's the matter? You've been sad for days."

"Have I? I hadn't noticed. Eat your pudding, Lizzie. You're too thin again." Lizzie was such a tiny woman that she worried overmuch about her waist thickening.

"And you're getting thinner by the day. Is it that man?"

Hope shook her head.

"They're not worth worrying about. Especially not that one. He looked so stern when I saw him leaving."

Hope looked at the warm concern in Lizzie's eyes. "Not all men are like Garth, Lizzie. They're not all bullies and beasts who hit."

Lizzie blinked. "No, no, of course they're not." She blinked again. "Belle does a good job of keeping that sort out of Perdition."

"Yes, she does."

"Gotta watch that Mr. Hutchins, though. He'd hurt a woman if he got a chance."

Hope was horrified. Mr. Hutchins was such a quiet, polite man. But Lizzie knew more about violence in men than Hope did. "Do you think?"

Lizzie nodded. "Not that I've seen anything, mind you, but there's a look in his eyes sometimes when he thinks none of us is watching him."

Hope decided to play closer attention to Mr. Hutchins from now on. "Think you should mention this to Belle?"

"I have. She said she's aware of it, but he has important connections."

Hope nodded. "Thing with important connections is, they'll turn on you faster than you can blink if they think you're gonna get them muddy. Belle has her own connections, anyway. If Hutchins has a mind for hurtin' girls, she'll know it soon enough."

"Still, he won't get an invitation to my room."

"Nor mine," said Hope, with a shiver for emphasis. Damn this life and the dangers it could pose. "Still, there are good men, Lizzie. Men who don't hit, who raise their children with a kind hand."

"Have you heard from him?"

"I don't expect Jed'll ever show his face here again. I showed him the truth and it's too ugly for a good man like Jed. I don't blame him."

Lizzie went red in the face. "You don't need him, anyway, not livin' here the way we do. This is a high life we've got here."

Hope told herself it *was* a good life, an independent life. A life a lot of women would envy.

Lizzie slid a dish of rice pudding along the counter to her. "Eat something," she urged.

"I can't. My stomach—" The door swung open again and Jed Devine stepped into the kitchen, hat in hand. "Jed! What?"

Lizzie stood in front of Hope. "What are you doing here?" Her back was rigid with anger, shoulders squared. Hope had the ridiculous notion she'd pounce on Jed rather than let him come any closer without an invitation.

"Please, Hope, I'd like a few moments of your time, if I may." He bobbed his head in a courtly way.

"You holler, Hope, if you need anything," Lizzie said while she stepped cautiously around Jed to leave them alone.

Hope turned to the sink and grabbed a cloth to scrub at the counter. "This kitchen is always in need of cleaning, with so many meals to prepare and I love to bake desserts myself, and the cook hates it when I leave a mess and I need to get this done, and then there's the laundry—" Jed's hand on hers, burning through her to her heart, cut her off.

"How, Hope? How did you end up here?"

She couldn't look at him, turned away. "Does it matter? I'm here. Have been for two years. What do you think of that?"

She thought she'd avoided this conversation, but even that wish was denied. But this was no time for self-pity; she'd had three days of that. "No more," she said clearly.

"What?"

"No more crying about the how or why of it. Truth is, I'm happy here. I have friends who care about me! Men, yes, *men* who enjoy my company! I have freedom to come and go as I choose. I visited Niagara Falls last year. All by myself, took a train when I got a notion to go and I went. Just like that. Do you know any other women who could do that?"

"No, can't say as I do."

He looked so perplexed by her outburst she wanted to laugh. What must he think?

"So, you're happy?"

He couldn't have asked a more loaded question. It speared

her through the heart, dragged every hope, every dream she'd ever had, ever buried deep, into the light. She cried out with the pain of seeing her dreams held up shiny and new, then dashed again. "I have to be! Can't you see that? I have to be happy here. It'll kill me if I'm not."

His eyes softened and his lips kicked up into a gentle smile that all but drew blood.

He opened his arms and took the two steps that brought him all the way to her. Tired of holding herself together, she went into them, to take whatever comfort she could.

6

Jed slid his arms around Hope and held her tight to his chest. She claimed to be happy in Perdition House, but he couldn't believe his ears. Her eyes said the opposite. He was sure she was only making the best of a bad situation.

The scent of her went to his head. Baked apples, cinnamon, and other baking smells wafted through her hair. She smelled of home and comfort and all the things a good woman should smell of.

He nuzzled at her hair to capture every last bit of her delicious, homey scent. Her breasts pressed soft and womanly against his chest. Her neck was so warm under his nose he set the tip of his tongue against it.

She stilled at the first touch of his tongue. He'd dared to hold her and caress. Did she dare to care for him?

He'd thought he'd seen genuine affection and interest in her gaze and even in the way she'd loved him. He had no experience of fast women and none at all with a woman who responded to a man's desire and passion. Maybe he'd misjudged, but then again, maybe he hadn't.

He touched her neck again in another experimental tasting.

She sighed and settled closer to his chest. With a tilt of her head she offered more of her neck so he could trace the outline of her ear with his tongue. Her breasts rose and fell, and the nipples hardened enough that he could feel the points pressing into him.

He pressed back and raised her chin. Her beautiful eyes swam with unshed tears and he held her face between both palms. Running his thumbs gently over her eyes he gathered the wet before laying claim to her mouth. In reverence, he gentled her mouth open with hesitant kisses and quiet nibbles.

He heard a near-silent moan come from her throat and she was his. All his.

He loved her. With all the passion a man could have. With all the hopes and dreams a man could bring to a marriage.

Hope tasted even better than he remembered as he fell into the kiss, fell headlong into love with her.

His heart thudded and banged against his chest wall, his ears rang with wanting her, and he felt again the warm welcoming comfort that was Hope.

His blood rushed to fill his cock and he buried himself deeper in her mouth. His tongue sought more of her and she opened, moist and needy. Her lips softened in a way that signaled her readiness for more. As soft as her mouth was, she'd be even softer, hotter, wetter below.

The thoughts that rushed through his mind held no confusion. He needed to get in.

In. Hard.

In. Straight.

In. To the heart of her.

And he had to do it now.

Before she could have time to think, to refuse, to consider all the strings he came with.

He lifted her to the counter by the sink, consumed with desire and heat. Her skirts were in the way, but he felt her try to open for him. He tangled his hands with hers as they both reached to lift her skirts. He pulled back and searched her eyes.

Her neck was flushed red, her eyes glowed with a woman's need, and she bit her lip prettily. He thumbed it.

And then she did the most arousing thing.

She opened her mouth and sucked his thumb, twirling her lips and tongue around it.

Hallelujah, she wanted him as much as he needed her. He went back to hiking her skirts to her hips. Somehow, he found himself exposed and ready to slide hilt-deep into her. She must have worked him free of his trousers while he'd been at her dress.

Hope leaned back on her elbows and wrapped her legs around his hips. "Jed, don't think, don't wait. Just do it! I want you so much!"

He didn't want to ask, but he had to. "More than any of the others?"

Her startled eyes widened at the question. "I've never wanted any of the others."

He stopped, thunderstruck by the honesty in her gaze. Not only was her body open and ready and vulnerable, so was her heart. Hope cared for him.

He saw it and believed it. How could he not? Her love was clear in her eyes. In the way she smiled at him, held still when his children giggled, the way she melted around him and showed her desire.

"Jed?" her voice sounded far away and half afraid.

"Tell me, Hope. Tell me what you want. How much you want."

"I want you every way you'll have me."

"Do you want this?" He slid two fingers into her without fanfare, without finesse, without tender preparation. What he found shocked him. She was so open, wet, and needy that he slipped in without a hitch.

He pumped his fingers in and out experimentally. She got wetter, slicker, more open. Her head went back and she closed her eyes in wanton pleasure. For the first time, he saw a woman honest in her need, willing to take her pleasure from a man.

His heart warmed and stuttered in his chest.

He tasted his fingers—the essence of Hope—and found her salty and juicy.

"Do you want this?" he asked before he bent to taste her flesh, soft and hot. He swirled his tongue around her outer lips. In a wild rush of scent, he knew her arousal was complete. She tasted of slick honey and welcome, of woman and heat, of need and lush acceptance. His tongue slid deep into her in a hot parody of the act he wanted most.

In. He wanted in. His cock throbbed, so he slid his hand up and down to keep from grinding into her too soon.

He'd never done these things before, although he wanted to with a fierceness that surprised him. The spice of her rose to him, the heat of her called to him as he licked and plunged and sucked up her juices.

He'd never guessed a woman could be so delicious. There. And here, and in here . . .

He wanted to lick her dry, wanted to suck the nub he found at the top of her slit. He tried a gentle suck and she bucked up toward his mouth with a groan so deep he felt it on his tongue.

"You like that?"

"Yes, Jed, do it again. Harder, faster—fuck me with your fingers while you suckle."

The words, harsh and earthy, rained down on his head as he did what she asked. He slid his fingers inside her again, deeper, harder, as his lips nibbled at the nub that peeked out of a tiny hood. Her voice encouraged and tantalized as Hope bucked and strained toward him. The nub, purple and turgid, rotated under his mouth as Hope caught a rhythm that would take her over a cliff into ecstasy.

He held his place and let her ride it out, thrashing and groaning, and with a deep slide of moisture and a long, keening wail, she rose to his mouth and came in a creamy gush.

He licked and swallowed as she came, thinking only of keeping her there at the pinnacle she'd found.

She only wanted him, had never wanted the others.

Hope wanted him as he wanted her.

No longer able to wait, he pulled her toward him and slid his cock in slowly, feeling her inner pulses as her orgasm completed. He bucked and rode into her, raising her legs to wrap around his waist as he plunged in and out.

His own come raged through him as he shot into her. At the height of sensation, he kissed her, spearing his tongue into the wet heat of her mouth. The feel of her, the taste of her juices mingling with her mouth enhanced his orgasm to breathtaking.

Suddenly, Hope bucked against him and held his ass still as she rode out another come. The grip of her pussy kept him on the edge for longer than he'd ever known.

The door to the kitchen opened and he heard a man clear his throat and a woman giggle behind them. But he didn't care, was too far gone to worry what anyone thought.

He had his Hope. There was nothing else.

But Hope had other ideas. She yelped, then hid her face in his shoulder. "Oh my heavens!"

He gathered her close to shield her and the other couple hurried through the kitchen without speaking.

"Are you all right?"

"I'll never be right again." She shook in his arms. "I'm so ashamed."

The irony was clear, but Jed was too sated to point it out.

Hope slid off the counter, and ran from the room, her face in her hands.

He followed her up to her room where he found the door closed and locked. He knocked.

Silence.

He knocked again and put his mouth to the door frame. "Hope, let me in."

"Jed," her voice came quietly through the door. She must be pressed against it from the other side. "Go home and please don't come back. It's too hard for me. I can't see you again."

"Don't deny me, Hope. I don't come with much to offer. Another woman's children to raise and a shop to keep means I'm not much of a catch, not for a woman like you."

"You're right. You're not what I want, Jed Devine. You and your children are not what I want."

He waited a long moment but when the door still didn't open, he tapped it once more. "I think we are. And we want you." More silence. "I'm going now, Hope. You know where I'll be."

"Hope, Mr. Clarke's here to see you," Belle said. The Friday-night dinner crowd was gathering. The guests milled about downstairs in the dining hall waiting for the ladies to appear. She held an envelope in her hand because Hope hadn't come to the office with the other girls. She tossed the envelope onto Hope's dressing table. Inside was Mr. Clarke's request to spend the weekend with Hope. They'd partnered before and Hope had been receptive to seeing him again.

Hope brushed out her hair with a listless stroke. "I'm not feeling well, Belle. Ask one of the other girls to see to Mr. Clarke." She patted her stomach. "I think I need a hot water bottle."

"No monthlies last for two weeks. Leastwise, I've never

heard of it, and I've heard everything," Belle said. "Mr. Clarke is a powerful ally, Hope, and he likes you. Surely you can spare him some time?"

"Dinner, then I make my excuses."

"Which are wearing mighty thin. Even with me. It's time you did something about Jed, Hope. Past time."

She left Hope with her mouth hanging open.

Did she think everyone was blind? The woman was love-struck.

Love. Bah, the bane of Belle's existence.

Love. Only fools fell in love. Only simpletons believed in it.

Jed was replenishing his stock of men's trousers when the bell over the door chimed the entrance of a customer. In the two weeks since he'd seen Hope, he'd prayed for her to come in to talk, but she never did. His sweet Hope had a stubborn streak he hadn't expected. He was a patient man, but even he had his limits.

He turned to see who had come in.

Belle Grantham, the madam of Perdition House, stood just inside the door, waiting like a queen for his attention.

If a woman could be arrogant, then Belle Grantham was. Used to men jumping to her every whim, her confidence showed in the way she held herself. He saw it in her straight shoulders, the proud bearing of her head. She was a rare beauty and from what he'd heard, an untouchable woman.

Rumor had it ice water ran in her veins, while she kept a steady rein on the girls and clients at her house. He had no idea what she wanted, because her expression gave nothing away.

"Can I help you?" he asked, feeling wary. Not many women made him cautious, but Belle Grantham on a mission was a woman to be reckoned with. "Or did Hope send you?"

"Of course not." Her gaze was coolly appraising as she glanced around the shop.

Until that moment he'd felt the store was in pretty good shape. While she took silent inventory, he reminded himself his displays were neat, his shelves organized into areas for the home, the farm, the kitchen, and clothing.

His belly clenched. "You know her better than I do. Why hasn't she come to me? I've waited two weeks."

"She's not well. Upset. Off her food. You have to tell me what happened between you." She sighed, looked at the ceiling. "She won't say a word."

"If she didn't talk to you, then it's wrong of me to speak."

"I heard about the kitchen, of course, but not the why of it. Hope doesn't behave that way normally and—"

"Neither do I. I'm not sure what happened. I care for her. But she won't answer my calls or my letters."

"I'm aware of the calls and letters. After two weeks most men would give up." She eyed him in much the way she'd looked over the store. He straightened as if for inspection.

"I'm not a quitter, Miss Grantham. Not by a long shot. Has she spoken of me at least?"

"She won't even talk to Felicity and that girl can get information out of anyone."

"Should I come now? I planned to show up at your door anyway. See if I could catch her unawares."

"You might try." She smiled, obviously relieved. She gave him a bold look up and down. "You've got mettle under those shopkeeper's clothes, I'll give you that."

"Do you have any idea why she won't see me or even answer my letters?"

"I've got a hunch." She took a turn around the store, looking at everything, running a hand across the stacks of denim work pants and along the toes of the work boots he had on display. "You've got a nice shop here, and from what I hear, a flock of children upstairs."

"Yes, ma'am, I do."

"And no mama for those kids."

"My wife, Eloise, passed on about two years ago."

"You got any prospects for the next Mrs. Devine?"

He shook his head. "I've got Hope. She's all I've ever wanted in a woman."

"Well." She eyed him again, looked thoughtful. "You sure?"

"I want her."

"Then that's the problem."

"How can that be? I'd have thought a woman in Hope's position would be thankful—"

She held up her hand, cut him off. "Hold up there. I don't think you grasp the situation out there at Perdition House."

He was getting tired of the waiting and the hide-and-seek Hope was playing at. He wanted her. She should be happy and accept him. "Not every man would be able to accept what Hope's been doing," he said. "I'm willing to forgive all that."

"Forgive? I see. And when you're feeling all that forgiveness, will you remind her once in a while how you rescued her? Or are you willing to forget as well as forgive?"

He wasn't sure he liked her tone, but he understood her point. "I won't make her feel less wanted because of her circumstances when we met. I've had a lot of time to think about everything, including the life I had with my very righteous wife. I wouldn't be that way with Hope. She's got the soul of an angel and that's all I see."

"That's so, and I'm relieved you know it." She eyed him some more, but now her gaze held approval. "Hope came to me out of desperation. Her husband had been beaten and left for dead for cheating at cards. She held out as long as she could, but in the end, I was the best choice out of many worse ones." Her tone softened. "She asked for a job. I gave it to her, but she's never been happy in her work, if you catch my meaning."

He remembered the startling revelation that Hope never wanted the men she took to her bed.

But she wanted him. He knew it, felt it, saw it in her eyes, felt it in her deep clenches that came with her release.

"She wouldn't tell me what happened, even though I asked."

"She never wanted to live this life. It shames her. You're the kind of man she always wanted but feels she can't have now. Hope loved her husband, gave him everything a man could want, and he threw it away on a game of cards."

It pained him that Hope had loved before. But her first husband wasn't worthy of her. He only hoped he'd do better. She deserved the best.

"I'll be there at 7 o'clock," he said. "Warn her if you want to, or not."

"I think not."

Hope slid into the hot tub of water and submerged her entire head. She loved bathing and Perdition House had lots of hot water. There was a boiler for every third bedroom, more than enough to supply all the girls.

She'd been doing that lately, reminding herself of how heavenly life was here. All the little things Belle had added to the house for the girls' comfort added up.

It was far better for her to think about these things than to think about Jed. What he'd said through her bedroom door the last time he was here still stung.

Imagine a man like Jed, kind, decent Jed, thinking that he and his children would be a burden to a woman. There was nothing more precious than to be entrusted with the care of another woman's children and she couldn't believe he would be willing to offer himself and his children to her.

But it would haunt her forever if she ruined all their lives. She loved Jed too much to wreck his life and the lives of his children.

What chance would that dear blond sprite have if folks knew what her stepmother was? No chance, that's what. None.

She went back to her inventory of reasons to stay in Perdition House. She figured if she kept counting them off, they might eventually total to something worthwhile.

Annie's innovations helped everyone. From Felicity's contraptions to the peepholes she'd had the girls secretly install.

Slowly, the bath gentled her thoughts and Hope felt better as she scrubbed and soaped all over. She washed and rinsed her hair, then wrapped it in a towel. Yes, there were lots of reasons to stay here, and even more reasons not to go to Jed.

She stood and stepped out of the tub, dripping water and leftover bubbles.

"Hope?" Jed called to her from her room.

She lifted a towel off the rack and tiptoed across the floor to where her bathrobe hung on a hook. But it was too late.

Jed peered into the bathroom and stared at her, taking in her nakedness.

"What are you doing here?" she asked as she reached for her robe. He snatched it off the hook before she could get it.

She clutched the towel to her chest, but it still revealed too much.

It hurt to look at him. Her heart pounded painfully. "Go away, Jed. I can't talk to you right now."

"But I need to talk to you."

"There's no point." She turned and headed through the doorway into Annie's room, a clever design that Annie had come up with so two girls could share a bathroom.

Jed followed.

She turned. "I said no." Then she ran out into the hall, thinking to double back into her room and lock him out.

But he was fast on her tail, his eyes ablaze with determination and temptation. Oh, the temptation!

"Don't come any closer." She whirled away, but he didn't stop.

She dashed down the stairs to the landing, but Jed kept coming. She took a second to wrap the towel around her body, then took off again.

At the bottom of the stairs, she belted toward the front door, but it opened and two men walked in. She slid to avoid a collision with the first one, then careened off toward the kitchen in the nick of time.

Jed's heavy footfalls followed again.

The men called out to her and then again to Jed as he strode past. "Go get her, friend!"

"Yes! She's worth every dime," came another call, making Hope's ears burn with humiliation. She took a quick glance behind her. No, she didn't know him. Small mercy.

Jed stopped and took three steps back to the men. "Who said that?"

The younger of the men, a boy barely out of college, laughed. "She's a beauty, I've had a hankering for her myself."

Jed punched him in the face.

The young man sagged against his friend, then slid to the floor, out cold.

Hope screamed.

Jed scowled.

Hope ran.

7

Jed's knuckles stung where they'd connected with the young buffoon's face, but still, it felt good to let fly with the solid punch. He glanced to make sure the man was breathing, then took off after Hope again.

She'd gone into the kitchen. He could take his time now. She had nowhere else to go.

Maybe he could coax her into the pantry so they could have some privacy to talk.

But when he walked through the kitchen door, she was slamming the door to the side yard. She was outside, running through the gardens in nothing more than a towel. Damn the woman's stubborn streak!

She'd catch her death of cold that way, not to mention the added embarrassment of her hither and yon dash for freedom.

He picked up the pace from a fast walk to a trot. Then when he saw her head for the cliff he started to run.

Oh! God, no! She wouldn't jump, she couldn't. Was she that delicate of spirit?

He didn't think so, not after what Belle had told him, but no man could know the way of a woman's mind. They were strange creatures at the best of times.

And these were not the best of times. Not for Hope.

He'd frightened her with his lust. She'd accepted him as a lover, but he wanted more than that and for reasons of her own, she felt they were doomed.

"Hope! Stop!" But it was too late. She disappeared down the cliff side at a dead run.

Heart pounding, feet thumping the earth, he ran hard to the spot he last saw her. As he drew nearer he saw a railing.

Stairs! She taken a set of stairs down to the beach.

He followed, angry at her foolish behavior and relieved beyond measure that she hadn't jumped.

Fool woman! What the hell was she up to?

As he caught at the railing, he heard more ruckus behind him. The entire household trailed along, yelling and calling.

Women in their house robes, gentlemen in their shirt sleeves (and one in a lady's underthings that he refused to accept he saw) all ran across the lawn helter-skelter and from all directions.

Below him, past the first landing and well onto the second set of stairs, ran Hope. The towel on her head hung down her back, the one clutched at her chest threatened to fall.

He followed her down the cliff, mind racing, heart racketing a steady tattoo.

He had no idea what to say when he caught her.

Hope headed down the next flight of steps, hellbent on getting to the bottom and running as far and as fast as she could go.

Didn't he see she didn't want to speak with him? Couldn't have him in her life? This was just one more torment she'd been given.

Jed Devine: even his last name mocked her.

Her breath was coming in hard gasps now, pain coming with each one. Her heart thudded and thumped, which surprised her because she was certain it was broken so badly it wouldn't work.

But it did, pumping and thumping and reminding her she was alive and would be for a long time to come.

She tore the towel from her head. It was wasted weight, tiring her uselessly.

She felt a splinter dig into her right foot. Great! She'd landed hard on her left foot on her way off the porch step so that ankle was none too dependable, but even if she had to hobble she'd keep going until that fool man behind her gave up.

In the end it was the sharp pebbles and rocks on the beach that did her in. She fell headlong into a pile of dried seaweed that stank of dead sea creatures and buzzed with flies.

She got to her knees, but the towel snagged on a piece of driftwood. She tugged but it wouldn't come, so she pulled free of the towel, got to her feet, and started up the beach again.

"Hope, for God's sake! You're naked."

Jed! He was closer than she thought. He was wearing boots so the stones hadn't slowed him down.

She turned, hair loose and blowing, the front of her covered with dirt and bits of debris from the seaweed, but she didn't care.

"Jed, go away. Why won't you go away?" Her voice broke in between her heaving breaths.

She dropped her head, placed her hands on her knees so she could stay on her feet while she caught her breath. She felt a dry heave from her belly, but controlled it.

A loud cheer went up from the people that lined the cliff above. She'd never live this down. Even if she lived for eternity, she'd be reminded forever about her naked run to the beach.

She stared down at her feet, straining for each breath, willing her heart to slow when a pair of men's boots appeared directly in front of her own naked and bleeding toes.

A jacket landed beside the boots, quickly followed by a shirt. Trousers and dangling suspenders slid down to cover the boots.

"Oh, my Lord, what do you think you're doing?" she gasped out as she rose to full height.

Jed lifted a foot and removed his boot and sock. Then he did the other foot too.

"If you want to shame yourself this way, then I can't let you do it alone. You don't have to do anything alone ever again, Hope."

The catcalls and jeers from the cliff top quieted as Jed stripped off his long johns and joined her in her nakedness.

He was magnificent.

Sculpted muscles, trim waist, bleeding knuckles. "You're hurt!" She raised his hand to her lips and kissed each broken patch of skin. "You punched that man. I don't know him. I've never . . ."

"I know, but it wouldn't matter to me if you had." He pulled her to his chest and against her better judgement, she went. His body heat felt like salvation and she shivered. "You're cold, Hope. Let me give you my jacket."

"We'll share."

In the end, he swaddled her in his shirt, then hung his jacket from his shoulder so he could carry her over the rocks, up the four flights of stairs, and to the back of the house.

By some odd emotional trickery, the crowd had dissipated, wandering back to their own pursuits by the time they reached the lawn. Perhaps Belle had convinced them Jed and Hope needed their privacy.

Jed set her down on the soft grass and they walked together, arms wrapped around each other.

They found no one in the kitchen, nor the front hall, nor on the stairs. When they finally got to her room, Jed slid his forehead to hers. His eyes filled with concern and a deep love Hope had no choice but to deny.

"We have to talk," he said.

"Let's get warm first." She stalled and turned toward the bathroom centered between Annie's room and hers.

The tub steamed with fresh hot water. The scent of lavender rose into the air. A tray with mugs and a pot of coffee sat wrapped in a towel on a stool beside the tub. Next to the coffeepot was a flask of brandy for added measure.

"Annie must have done this." She'd find a way to repay this kindness some day.

"You have good friends. People who care about you," Jed commented with a touch of a finger on the coffeepot. He lifted the flask and took off the top. Sniffed.

He cocked an eyebrow at her. "I'm not much of a drinker, but this is a rare occasion." The humor in his voice was unmistakable.

"Yes, it is. I've never run naked across the lawn before, but I promise I'll never do it again."

"That's good. I don't think I could carry you up that cliff again." He poured a measure of brandy into both china mugs on the tray.

Hope turned her face away to hide the smile that split her face. She couldn't imagine any other man doing something so outrageous. The staid shopkeeper and father of four. She shook her head in wonder at the sight they must have made.

She slid off his shirt and slid into the tub of water. The hot water stung the grazed skin on her toes. "Join me?" she asked with a wince at the sting.

"Another first for me. Bathing with a woman. When will they end, I wonder?" His smile caught at her heart.

He joined her in the tub, his back to the water faucets, his long feet on either side of her hips. His knees poked above the water's surface like little Mt. Rainiers, without the snowy tops.

Because the coffeepot and tray were closer to him, he poured them each a mug and passed her one. The brandy changed the scent to spicy and she breathed it in before trying a sip. It warmed her down to her belly.

"Why did you run?"

"I don't want this." She waved her hand at him then placed it over her heart. She probably shouldn't have, because the gesture put a knowing smile on his lips.

"You don't want us to make love anymore? Or be in love anymore?"

"Love has nothing to do with what we do with each other. Love doesn't belong in Perdition House. Not ever."

"Why not?"

"Belle says it's bad for business."

His roar of laughter shook the coffeepot and sloshed bath water dangerously close to the top of the tub.

"If she thinks love will make a woman leave the house, then, yes, I guess it would be bad for business."

"Leave the house?"

"That is what we're talking about here, Hope. I want you to leave Perdition House."

"And why would I do that?"

"Because I want to marry you. Give you a respectable home."

She sagged so deeply she felt the water less than an inch from her nose. She blew bubbles in the water to give herself time to frame a response.

Eventually, she did. "You don't mean that. You can't take me home to those children of yours. Can you see me behind a dry goods counter if a man came in who recognized me? How about imagining me in church with your children? What would your wife's family say, her friends?"

"I don't much care what anyone says. And I think I proved that when I stripped to buck naked down on the beach." He sipped at his brandied coffee.

"It was the first time I saw you like that." She felt heat rise from her loins to her nipples.

He noticed.

He leaned so he could skim a finger across the bobbing pink bud. "I've never see you in the altogether until today either. Up til now, we've kept most of our clothes on. You're more beautiful even than in my dreams."

"You dream about me?"

He leaned back, left her breasts to float untouched on the surface. "For weeks now. Day, night, doesn't seem to matter. You're all I think about."

"Well." She considered everything he said. "That has to stop."

"I think marriage will take care of matters nicely."

"I have a better idea for both of us."

"That is?"

"You come to see me whenever you want. I can call you, too, and invite you, of course."

"I could do that anyway."

He had her there. "True. But this is different. We'll be lovers, no business between us."

"Won't work."

"Why not?"

"I can't share you."

"But it wouldn't be sharing. At least not here"—she tapped her chest over her heart—"where it counts."

"The hell it wouldn't. I can't bear to think of anyone else being where I've been, doing what I've done with you. Look into your heart, Hope. Could you feel the same about me if I was with one of the other women? Or how about I ask for your friend who left us this coffee?"

"Annie would never do that. Not when she knows how I feel."

His face closed, went hard. He'd made his point, she supposed. "But I still won't marry you."

8

"This stubborn streak of yours will be the death of me," Jed said. Hope would have to come to her decision in her own time. Sooner or later, she'd get around to explaining the real reason she refused him. But still, he wasn't a patient man for all his good intentions.

But, right now, with her breasts floating on the surface of the bath water and her toes wriggling just under his sac, his mind went in a different direction.

Hope watched Jed's incredibly readable face and knew the exact moment when his cock responded to her teasing toes. His expression turned intent. When his knees opened to lean against the walls of the tub, she knew he'd forgotten about pressuring her into marriage.

It was a ridiculous idea. An upstanding man sacrificing his good name and reputation and the future of his children by marrying a prostitute. She'd never heard such nonsense.

He shifted one foot from the outside of her hip to the inside of her thigh and she melted in anticipation.

"Two can play at this game, *Miz* Teague," he said on a soft, sensual tone.

His big toe tapped delicately at her center. A thrill shot up to her womb. She softened between her legs in readiness.

Her own knees widened of their own accord.

His grin said it all. This was a test of wills.

He cocked an eyebrow at her. She lifted one right back.

"My, my, the brandy in the coffee has made me very warm. You? Mr. Devine?"

"I'm hot as Hades, Miz Teague."

"Heat crawling under your skin, making you burn?"

"Yes, ma'am, I'm burning." He slipped his hand under her heel and lifted her toes to his mouth.

The sensation of having her toes sucked went straight to her nether region and had her shoot out of the tub. "Oh, my! That's . . . a lowdown dirty trick, Mr. Devine . . . oh, my word . . ." Her head sank back onto the edge of the tub. The world went dark as her eyes slid shut. Filled with the heady sensation of each toe being drawn into his hot, wet mouth, his bottom teeth scraping across the sensitive pads, heat filled Hope's lowest belly. Her nipples tightened into hard pebbles and her hand slid to the foot he had placed oh so close to her core.

She touched the top of his big toe and pressed it against her hottest button.

"You like that?" Jed asked from someplace filled with sex and images and sensual excess.

Hope shuddered and rocked her pelvis toward his marauding, tapping toe. Pleasure beyond bearing rose up her belly to her heart, where it threatened to explode out of her chest.

He kept up the suckling while his toe continued to pleasure her beneath the water. The more she thrashed, the harder he sucked and tapped.

Revenge.

This type of torment needed revenge!

"Uhh," she moaned and felt the telltale swell of her clit as she got closer and closer . . .

Suddenly her world was awash as Jed dragged his foot back and positioned himself on his knees before her. Strong hands hoisted her to the tub rim, the water draining away from her body, leaving her exposed to the air.

Exposed to the wickedness of Jed's mouth and tongue.

His face changed from lover to marauder as he balanced her on the edge. She lifted her feet to the rim on either side of him and held herself steady.

Jed dived face first into her honey and lapped and speared her with his tongue. Arching wildly, she offered every secret she possessed for his delectation and he took full advantage of her precarious balance.

She had to work to stay on the tub rim and that gave him ample opportunity to keep her from coming. Delicate touches of his tongue had her begging for more, deep intrusion gave her hope that he'd take her where she needed to go, but he withdrew just short of orgasm.

"You're a devil, Jed Devine." Who'd have thought a mild shopkeeper could be such a toe-sucking, honey-eating wonder?

He growled as she shifted and rocked toward his seeking mouth. His arms encircled her hips to help her balance.

With his help, she was able to let herself go and fall into an incredible orgasm. She gushed and he drank of her juices thirstily.

"Oh, Jed! Yes!" She keened a cry of such urgency he took pity and held the flat of his tongue against her clit so she could rub and rock against it. His fingers finally entered her as her inner walls clenched and released in fulfillment.

When her shudders eased and she could no longer stay on

the rim, Jed lifted her in his arms and carried her to the bed in her room. She sprawled, sated, while he went back into the bathroom to fetch towels.

He dried her gently, front and back, before tending to his own dripping body.

She slid under the covers, holding them up in invitation.

He sat on the edge of the bed instead.

"No, Hope. This is it. You decide now. I want to marry you. I want a life with you and until you say yes, I can't come back here. I won't make love to you again."

She sputtered in disbelief. "All I ever wanted was to be married, to have a family, be a wife. But Jed, it's too late now."

"It's not. I want all that with you."

"Let me finish, please. All my dreams were dashed by Jonathan's gambling. That was hard, but when I entered Perdition, I gave up that foolishness. I don't have the right to even wish for it now. Not after what I've done, what I've become."

"Hush now, Hope." He looked pained. "Don't dwell on the things you've had to do to stay alive."

"It isn't just living here. I can accept what I've had to do. It's what my history will do to you if it comes out. You'll be ruined!"

"We'll move away. Go where no one knows either of us. Maybe Alaska. Or if that's too cold, we could try Vancouver. We could be happy in Canada."

She didn't want to tell him about the Canadian politicians who'd made the trip to Perdition. The house's reputation was known far and wide and in the most influential and exclusive circles.

It wouldn't be easy to convince him, she could see that clearly. "Your children deserve a mother they can be proud of."

"My children are already intrigued by you."

"How? I've never met them."

"We have a hidden spy hole between floors. It's so the children can watch when the store's empty or I need to run upstairs for something. They've watched you smiling at their antics and have asked about you. You have a much warmer smile than Miss Spencer does."

"Who's Miss Spencer?" she asked tartly.

He smiled. "A schoolteacher who's set her cap for me."

"We'll see about that!"

His smile went sly.

"Oh! You mentioned her just to get my goat." Piqued at how easily he could expose her weakness, she scowled.

"No, I didn't, but I'm mighty pleased with your reaction. I can only imagine what hers would be if she knew about you." He pursed his lips together and knit his brows, while flaring his nostrils.

Hope chuckled. "Is she all that bad?"

"Horrible. Doesn't like children. She scowls whenever she hears a peep from mine upstairs. I believe she's of the 'children should be seen and not heard' school of thought. I can't figure why she thought to be a teacher."

"Because she wouldn't be a whore."

He pinched the bridge of his nose looking for all the world like an exasperated man.

"Look, Hope. You've got to forgive yourself for the choice you made. You had no alternative."

"This Miss Spencer. Is she pretty?"

"She's got brown hair. Taller and thinner than you. Wears spectacles to read. Forbidding and cold. And she has a tight, pinched mouth. A very unkissable mouth."

Hope giggled and felt oh so much better.

"Does she have a family?"

"She lives with her parents, if that's what you mean."

Hope sighed. Parents. Maybe if she'd had her parents, her choices would have been different. "I don't have any."

"Parents? I'm sorry. When did they die?" He leaned over

her, his dear, kind face sorrowful. She felt loved and wanted, coddled and cared for.

Oh, God, why did he have to make this so hard? But she pulled out her last bit of ammunition and took aim.

"I don't know that they are dead. My parents left me in an orphanage when I was a toddler. I don't remember them. It . . . it caused a lot of commotion in Jonathan's family when he wanted to marry me. He was disowned."

"Why?"

"He came from a good family, upstanding in their community, and they didn't want an orphanage brat to ruin that standing. They wanted a woman of good breeding and since mine was suspect they didn't think I'd have the high moral standards needed to be a Teague. They were right."

She gathered her strength. "Marrying me ruined Jonathan. We had to struggle on a bank clerk's salary. We scrimped and saved so we could move to Butte. That's in Montana," she explained, in case he hadn't heard of the worst hellhole in the country, "where his uncle owned a mine. Jonathan got a job as bookkeeper and we thought we'd be fine. Then I lost . . . Our baby died, and Jonathan started visiting the card tables." She twisted the top blanket in her fingers, finding it hard to catch her breath and harder still to keep her eyes from filling with tears.

"If he had never married me, Jonathan would be married to someone else, still in the bosom of his family. He'd be happy!" She sobbed, once, then snapped her mouth shut tight. She'd said enough.

Guilt, ugly and sure, rose up like bile from her soul.

Surely Jed would see the folly in pursuing her now.

She wiped an errant tear on the sheet.

Jed gazed at her, looking watery through her tears. Or were they tears of his own?

"If you'd had a family, you'd have had somewhere to go when he died. If you'd chosen to starve to death instead of going to Belle for a job, we'd never have met. If my wife weren't so cold in bed, I might have remarried sooner. But I didn't know what I was missing until you took me inside you and turned me inside out. Hope, don't turn me away now."

She covered her lips with her fingertips. Held in another sob.

"Oh, Jed."

"Too many ifs in our lives, Hope, to let any more of them in now. I love you. And you love me."

He leaned over her, trapping her on the bed, holding her in place with nothing more than his serious stare. How could she refuse him when he was so right?

"Marry me, Jed, and we'll have no more what ifs. I love you so. I'll love you forever."

"Forever."

Faye woke with a start, tears trickling onto the pillow. She was in Mark's bed, *at the hotel*.

Touched as she was by Hope and Jed, she should have been safe here. Should have had a good night's sleep.

Mark struggled to rise on his elbow. They'd spooned in the night and his hand cupped her breast. Her nipple lay between two fingers. He squeezed them, bringing the nipple to a bud immediately. "What's up?" he asked groggily. "Aside from my cock?"

Which she felt nudging at her backside. Deliciously available and ready.

"I had a dream. A very sexy and arousing dream." She was soaking wet and ready to come. Belle had told her she probably wouldn't dream while she was away from the house, but obviously Hope hadn't bothered to wait.

Normally, after one of the dreams, Faye would have her hand on and in her pussy. But this morning, she had Mark. She shifted to her back and stroked his cock, hot and eager.

An early morning kiss turned avid and she burrowed into his heat.

She slid down the bed until she found his hard-on, already wet at the tip. Tightening her mouth around him, she tasted his hot flesh and licked him from sac to tip. Then she pushed Mark to spread-eagle on the bed. No finesse, no slow teasing.

"Great way to wake up," he murmured as he guided her head to take more.

Too randy to wait, she got him good and wet, then squatted over him, balancing on the balls of her feet. "Look, Mark, look at my wet pussy as I slide onto you." The dreams made her rapaciously horny and she needed to act now. Heat skimmed under her flesh, rousing her to near ecstasy.

He still looked bleary, but was waking fast. "I can see it. You're dripping and I can see those deep pink inner lips I love to swirl with my tongue."

Faye, head still reeling, dropped her hand to her outer lips and opened them. She spread her hood to expose her pulsating clit. She tapped it with her forefinger.

"Let me see my cock slide in, Faye." He took over the tapping on her clit so she could balance. Surges of sensation rose and zinged around her belly and up to her heart.

She guided the bulbous head of his cock to her clit and swirled it in circles, to tease and prepare her for the plunge to come. The incredible combination of her dream-aroused state and his morning erection made her wild. His avid expression as he watched had her rocking back on her heels so he could see more.

"I don't think I even need to fuck you to get off this morning. Just seeing your hungry face is enough to make me come," she said in a saucy tone meant to arouse and tantalize him. Her belly clenched with need, her pussy dripped with readiness.

"Fuck me. Slide down on me, Faye."

She let him in about half an inch, not enough to take the whole head, but enough for him to feel her heated channel begin to envelope him. The sensation was exquisite torture. The almost-there feel of him, the titillation of her clit, the throbbing of her vaginal walls.

She couldn't take another moment.

But she could take all of him in one deep slide. She rocked once, twice, making sure her clit rubbed hard on his pubis and that his jutting cock hit home.

She came in a mad rush of release the moment he cupped both breasts in his hands. He spiked the orgasm by squeezing her nipples when she moaned and panted.

Mark grunted with his own orgasm and rose even deeper into her as he held her still. She reached around to squeeze his sac gently to heighten his sensation. He groaned, head thrown back.

When he finished, she slid off to cuddle into his side, blowing her bangs off her forehead.

"That was great! You're a wild woman, Faye."

She agreed, happily.

He cupped her cheek. "I want to see you tonight. I already want more."

"I can't. I've got a million and one things to do. Did I tell you I'm opening another TimeStop? I need to go hunting for another location."

He took her refusal in good humor. "You'll be as busy as I am over the next few weeks."

It pleased her to see he didn't expect her at his beck and call. She had a business to run and he accepted her career would interfere on occasion.

"Maybe both of us being busy is a good thing. We've kind of skipped a whole lot of the 'getting to know you' stuff that most people do."

"Are you ready to get to know me? Last night you wanted to keep this light."

"There's light and then there's light." She rose to her elbows. "I want to know what's happening with you, interested in your expansion into retail. All that good stuff."

"You're sure about tonight? I'm catching a plane home first thing in the morning."

She frowned. "I didn't tell you, but I've decided not to sell the house I inherited. I'm living there instead. That's why I need to expand into a second store. So between cleaning and repairs and the new location . . ."

He nodded and kissed her lips lightly. "A head for business on top of a dynamite body. How'd I get so lucky?" He nuzzled her neck. "I'll call from Denver. I've got to sell my place there."

"Then we can explore the infinite possibilities of phone sex." She thought the girls might get a kick out of that one. It was a pretty sure bet they hadn't done it that way, ladies of the evening or not.

"Not nearly good enough, but we'll manage. I'll be back and forth from Denver a couple of times at least." He grinned, and rose from the bed. He held out his hand.

"Great! Just call ahead. I'll see if I can clear my schedule," she teased.

With a growl, he picked her up in his arms to carry her. "I'll give you notice, if you promise to end up here for the night. I don't care what time you show up, just be here for the morning. Oh, and save those wild, horny dreams all for me. I like the way you wake up after one."

"I'm having them more and more often," she said. "It's disturbing." She slid to the floor while he adjusted the faucets for their shower.

"You mean they're not all about me?"

She laughed. "No, they're about people that must have been alive back in the early part of the nineteen-hundreds. Judging by the clothes and the cars I see, maybe even before the First World War."

"That is weird. What are they doing?"

"Having sex, falling in love. They play out like movies. There's a beginning, middle, and end."

He held the shower curtain open so she could step in before him. The roar of the water filled her ears and she thought the conversation would die as he reached to soap her all over.

"I'm not surprised you'd dream about movie people. You do own a clothing store full of old Hollywood clothing. Obviously, you love the history of Hollywood and old black-and-white movies, right?"

"Right. I guess that's it." His hands lathered her chest, making her skin slick and warm. When he slid his fingers across her slit she lost her train of thought.

His fingers rubbed and tugged between her legs. "And you've been taking sex lessons, so put it all together and . . ." He plunged two fingers into her and let her ride his hand, bringing her to an exquisitely joyful orgasm as the water streamed around them.

This time, the arousal was all hers, not influenced by a dream or some other bit of spirit trickery.

His response to her comment about her dreams showed her a pragmatic side that might or might not become bothersome. She doubted a pragmatist would accept being haunted.

9

"Hope was eager to move on. That's why she told you her story while you were away from the house."

"What do you mean, 'move on'?" Faye wrung out her wash rag, then lifted the bucket of blackened water to carry through to the kitchen to toss.

"Jed was waiting for her."

The water bucket sloshed as Faye stopped in shock. "So, Hope's gone?" Never to be dreamed of again.

"Yes. Apparently."

"Oh." Faye didn't know what to feel. No more cinnamon and apple smell wafting around the kitchen. But that was self-ish, she realized as she tilted the bucket to drain it down the sink. Hope was with Jed now and she could never wish them apart. "Why didn't she go before? Surely she told the end of her story to Auntie Mae?"

Belle pursed her lips and looked resigned. "Your aunt learned to block out the dreams."

Interesting. "So Auntie Mae kept Hope here? Kept her and Jed apart?"

"In your aunt's defense, none of us knew that telling a story to its happy conclusion would release the spirit to move on."

"Do you think that's how it works? A happy ending means the spirits get to move on?" Made her wonder what an unhappy ending would mean. She shivered.

This did not bode well for a good night's sleep. She'd had hints that more of the girls fell in love. Now that everyone knew Hope had gone to spend eternity with Jed, Faye and her sleep patterns were in for a rocky road.

"I'm already sleep-deprived and oversexed. How much longer can this go on?" The great sex was well, great, but the lack of sleep was miserable.

"As long as you can, my dear."

"I need a couple of nights off. I'd hoped to have a good night's sleep at Mark's hotel last night, so now I'm dragging my butt around here."

She filled her bucket with more hot water and cleaning solution. "I have so much cleaning to do and I also need a clear head for business. But I'm a zombie. Think the other girls can be patient?" Or she'd have to figure out how her Auntie Mae had blocked out the dreams. "You wouldn't care to tell me how I'd do that, would you?"

"Would you want to block out dreams that might help your friends move on?" Belle looked disappointed.

"No, of course not." Rats! A conscience could be a real pain sometimes. She grabbed a clean wash rag off the drying rack and headed back into the dining room.

Annie slid down the draperies from the ceiling. She was dressed in dungarees again, like when Faye first met her. "I can wait, Faye. I remember what it's like to need sleep. When we were building this place, I'd stay up half the night going over the plans. Learned how to read blueprints that way."

"Thanks, Annie. Between these lusty dreams and trying to

find a location for TimeStop and bouncing between Mark and Liam, I'm a wreck."

"You gotta give up something, and it shouldn't be sex, and it can't be the location-hunting, so it's gotta be the dreams. I'll go last, if that'll help."

Faye thought a minute. "So, that means you found love at Perdition House, too?"

"I surely did." She rocked back on her work boot-heels. "My man Matthew's waiting, but he's patient. Always was."

Faye could almost see a piece of straw hanging out of the corner of Annie's mouth. The mischief in her eyes was contagious.

Belle laughed. "Matthew Creighton had to be patient. Annie wanted to sell her cherry to the highest bidder, all the while ignoring Matthew."

"And Matthew waited, knowing about the bidding?" This was too delicious. Selling her cherry in a house like Perdition must have caused a stir. The men who visited here were wealthy beyond well-to-do. The bids must have been astronomical. Annie was a beautiful tomboy, with lustrous, curly hair, a trim, athletic body, and energy to burn.

She'd have been quite a prize back in the day.

Annie grinned, lifted her hat, then settled it back on her head. "First off, he had to figure out I was a girl. That took some time."

"I bet it would. Especially if you looked like that. Lift your hat again," Faye said.

Annie obliged and held the brim of her hat in her hands.

"Your hair's short. Like a man's." She really had presented herself as she'd been when she first arrived. "How long did you wait before deciding to offer yourself for auction?"

"I met Belle when I was eighteen. We spent most of a year

building the house and settlin' in. Then we set up the business and right away wanted to build additions."

"How long?"

"Three years."

"How long was Matthew here?"

Annie blushed and the rosiness in her cheeks destroyed the masculine image she wanted to portray. "I said it took a time for Matthew to see me as a woman, didn't I? If my hair was long, pfft, he'd'a seen me for a girl right off."

"So you hid yourself under these clothes and kept your hair cut?"

Annie shuffled her feet and hung her head.

"Well, damn," Faye said, "now I want to hear this story right away."

Belle chuckled. "We've all waited this long, Faye; we're happy to wait awhile longer. Making you suffer is not what we want to do. Not at all."

"Besides," said Annie, "you've got to get down to your own business. Forget about us for a while. We'll still be here when you're ready to hear more."

But Faye could see the anxiety underlying Annie's good-hearted offer. She wanted to see her Matthew again. What's more, she deserved to.

Felicity's voice echoed through the room. "I agree."

"So do I." Lizzie, the practical joker of the bunch, called from a distance. She preferred hanging around out in the garden. She only came into the house when she had to. "If we have to tell how we fell in love, then I think Annie should go before me. She waited a lot longer than I did."

Belle smiled indulgently. "Yes, but your story's such a good one, Lizzie."

Lizzie blushed. "It is, isn't it?" She sighed.

"See? This is making me crazy," complained Faye. "I need to sleep without dreams, I need to find a store location so I can get Perdition House repaired and maintained, and I've got two men keeping me so hot I can't think straight. What am I supposed to do first?"

"Find your store location. Without a second store, you'll have to sell the mansion. None of us wants that," Belle suggested.

"Agreed," said Lizzie.

"Me, too," said Felicity.

"And me," said Annie. "We'll wait."

True to their word, the girls left her to sleep dreamlessly for a couple of nights. It was heaven in Perdition again.

On the third morning, Faye sat in the gazebo and read the retail lease listings to find the right location for a second Time-Stop. She enjoyed the faint strains from a gramophone that Lizzie conjured while she read. The girls needed something to do to fill their time while they waited. Annie was constantly measuring things and advised her on repairs that needed to be done, while Felicity fanned herself on the front porch and read old dime novels.

For the most part, she found them cooperative, but they all missed Hope.

She ran her eye down the listings again, but nothing appealed to her, so she flipped open her cell phone and called in reinforcements in the form of her friend and assistant manager, Willa. "I need help. How soon can you get here?"

"Kim?" Willa called with her hand only half covering the mouthpiece so Faye could hear. "I'm headin' up to the la-di-dah mansion to help Faye. You handle things. Don't forget that shipment that's going to Delaware."

Kim's response was too soft to hear, but Faye could guess

what it was. Since Kim had been the one to get the Internet side of the business going, she never liked to be reminded to take care of the shipping for the great orders it brought in. She figured Willa should have more faith.

Faye agreed. Kim was a godsend to TimeStop. To have two employees who took such pride in the store was incredibly lucky. She valued both women.

Within hours, Willa arrived in a flurry of spandex and sequins. The woman wouldn't know the meaning of subtle if she was hit over the head with it. She strode into the front hall, slapped her oversized bag onto the table and wrapped her arms around Faye in a bear hug Faye couldn't resist. "Oh, girl, how you doin'?"

"Oh!" She felt the soft squishiness of Willa's chest and took comfort in the familiar scent of her talc. "The hug is for my breakup with Colin?"

"Of course it is," Willa said with a deep squeeze that threatened to accordion Faye's rib cage.

"He was fucking his receptionist when I walked in. And not particularly well, either." She laughed in between squeezes. Willa had never liked Colin.

"I always wondered what you saw in him. I figured it had to be good sex, but even that was wrong." Willa leaned back, gave her a steady look. "You lookin' good, girl. Something's agreeing with you here."

"Great sex will do that for a woman."

Willa's eyebrows shot up. "You got that right, honey." The grin that split her friend's face was lascivious. "So, you found some revenge sex? Feels good, doesn't it?"

"You could say that," Faye hedged through a chuckle.

"Hmm, don't want to talk about it, either." Willa eyed her again. "Okay, so why am I here?"

"I've decided to live here permanently."

Willa frowned. "No way." She peered around Faye and took in the expansiveness of the front parlor, hallway, wide formal staircase, and huge dining room. Then she looked up to the second floor and turned in a circle to track the wraparound hall upstairs. All the bedrooms opened onto the hall and overlooked the front entrance. "This big place? You in here all alone? That's crazy."

Her tone said she thought it was a dump, too. But Willa would wait to expound on that.

"And I need your help finding a second location for Time-Stop. It's the only way I can keep this place. It, ah, needs a lot of work."

"I'll say. Girl, you are crazy." She ran a finger down a newel post and sighed when she saw a heavy coating of dust.

Why, oh why, couldn't Belle make the place look clean, the way she had when Faye had first walked in?

"You want my opinion?"

"You just gave it to me. And I agree, I am crazy, Willa. But, it's a good crazy. I fell in love with this house as soon as I saw it. And I fell out of love with Colin at the same time. This is what I want to do and this is where I want to do it."

"So you think a second store will keep you in fine style here?"

She nodded. "With your help. You've got a great understanding of what our clients want. No one knows the vintage clothing market better than you. You'll help me find the perfect spot, right?"

Willa's cheeks flushed at the compliments, but she already knew how important her expertise was to the store. "Thanks, I'll try."

"Come into the kitchen for a cup of coffee. We'll talk about what I'm looking for. Then we'll hit the streets of Fremont."

"I thought I was going to die of caffeine withdrawal. What

took you so long?" Willa kicked off her shoes with a relieved sigh and followed Faye through the dining room into the kitchen, looking at every piece of furniture with a jaundiced eye.

She didn't like the mansion, that much was clear.

"My mama worked in a house like this when she was a girl."

Which explained a lot.

Faye grinned. "I've met your mama, and believe me, she never worked in a house like this one."

"And I'm saying she did. Fancy houses this size need a lot of maids." She ran a finger along the top of the sideboard. "This place is filthy. Look at those drapes! They're ready to fall off the rods, they're so rotten."

"You're right. This is why I need another store. If I plan to live here, the place needs a lot of upkeep. I can't do it myself. I have to hire a housekeeper and a gardener." People who wouldn't mind sharing space with ghosts who had a habit of invading dreams and siphoning the orgasms of the living.

Willa sniffed and made a disparaging face at the dusty drapes. "Maybe more. And you expect a second location to pay for the upkeep around here?"

"Exactly."

"Not gonna happen. You'll need more money than the income from two small stores. You'd need a chain of six or seven stores at least and we can't scrounge that much inventory."

"I may have a fresh source," she said with a glance to the ceiling. The attic still needed an inspection but something told her she'd best do that alone. Willa would be great on the location hunt, but probably wouldn't want to dream any dreams of sin and seduction.

They spent the rest of the day roaming the streets of Fremont looking for available lease space. Nothing appealed and at seven, they stopped for a bite to eat, before one last stroll around the neighborhood.

"So, you ever plan tell me about the man you're seeing?"

Faye fortified herself with another sip of Sauvignon Blanc. "Plural."

"More than one?" Willa leaned in, all ears. They sat at a bistro table at an outdoor café. Across the road was a pretty lake ringed by a walking trail. "Woman, you've got my attention! Spill!"

"Mark's a wholesaler who's moving into retail and we met a couple weeks ago."

"Uh-huh, while you were still engaged to Colin?"

"Colin and I were in trouble and um, spending time with Mark made me realize it wasn't worth trying to fix the trouble." She didn't think Willa would ever be ready to accept the truth, so she watered down the facts from fire water to ice water.

"And who's the other one?"

"My lawyer's son, who's also a lawyer in the same firm. Liam. He's fun and sexy as hell and a sweet guy."

"Uh-huh. Sexy? That all?"

"Hung like a bull. I mean *H-U-G-E*." The wine had gone to her head, but Willa was a close friend.

"What are you going to do about these two great guys?"

"After the mess with Colin, I'm not ready to settle down. So, I've sort of taken two lovers."

"And you're not feeling guilty?"

"No, we're adults and since one of them is out of town for the next couple of weeks, I don't see a problem. None of us want anything heavy for now."

"Right. You think both men would accept you being with the other?"

Sometimes straightforward friends could be a pain in the conscience. "Not happy, no, but I'm keeping it light and friendly for now. I just don't want anyone to get hurt."

"Especially you."

"Especially me." Hell, even hookers in bordellos ended up happily with the men of their dreams. But that had come after a helluva lot of sampling.

Faye studied Liam's handsome face as he settled into the driver's seat. Square jaw, great soft eyes, healthy glow. He'd nicked a spot on his neck shaving. He was always so careful not to have bristles on his jaw. Didn't want to scrape her tender flesh. He was in every sense of the word, a gentleman. A gentle man. A gentle, yawning man.

He turned the key in the ignition. "Sorry."

"Don't apologize, I can tell you're not bored—you're hard as a steel rod. A hard man is not a bored man. Tired?" Faye asked. She patted his knee and let her fingers trail up his thigh to cup him. Mmm. The man was solid.

"No sleep for two nights." He turned toward her. Signs of strain around his eyes and faint dark smudges beneath each eye proved his exhaustion. "Weird dreams."

"That's odd." She kept her voice calm, light, but stroked him through his khakis.

He slid his hand to her cresting nipple. She loved the way sensation ricocheted from her breasts to her crotch when he palmed her there. She opened her legs in invitation and let him skim his other hand up her thigh to feel how wet her panties were. "Let's go inside. I want you."

The side of his mouth kicked up into a sexy grin while the tap of two fingers at her entrance made her breath catch.

"We could stay in tonight," she suggested. "Go to bed early."

He looked up at the house through the windshield. "No, I don't want to sleep here. Not tonight. I have a feeling these dreams will be back tonight. It's like a movie unfolding. Every night more of the story's revealed in bits and pieces. I thrash around in my sleep. I'm better off at home."

She felt a shiver go through her at the expression in his eyes. He was worried, maybe even spooked about something.

He removed his hand from between her legs. "Ever had a dream you tried to back out of, but couldn't?" He reversed out of his parking spot and continued around the circular drive.

"Yes, I have. Pretty recently, too." She thought better of telling him about the screaming woman. He had his own dreams to deal with. He didn't need to hear about hers.

Faye glanced back out the rear window to the house's second story. For what, she wasn't sure. The girls didn't need to open the draperies to look out the windows. Still, she felt a chill cross the back of her neck.

Foolish, she thought, *worrying about a screaming hooker.* After all, who could possibly be affected today by something that happened eighty years ago? No one would care now. No one living, anyway.

The limbs that stretched across the drive parted before the car, a nice trick of Belle's that she appreciated. Liam stopped the car at the end of the drive, checked for traffic, then turned right onto the road.

The moment they left the driveway, Faye's inner tension eased. "Ever get the feeling when we're at the house, that we should stay at the house?"

"Yes, now that you mention it. Whenever I turn into the drive, I get rock hard and ready. Sometimes it's all I can do not to throw you to the ground."

"Sounds like fun," she teased. The farther they drove away from the end of the drive, the easier it was to keep going. "Sometimes it's all I can do not to drag you upstairs to bed."

He slanted her a glance. "We could just give in to these urges, but I want more than just sex, Faye. The only way to get more is to share other things." He shook his head. "I can't believe I'm saying this. Turning down the hottest sex I've ever had with the sexiest woman I've ever known to go out for an evening."

"I'd like more, too." She smiled and rested her palm on his thigh. "But we can have both—hot sex and great conversations. As long as we get clear of the house first."

"Stay at my place tonight."

She patted her purse. "Have my toothbrush and fresh panties all ready."

"Good. Let me know if I talk during these nightmares. Maybe I'll say something that'll help me figure out what's going on."

"You said the story seems to unfold in episodes?"

He nodded. "Yes, like one of those old serialized black-and-white movie shorts."

"Ah, right. The ones that ended with cliffhangers every week. My grandmother talked about them. They were short and full of action and adventure."

"Yes. And I think you're right about the cliffhangers, too." He frowned.

"Do you remember much when you wake up?"

"No, I just know they're making me tired and . . ." His attention was diverted by a series of skateboarders at the side of the road. He slowed as he passed them.

"They make you tired?" she prodded.

"Yes, and anxious. When I wake up, I'm anxious, but I don't remember why."

"Weird." At least he wasn't waking up pleasuring himself, the way she always did. Maybe he wasn't being haunted by Belle and the girls. Maybe his were just plain, ordinary dreams.

"But the more I think about it, the more it seems the dreams have something to do with you." He cocked an eyebrow in her direction.

The best way to get rid of anxiety, Faye realized, was sex.

"You must be waking up horny," she said blithely. Her mouth watered. "I always think of giving you a blow job when we're driving," she whispered into his ear. "Want one?"

His grin went wild and his eyes lit. She unzipped him and dropped to his lap, enjoying the wild thrill of danger that came with her experiment.

He moaned as she swirled her tongue around the head of his cock, licking and nipping everywhere she could reach. Which wasn't nearly enough to satisfy.

The roar of traffic changed from city streets to the steady hum of the freeway. "Gotta pull over," he said. The car slowed and she felt the gentle movement as the car braked to an easy stop.

"Gotta taste you now," he said and raised her head so he could maneuver her onto her back.

With lightning speed and precision he opened her legs, set one to hang over the seat back and put the other foot on the dash. She arched to him with a squeal of delight and didn't care that traffic roared by.

To her there was nothing in the world but Liam. His tongue, lips, and fingers centered and grounded her. Took her to heights she hadn't felt before as the element of danger spiked her arousal to sky high.

Liam's tongue swirled around her clit, speared into her slick channel, and took her over the top quickly. She moaned, arched her hips toward his mouth, and came in a wash of release she craved more and more often. Oh, the man was good. So good.

The spirits had turned her into a sex maniac. Anywhere, any time, she was ready. "I'd wondered if you were telling the truth about sex whenever and wherever the mood strikes. I'm not wondering anymore."

"If the woman's into raging quickies, it works like a charm; if she's not, it's tough."

Her liquid insides proved she was definitely into raging quickies.

"The ability to come fast is a major part of the experience." He shifted away from her and shucked his cords to his knees. "Now climb on and fuck me."

"Yes, sir." She hiked her Sophia Loren skirt up to her waist and straddled him, knees wedged into the seat back. She slid with exquisite care down the full length of him, each millimeter robbing her of breath and sending shockwaves of sensation through her body. "Oh, that's good. You feel so wonderful."

"You're tight and wet," he said before nipping the skin of her neck between his heated lips. "Fuck me, Faye, before I lose my mind."

She rode him faster and harder than any time before, until she screamed with another come, her inner muscles clasping him hard and deep.

Her scream echoed in a blast from a trucker's horn.

"The windows are steamed." The roar of traffic right outside the car muted the sound of her voice.

10

Faye bent her head to avoid banging it on the car roof. She nipped Liam's ear and growled into it when he gushed into her with a buck that held her immobile. Her still-pulsing channel milked him empty as she felt the tension ease from his naked thighs. She smiled with the afterglow.

"You're incredible," he whispered against her neck. She could hardly hear him with the rumble of traffic speeding past.

"But we've got to get out of here before someone reports us."

She lifted her hand and languidly wrote the word *incredible* on the steamed up window. Under it, she put *you.*

"You think I'm incredible?" he asked with a nuzzle at her breast.

"Of course. I only sleep with incredible men."

"How am I incredible?"

His question was an obvious fish for a compliment, but hell, the man deserved more than she could think of. "Aside from the fact you're endowed with the largest, thickest, longest cock I've ever seen?"

He flushed from the neck up to his ears. "Well, yeah, aside from that."

"Hm," she hummed for effect, then wiggled on his lap, letting him understand how much she appreciated his physical attributes. She slid off him and found her panties hanging from the rearview mirror. She struggled to slide them back on while Liam adjusted his clothing. Several other horns honked as they dressed.

Sooner or later some uptight citizen would use a cell phone to report the steamy windows.

"How's that case with the woman working out?"

"You mean the custody case?" He started the car and turned on the air to clear the windshield. "The woman with the drug dealer ex?"

"Yes, her. I like that you took her case. How's it going?" She checked her lipstick in the rearview, found it gone, and opened her purse to slick more on.

"The ex has connections somewhere. I'm having a hard time proving he's as dirty as she claims." He frowned.

"Still, I'm very proud of you. It shows a lot of heart."

He grinned. "So, I am more than just a hard cock when you need one?"

"Definitely." She remembered a snippet of conversation from one of her recent dreams. "And connections will turn sour if they're made public." The conversation may have been decades old, but the advice still sounded true today.

He thought for a moment. "I'll see what I can find out about the men he's friendly with. Maybe they'll put the squeeze on the guy to leave his ex-wife and children alone. Domestic problems have no place in his kind of business. If his connections think their reputations will be tarnished by association, they'll tell him to lay off his wife." He frowned and thought for a moment. "It's a delicate situation."

"I'm sure you'll handle it like an expert."

"Thanks."

"Glad to be of help." She straightened her clothing and waited for him to pull out into traffic.

"We found a location for my second store today. It's just come up for lease and my assistant manager, Willa, found it when we went out scouting. It's perfect."

"I'm glad you're staying," he said, pulling into the first break in traffic. The car kicked into passing gear smoothly and their escapade on the roadside was over.

"Thanks, I'm glad I am, too. Although giving up millions to keep a rickety old mansion must say something about my mental health." She laughed. "Oh, and Willa tells me I'll need more money to keep the mansion in repair than the income from two stores."

"She's an expert?"

"She's got a unique perspective on the costs of maintenance."

"Like I said before, you could sell off some of the surrounding acreage." He held up a hand in surrender. "It's only an idea. You don't need all those gardens. Although I have fond memories of the gazebo."

"I can't sell. Perdition House wouldn't be the same." The setting was elegantly private, with a long driveway, deep side yards with gardens, a gazebo, and a thick ring of trees that provided complete privacy. She couldn't think of one half-acre she could do without.

"Still, it may come down to that." His chin took on a stubborn set.

She reacted to it. "I'll think of some other way to make more money." The girls were depending on her. Just because Hope got to move on to be with Jed didn't mean it would work the same for all of them.

Besides, Faye loved her family home just the way it was. Spirits and all.

"You have to realize how old the structure is. It could be unsafe."

Her hackles rose. "It's safe. We were even out on the widow's walk, remember? It's solid as the day it was built." Her irritation showed in her voice. "Great way to ruin a perfectly good after-sex glow, Liam."

"I thought I was pointing out the obvious." He glanced at her, humor in his eyes. "I guess that means no blow job?"

The teasing glint in his eye had her smiling.

"You're incorrigible."

"I'm not. What I am, is already hot for you again."

She laughed, eased the shoulder harness off her shoulder, and leaned down to him.

She didn't know why she'd always thought of Liam as the straitlaced lover and Mark as more adventurous. It wasn't true. Liam was the one who'd enjoyed rough and ready sex in the gazebo with spirit laughter coming from the trees. He'd heard the feminine giggling and it hadn't stopped him from laying waste to her within minutes of saying hello.

It had been Liam who'd loved her like a queen on his desk with his receptionist on the other side of the door. He loved to take chances, enjoyed the spicy headiness of being close to discovery.

And now, his wonderfully huge cock was already responding as she inched down his zipper fly. She undid the tab of his slacks and brought forth his fresh hard-on.

She nuzzled him with her nose, taking in the musky scent of her own sex on his hot skin. "Hold on," he said, "there's an exit ahead that'll take us to a quieter stretch of road."

Since she didn't much like the idea of causing a thirty-car pileup, she waited, balancing an inch away from the tip of his cock. The car did a wide arc around an exit ramp and straightened out again.

The roar of traffic slowly fell away and Liam positioned the car away from other vehicles. His hand rested on top of her head, fingering her hair as she waited to please and tease him.

Faye took his cock into her mouth in one long slide, the spice of her own juices adding to the heady flavor. He reacted by pressing the accelerator, then quickly backing off. She chuckled.

"Oh, yeah, do that again. Your mouth's wet and hot and when you laugh, I can feel it."

She hummed and swirled her tongue, lapping and cleaning every wide, heavy inch of him. "I can't get at your sac this way."

"If you did, I'd go off like a rocket and I'd like this to last a bit. There's a long stretch of road ahead. We could end up in Canada."

She teased and tickled and sucked and licked until his fingers started to contract in her hair. Time to relieve the man, she decided, and with two powerful surges, took him over the edge.

The car swerved, but he took the wheel with both hands and let her carry him to heaven.

She couldn't for the life of her understand why she'd thought of him as Mr. Straight Arrow. He wasn't like that at all.

She wiped delicately at her lips and zipped him back up.

His face, when she saw it, was mellow and easy.

"Home, Liam. We need to go home now," she said, thrumming desire turned her voice husky.

"I just hope my only dreams are of you."

"I plan to wear you out so you won't dream at all."

Something hit her arm. Hit her again. Faye rose to her elbow and looked over her shoulder at Liam.

"Mmfpf. Get off! . . . mmfpf . . . her!" His legs shot out straight to the end of the bed and he kicked off the sheet. He rolled away from her and struggled when the sheet tucked in around his arms. He yanked and pulled in frustration.

Then he yelled, "Bastard! Gotta get . . . mmfpf."

Great, another ruined night's sleep. If it wasn't hot and horny dreams at Perdition, it was Liam, thrashing around like a lunatic.

She touched his shoulder, but he ignored her and kept trying to get himself free of the sheet.

She tugged it out from under his shoulder and unwrapped him as well as she could, considering he started to flail his arms as soon as he was free of the sheet. It still tangled around his legs, but she was glad he was under wraps. She didn't want to be kicked. She was having enough trouble avoiding his hands.

"Liam! Liam, wake up," she said, giving his shoulder a shake.

He rolled to his back and opened his eyes. Staring straight up at the ceiling, he went rigid. Still.

She leaned over him, and searched his face, but saw no sign of recognition. He didn't even see her. She shook him again, concerned when he was still stiff and unyielding. "Liam, sweetie, wake up!"

He blinked, looked at her, and smiled. "You're so beautiful," he said.

"Thank you, now—"

He grabbed her by the shoulders and tossed her to her back, cutting her off in mid-sentence. His weight on her chest pressed her into the mattress, making it hard to catch her breath.

His eyes looked wild and gleamed in the moonlight that filtered in through the slatted blinds. Without another word, he spread her knees with his stronger legs and shoved two fingers inside, pumping twice. She barely had time to register a response before his cock found its mark and slid home.

No finesse, no gentleness. Hmph. She'd give him what for in the morning, but right now, the slick push-pull of his cock on her inner walls was delightfully rough.

He tucked his hands under her ass and tilted her higher so he could get deeper inside. It worked and she felt her desire rise to meet his thrust for thrust.

"See? See I told you you'd like it."

"Fuck me, fuck me hard!"

And he did. Slamming and writhing on her, Liam rode her harder than he ever had before.

She crooned to him, trying to gentle his thrusts, but soon got carried away on a rising tide of arousal. She crested suddenly and completely, barely aware of his sudden, deeper, harder plunge that carried him over the edge with her.

With their hearts pounding as one, she trembled in his arms while he pumped into her, finally going slack and sliding off next to her.

His breathing changed immediately into quiet snores and with a soft snuffling sound, he was deeply asleep again.

"What the hell was that about?" she asked the sleeping man, expecting—and getting—no response.

Faye dialed the number for TimeStop and waited. She sat in an ancient love seat that had creaked with her weight, but held firm. Belle's favorite sanctuary was quickly becoming hers, too. The back veranda outside the kitchen door had just enough room for the love seat and a couple of wicker wing chairs that ringed a wicker coffee table. Luckily, the veranda had a deep awning so she could even sit outside on a rainy morning without getting wet.

She waited for three rings before Willa answered from her end. "TimeStop, how may I help you?"

"Hi, Willa, customers gone?" She could hear Kim in the background thanking a customer for coming in.

"For the first time all morning. What's up?"

As happy as she was that the store was busier than ever, she wanted Willa's complete attention.

"It's all ours," Faye said. "We can start renovations on the first of next month."

Faye tried to hold in her excitement but Willa whooped like a cheerleader. Her tension broke like a ray of sunshine through clouds. *She was really going to do it!*

She hadn't felt this combination of fear and excitement since deciding to open the store in the first place.

Faye could hear Kim exclaiming in the background, too. "It's so close to perfect, we should be able to open on the fifteenth," she added through the whooping and hollering. She laughed, giddy with the thrill of anticipation.

"I'll get an ad written for more staff right away."

"Thank you. We'll need at least three to start with. We'll train them first, then take on more as the shop gets established. I'm not sure how many hours I'll be able to give to each store, so I need people I can depend on."

"Well, honey, Kim's about to pee her pants here. She's hoping to get a chance to manage. Hey, let go—damn, girl, you about broke my nail!"

"Faye? Could I try? I'll be happy to move closer if you want." She'd obviously grabbed the phone from Willa.

Kim had been with TimeStop for close to two years and Willa swore the girl knew more about the up and comers in Hollywood than anyone else. Plus, she'd been the one to get them set up with a Web site and e-mail list. She was more tech savvy than either Willa or Faye.

"Are you sure, Kim? You want to try your hand managing? It'll be longer hours, and you know what a bitch I can be." Faye laughed.

"You? Never. That's one of the reasons I hang around. You and Willa are great to work with!"

Kim didn't have a lot of family and Faye sometimes wondered if she put more into her job because of it. She and Willa were very close.

"I can't pay you much more until we see how the new store does. You know I'd like to—"

"No, don't worry about that," she interrupted. "I just want the chance. We'll work things out, you'll see. Besides, I'd like to move up that way. Get away from things here."

"You mean get away from Jason? This sounds like a breakup."

"A permanent one this time."

Faye had heard that story before. But, maybe, with a new focus and a new location, Kim would move on. "Then, we'll get you up here as soon as we can. You could stay with me while we're renovating the store if you'd like. I could use some help around the house for a few days, anyway."

"Willa needs to hire a person for this store, but as soon as we do, I'll be there! Thanks so much, Faye. I appreciate the chance. I'll do great, you'll see."

"I'm sure you will." She rested her feet on the edge of the table and pulled her sweater tighter around her. The air was chilling, with more rain on the way, but she wanted to stay outside to finish her coffee before heading back indoors.

"Perdition House has been swallowed by dust. My aunt was old and frail when she passed away and I'm trying to bring the sparkle back to the place."

"I'll be happy to help, Faye. Just give me a scrub bucket. I'm on it."

Faye closed her eyes in a silent thank-you. "Kim, you don't know what this means to me. I've been overwhelmed here."

"Willa told me how big the place is. It's no wonder you need help."

She sighed with relief at the offer of help. Auntie Mae had lost her battle with the dust mote army years ago.

Faye thanked her again and hung up with a smile. Her friends were behind her and supportive of the expansion. Confidence restored, Faye finished her coffee, content to wallow in the good-news morning she'd had.

Belle whispered into her ear. "This is a good location?"
"Yes, it's perfect." A suspicion crossed her mind. "Willa walked into a store she thought would work and wouldn't you know it? The owner was in there."

At Belle's surprised, "Really?" she went on. "Yes, she was. Willa said the woman mentioned wanting to retire and the conversation went from there. You wouldn't know anything about that, though, would you?"

Belle fussed with the hem of her gown, then conjured a fan to flutter in front of her face. "Of course not. I'm sure the store owner was planning on retiring at some point."

"If you helped bring the idea to the forefront of her mind, thank you. I appreciate the help." Sometimes living with meddling spirits could work out nicely. But only sometimes.

Belle's smile was enigmatic.

It was small consolation the ghosts couldn't create something from nothing. If the store owner hadn't been thinking of retiring, Belle couldn't have forced her to.

"Would you like to see the attic now?" Belle asked. "You might find something to use for inventory in the new store."

The shoes! Open-toed slingbacks from the 1940s, her favorites. "I forgot. Thanks for reminding me." The news just got better and better today.

Once inside, Belle floated up the stairs ahead of her, dressed in a peignoir set that had once been green. Faye saw flashes of color in the folds as they fluttered behind Belle's otherwise monochrome beige. Being outside in the gray overcast light and with the faded gray wicker at her back, Faye hadn't noticed Belle's lack of color.

It wasn't like her to be beige. Something must be wrong. "Are you upset at the idea of my inviting Kim to the house?"

"No, of course not. I have a feeling Kim will be very entertaining."

11

"You will leave Kim alone," Faye said firmly to Belle, whose knowing smirk irritated the hell out of Faye. "She's not to be jazzed up in any way. While she's here, she'll be working, either helping get the new location ready or searching out new inventory. She's not a plaything." If they messed with Kim, Faye would lose her for sure.

Faye heard a deep sigh come from the wall beside her. She stopped and put her hands on her hips, spun toward the long-suffering sound. "I'm not joking, Lizzie. You leave her alone."

With Lizzie's penchant for practical jokes, Faye was afraid the spirits would go too far and she'd lose a great employee. Not to mention a friend.

There must be a state law against terrorizing the help. Just because she had no problem being surrounded by spirits didn't mean Kim would be okay with it.

"All right, I promise," agreed Lizzie from somewhere deep inside the wall. At least it sounded like she was inside the wall. It might have been the ceiling.

Now, all she had to do was make Annie and Felicity promise

to leave Kim alone and she'd have an easier mind about Kim living here for the next few weeks.

"But the minute one of you pulls something on her, I lose my help and you'll be sorry," she threatened, loud enough for all of them to hear. What good threatening the dead did, she didn't know, but it was worth a shot.

The attic entrance was in the ceiling of a back hall corner.

Belle stood to the side while Faye tugged on an ancient rope. The stairs folded down from the ceiling with the groans and squeaks that were to be expected from hundred-year-old hinges. But once the stairs got moving they opened easily enough and Faye climbed up, surprised by the sturdy feel under-foot. "What," she slanted a glance at Belle, "not coming with me?"

"I'll meet you there."

"You being afraid of heights seems a little weird. You can't exactly get hurt."

Belle blew her a raspberry.

As soon as Faye set foot on the attic floor Belle appeared seated on a trunk in the corner. Dust flew everywhere, but for all the years of neglect, it smelled clean enough. There were no obvious signs of animal or bird infestations.

No bats, either. She hated bats. They flew so erratically.

From the central staircase opening, the attic went off in every direction. From here it was clear how large the house was, because the entire floor area was open. Dormer windows were evenly spaced around each wall, including the additions that were built on later. There was an octagonal area that was obviously over the conservatory.

Each dormer wall had hooks on the walls. Some even had tiny closets built in.

"What went on up here, Belle? These sort of look like cubbies or partitioned areas."

"Staff slept up here if they didn't have homes to go to. Beds were tucked in under the windows and there was a stove by the stairs for heat in the winter. It wasn't unpleasant."

She took a closer look and saw curtain rings on poles stretched across the openings to each dormer. "How large a staff did you need?"

Belle shrugged. "Four or five live-ins. More in the summer to tend the garden. We had a laundress, eventually some kitchen help, but mostly the cook's son, Henry, at first."

Four or five live-ins. Willa was right. She was going to need more help than she thought. Even with modern equipment like a dishwasher, vacuum cleaner, and a washer and dryer, Perdition House was too big for one person to keep up. Especially one person with a business to run.

"Did Annie work in a cathouse in Butte when she ran away from home?" She might have suggestions for efficient use of Faye's time.

"Yes, and it wasn't anything like working here. She'll tell you that!" Belle chuckled and the green in her gown returned.

"You're feeling better."

"Why, yes." She cocked an eyebrow at Faye in query.

"You were beige. First time I've ever seen you so colorless. Is something worrying you?"

"Nothing for you to be concerned about. I may have a renegade in the ranks, that's all."

"Renegade?" She laughed, finding the idea funny in a weird way. "A renegade ghost. Ooooo, scary."

Belle frowned. "Until now your experiences have been pleasant, haven't they?"

"You mean things could get nasty?" The thought of a ghost going postal suddenly scared the bejeebers out of her.

"I said it was nothing for you to be concerned about. Let's get to the matter at hand, shall we?" Belle's expression said the discussion was closed. But the green remained, lustrous and emerald.

Belle never spoke without thinking. She'd meant for Faye to know about the renegade, but typically, wouldn't explain things in a straightforward manner.

Dealing with the dead was a royal pain. Their sense of time didn't exist. Neither did concern for life and limb. They couldn't remember sensation unless it was sexual, so it didn't much matter to Belle and the others if Faye felt hot or cold or simply worn out.

"Fine, back to the trunks. I hope this isn't a waste of time." Her tone was snarky, because pursuing the subject of a renegade spirit was useless.

She stalked over to a line-up of trunks in the far corner and lifted the lid off the first one she came to. Inside, she saw shoes, hats, purses, and even a couple of fox stoles. "Oh! This is fabulous!"

Belle moved up close, bringing a sharp chill with her. She looked over Faye's shoulder at the loot. She smiled gently and her eyes lit with recognition. "Happy?"

"This is a treasure trove! Instant inventory for a vintage clothing business." She lifted the stoles out of the way so she could paw through the purses and shoes. "It all looks brand new."

She draped a stole around her shoulders, petted the still silky fur. "You're not just making them look this way, are you?" She wriggled her nose in imitation of a television witch.

"No, I'm not. We only wore the best and changed with the styles. Nothing was worn for long."

Faye held up the end of the fox stole. "I hate seeing their little pointy noses dangling there like that. What were women thinking slinging these cute little guys around their shoulders?"

Belle cocked an eyebrow. "Maybe they felt a chill?"

She felt her cheeks heat.

"Fashions change," Belle said. "Just because wearing fur is

considered gauche today doesn't mean it wasn't all the rage back then." Belle sniffed.

"You had one." *This one.* She stroked the fur and dropped the end, trying not to look at the lifeless, shrunken face.

"Of course. Everyone who was anyone did."

"Mink, too?"

Belle put her hands into surrender mode. "Guilty." She glanced toward an oak armoire. "It's in there. Don't worry, it's cedar-lined."

Faye's eye for profit roared to life. "There's a growing market for fox and mink in the vintage business."

"And they died so long ago, what difference does it make now?" Belle asked huffily.

"Right. I guess." But the conversation reminded her of the dream she'd had the other night. The dream with the screaming woman. Whatever had happened in that room to that woman was so long ago it couldn't possibly affect anyone today. No one involved was still alive after all this time. Liam had agreed with her, but Belle might have another idea.

"When I found the secret passageway and Annie showed me the peepholes, I felt the same way about the murder victim. But, when I dreamed about peering through the peephole and seeing the woman and her lover, it got me to thinking. Why bother showing me anything if you want me to forget all about it?" She couldn't see the point.

"Who said I'm the one who encouraged you to look through the peephole?"

"Who else then?" She considered the possibilities. "The renegade?" A nasty renegade. "Who else is here? I thought I was surrounded by friends, and now you're saying one of them wants to torture me with dreams of murder?" If Belle were alive, Faye could grab her by the shoulders and shake the truth out of her.

Belle blinked out and disappeared. She could be testy when Faye pressed an issue.

"You won't stop me," she called. "I'll find out eventually. What harm can an old scandal do today anyway? It was decades ago." She shivered as a new thought crossed her mind.

Liam's dreams.

The episode in the night had all the earmarks of a ghostly visitation. Not that she'd seen one before, but the way he'd behaved was nothing like him. Did she thrash about during her dreams too?

Mark didn't mention her rolling around or mumbling in her sleep and he'd been with her during her dreaming session about Hope and Jed.

She smiled. He'd responded well to the way she'd woken him with her tongue. Her dreams made her horny. With Liam's behavior so fresh in her mind, she could easily believe he'd been visited by a spirit.

Not that she minded the rougher side of sex on occasion, but someone else had been in Liam's body. Her own body had responded with lusty appreciation immediately, so she hadn't mentioned the sexy grab this morning.

Now that she thought about it, Liam hadn't mentioned it either.

Maybe he didn't even remember.

And maybe the renegade Belle had spoken of wasn't one of the girls. Maybe the renegade was a man.

The girls had been siphoning off sexual release from Faye's orgasms ever since she moved in. There was no reason a male spirit wouldn't do the same with Liam's.

No wonder they were so hot for each other. Neither of them was alone in their libido.

Her thoughts whirled in so many directions at once, she couldn't hold one steady. Until one ugly one popped into her head.

What if the victim's body was hidden somewhere on the property? In the garden? Under the gazebo? The roses?

The attic.

Faye shivered again and looked up at the rafters, half expecting to see a desiccated corpse grinning down at her from above. She jumped when Annie floated in through the round window on the end wall.

"You're being silly. There's nothing here like that. We shipped her home to her people."

Faye could swear her heart stopped. "Who did you ship home?"

"Lila, my cousin. She had a baby, got sick, and died. End of story." Annie ducked her head. "I made sure we did right by her, though. Told her folks she was a housekeeper here. I said she was a righteous woman and they should be proud." Her voice spoke of her grief, quiet and desolate, even after all these years.

Faye had been wrong. Some of the ghosts remembered emotions. Sadness, regret, grief. More than that, they remembered love.

"Were they proud of her?" Annie's father had been a hard line Temperance man, unforgiving and stern.

Annie shrugged. "I doubt it. My pa took care to ruin my name and when Lila joined me here, he ruined hers too. I never heard from Lila's folks. I hope they gave her a Christian burial."

She'd have liked to offer Annie a hug, but the dead weren't able to feel them, not even when they were at their fullest consistency, which she likened to marshmallow.

"That's okay. It's the thought that counts." Annie sniffed. "There are dresses in those wardrobes over there. Pretty ones we wore for dancing. Some flapper dresses, too." She smiled, her somber mood gone. "The twenties were a lot of fun!"

"Were you here that long?"

"Matthew and I lived close by and we'd come over for parties and the like. Matthew wanted the business contacts and I missed my friends."

"A contractor often builds his business by networking," Faye said.

"I don't know about that, but his name got passed around a lot and he did very well that way. We had a good life, Matthew and me."

Faye yawned and tried to cover it. "Between Liam's thrashing and some great sex, I didn't sleep much last night. If I took a nap, you could tell me about how you met Matthew and fell in love." Maybe somewhere in Annie's story there would be a clue to the renegade's identity.

"I have no idea who the renegade is. Belle keeps her own counsel," offered Annie in response to Faye's thought. "I've never read Lila's diary. Maybe there's something in there."

"There's a diary? Show me. I'm sure it's fascinating."

"All right."

She took another look around the room and yawned again. "I'm impressed with everything I've found up here. The condition of the clothing is immaculate, but I need help to go through it all. When Kim's here, we'll go through everything together. And"—she grinned at Annie—"I think I'm ready for a nap."

Anticipation and arousal grew, and whether it was under Annie's influence or not, Faye didn't care. She was already moistening and ready for another erotic dream.

She headed downstairs with Annie, who led her into the bedroom beside the secret passage. "This was Lila's room for a time. Her diary's under that chair."

"This is the room with the peephole." She walked to the heavy gilt-framed picture. "It was clever to put this hole in the frame. It blends into the intricate carving perfectly."

"Thank you. Belle was pleased with the design. There were times she kept an eye on certain customers."

"For blackmail?"

"Of course not. We thought of it as security."

Faye felt a chill of recognition. This was the room where the screaming woman was with her lover in her dream.

12

Annie glanced at the bed. Suddenly the linens folded down in invitation.

"Oh, that's creepy," Faye said. "I wish you wouldn't do things like that."

When she'd first arrived the mansion had been immaculate and she'd been tricked into thinking it was in perfect repair. Gradually, the truth had unfolded and she'd finally seen the house as it actually was. Dusty, dirty, and frayed around the edges.

But by then, it was too late. She already loved the place.

As Belle had known she would.

She sighed. That had been the first instance of Belle getting her own way.

She stripped down to her panties and bra to settle under the covers. The peephole was trained on her. If anyone cared to look, they could look. Sleep rolled over her like a comforting wave and she rolled with it into a deep, calm place.

* * *

Annie Baker learned three things when she disguised herself as a boy and ran away from home.

First, a smart woman didn't need a man.

Second, a smart woman learned quickly how to pleasure herself.

Last, and the rule she was having the most trouble living by, a smart woman saved her cherry and waited for the right price before selling it.

Annie was still waiting.

But Matthew Creighton tested her resolve each and every day. The same resolve that kept her doing what she loved more than anything else in the world. The resolve that defined the person she wanted to be.

The resolve that crumbled more every time she looked at him.

Today was no exception. He'd taken to going for a swim at first light. So, every morning found her gawking at him as he came back across the lawn.

Matthew's wet hair was the first thing Annie saw. Then his face and still-dripping shoulders rose up to lawn level as he climbed the stairs from the rocky beach below. Rising like a sea god from the depths, he got to the top of the cliff and stood there, long-limbed, lean, and wet from the top of his head to the tips of his toes.

The saw she'd been using on some two-by-fours dangled from her hand as she watched, dry-mouthed, as Matthew toweled off.

He assumed no one was watching and scrubbed the towel roughly over his hair, then down his arms and finally, he bent to dry his legs and feet. His form, outlined by sunshine, was perfect. He had a trim, flat belly, broad shoulders, long legs and strong arms.

Annie sighed and thought of helping him. She would run the

cotton toweling down his well-sculpted chest, around to his back. Soon, her nearness would register with him and he'd respond by trapping her arms around his back. Then he would lean down to kiss her. She closed her eyes to savor the touch of his lips to hers. The pressure, the taste of him, salty from the sea water at first, then sweet inside.

Her fingers traced her lips where his would be. He would press gently to open her mouth, then coax her tongue aside to make room for his. Once inside he'd plunder and tease and take everything she had to give.

She let sensations long forgotten tumble through her. Thrills chased from her belly to her heart and back down again. *Oh, Matthew, touch me. Touch me the way I dream you do.*

It had been years since she'd been kissed, and never with the skill a man like Matthew would bring to the task.

But Matthew, oh! That man had the best hands Annie had ever seen. Long fingers with square tips, clean nails, and just the right sprinkling of hair on the knuckles. His lips were full and kissable.

She didn't want to think about his body this way. But, working with him side by side on the building of Felicity's conservatory had strained her good intentions.

Right now, watching Matthew's easy stroll across the back lawn toward her made her wet and open in a way she never felt when she rubbed at herself.

His bathing suit was still wet and clung at all the right places. His cock and balls swayed with each step he took and she couldn't take her eyes from his body.

One flick of a finger and she'd be his, the value in her cherry forgotten, her decision to sell it gone.

Being a virile man, he'd take what she offered and go on his way to the next woman. She was under no illusions about men and their needs. As intent as they were on bedding a woman, they were just as intent on escaping her.

She would not be used and tossed aside. Not for free, anyway.

Oh no, Annie Baker was too smart for that. And all she had to do was remember it.

He was so close now that she had to pull out of her reverie and put on a show of working. If she didn't, he'd see her watching him and might catch on that she was lusting.

Thank God he knew her as Andrew. It was her only protection from his appeal.

Hiding behind a young man's disguise had worked well. Working like a man had made her strong and capable. She had even learned how to read blueprints. To keep up the illusion, she kept her hair short and her breasts bound. Work pants and a laborer's cap topped off the disguise perfectly.

Something was on Matthew's mind this morning. She could see his worry in the dark circles under his eyes and his weary expression. She'd seen both too often lately, but he wasn't the kind of man to share his inner thoughts.

It wouldn't do to let him catch her watching him. Still, she took one last glance at the man who'd captured her lustful attention, and, in the middle of sawing two by fours, moistened at the thought of running her tongue across each perfectly indented slope of muscle on Matthew's chest.

It was sinful, the way that man was built for licking.

She tried to focus on the draw of the saw across the wood, but her thoughts were still on using her tongue on his body. She could run her tongue down to his belt buckle. Below the buckle she'd go, to where the sprinkling of coarse hair covered his manhood.

"Andrew?" Matthew said.

The saw dropped with a clatter from her nerveless fingers.

"Yes?" The man had a knack for knowing when her mind wandered. She bent and picked up the saw, ducking her face so he wouldn't see her embarrassment.

"That lumber's not going to cut itself. Got something on your mind?"

"No! I mean yes. I'll get on it." She bent to the task, glad that she took the time every night to sharpen the saw's blade. She used any trick she could to do the jobs he needed from her. A sharp saw blade made the work easier which, in turn, made her look stronger. Strong as the young man she pretended to be. "I could ask you the same question. You look mighty worried this morning and it's too fine a day for worry."

She tilted her cap back and looked up at the clear blue overhead.

Matthew studied her face in much the way he'd been doing for months. Then he grinned to himself and shook his head. "When you're done there, see if you can help Jack with that mortar. He's still getting over a night with Lila and needs a hand."

"Yes, sir." Once in awhile, Annie would nick her chin to make it seem that she'd cut herself shaving. But the way Matthew studied her nowadays she wondered how effective her subterfuge was. Her nipples beaded at his intense focus and she worried he might notice.

She worried more that there were times she forgot to bind her breasts tight enough to pass an intent inspection. Like the one he was giving her now. She felt her cheeks warm and prayed he wouldn't notice her feminine color.

Matthew's gaze shifted away as he swiped his towel across his brow, taking in the half-built addition to Perdition House.

"This conservatory's a beauty." His voice sounded hollow. He cleared his throat.

"Yes, sir. As beautiful as Felicity herself," she said, because Felicity had been the one who wanted the addition. "What Felicity wants Felicity gets," she said. Men included.

Matthew made no comment. He never did, no matter how many times Annie mentioned one of the girls in the house.

Matthew never enjoyed their charms, never took one to his bed.

He'd had offers aplenty. Some of them for free, too, but he kept to himself every night.

He used a tent as temporary quarters and building-site office, even though he could find a bed in the house from any one of the girls.

"If Belle would allow us to work past three on Fridays and on the weekends we could be finished weeks earlier. I could move on to my next job."

"Do you want to leave so bad?" Damn her shaky voice. She sounded stricken when what she should do is encourage him to leave. She bit her lip and stared down at the sawhorse.

"It's past time this job was done, but Belle won't allow construction to ruin the peace of the place. Weekends are the busiest time."

The crew was dismissed Friday at three and not back on site until ten a.m. on Mondays. The laborers loved all the free time, while Matthew chafed at the slow pace. He used the downtime to study more on architecture and design.

Lately, he'd been teaching Andrew more about those subjects, too. While Annie was dying to teach Matthew about the art of seduction.

Of all the dumb mistakes a woman could make, bedding a man to ease herself was the most stupid.

If Matthew ever learned that Annie was a woman who wanted to spend her life designing and constructing buildings, he'd think she was unnatural. He would never teach her another thing.

Taking him to her bed would ruin her best chance to learn everything she wanted to learn.

So, she had no choice but to saw two-by-fours and pound nails during the day and dream of Matthew's hands and fingers and kisses all night. She heaved a heavy sigh and got back to work.

"I've been getting a lot of interest from the guests," Matthew commented. He shrugged out of the shoulders of his bathing costume and slipped into a shirt he'd left by the sawhorses.

He took a quick glance around, then tugged off the bottom of the suit. His balls bounced and swayed while he held one foot up to fight with the wet material.

Annie swallowed hard and did her best to not look straight at him, but she still got a good view out of the corner of her eye.

"A couple of commissions have come my way because I took your advice," Matthew was saying as he yanked on his work pants.

He worked at the fly and belt with deft fingers.

Annie's mouth was too dry to speak. She swirled her tongue around to test, but it felt like sawdust.

"Office buildings and even a bank," he said. "I'm glad you pestered me to mingle more. But now I've got more jobs lined up than ever and Belle's holding me up."

Now that he was fully dressed, her power of speech returned. "You sound frustrated. Could be you need to make use of one of your admirers." The whole crew had teased him for weeks now because so many of the girls had offered him their attentions.

"No, I don't." His firm tone put the end to that conversation, but cheered Annie to no end. He turned and headed toward the house. "I have to see Belle. Don't forget to help Jack when you finally get these two-by-fours cut in half."

The insult to her work ethic spurred her to bend to her task again.

Pleased that he'd refused to have anything to do with the women in the house, she whistled a ditty she'd learned from one of the carpenters. She didn't want to think of Matthew with gentle Hope, or skittish Lizzie, or adventurous, inventive Felicity. Or any of the other women who came and went as Perdition House's reputation grew.

She didn't want to think of Matthew with any woman but her. The danger in that thinking frightened her.

While Matthew treated his men fairly, and respected Andrew's desire to keep learning, Annie knew sure as the sun set that he'd never, ever let a woman work with him. He had strict notions about where a woman belonged, and a construction site wasn't one of them.

Even when he wanted to speak with Belle about the conservatory, he went into her office. He never asked her to walk through the actual addition. Maybe he thought structure, form, and angles were too much for the feminine brain to comprehend.

Frustrated with the way of the world and stubborn men in general, she snorted.

Annie had to remain Andrew, no matter how hot Matthew made her. No matter how her body screamed for his. Andrew she must stay.

Life at Perdition House would be perfect if only Annie could take care of this itch.

She wanted Matthew deep in her bones. But having him would be a huge disaster.

So, if she couldn't have Matthew, she reasoned any man would do. Selling her cherry was the wisest course of action. If she got rid of this itch with someone else, then she'd be able to continue working with Matthew without giving herself away by mooning after him.

She'd bind her breasts so tight, they'd pop out the other side. She'd work harder than she ever had, work her muscles to the point of exhaustion.

And she'd sleep at night instead of dreaming of a man she could never have.

Belle had promised to help her find a man when the time came—and Annie's time had come.

Matthew's hands shook as he walked away from Andrew, determined to have this out with Belle once and for all. He held his hands out in front of him, then flexed his fingers long and wide.

Finally, he shoved them in his pockets, disgusted that he couldn't stop the tremors. They had begun weeks ago. There were times his palms itched and sweated and craved. He knew men like this existed, but, like the rest of society, he considered them abominations.

Never, ever did he think . . . the thought was too horrible to bear.

Whenever Andrew was around, Matthew's gut ached, need rose. He was sick. Sick!

The slope of the boy's neck, the seductive way his dungarees swayed when he walked, even the smoothness of his facial skin called to Matthew. His urge to touch the boy appalled him, and his needs had begun to override his good sense.

He'd lost weight, couldn't stand to drink in fear he might act on his wild impulses. He'd gone mad and his only salvation was to leave. He hated the idea of walking out on a half-completed project, but he'd be sent to damnation if he stayed on to finish.

He hadn't slept a full night in weeks and the swimming wasn't helping.

Worse was the sure knowledge that Andrew saw and responded to Matthew's unnatural interest. God help him, he'd seen the boy watching him out of the corner of his eye. And the way his cheeks had gone ruddy had nearly flattened Matthew.

Perdition House was right.

It was hell working here.

He loved women. Their scent made him wild, their kisses enticed. Their eyes flirted and cajoled him into stupid declarations he'd never meant.

But with Andrew . . .

He had to get away. And he had to go now.

Today.

He strode through the kitchen and headed into her office to tell Belle he'd be leaving Andrew in charge of finishing. They seemed to have some kind of connection, a deeper friendship than a woman might ordinarily have with a handyman, so she might see her way clear to give the young man a chance to prove himself.

"That won't work, Mr. Creighton. Andrew's not the man for a job like that. He's young and untried." Belle smiled serenely up at him, but her blue eyes were sharp as glass.

His gut clenched. "Andrew's a fast learner and he's well prepared. I wouldn't suggest him if I didn't think him capable."

Her smile turned to amusement. "He'll be glad to know it. But are you sure the entire crew agrees with you?"

A contractor had to have the support of his men and Andrew was younger and smaller than all of them. As bright and eager as he was, he did not cut a commanding figure. In a contest of wills, with a man's pride at stake, Andrew would lose.

He frowned.

"I see you understand me. If it's a matter of money, I'd be happy to discuss terms, but if you're eager to leave for another reason, I'd like to know it."

"I have other commissions that need my undivided attention."

"Commissions you got because of the time spent here, I understand. These commissions came to you from my own clients. It would do you well to stay in my good graces. Leaving me without a contractor in charge with a half-finished conservatory would not keep me happy."

"Then I need the crew to work a full day Fridays. Saturdays, too."

"Hire more men if you need to." She reached for her telephone and picked up the receiver. Looked at him with one perfectly shaped eyebrow arched. "But I won't extend the work hours. Perdition is a retreat from the workaday world, not a construction zone."

He couldn't ignore the dismissal. He turned and left the office. Beautiful as she was, Belle Grantham was a consummate businesswoman. She used her beauty to disarm a man, then cut him off at the knees. Her bull-doggedness had been pointed out before he'd come here but until now, he hadn't seen it.

He had too much pride to let this project be built in a shoddy fashion. While Andrew had the necessary skills and experience to build the conservatory, he couldn't lead a crew.

Belle had seen the lack of leadership, while Matthew had been blinded by his troubled reaction to his sick urges.

He'd stay until he could find a new foreman. He had resources to call on, but it would take at least a week for Ben Pratt to get here. If Pratt wanted the job.

He could last out another week.

He had to.

"You're sure you're ready for this, Annie?" Belle looked concerned, but a gleam in her eye told Annie she was also seeing dollar signs. No mistake Belle was mercenary, but she also had a heart on occasion.

"I'm sure." Heat suffused her skin from waist to hair roots, but Annie was determined. "I've known since I worked in May Malloy's place that my cherry was valuable. She told me not to sell too cheaply and I've taken her advice. I almost gave it up for free before I got to May's. I see that as a close call now."

"May gave you good advice." Belle hesitated, eyeing her closely. "I just didn't see you joining the other girls here, Annie. I always thought you'd move on." She pulled a book out of a side drawer in her desk.

"When I found out you planned to build your own place, I had to join up with you. It was a dream come true for me. This was the only place I could learn everything I have. Maybe someday I'll find a man who'll appreciate what I can do and not try to hold me to a kitchen." She made a face.

Belle opened the book, which, from Annie's side of the desk looked to be pages of names and addresses in columns. All the men who'd come for visits, Annie guessed. "The odds of finding a man willing to let you swing a hammer are damn slim," Belle said.

"Exactly. This way, if I work at Perdition House, I can stay and oversee whatever else goes on with the building. The men I bed will have no say in what I can and can't do."

Belle glanced up from the columns of names. "Got an itch for anyone in particular?"

"No, there's no one." She shifted, her secret heat moistening her underwear.

"You don't spend a lot of time with the guests but have *any* of the men caught your eye? Maybe someone on the crew? You work with them every day. We could start there."

"No." She hesitated before adding, "But, I don't want Matthew to know about this if we can help it."

"I already figured on that. He won't let you work if he finds out you're a woman." Belle chuckled. "But he does think Andrew is very skilled and capable."

Annie heated up even more but didn't care that Belle would see the blush. After all, Matthew was complimenting her carpentry skills, not her feminine wiles. "Does he?"

"He told me so just this morning. He's looking to move on, but I insisted he finish the conservatory first. At least to a stage where I'll feel right with someone new in charge of the laborers."

Annie could imagine how that conversation had gone. Matthew had been in a foul mood all day, so difficult she didn't even care that it wouldn't be him who took her the first time. Let someone with a cheerier frame of mind do the honors.

Belle ran a finger down the columns of names. "If memory serves, I've had a few of our gentlemen specifically ask about virgins." She tapped a name. "Yes, we'll start here. Tomorrow at dinner we'll make the announcement."

Annie gulped. "Right. Friday dinner."

"You'll be there, dressed appropriately. Bidding will commence after dessert."

"Like a cattle auction?"

"Don't be ridiculous. There's a protocol to follow. We never display bad manners at Perdition. Never."

Annie's belly flipped, then righted itself. She raised her chin. She'd do this with all the grace she could muster. She just hoped she remembered how to walk in skirts.

The delivery boy left the telegram and Matthew hesitated for another minute before opening the message. "Thank you for the opportunity. Will arrive Sat mid-day." Signed Ben Pratt.

Matthew crumpled the telegram then smoothed it again. Ben would be here Saturday. Tomorrow.

They would spend Sunday bringing him up to date with the project. Monday, he'd meet the men and spend the rest of the week with Matthew, meeting suppliers and keeping the crew in check. With a new man, he expected some grousing from the crew, but given a few days, Ben would take charge. He would command respect, where Andrew couldn't.

This was the best choice to make.

The only choice.

Something odd was happening with Andrew. He was off in

another world most of the time, but Matthew was afraid to ask what he had on his mind. He was afraid of getting too close to the boy. Afraid of himself.

But his first order of business was to let Belle know.

He took off at a trot to get into the office before the crew headed home for the day. The sooner he told Belle about Ben, the sooner the crew could be told.

And then he'd have to find Andrew.

13

Belle read the telegram Matthew handed her. Her lips pinched in an unhappy scowl at his news.

"And you went to school with this Ben Pratt? You vouch for him?"

"I do."

She frowned and folded the telegram, tapped it against her chin while she thought. "You haven't given me much time to consider all the ramifications. There's more here than you know about."

"If you're thinking of other projects, then I think it would be best for you to discuss them with Ben. He's looking for a new start and would like to settle out here."

"If I approve of him, I'll pay him three-quarters of the remainder due you."

"He'll be doing one hundred percent of the job."

"But this Ben Pratt is not the man I contracted with, is he? He's a substitution. And for Perdition House, substitutions are second-best. We don't pay top rate for second-rate work."

"You won't get second-rate work from Ben Pratt. I guarantee it." He met her gaze straight on and during the long seconds she took sizing him up, he wondered how Ben would fare with her.

Her pale blue eyes saw far more than he wanted to show and her keen mind catalogued each nuance on his face.

Finally, she blinked and smiled easily, as if at a joke only she knew and would never share.

"Very well," she said. "When he gets here, bring him into the office to meet me." She walked around her desk and crossed the room to the window overlooking the driveway. Outside he heard the sounds of automobiles on gravel. Weekend guests were already arriving.

"We'll be seeing some interesting events in the next couple of days. You'll want to see them." She went to the bell pull. "Tea? Or something stronger, perhaps?"

She was a beautiful woman, but hard-headed as any businessman. It was clear he wouldn't get his due until he'd witnessed these upcoming events, whatever they were. "Scotch, if you have it."

"Of course." Her smile only confused him more. "I don't believe I've ever seen you drink anything stronger than coffee, Matthew."

"On occasion." Maybe the scotch would steady his nerves. He looked at his right hand. No tremors for the moment. But that would change at first sight of Andrew.

"Scotch it is." She went to the drinks cabinet and pulled out a bottle of twelve-year-old scotch. His favorite. "You don't often join us for dinner, Matthew. Make an exception tonight."

It wasn't a suggestion, more like an order. She knew something he didn't and since she'd always been straightforward with him, he allowed her to think he hadn't noticed the high-handedness in her tone.

"I'll do that," he said.

He accepted the glass she proffered. Her expression of delight intrigued him. "Any particular reason?"

"I think you'll find plenty of reason, Matthew. Now, please excuse me, will you? I have to chase these girls." She swept from the room and clapped her hands out in the hallway. "Felicity! There you are. We need your assistance upstairs immediately. Please come with me. Hope, go find Annie, will you? She's disappeared outside. Run like a scared rabbit."

Feet scurried overhead, and he heard feminine giggling and shrieks of laughter. The female hubbub that ensued made him smile into his scotch.

Annie was a new name. He hadn't heard of her before. If she had run, she must be young. If she was smart she'd keep running. As far away from this life as she could get.

Women belonged at home, with children and men to care for. Not at the beck and call of wastrels and brutes.

Women. Their mysteries intrigued him. Their soft skin called. Their gentleness soothed.

And then there was Andrew.

He downed the scotch. Poured himself another. It heated and smoothed down to his gut.

He relaxed. Tomorrow, with Ben here, he'd feel like himself again. In control.

Matthew had confidence he would leave the project in good hands, but Belle had to see that for herself. Fair enough, she was the client; she had that right.

Hardheaded as she could be, he'd also seen evidence of deep kindness in her heart. He wondered at the friendship she had with Andrew. Belle was too young to have a son Andrew's age, but he could be a nephew or someone she'd taken under her wing.

The only fair thing for him to do was tell Andrew of his decision to leave. Then he'd tell the crew before they left for the weekend.

Checking his hands for steadiness one more time, he finished his drink and let himself out of the house. This would be a quick conversation, no time for explanations. Let Andrew think what he wanted.

He found him hunkered down by the south wall smoothing a line of mortar and looking happy with the result. Sunlight lit his slim shoulders and glistened off the smooth jaw Matthew had fought so hard to ignore. The tremors began immediately. If he didn't leave soon he'd shame himself and the boy.

Lizzie skittered to a halt behind him. "Annie's wanted in the house right away," she said.

Andrew's eyes flared wide. "I'll tell her. She went by here a couple of minutes ago."

Lizzie laughed, pretty as a sprite. "I'm sure she did. You let her know for me."

Andrew nodded and turned his attention to Matthew. "Yes? You needed me?"

Annie caught a look of longing on Matthew's face. A pulsing, yearning heat in Matthew's gaze pulled at her. Need and desire rushed from her core to her heart and set it to beating in a wild rhythm. Drawn to him by the tugging of her own traitorous heartstrings, she stepped close.

A cord stretched from her heart to his, the strain of want a pain in her chest.

Matthew's raging need seemed in tune with her every desire.

"Matthew?" she whispered. But there was no question to ask, no answer to be given.

His square jaw twitched and she caught the movement as his fingers flexed into fists. He opened his mouth to speak, but no sound came.

The man was in torment. Over her?

He must know she was Annie, not Andrew, her secret exposed when Lizzie had blundered in. Her time as Andrew was over.

She had nothing to lose now. She did the only thing she could think of to let him know it was all right.

Annie raised to her toes and pressed her lips to Matthew's in a tentative, gentle caress.

He groaned as if hell itself had swallowed him. She wanted so much to feel her breasts against his hard chest but her binding had made her almost numb.

She gave him everything he asked for with her mouth. Deep kisses of longing and need. She swept her tongue between his lips and tasted his incredible, uniquely Matthew flavor.

Oh, she wanted him. Wanted to climb up his body and settle her legs around his hips. She crooned into his mouth while he groaned into hers.

She swished her bound breasts against his chest in frustration. Oh! To let him feel her softness. Her nipples peaked hard against her binding. Her flesh itched and burned to feel him against her.

Damn!

Thoughts spun and sensation took over until all she knew was her need to have him inside. Taking her, thrusting into her. Breaking his way through her barriers to her soul.

No! It was too much! She'd changed, wanted more than just his body. She cried out and pulled back.

She wiped her lips to cleanse herself, to clear out her heart where Matthew had taken up residence. She couldn't give herself to him.

She mustn't.

Before she could speak and give her heart away, she bolted for the kitchen door.

Stupid woman! Falling in love. She ran, terrified he'd give chase. But she heard no footsteps, no protest from him.

She ran through the house and straight through to Belle's office behind the front parlor.

Her virginity was all she had to set herself up for good. If she gave it away now, she'd have to work a lot harder to get a good stake. And it would be doing work she didn't much care to try. She wasn't cut out to whore.

Sex, for her, was about love. *Bah!*

That's why she'd waited. Not to make money, not to earn her keep, but to find the right man. Not the right price.

She felt like a tightrope walker she'd seen in a circus once. One false step and she'd fall, a long agonizing fall on her face. Her years of hard work and everything she'd learned would be for nothing.

She careened into Belle's office and caught her just as she was putting the telephone receiver back in its cradle.

"What's wrong?" Belle said, leaping to her feet.

"You gotta find me a man, Belle, and it's gotta be quick." She slid to a stop in front of the desk. "Tonight."

Belle rolled her eyes. "Calm down. What's happened?"

If Matthew thought she'd joined the girls in the house, he'd leave her alone. Once he was gone, she could put on her Andrew clothes again and continue work on the other additions Belle had planned.

If he thought she loved him, he'd want her to give up building. To have her heart's desire, she had to give up her heart's content.

She had to give up Matthew.

She wasn't sure she had the strength. But she had to try.

"The auction. I want it completed tonight."

"No," Belle said firmly. She clasped Annie's shoulders. "We finish next week. You'll make more money than you ever dreamed. We both will."

Belle's grasp was firm and helped clear her head. "You're right. This is about money." She'd nearly forgotten. "It always was."

"Now, why don't you tell me what's got a bee in your bonnet." She tapped the peak of her cap.

"I kissed Matthew is what happened. And I've gone all soft. If I'm not careful, I'll end up giving it away!"

Belle smiled. "You'll do no such thing. Now get upstairs, Felicity's waiting to do your hair."

"Are you laughing at me?"

"No, of course not."

"I'll be able to say no if I don't like the gentleman who wins me?"

"Of course." Belle put an arm around her shoulder. "That rule will never change. It's always up to the girls. However, it's in your best interest to be happy with whomever bids the highest."

She thought hard about that. Her heart still pounded from Matthew's kiss. Her panties were wet and her secret place felt open and achy with need. Her skin felt hot to the touch and her thighs weak.

"And," said Belle, "it's time you got out of those dungarees and dressed like the woman you are."

"But—"

"No buts, Annie. You've got to show the assets if you want to make a splash. I've already been in touch with several of our clients. They'll be here for dinner tonight. Bids will come in from clients who live farther away, too. It wouldn't be fair to exclude them from such a momentous occasion."

Annie's head spun. Surrendering to Belle's plans was her best option because she couldn't trust herself alone with Matthew.

"I'll go upstairs and get myself gussied up." She yanked off her cap. "What'll we do with my hair?"

"Go see Felicity. She's waiting to curl it."

"You've thought of everything."

"That's my job, Annie, to think ahead." Belle smiled. "Besides, Felicity's been saying shorter hair is coming into style anyway. This will give her a chance to try out some techniques. You know how she loves new fashions."

"And gadgets." Felicity had requested several pieces of equipment modified, like her rocking chair, or brand-new designs, like her swing.

"What about Matthew, Annie? When he sees you he'll see the truth."

"He already knows. After all, he did let me kiss him. My time working with him is over, Belle. He'll never want me out there again. I might as well make my money while I can, so that when he's gone, I can take over building Felicity's Conservatory."

She slipped her cap back on her head and left the office to head upstairs and turn herself into the most delicious virginal offering Perdition House would ever see.

14

Matthew, shaken to his soul, stumbled back against the wall trying like hell not to lose his lunch.

Andrew had kissed him.

Kissed him like a woman, and he was so aroused he could hardly believe the ache in his belly.

He rubbed his hand over his mouth, unable to credit the softness he'd found. Andrew was soft as a woman, his hips flaring out from a narrow waist, but his chest was flat and hard.

Something wasn't right. The boy smelled soft, felt soft, kissed soft.

He never should have had that scotch. It had befuddled him, made him see a woman where Andrew stood.

If he didn't know better, he'd think—hell, he didn't know what to think anymore. But whatever was causing this aberration had to stop. Or, he'd get his revolver and stop it. He would not go through his life an abomination.

No, he'd rather end his sorry state now. His only salvation was Ben's arrival tomorrow. He wiped the sweat from his brow and ran to his tent.

He'd swim the scotch out of his head, then find Andrew to apologize and let the boy know he wouldn't have to deal with any more advances.

It wasn't until he'd swum his full twenty yards out from shore, that he realized it had been Andrew who'd kissed *him.*

The temptation to let the waves slide over his head was almost too much to resist.

Dinner was served precisely at seven, so at six fifty-five Annie made her way down the staircase with a demure tilt to her head, ready for the first time to be introduced as herself.

Her gown was peach-colored silk, her cheeks lightly rouged, although she didn't need it. She was aflame all over. Felicity had taken hot irons to her short hair so that she had tight curls. For the first time since she ran away from home, she wished for her long hair.

Stomach fluttering with nerves, she descended to the second landing. Now the time was here, she wondered how she would be received. Was she pretty enough? Bosomy enough? Did either matter to men who wanted to be her first?

She held her hands up in front of her. No amount of fussing had gotten rid of the work she'd done for years. She even had one blackened nail from a hammer blow three weeks ago.

A hammer blow she blamed Matthew for. It was the first morning she'd seen him return from a swim. The sight of him had so distracted her, she'd hit her thumb with the hammer.

Matthew. Would he ever guess her true feelings? Or would he see only what she wanted him to, that she'd joined the ranks of the working girls at Perdition? If that was all he saw, she'd be well rid of him.

She didn't think she was interesting enough to catch and hold the attention of some of the most powerful and wealthy men in the state. Her hands trembled with trepidation.

At the landing, she paused to gather her nerve. Matthew

stood in the archway between the dining room and the front hall. He talked with a man she didn't recognize.

It was too much to expect her to go through with this with Matthew in the room. Her belly dropped to her toes.

Full of dread, she turned to head back upstairs to escape, but Felicity stared her down from three steps above.

"Don't you dare! Not after all the work I did to get your hair to curl."

"But Matthew's right there."

Felicity lowered her voice to match Annie's harsh whisper. "And don't you feel the fool for pulling the wool over his eyes for this long? It's a terrible thing to have done." She clicked her tongue as if she hadn't done her share of terrible things. "I've never understood your need to parade around in overalls talking about roof trusses and the like. You're the queerest woman I've ever known, Annie Baker." She sidestepped to block Annie's attempt to get by.

"And it's time you put away your weird ways. It's time to be a woman."

"Oh, I'm happy to be a woman!" Her need and desire for Matthew could make her nothing but happy to be a woman. "It's being a lady I have issue with," she stated.

Felicity's eyes opened wide with shock.

"Fancy clothes and fancy talk have never interested me," Annie explained. "Oh! Fuck! You'll never understand."

Felicity's eyes fairly bugged out at the rude word. She pinched Annie's earlobe. "You've been around those rough workmen too long, Annie. Now get down those stairs before I boot you down."

"I'd like to see you try." The image of Felicity kicking anything made her grin. She hiked her hem to just below her knees and walked the rest of the way down, keeping her face turned away from Matthew. Blood rushed in her head, making her woozy.

She'd keep away from him. He'd probably forgotten about their kiss anyway. And she didn't care if he did remember it! It was only a kiss, a minor one at that.

Felicity walked beside her, arm in arm, not out of friendliness, but determination to keep her moving. "I'll eat my dinner, then leave the table right away."

"Yes, that's best. It's unseemly for you to hear the bids."

They were auctioning off her cherry and having her hear the actual bids was unseemly? She shook her head at the convoluted notion.

Annie planned to rise from her seat in one smooth motion, then flounce out of the dining room as much like Felicity as she could manage.

She knew enough about men to know that Matthew's response to her kiss didn't mean he liked her enough to spend good money for her time. His disdain of the working girls was what she was counting on.

He had to leave Perdition House so she could get on with her life. The longer he stayed, the harder it would be not to fall in love with him.

At the bottom of the stairs, Annie kept her face turned away while Felicity boldly looked at the newcomer. The men's conversation faded away.

Inwardly, Annie groaned. Why oh why must Felicity search out the favor of every man who came through the front door? The woman had no concept that a man might not want her. No concept at all. With good reason. To Annie's mind there wasn't a man who'd ever come to Perdition House who didn't want Felicity.

Except Matthew. Annie's lips curled into a quiet smile.

The stranger introduced himself to Felicity. His tone warmed and Felicity simpered the way she always did.

If the floor would only open beneath her, Annie would

gladly fall through. Even that would be preferable to standing here under Matthew's watchful gaze.

She caught sight of him, tall and wary, in the corner of her eye. Quickly she turned her head farther, but he sputtered in recognition. A second sputter followed.

She looked at him square on then, prepared to tell him to stop making a scene.

Before she could speak, he snagged her upper arm and tore it from Felicity's loose grasp. "What the hell's going on?" he demanded.

"Ouch! Let me go!" Annie spat, suddenly afraid of the intense anger in his face. This wasn't Matthew. Not her gentle Matthew. Except he wasn't hers, she ruthlessly reminded herself.

He dragged her close to his face. "You!"

Her heart stopped but she refused to show the fear that battered her innards. "Of course, it's me. What did you think?"

He went pale as fresh-cut lumber. "I thought—never mind what I thought! What are you doing here dressed like this?"

"I'm ready to join the other girls, that's what."

His voice rose to decibels she'd never heard before, not even when her father was in one of his most righteous rages. "Join the—" The sound cut off while Matthew's mouth worked, but no noise came out.

He'd never been at a loss for words before.

Felicity abandoned her man and headed through the doorway into the dining room, calling for Belle.

"You have to let me go now, Matthew," Annie said, keeping her voice calm. "I don't like being manhandled." She tilted her chin the way Felicity would when she was in a snit.

"Manhandled!"

Instead of letting her go the way any sensible man would, Matthew quick-marched her into Belle's office. She tried dragging her feet, but he wouldn't have it.

The office was empty. She whirled to run back out to the hallway, but he slid the pocket doors shut. She heard Belle knocking, but Matthew ignored it and turned to her. "And I don't like being made a fool of!"

She heard Belle through the door telling everyone to take their seats at the table. That Matthew and Annie had something to discuss.

She backed up, gauging the distance to the open window. She'd never get there before him, not in these stupid shoes, dragged down by these even sillier skirts. "What do you mean?"

He dragged her close, her skirts swirling around them. Her breasts, finally free of their tight binding, smashed up against his powerful chest and immediately peaked.

His eyes were so angry, his mouth so hard, she couldn't believe they were Matthew's. He claimed her mouth with insistent pressure.

Oh! Yes! Glorious kisses rained across her lips, her chin, her eyelids and around to her neck. She tilted her head to let him nibble and bite, while thrills chased around her belly and went deep. Anger and need warred inside, finally blending into a physical ache.

Giddy, she allowed him to walk her backward against the desk. There, he laid waste to her mouth, her neck, the sensitive flesh behind her ear. His hands tunneled in her hair, destroying the artful curls Felicity had taken such pains with.

"Oh, Matthew, you kiss like you mean it. Touch me, touch me everywhere," she pleaded as he undid her blouse and reached in to scorch her breasts with his palms. "Oh, yes, I'm burning up."

"You're so soft, so full," he said, a second before his chin nuzzled the material away from her breast. Finally freeing it, he suckled at her nipple and she offered herself openly.

Deep suckling produced the most interesting surges to her

belly and lower. She flowered open and moistness oozed into her slit as she felt the heat of his hands under her skirt.

She set her feet wider apart and sagged down onto the desktop to give him as much room as he needed to touch her. She ached and burned with each scorching kiss.

Matthew drew on her nipple strongly, pulling her belly up with each suck.

His other hand reached her inner thigh and she pressed toward him, seeking his touch at her most secret entrance.

The man was slow as molasses in January.

"Touch me!" she begged. "Touch me where I burn for you."

And, finally, he did.

In a melting ball of need she felt his finger brush once, twice against her sensitized flesh. Jiggling her outer folds in a way that made her gasp for air, he played her. At the feel of his fingertip at her entrance, she caught her breath.

"Don't! You've got to stop." Aching as she was, she hadn't lost complete hold of herself. Any further in and he'd ruin her.

She was no foolish young girl to give this away.

For what? Passion that would burn out in no time. She'd seen it all too often.

Annie Baker was no rube. She knew what she wanted and it wasn't a quick fumble and run.

She wanted Matthew here, right now, but more than this terrible desire was her need to live her life on her terms.

But first, first, she wanted the feel of his finger as it swirled around her outer folds, tantalizing her petals of sensitive flesh. He got so achingly close she wanted to cry her need. But close was not penetrating and for that she thanked him.

"Let me in." His demand, coupled with a touch against her nub, made her wild with yearning need. "You want it too. I can feel how wet you are. You're as ready as I am." He took her hand and placed it over the bulge in his trousers.

Full, hot, ready, Matthew was all man. And all hers.

"Will you let me work with you the way I've been doing?" His eyes were desire-befuddled. "What?"

"I have to know. Will you let me work with you?"

He pulled back, stared hard into her eyes. Finally, she saw the anger that drove his passion. "You're a woman and a construction site's no place for you. All those men. All that talk."

She caught her breath, heard her own heart slam against her ribs. "So you'd want me to stop, then."

"Hell, yes." He stepped back two paces, but kept his fingers between her legs, gently swirling. His expression tensed with arousal and it was clear he wanted her as much as she wanted him. "You can't work out there anymore, not now." He ran his other hand through his hair, mussing it the way he'd mussed hers.

He tried to kiss her again, but she turned her head to the side. "Matthew, I want you, there's no denying it." Even as she spoke, she melted more juice onto his fingers, felt the deep tension build inside her.

"But I don't want to live in a kitchen or a front parlor. I won't warm your bed at night if I can't work with you in the day."

He removed his hand from her. Let her skirts fall back down to hide her trembling legs.

He moved back farther, leaving her cold, abandoned.

"None of this makes sense. You're a woman. I'm a man. We want the same thing." He shook his head. "There's a right and wrong to this, but I'll be damned if I can figure you out."

She slammed her open palm to her chest. "I'm the same person I was in dungarees and suspenders, Matthew. Except I'm in skirts now. But my brain's the same, these eyes are the ones you taught to read blueprints, these hands are the very same hands that saw lumber and hammer nails." She raised her work-worn hands so he could see, so he could recognize Andrew under the clothes.

He placed one palm against one of hers. Tears swam in her eyes. He intertwined his fingers with hers. "I wondered all this time, how such delicate hands could be so competent."

He blessed her blackened fingernail with a feathery kiss.

"Competent," she repeated. "I can do everything you've taught me. Why won't you let me continue as I've been doing?"

"It's wrong," he blustered.

She pulled her hand from his. "I thought you were different. When we kissed earlier, I hoped that you might understand."

"Don't talk about that. It sickens me."

"A kiss sickened you?" Hurt beyond bearing, she blinked back her wasted tears. "After these few moments in here you must be at death's door."

He glared. "Don't pretend you don't get my meaning. You pretended to be Andrew!"

"I don't understand." She dismissed the confusion. "I want you, but I also want to work at building. If I can't have both, I'll find a way to live my life my way."

She raised her shaking hands to her hair and did her best to put her curls to rights. Felicity would have conniptions when she saw the mess Matthew had made.

Which was nothing compared to the fits Matthew would soon have when he learned Annie's cherry was on the auction block.

The cherry he could have had for free if he weren't such a stubborn, wrongheaded man!

15

Coffee and cake were served, but Matthew hardly noticed. He was still so hard he ached with it and angry with the woman he'd realized was named Annie. He'd had his hand up her skirt and hadn't even bothered to ask her name.

The hurt he'd seen in her eyes when he'd denied her wish to keep working still stung. But the woman was touched in the head to dream her kinds of dreams.

Women didn't understand building and tools and design. Their brains didn't work the same way as a man's.

Everyone knew that.

Belle stood at the head of the table. She waited, serene and regal, until all eyes were on her. When everyone had quieted, she looked around the table fondly, as if at a large, loving family. "As you're all aware, we're having a special celebration meal because of a rare event."

A few men cleared their throats and a couple of the women tittered and giggled.

Nothing of import to him. He fell to his own thoughts again.

He ran his hand over his mouth and found the arousing scent of Annie on the fingers he'd used on her. His cock reacted to the enticing scent. He had to shift himself for comfort while he stared across the table at her.

Her cock-eyed curls danced on her head as she glanced around the table. Her eyes settled on his and they widened and held. She set down her coffee cup.

Her glance softened, her chest rose and fell, and the telltale nubs of her nipples rose to attention. She'd admitted how much she wanted him. He'd felt the evidence of her moistness in his own hand. The scent of it called to him now.

She watched, wide-eyed, as he slid his tongue along the outside edge of his fingers. Her eyelids drooped as he tantalized her with another long, slow lick, lapping at the remains of her juices. She knew what he was doing. Knew and responded.

The taste of her, salty and delicate, aroused him to the point of pain.

Annie. Her name was Annie and he'd never wanted a woman more.

The shock of learning that Andrew was actually Annie still resonated, but his relief at not being one of those men who preferred—well, he needn't worry on that score again. She sat across the table from him, smart, proud, aroused, and available. As soon as this dinner was over, he'd take her by the hand and finish what they started.

Surely a woman whose lips were as soft and giving, whose secret flesh was as wet, pliant, and needy as hers would get over her insane urge to think and act like a man. Annie was built for a man's loving. Built for Matthew. If she thought he'd allow her to join the other women for a life of degradation she was addled in the head. She was his.

He let his mind wander over the first hour of having her in his bed. He couldn't think of anything more arousing than taking her where she wanted to go.

His cock tented the linen napkin in his lap as he saw Annie turn to look at Belle at the head of the table. Her fine delicate profile and jaw line enticed. He could see her femininity now and it pained him that he'd been so blind.

He took a sip of cold water as he tried to concentrate on what Belle was saying.

A loud cheer went up and Annie suddenly rose, pink-cheeked and lovelier than any woman here. He had no idea why everyone was congratulating her, but she ducked her head demurely, as ladylike as he'd ever seen a woman, and slipped out the door to the hall.

He made to follow her, but Felicity put her hand on his arm before he could rise from his seat.

"No, Mr. Creighton, you lost your chance with her," Felicity said softly. "Now you'll have to bid like the others." Her voice was calm, but forceful, her eyes lit with sharp humor. She was laughing at him.

"Bid?" He looked around the table. "What did I miss?" But no one answered him.

"A thousand!" said the senator who usually spent his money on Felicity. She looked delighted with the bid and clapped her hands.

"Twelve hundred," said a banker Matthew had a contract with. He was still working on blueprints that would allow for the most up-to-date wall safe available. The banker would bid money like this, but refused to spend a dime for reinforced floors.

"What are they bidding on?" he asked Felicity.

"Annie's deflowering, of course. She feels it's time. Since you wouldn't grant her dearest wish, she's chosen to live the way she wants to."

"Her what?!" He roared over the chatter and ever-rising bids. "She's mine!"

He stood, kicking over his chair, and stepped toward the

door, but it was barred. And a burly man he'd never seen before stood in front of it, arms crossed. He had the broken nose of a pugilist and arms and fists the size of pile drivers.

"No man gets to Annie for seven days, Matthew," said Belle over the suddenly hushed table. "That's when the bidding ends. We have to be fair to our gentlemen from farther afield." Her reasonable tone outraged him, while the comment created some grumbling from the other men.

Matthew's heart constricted in his chest.

This—he'd brought Annie to *this.*

There was no doubt this travesty was his fault. If he'd allowed her to continue working with him, he'd have had her in Belle's office. She'd made it plain she was his for the taking.

If he had compromised on everything he believed to be true about men and the rightful place of women, she would have been his. But to compromise on something that went against human nature was impossible.

He headed for the drinks cart and poured himself a stiff scotch. He threw it back in one gulp.

Warmth flowed through him as he poured himself another.

He looked from one man to the next. His competition included a banker who was peering down the new girl, Faith's, bodice. A senator whose eyes were closed, glorying because Felicity had her hand beneath the table and was leaning in to whisper in his ear. There was a powerful lawyer with political ambitions next to the senator, and the chief of police chatted amiably with Belle.

And these weren't the only men who would bid. No, Belle had contacts all the way to Washington and she'd have no compunction about using them. He had to come up with more money than Midas in seven days.

Impossible. He'd have to find another way to make Annie his.

* * *

Annie sat by her window, hands clasped in rapt attention as Lizzie described what to expect next.

"They tend to like you to lick them clean and swallow it all down. Some of the girls have to spit, but I find it tidier to swallow. Less fuss when it's over."

"And what about when a man wants your back door?" Annie asked.

Lizzie looked surprised. "Not all of them do."

She considered that with some relief. "A few years back, at May Malloy's, I saw a friend of mine take on two men at once. One liked the back door; the other took her mouth." It hadn't looked comfortable at all. She wasn't sure it was something she could do.

"Your friend was older?"

"Yes. She was pretty far past her prime. Liked to drink some, too."

"Some women do more things the younger ones don't have to do just to make a living." Lizzie smiled sadly. "But here, we don't have to worry about that. I've already got a nice nest egg set aside, thanks to some of the tips Belle's friends have passed along."

"Really? The house has only been open a couple of years." She'd put that time into learning everything she could about construction.

She sighed. If only Matthew had understood, she wouldn't be stuck here, like a princess in a tower. She chafed with the restrictions Belle had put on her.

No going outside alone.

No wandering down the back stairs to check on the construction progress.

"What have you heard about Matthew's friend, Ben Pratt? Have you met him?"

"Seems nice enough, I suppose. He's big and rough and

ready. Belle thinks he'll take charge well enough and the conservatory should be built on time."

"So, Matthew will be gone by the weekend?"

"Looks like it. Will you miss him?"

Something awful. "No. He taught me a lot about construction, but now he knows I'm a woman he won't allow me out there."

"Men think they own the world."

"That's because they do own it." But the truth didn't make Annie any less frustrated. "Do you think Ben Pratt's any different? Would he let me work, d'ya think?"

Lizzie shrugged. "I'll ask him after Matthew leaves."

"Once Matthew's gone, things will change or I'll go to Belle and make 'em change."

She hadn't set foot outside the house in three days. From her window, she could see Matthew's tent. She knew when he woke each morning and when he went to sleep at night. She tried not to watch him during the day, but she couldn't stop.

She should have had him when she had the chance.

The ache between her legs grew day by day. Recalling the way his tongue ran along his fingers at the dinner table made her wet. He'd been tasting her on his flesh and she'd been able to think of little else.

She shifted around the warm need in her belly. "Got any ideas on how to live without the man you crave?" she asked.

"Me?" Lizzie gave a bitter laugh. "No. Since I've never craved one, I can't help you."

"You mean there's never been a man you wanted more'n any other?"

"Garth beat that out of me. I was only with him six weeks, but that was still more than long enough to clear my head of foolish thoughts."

"He mean?"

"As a snake. And big, too. But I took care of him in the end." She shuddered. "I just hope the law never finds me."

"My pa was mean *and* righteous. Never could figure out how he made sense of that, but he did. He told me I was gonna burn in hell for being so pretty, for turning men's heads and making them think dirty."

The sun danced off her friend's Gibson Girl hair style, making a halo to frame her tiny, perfect features. "Oh, Annie, did he beat you?"

She shivered in remembrance. "Some, but mostly he dragged me out to the root cellar and locked me down there."

Lizzie's horror flitted across her face.

"I didn't mind being dragged so much as gettin' thrown down those steps. It was dark. So dark." She rubbed at her arms to dispel the remembered dankness of the earth walls.

"How'd you get away?"

She brightened. "Well, see, since I liked to see how things are built, I studied the joists and support beams in the floor overhead. I could hear my ma up there in the kitchen. I had to be careful how I dug so's not to weaken the structure. Took weeks but finally, the last time Pa tossed me down there, I was ready to finish digging my way out. I had a pack of clothes and some food ready to go. Dived into a hay wagon heading to Butte."

Lizzie's expression made Annie laugh.

"Don't look so surprised. I figured a way out of a bad situation and took my chance. I'm never going to live under anyone's thumb again."

"That's why you're holding out now."

Annie nodded. "But, Lizzie, I've never done anything worth getting the law after me for." Her tone softened to invite Lizzie's trust and confidence, but Lizzie pursed her lips.

Suddenly, her own worries seemed shallow, so when Lizzie changed the subject, Annie let her.

"You're not planning on working full-time with the gentlemen anyway," Lizzie said. "You want to go back outside to your hammers and nails."

"I want to supervise the building and repairs around here. If the world were different, I'd go to school to study architecture, but that's not likely to happen in my lifetime."

"No, you're right." She set the tea pot down onto the tray. "How did you feel working like a man? Being treated like one of them?"

"I felt free. Like I could do anything I wanted." Oh, to have that feeling again. Being cooped up inside the house was killing her. At least it was bright and cheerful, but the walls were beginning to close in. "Before this crazy business I felt as if I could go anywhere I wanted."

"Did you? I can't imagine feeling free as a bird. I was raised to obey my husband, bear his children, and think of God and country when he demanded his marital rights."

Annie laughed. "So was I, but my pa never stopped telling me I was bound for hell. When I ran off, I expected that was exactly where I was going, even kind of looked forward to it just so I could thumb my nose at Pa like I didn't care. Instead, I landed in Perdition, which has been heaven to me."

Lizzie joined in laughing. "Have you ever heard the word ironic?"

"No, what's it mean?"

Three days. Matthew had spent three days studying his problem with Annie. She stayed inside the house as if it was under quarantine.

He'd only been inside for brief meetings with Belle to introduce Ben and get them on a familiar footing so they could work together. Those meetings had been charged with static. He wasn't sure Ben and Belle could work together, but that wasn't his problem.

He was happy leaving Perdition in Ben's hands.

"That woman's going to be a pain in the ass," Ben said, staring at the front door of the house.

"I don't know how to keep her away from my sites, but I'll think of something." For now he had to concentrate on finding a way to get to Annie in the next few days. All during the time she'd been masquerading as Andrew, Matthew had enjoyed the company. But now, he couldn't allow Annie to run around in skirts in the middle of an unfinished building. It was too dangerous.

It gave him heart palpitations to remember he'd sent her up on scaffolding to help the carpenters install roof trusses.

"What sites?" Ben frowned at him.

"You're talking about Annie, right?"

"No. It's Belle. She's a hard woman to read."

"I never have any problem." He looked over his bills of lading to check some figures. He'd been shorted on lumber again. "We need a new supplier. I'll put a call in to Bart Jameson, the man who's sweet on Lizzie. He seems fair enough. The type who won't stiff us on delivery."

"Lizzie? The tiny one?"

"Don't let that fool you. I heard she laid a man out cold, once. Maybe killed him."

Ben looked impressed. "Maybe Belle's not the toughest one of the bunch."

"Belle's just hardheaded when it comes to business. What you have to realize with her is she thinks like any man who's out to make his fortune."

Ben's expression dismissed the comment.

Matthew laughed. "You'll learn how she thinks soon enough. Never met a woman like her. Sharp as a tack."

"Sure is a fine looker." Ben cocked an eyebrow in question.

"Yes, she is. Never heard of her in connection with a man, if that's what you're getting at. She keeps to herself that way."

"Maybe she's discreet."

"In a henhouse? Not likely. She's too busy keeping a close eye on each aspect of the business. She runs the house like it's the Taj Mahal. Everything in the place has her touch to it."

In a way, Belle Grantham was more fixated on business than a lot of the tycoons who used the place. At least when the men got here, they unwound, left their businesses behind. Belle never let up, not for an instant. "You'll soon see her in action yourself. Belle's a wonder. You go in there with a problem and she'll find a way around it by the end of the day. This whole addition is right on budget, in spite of our suppliers thinking they could bamboozle a woman."

"You're telling me to watch my step."

"I don't have to. You're old enough to recognize a smart woman when you meet one."

"I always was partial to the smart ones."

Matthew snorted.

"So Belle's the one that wanted this conservatory." The shouts of the glazier installing the windows rang around the enclosure. Once the windows were in, all that would be left to do was the interior finishing.

"No, Felicity misses the one in her family home. She's a Boston gal, wants to sit out here in the storms." He swung to encompass the conservatory. "But make no mistake, this has Belle's touch, too. Nothing happens in Perdition House without her either causing it or approving it."

"Felicity's paying for this?"

"In partnership with Belle. But Belle's in charge of dealing with the crew. Felicity's got a head for numbers, while Belle knows men and business."

"There isn't a woman here who's normal."

Matthew laughed. "I think you're right. We're in a hornet's nest."

"And you've been stung, my friend." Ben clapped him on the back. "So, how will you get around Belle to get to Annie?"

He set his hands on his hips and stared up at the three tall stories. "Hell if I know. But I will."

"Time's running out," Ben commented, as if Matthew hadn't been counting every blasted day.

"I know." The house was abuzz with news of the bids every time a new milestone was reached. The numbers both staggered and disgusted him. "You hear some congressman offered ten thousand the other day?"

"Yes, I did. Some fools have more money than sense."

"And more of them are coming out of the woodwork. Telegrams arrive every day now." The house's reputation was growing, but this was over the top.

"You've got to do something soon," Ben said, scratching behind his ear. "You say the word and I'll back you up. Maybe we should storm the house, push our way upstairs to her room."

"And what? Sling her over my shoulder kicking and screaming?" Although the idea of sweeping Annie off her feet and away from a life of ruination had its appeal, he couldn't do it. Annie would never forgive him.

Without her cooperation, life with Annie would be hell, not the Heaven he wanted. But, Annie was his, and it was time the whole of Perdition knew it. Including her.

A new thought struck and he turned to his friend, stared at him with a new understanding. "Or do you just want to go toe to toe with Belle Grantham? Get her riled to see what she's made of?"

"Oh, I know what she's made of, and it isn't sugar and spice." Ben turned and walked out the only window frame left that still had no glass in it.

He shook his head at Ben's folly. To be interested in Belle Grantham was a waste of a good man's time.

He went back to studying the house, embroiled in thoughts of his own folly. The wall under Annie's window stared back at him.

Well, damn, his answer had been in front of him for days.

16

Annie watched out her window as the lamp dimmed to darkness in Matthew's tent.

The bidding was over tomorrow and he hadn't even tried to get a note to her, let alone get into the house for a personal visit. Damn the man.

This just proved she was right to sell her cherry to the highest bidder. Once she got this bit of business out of the way, she would be free of Matthew Creighton and any other man who wanted to tell her how to live her life.

When Ben Pratt saw how much she knew about building, he'd better let her go on the way she'd been doing.

Belle would insist on it, and Belle always got her way. Especially with men like Ben Pratt. It was all over the house that sparks flew whenever he was in a meeting with Belle.

Silly man. Belle would soon have him eating out of her hand. Many's the man who'd come to the house and fallen for her. She was a rare beauty and far too smart to let her heart dictate her actions.

Annie would be like that, too. Hard-hearted and cool to

every man who gave her a second glance. After making a fool of herself over Matthew, she'd learned her lesson.

She studied the corner of the conservatory, all she could see of the new addition. She enjoyed a moment's pride that she'd had a hand in building it.

Tears threatened when she recalled the day she and Matthew had first broken ground together. She'd been so careful not to stare at him in awe.

He was so handsome! Talented and smart, he controlled an entire crew of men effortlessly. There was nothing they wouldn't do for Matthew, because he was better at everything than they were. Carpentry, mortar, design—Matthew had done it all. He was a builder's builder and she'd been smitten at first glance.

But she wasn't a silly girl any longer. She was a woman with needs and she was about to see to them. Tomorrow.

She'd finally be made a woman, and with a man who'd paid a handsome sum for her, too. She thought to feel some measure of pride in the fact, but fell short. Rather than pride she felt loss.

"Oh, to hell with Matthew Creighton," she said to the empty room. He could take his work-worn hands and strong jaw and go straight to hell. That's where she was going. *Well, Pa, you were right all along.*

The windows in the conservatory gleamed in the bright moonlight. For once there was a clear night sky overhead. The summer had been wet and gloomier than most.

But that couldn't take away from the joy she'd felt working on the conservatory. Now that the glaziers had installed the windows, it would be down to interior finishing.

She could handle that through the fall.

With Felicity adding a widow's walk to the roof, she must plan to be here for the rest of her life. Maybe Annie would stay forever, too.

With Matthew gone, the craving for him would stop and she'd have everything she wanted, except his hands on her again.

Craving Matthew was the worst and most unexpected thing that had ever happened to her.

She thought being bedded by one man would be much like being bedded by any other, but now, she wasn't so sure. Lizzie seemed to think all men were the same, but Hope certainly didn't. She'd told Annie being with Jed had been the most spectacular time she could remember. That love brought a new dimension to the bed that money couldn't buy.

But love had no place in Annie's decision.

Aside from the money the house would lose, she'd promised Belle to go through with the auction. Important men were heading here now just to—

A movement by Matthew's tent caught her eye. He was there, in the moonlight, standing in front of the tent flap, staring up at the house. With a quick glance left to right, he started across the lawn, his very movements full of purpose and intrigue.

When he got close to the house wall, she couldn't see him. A scratching noise caught her attention and she opened her window. He was climbing the trellis.

"What the hell are you doing?" she whispered as loud as she dared. It was fine for Andrew to say hell, but Annie shouldn't. Oh, damn. Life as a man had even changed the way she thought.

"Climbing up to your window." His tone was amused but throaty. It was taking some effort to hoist himself up the slender trellis.

"That trellis was built for roses, not full-grown men." She should know; she built it. A thrill rose that he'd finally taken matters in hand. "Be careful," she hissed.

"You just get ready."

The thrill she felt turned into a trickle of alarm. Her breath caught. "I'm more than ready," she snapped back at him.

She closed and locked her door, then headed back to the open window, half afraid she'd see him in a tangle of limbs in the flowerbed below.

Leaning out again, she found him close enough to touch, so she leaned farther out and grabbed the back of his jacket collar to steady him while he swung his leg over the windowsill.

"Let go, I can't get in with you in the way."

She stepped back, flustered by his unique entrance and overbearing way.

He hopped over the sill and landed sure-footed on the floor.

Wary, she stepped back a couple of feet, out of reach.

Now that he was safely inside she let her irritation show. "Took you long enough!" Six days. "I've been stuck in this house since last Friday."

His brows knit into anger. "Me? What about you? Allowing this farce!"

He had no right to be angry. He'd tossed her to the wolves by being stubborn and stupid. "Farce?" She crossed her arms to keep from reaching out. "Is that what you call a rational decision?"

"Rational." He made a disgusted noise. "Females aren't rational. They're emotional, fragile creatures who need to be guided. That much has been brought home to me very clearly these past few days."

He wasn't here to make peace. He was here to demand she bend to his will. Like a good little woman.

"So that's what you think of me. After all the hammering, the measuring, the lifting I've done for you? I built that trellis you just climbed up on." She pointed at the window, as if he'd forgotten where it was. "Fragile, my eye!"

Oh, she wanted to punch him. Right in the nose. But she was too smart to get that close.

If he touched her, if he pulled her close, even if she got near enough to smell him, she'd be lost. What had become of her mind, her will?

She heaved in another breath, grabbed onto what was left of her resolve. "You have to leave."

His gaze caught hers when she looked at his eyes. He'd gone still. And silent. His eyes, no longer amused, focused hard on hers.

Uh oh.

She backed up two steps. He advanced three.

She took one step to the side.

He took two.

"You stay where you are." She held up her hand, as if a man who'd climbed a rickety trellis would stop at a hand gesture.

"No." He advanced.

She retreated. "I'll scream."

"No, you won't."

She looked to her bureau top. Her brush was there. She picked it up.

He stilled, eyes glittering in the lamplight, mouth twitching. "Go ahead, throw it at me. I don't care. I also don't care about the bids. They don't mean anything."

"They do to me." She thumped her chest. "They're my ticket to freedom."

That caught him up short. His hard lips went harder. "Freedom?" He cocked his head as if it was a new word. Maybe applied to a woman, it was.

"To live my way. Freedom to be who I am. You want me to change, to be a lady or some damn fool thing I'll never be."

"I just want you, Annie. *You.*" He ran his hand through his hair, leaving it in spikes. "These men who bid on you want a beautiful virgin, while I want *you*, Annie Baker. I know you better than any of these other men ever will."

That was true, she thought, but kept it to herself.

"I know what makes you laugh. I know that every time a flock of geese flies overhead you stop whatever you're doing to listen to the honking. Hell, I've even heard you honk back." He waited for three heartbeats before he added, "I know you watch me the way I watch you."

He straightened in a pose that no longer threatened. He wouldn't pounce. He didn't need to pounce. He could sweet-talk her into walking into his arms.

The sly bastard.

"I know what to expect from the others, Matthew Creighton. But what do I get from you if I give in to your persuasions?" Which was looking more and more likely as the minutes and slow tension stretched between them. Moisture already seeped, breaths already deepened, need already pulsed.

"I'll give you a good life, Annie. I'll provide for you, give you my heart, give you children to love. I'll give you the life every woman wants."

"You'll give me chains." The pain of his truth cut into her.

He stabbed his fingers through his hair. "What is it that you want then? Tell me and I'll give it to you. Just make sure it isn't life in men's trousers."

"Oh, you make me so—" And then she realized. The man was dense as a post, but he thought he loved her.

He didn't know her at all.

She pulled herself up to her full height. "This dress, these curls, aren't me." She lifted her skirt, fluffed the hem, and lifted it to her knees to show him her best pair of work boots. "I might be wearing a skirt, but underneath, this is who I am."

She ran her brush through the silly curls Felicity had fussed with again. Hairstyle ruined, she glared at him, daring him to see the real her.

He stared at her as if she'd sprouted a second head.

"What are you doing?"

"You see Annabeth, the girl my ma wanted me to be. The woman I've never been and never want to be." How could she explain so he'd understand? "I don't know why I want to work with my hands and use my brain, but I do. To deny that part of me would kill me. If you don't see that, then you don't see *me*."

She patted her chest over her heart. "I love you, Matthew, but I'd never want you to be different. I don't want you to be a farmer, or a policeman, or anyone else but who you are."

"Annie, I—"

She held up her hand to stall him. "Please, if you love me, do me the same courtesy. Accept me for who I am, what I am. A woman who wants to work with you, beside you. Let me be Annie.

"I'm not asking for life in trousers, although they're easier to live in. I don't understand how you can deny me the joy of building. You know how much I love to see the structure take shape, the pride I share with you."

He gritted his teeth so hard she thought his jaw might break. "Share with me. Yes. Annie, do you truly feel pride in the work? The way I do?"

"Haven't you seen it?"

He dropped his chin and for a long moment she waited, wanting to reach out and smooth the thick cap of dark hair he'd ruffled into wild peaks. Instead, she held her breath and hoped he'd recall every time they'd stared at a wall, at bricks, at a well-built foundation, and grinned together like children.

"Yes, of course I have. I'm, I'm . . . sorry, Annie."

She'd never heard Matthew apologize to anyone before. Certainly her father had never done it. She froze, not sure if she heard him right.

"For what?"

"For not loving you enough to see through Andrew, for not

seeing the beauty of who you are. All I want is you, any way you are. Anyone you are. If it pleases you to hold a hammer instead of a soup ladle, that's what you'll do."

He opened his arms. "Just be mine, Annie. Mine."

Her heart, denying everything she'd been telling herself, cried out, *I am! I am!* Throwing self-preservation aside, she walked into his arms.

Heat and strong arms enveloped her. His eyes, so close, searched her face. She allowed a small smile before she tilted up for a kiss. His lips dropped to hers and the need for words was gone.

Desire swooped and dived to her deepest reaches with every touch of his hands. Matthew smoothed her back, her arms, her chest with his callused, powerful hands. Oh! Her chest!

"Oh, yes, feel my breasts. They ache so."

He cupped each one, hefting the weight of her flesh. His thumbs circled each nipple, sending deep charges of heat to her loins. She sighed and moved against his hands in a tantalizing fluidity.

"How did you hide these?" He rolled her nipples between his thumb and forefinger, sending arrows of want south.

"I bound myself. Many was a morning I wanted to leave the binding behind, to let you see, but I wanted to stay at work even more." Something he'd said niggled at her. "When you said you didn't see through Andrew, are you saying when you kissed me last week, you thought . . . ?"

"Hush, now, and let me love you." His lips burned a trail down her neck from her ear to her shoulder.

She giggled and promised herself a hearty laugh at his expense . . . later. Much later. When they were old and gray and it wouldn't matter anymore.

With shaking fingers, she undid his shirt buttons and swept open his shirt. Finally able to feel his muscles under her heated palms, she reveled in the hard strength of him. "Oh, I've wanted to touch you here," she murmured.

Hot flesh over hard muscle. She couldn't get enough of the heated sparklers of desire she gathered in her palms. Wildness rose as he devoured her with gentle kisses and firm strokes.

"Annie, I can't get at you fast enough." He dropped to his knees in front of her and laid his head to her chest. "Love me, Annie, I'll burst if you don't."

She chuckled and held his head, feeling the bristly ends of his fresh haircut. "I do love you, Matthew, and I need you more than anything."

She took one step toward the bed and he rose to his feet again. She held her hand out to him and he took it as she led him to the bed.

They faced each other. He set to work untying the bodice of her Gibson Girl blouse while she undid the buttons on his fly.

"We have to slow down. I don't want to hurt you," he said on a harsh breath.

"I don't imagine you will. I'm so juicy I feel like I could slide off the bed."

He laughed deep in his throat. "Oh! Annie, you're priceless."

"I don't think the bidders would agree."

"Love has no price," he whispered as he knelt on the bed and pulled off his shirt. "Belle will be angry when she finds out about this."

She reached for his waist and helped him shuck his pants, boots, and socks. "I don't think she'll be all that surprised. Knowing Belle, she's probably already planned for it."

Finally, he was naked and clearly more man than she had imagined. "Oh, my," she murmured when she saw the size of him.

She was familiar with men's parts. She'd seen plenty when

she worked in May Malloy's whorehouse, but knowing Matthew would soon slide his parts into her parts brought a new light of knowledge and delight.

"Why the strange look, Annie? Never seen a man before?"

"I've never seen *you* before. And you're the one I've always wanted, even before I knew what it was I was itching for."

"Let's get your clothes off, too. I've waited a long time to see you as a woman, Annie. Before, all I could think was that you were one funny built man."

She laughed at that and reached for the button closure on her hobble skirt.

"Your hair was always so clean and soft," he said as he watched her with delight in his gaze. "The sun would dance off your perfect smooth cheeks. Your hips swayed when you walked and your wrists . . ." He took one in his hand, lifted it for a kiss. ". . . so fine-boned. I often thought they'd break under the loads you carried."

She tugged, one-handed, on her skirt. Finally, it slid down to her ankles. She stepped out of the puddle of cloth and started to work on her underclothes.

Naked, she rose to her knees to face him on the bed. For a long moment, he looked his fill. Then, he traced the skin of her left cheek, followed the line of her neck to her collarbone, then plumped her breast with three fingers. He lifted the flesh again, high, then dropped it, apparently fascinated by the fluid, jiggling movement.

She shook her breasts from side to side, enjoying the freedom of no binding. She lifted her breasts in her hands and offered them to his mouth.

The suction pulled down to her womb and she softened and opened with desire. On their own accord, her knees widened on the bed, offering a perfect triangle for his hand. She was beyond thought and jerked hard with the tender feel of his fingers between her legs.

He stroked and petted the curls while he suckled and nipped at each breast in turn. She could only stay upright by leaning on his shoulders.

She felt a fine tremor go through his body when she groped for his shaft. So hard, so smooth. The tip felt like velvet as she slid her thumb to the bead of dew she found.

"What's this?"

"Taste it."

She watched his eyes darken to thunder when she licked her thumb. Delicious and wicked, the taste of him delighted her.

"You don't know what it does to me to see you do that." His voice was rough around the edges and curled into her heart.

"Tell me."

"I'd rather show you."

With that, he settled her on the bed and straddled her chest. From this angle, he loomed large in front of her and again, she slid her thumb across the tip of his cock.

Farther down, she felt the sway of his balls and cupped them gently while he played with her nipples. Settling each nipple in the apex of two fingers, he jiggled the flesh, creating spears of heat that traveled to her womb.

She opened her legs, streaming from her pussy onto the sheets. "Matthew, I can't wait any longer."

"I have to taste you first, before I've been inside. I need to taste the juices you've saved for me."

He moved so quickly, she felt an ache as he tore away from her. But the ache was short-lived as his hands spread her knees wide and he looked at her. "You're glistening here . . ." She felt his thumb on her outer lips and raised her hips in a plea for more. ". . . and here." His fingertip entered her delicately.

She bucked upward in demand, but he swirled lightly rather than plunging in. "Oh, Matthew, you're making me crazy with wanting you."

He lifted his finger to his mouth and licked it clean. The other hand pumped at his cock rhythmically. She watched the slow up and down motion of his large, square hand on his thick shaft. Her mouth watered at the sight as she imagined the joy she'd feel as he slid in and out of her in a rhythm they would find together.

No other man's rhythm would be like Matthew's. No other man's cock would taste like his, feel like his, burn like his. She shifted on the bed, anxious to speed him along.

"Is it always this slow? Can't you just put it in?"

He chuckled. "No. Not the first time. You need to be ready. Slick and wet and open."

"But that's how I feel. Honest."

"This nub, right here . . ." He pressed and tapped on her clit, drawing out a moan she didn't even recognize. ". . . will be rubbery soon. When that happens I'll lick it, get you wetter, taste your juice."

"Oh, Matthew! This cherry-popping business takes too damn long!" She thrashed her head with frustration while he continued his delicate torture. "Arrgghh!"

The sensual assault on her pussy went on and on while she melted on his fingers. Her face was hot and her skin burned from the waist down. He swept his thumb over the sensitive bud near her top, then delved into her channel, to prepare her for the length and breadth of him.

"I'm ready now, Matthew. Take me," she crooned. "Fuck me the way you want to. I'm yours."

Finally, he settled his face between her legs. She raised her hips and offered her pussy to his questing tongue and fingers. Delicious sparks rose from every spot he touched, licking and sliding and spearing his tongue into her. "Oh, oh, ohhhh!" Incredible tension rose, taking her higher than high.

She'd pleasured herself many times, but it didn't compare to the heat of Matthew or his strength. His command of her body made her want to cry out as the tension spun away, taking her with it.

A crest rose like a rip tide from her depths and shook her pelvis, her chest, her shoulders, and down her arms to her fingertips. She bucked and lunged with the crest and rode it high until she could ride no more.

At the pinnacle, the sudden weight of Matthew on top of her felt right and proper and she welcomed him into her in a long, slow slide of possession. She was still open and cresting when he pushed past a barrier she was glad to let go.

She came down to earth with the heavy weight of Matthew pressing her into the mattress. She slid her legs up to his waist and locked her ankles around his back while he seated himself deep inside. He filled her, stretched and pulled at her delicate inner walls. Each drag of flesh against flesh took her higher and higher along a path to another crest.

Mind gone, she rocked him in the cradle of her hips, held him in place with her legs as he slid and plunged again and again.

He set his lips to her neck, her ear, her mouth as she moved with every pump and grind. With the feel of her open and ready beneath him Matthew moved more surely in and out of her.

He stiffened suddenly and held her at another peak before she plunged over the crest once more.

He cried out, neck straining, face flat with awe at what they'd found together. Tears slid from the corners of her eyes, down past her ears to the pillow.

"Oh, Matthew. My father was wrong. I won't burn in hell for loving you. We have Heaven right here on earth."

Faye woke from her nap in Lila's room, with her fingers dancing across her clit, halfway to orgasm. She pressed harder and took the rest of the journey.

"Oh, that was nice," said Belle. "Quite a good one." She sat

on an incongruous Shaker chair beside the bed and waited
while Faye's heartbeat returned to normal.

"Why are you in here?" Belle asked. The plainness of the
simple chair emphasized the extravagant peacock display of
blues and greens she wore. No more beige.

Faye rolled her eyes. "Like anything goes on in this house
without you knowing about it." She sat up and finger-combed
her hair.

Belle had the grace to blush. "Lila's diary is under this chair.
Annie designed secret drawers all over the house, including in
the furniture. She was the only one who kept track of them all,
though, so it's been a good lot of fun looking everywhere."

Annie. Gone for good with Matthew. "Annie and Matthew
were happy?"

"Delirious." Belle's dry tone spoke volumes.

"Matthew was right about the auction, Belle. It was disgust-
ing."

"Oh, pooh, you don't think I took those bids? I'm of-
fended." She sniffed, haughty and dismissive.

"So you never planned to auction off Annie's cherry?"

"I never believed she'd work with the other girls. She didn't
have the heart for sex for money. Never did." Belle stated. "Not
to mention the men's clothing she insisted on wearing."

Faye laughed. "She wasn't polished enough?"

"Never." Belle shook her head and suppressed a chuckle.
"Even I couldn't make a silk purse out of a sow's ear. Annie
came from a strict farm upbringing. She was so worried about
hell and damnation that she hid inside Andrew. There's no
telling how long she'd have kept up the illusion if Matthew
hadn't fallen for her. Him. Her." She waved her hand in languid
insouciance. "Whatever."

"It must have been horrible for a man as heterosexual as
Matthew to have his sexual identity so shaken." Horrible, but
funny now that she thought of it.

"Poor man didn't admit it to her for years, but of course, Annie figured it out that first time. But once the truth came out, he took a lot of good-natured ribbing."

"I'm glad he got over his old-fashioned notions about a woman's place."

"Those notions were not old-fashioned for the times. He was a real man with a capital *M* to make the concessions he did. To Matthew's credit, he never regretted having Annie work with him."

Felicity floated in through the door. "Oh, Annie and Matthew? They were a funny pair. Annie refused to put on a dress and admit she was a woman and he kept denying her femininity because he was so upset with his reaction to Andrew. And her hair! I had the devil's own time to set it to rights."

"You're a softie, Belle Grantham." Faye warmed with familial affection.

"I'm not." Her chin rose and her back stiffened. "I'm a madam and I knew Annie would never work for me. This was a way to cut my losses. I couldn't keep paying for meals for a woman who wouldn't lie down!"

"Right. Of course not."

A gentle laughter echoed from the walls as Felicity and Lizzie chuckled along with Faye. Belle clicked her tongue.

Faye climbed out of bed and reached under the chair Belle was on. Sure enough, she found a pocket tacked onto the bottom.

Belle disintegrated and left Faye to tilt the chair over. A red leather-bound book slid out of the pocket.

She settled back onto the bed to read Lila's diary.

17

Lila's diary was a fast read.

Six weeks after arriving, comfortable and happy with her work, she was forced to confess she was pregnant. It seemed Captain Jackson noticed her belly and went to Belle, concerned.

Annie held Lila's hand in Belle's office and asked Belle to let her stay on until the baby was born.

She was four months along by her figuring and had a vague dream of returning to her parents with her child. Faye rolled her eyes at the childish entry.

A new arrival caught Faye's interest.

A Stella McCreedy arrived at Belle's invitation.

Stella was a midwife and took over Lila's care when things took a dark turn. Lila may have been alarmed but from Faye's perspective, Stella was a godsend. Determined not to have any more "mistakes" occur at the house, Stella provided the girls with rubbers. Until then, Belle had stocked a supply from France, but Stella's were better. U.S. Army issue, they'd been designed to "prevent disease."

The days turned into weeks and the entries became more sporadic and dreamy. It became clear Lila wasn't the sharpest pencil in the box.

In a flash of maturity, Lila rallied at the end with a note to her baby. Faye could hardly make out the words through her tears.

"And you call me a softie," said Belle when Faye closed the too-short story of Lila's life. "It was easy enough to send her back to her folks with a story about her having been ill."

One mystery solved, but Faye was no closer to learning about the screaming woman.

The phone rang and she glared at Belle, convinced the spirit had arranged the call to happen just at this minute. She ran through the room, down the hall, and into her bedroom to answer.

Out of breath, she picked up. "Hello?"

"Hey, babe," came a voice she could hardly hear over her labored breathing.

"Liam?"

"No, it's Mark."

"Hi!" *Oops!* She plowed over her slip of the tongue. "It's so good to hear your voice. I was hoping you hadn't forgotten me."

He laughed, deep and sexy, the sound warming to affectionate. "Not likely. I've been tied up trying to get my house listed when I should be in Seattle working on the expansion."

"What's the hold up?" Anything to do with real estate caught her attention these days.

"I'm a bachelor." He sounded frustrated.

"That's good, considering how we spend most of our time together." She chuckled. "How is that a problem?"

"Bachelors live like men alone. My listing agent is bringing in a home stager to redecorate. They say I have no style. It'll take a week before we can get the house on the market."

She could imagine Mark's decorating. Heavy black leather lounger front and center, and a widescreen television permanently turned to a sports network that showed football twenty-four seven. "Do you have black leather in your living room?"

"How'd you know?"

"A wild guess. But this means you won't be here for a while." He'd already been gone for days. Disappointment rang down the line and she hated that she sounded that way. "Sorry, I don't mean to sound clingy, but I—"

"You don't. You sound hot. I wish I was there."

She warmed to the underlying arousal in his tone. Her voice went husky. "So do I."

"I thought about hooking up last night, but—"

"We're not exclusive," she interrupted to reassure him. Maybe to reassure herself. "I understand if you need a woman." She closed her eyes and hated that she didn't want him with someone else when she couldn't make the same promise.

But Mark didn't have a house full of horny spirits directing his sex drive.

"Thanks," he said. "No pressure." He paused. "If I were the one who'd walked in and saw my fiancé with someone else, I'd be fucking everything in sight. I'm not even going to ask who Liam is."

She closed her eyes and wondered if Belle had made Mark this understanding. In the end it didn't matter. He was letting her know she was free to continue to explore her sexuality. "Thank you. I do have some things I need to work out."

"But for now"—she settled on the bed—"I've got a great idea if you're game."

"I'm game."

And horny. "You were thinking of hooking up last night and didn't, so that must mean you're tense."

He chuckled and the thrill of the deep sound rolled down her spine. "Tense. Yes."

"I'm on my bed. I might be able to help with that tension."

"Describe the bed."

She laughed. "I should have known you'd catch on quick. My bed is totally feminine. A four-poster with a snow-white eyelet lace down duvet. It's deliciously sexy."

"Does it have a canopy?"

"No, but it has one of those antique headboards made of wrought iron."

"Put one hand on the top railing of the headboard."

"Okay."

"How does it feel?"

"Cool and hard. It's about as thick as your cock, come to think of it."

He chuckled. "Good, now I know. I can imagine you with both hands locked on that headboard and your head thrashing on the pillow when you come."

"Will I? Come?"

"Oh yeah, around the time I do." He let two heartbeats pass before he said, "Ready?"

"Yes. Why do I get the feeling this is now your idea?"

"Why do you think I called?" His smile came through his voice and she melted. He had the sexiest, hardest lips she'd ever come across. Figuratively and literally. She shifted her legs on the bed, more than ready to follow his lead.

"I don't know if I should feel flattered or not," she said.

"Be flattered. There's no one else I would ever do this with," he said. "Now, in my mind I see you wearing that hot dress you had on the night we met."

"Yes, it was silk and draped down my chest." It had seemed to leap into her hand from inside a box of fedoras. She now realized Belle had arranged for the dress to catch her eye.

"You looked like a cross between Marilyn Monroe and Jayne Mansfield in that dress," he said, obviously caught in the same memory she was.

"I felt fire burn through me as I walked into the Stargazer. Sexual need exploded out my fingertips, my hair, and my skin."

"I know, I saw it. You had this red-hot glow all around you. You moved across the floor like you were halfway to a come. I couldn't resist the look of you, the scent of hot woman, the desire in your eyes. I've never been so turned on in my life."

Mark had responded like a bull to a red cape.

She dropped her head back in memory of his hands and mouth skimming down her neck to her chest.

"You leaned forward to let me see your cleavage. It shimmied and moved and all I could think of was sliding my cock between your tits."

"Oh, yes. I can feel it there. It's hot against my breastbone. Hard and thick, too."

"Press the sides of your tits together so I can slide right in."

"Oh yes!" Moisture pooled at the idea of Mark's cock sliding thick and heavy between her breasts. Her nipples peaked as he rode her chest.

"Put your hand on your crotch." The voice in her ear was breathy and uneven, as if he really was pumping at her.

"I will if you will," she responded with a husky burr.

"Way ahead of you, babe." She heard his breath catch. "Are you wet?"

"Streaming. I'm not wearing panties."

"You never do. That's one of the things I like about you, Faye—you're always so fucking ready."

These days, she loved sex so much she seemed to be thirty seconds from orgasm at all times.

"Where's your hand now?" he asked.

"Between my legs. My clit's sticky and I'm, *Oh!*, I'm rubbing."

"Put your middle finger inside."

"Oh, Mark! It's hot, so hot."

"Now, pump it in and out, Faye. Pump it hard. And rub your thumb on your clit. Feel it go firm?"

"Oh!" Her eyes slid shut as tension rose to claim her. More, she needed more, harder. "I put in another finger. I want you! I want you bad!"

"Fuck!" He growled into the phone and right on down to her pussy, where, liquid and needy, his voice roughed her nerve endings into a million shards as she came with him.

The receiver lay on her chest when she rode out the last of her pulses. Unbelievable! The man was still able to teach her things she never dreamed she was capable of.

She slid down the bed and cradled the receiver between her ear and shoulder. "Are you there?"

"Yeah. Man, that was hot. You're one in a million, Faye."

She stretched and yawned. Rolled to her side and pretended his chest was beneath her ear. "Thanks, but I couldn't have done it without you."

He chuckled. "I'll see you in a couple of weeks. Think about me." He hung up.

The dial tone buzzed after he disconnected and she dropped the receiver back in its cradle.

"What in the world was that?" Felicity asked from somewhere over the headboard.

"Phone sex. Did you like it?"

"I'm not sure. But in my day, the telephone was an instrument of communication."

"Oh, please. From what I've heard about you, you'd have invented phone sex if only you'd thought of it."

Felicity's light, feminine giggles made Faye laugh.

"You're right, Faye. I'd have tried anything and often did."

Faye rose and took a quick shower. Then she called Time-Stop to check in with Willa and Kim. Mark's comment about his expansion into retail had reminded her of a few points she needed to clarify for the help-wanted ad.

When she hung up, Lizzie stood in front of her, petite and agitated, the way she usually was.

She was such a nervous Nelly, Faye wondered how she'd managed to work.

"I closed my eyes and thought of myself in a lovely quiet field, picking daisies," Lizzie explained in response to Faye's thought.

Great, now they were all doing it.

"Sorry," Lizzie whispered, ducking her head.

"Never mind, I should be used to it by now," Faye said. "After all, anyone should be able to handle sharing orgasms with ghosts and having their thoughts read." She frowned. "Not to mention my sex drive tweaked into high gear every time I turn around. I haven't forgotten you got me together with Liam in the gazebo."

"He's such a well-hung man, how could I make him wait?"

"You mean how could *you* wait," she teased. Forgiving Lizzie was easy when she thought about the friendship she now shared with Liam.

But something about Lizzie didn't ring true. "Picking daisies in a lovely field. This is such bullshit, Lizzie. What gives?"

Lizzie's neck went a lovely shade of translucent pink, as if she'd been swabbed with a highlighter. Then the color moved up to her cheeks, giving her face a ghostly pink glow that became her. Lizzie, under all the nerves and shyness, was quite a looker.

"I took awhile to warm up to sex and all its delights. My first experiences were . . . unpleasant."

And then Faye remembered. Lizzie's husband Garth was a mean drunk. A virginal bride with a mean drunk for a husband made Faye cringe.

"But it got better?" She couldn't bear the thought of Lizzie being miserable for all the years she lived at Perdition.

"Oh! Yes! It got better, thanks to Belle. She taught me about my own body, and men's. I was the one to whom the gentlemen who needed to learn how to make a woman happy were sent." Her innocent green eyes went wide. "You'd be surprised how many men need help in that regard."

"Not at all," Faye said drily. Her ex-fiancé needed a lot of help, but he was too arrogant to know it. "So, which of the men made you blush so hot, Lizzie?"

"You noticed." She fanned her face with her hand.

"Ah, yeah." Faye held up her hand. "But Annie beat you to nap time this afternoon. Could this wait until tonight?"

"Of course. I didn't mean to make you think . . ."

"That you're eager to finish your story?" She finished Lizzie's thought for her. *For a change.*

"Yes, I'm eager." Lizzie grinned at the switch Faye had pulled. "I'll come to you tonight, as soon as you fall asleep."

She heard the distant ring of her phone and ran inside to answer. Busy place this morning, she thought as she picked up.

"Hi, Faye Grantham?"

She didn't recognize the man's voice, but her sexual alert went to high. She felt her low belly tingle and warm to the caller. "Yes, who's this?" She sounded husky. Appalled, she cleared her throat and told whoever it was trying to arouse her to back off.

"Grant Johnson. We met a couple of weeks ago?"

"Mark's friend. What can I do for you?" Desire gripped her low and hot and she ground her teeth to suppress it.

Back off!

"I'm in town again and—" He chuckled. "—I was so blown away when I met you, I was hoping . . ."

"I'm still seeing Mark, Grant, but the offer's flattering."

"Oh, I didn't realize."

Between the raging battle she was waging and this man's obvious disregard for Mark, she needed to let off some steam.

"Didn't realize what?" she said sharply. "That Mark thinks you're his friend or that I might not want to be passed around?"

"No need to take offense, Faye," he backpedaled. "I like you, think you're smart, funny, and beautiful. So does Mark. He told me you weren't on exclusive terms and—" His tone turned apologetic. "I've fucked up badly here, haven't I?"

"You have."

"Forgive me?"

His tone was so warm, so tempting. But she rallied just in time and fought back the arousal. "Forgiven. Now, I have a heavy schedule today."

"I'll let you get to it, then. I hope you don't think the worst of me. Mark and I go way back. I guess I've got a case of envy for the guy. Sometimes it gets the better of me."

"I won't tell him, but honestly, Grant, you're making more of this than you need to. I have a feeling Mark would understand." He'd told her that he and Grant had the same taste in women and that it had caused problems before. Like boys on any team, there were times they liked to keep score.

What was more important to her was that she'd overcome the sexual interference. Next, she needed to learn how to shield her thoughts from the girls. Then, she'd have her mind all to herself again. A refreshing change.

18

Lizzie picked up her envelope from Belle's desk and opened it, breath held. Every Friday before dinner the girls gathered in the office and Belle handed out their assignments. The gentlemen were allowed to request specific women. Often, couples paired for weeks until one or the other wanted to move on.

She pulled a square card out of the envelope. Everyone watched for her reaction. She glanced at Felicity out of the corner of her eye. "Stop smirking! Surely the man's got the hint by now. Even an ox has a brain."

She flipped open the fold and blinked. "Damn!"

Felicity tittered behind her hand. "Apparently oxen don't have brains."

Ignoring Felicity, she glared at Belle across the desk. "Do I have to spend another Friday evening with Bart Jameson? The man's a clod."

"Clod or not, he spends good money to enjoy your company. Did I say 'enjoy'? Perhaps I should say, 'suffer' your company."

Lizzie bit her lip at Belle's reprimand. All the other girls went silent.

"It isn't my fault the man can't take no for an answer." She leaned over the desk. "What's wrong with him? Most men never ask for the same woman again if they don't get what they came for the first time. Why does he ask for me week after week?"

Belle shrugged. "As long as I've been in the business, I've never seen the likes of Bart Jameson. He's got something other than sex on his mind, that's all I can think."

Lizzie couldn't imagine any other reason for a healthy man to come to a house like Perdition. He didn't talk to the other businessmen. He had tea with her in the parlor, then sat beside her at dinner. When all the other couples paired off for their evening's entertainments, she walked him to the front door and sent him away. It was tedious.

"Some men are beyond understanding," she said.

"Maybe he likes your conversation." Felicity shrugged and accepted her envelope from Belle.

She opened it and read. "Ooh, the senator again. Delicious. Who asked for you?" She turned to the newest arrival, who went by Faith, but had none.

While Lizzie stewed about Felicity's comment and wondered how she could put an end to the farce with Mr. Jameson, Faith responded to Felicity's question.

"Captain Jackson," Faith said. "Is he manageable?" She was fairly new and hadn't yet settled into the routine of a regular man. Once she did, she'd do nicely.

"I wouldn't know." Frost in Felicity's voice clipped off her words. She spun and marched toward the hall, back rigid, skirts swirling around her ankles.

"I'll gladly trade with someone," said Lizzie, half ignoring her friend's splendid exit.

"Trading isn't allowed, is it?" asked Faith, slipping her envelope into her pocket.

"No." Belle gave Lizzie a hard look she didn't appreciate.

In her role as teacher to the newer girls and even to some of the men, Lizzie often had a different escort each week. But with Bart's continual requests for her, she was facing a drought of activity.

He was so huge and intimidating none of the other men wanted to put in for Lizzie. Jameson had a clear field. She felt the pinch in her pocketbook, now, too, drat the man.

She was happy enough with her situation at Perdition but the work was often uninteresting. Her gentlemen were unskilled and it took great effort to teach them about pleasing women in bed.

Lizzie was good at her work, though, and took pride in how quickly the men left her behind to try their new skills on the other girls.

As a teacher, she'd learned to set her mind away from the excitement of the acts her body performed. As a consequence, Lizzie never found the pinnacle of pleasure her gentleman strove so hard to give the others.

Bart Jameson was big as a house and with his full beard he looked fierce, like a wild man down from the mountains. Which he was, Lizzie reminded herself.

He owned a logging outfit and was well known for knocking heads together on his crew. The man was violent, and the idea of spending another two hours in his company made her feel ill. She palmed her belly.

"It's been six weeks. What's wrong with the dumb ox that he can't see I'll never invite him to my room?"

Belle looked thoughtful. "For Bart, perhaps it isn't about going to your room."

"Oh, fie! What else could it be?" She leaned in, over the desk. "That's what they're *all* here for. That's why we're here!"

She waved her arms to encompass all the women, envelopes in hand, ready to pair off for tea with their gentlemen. Two hours of tea, music in the parlor, and small talk before dinner.

After dinner, the guests accompanied the women to their rooms if they were invited.

On rare occasions, when a woman felt unwell or the man was particularly loathsome, he was sent away.

To return, hat in hand, time and again was unheard of.

But then, Bart Jameson was an exceptional man. Quiet but clumsy, he excelled at nothing but hard work and making money.

Why he continued to ask for Lizzie was anyone's guess.

"I take his money and pass no judgement," Belle pointed out. "I suggest you do the same, Lizzie. Sooner or later, this will work itself out. He'll tire of your snubs or you'll find out what he's made of and change your mind about him."

"What he's made of? He's a bully and that's all he'll ever be." Her back stiffened at Belle's chiding.

She wanted to flounce out of Belle's office with as much starch in her back as Felicity, but she didn't have it in her. Bart Jameson frightened her too much.

She sighed and accepted one more Friday evening in the company of the ox.

Four weeks later, the dumb ox still appeared on Friday, shuffling and shy and big and cumbersome. The comments about his awkwardness were enough to stir pity in the most pitiless soul, even Lizzie. The gentlemen had taken to betting on what piece of bric-a-brac Jameson would break next.

None of the women could look at him without hiding a smirk.

The spectacle he'd made of himself was ridiculous. By extension, Lizzie felt the censure from the others that Bart ignored.

In a chair next to him, Lizzie smiled weakly up at his shoulder. She never looked at his face. He might take it as a sign she was warming. But neither could she be so cruel as to tell him straight out that he'd made himself a laughingstock.

Her husband had trained her well during their brief marriage. Impertinence and pointing out the obvious didn't pay. Except in bruises.

A man like Bart was too large. He could swat at a fly buzzing around her head and knock her out cold.

She shuddered so hard her teacup rattled against the saucer.

"Are you chilled, Miss?" he asked, setting his own cup and saucer onto the tea cart so hurriedly he sent the teapot onto its side, the plate of cookies onto the floor, and finally, with his wild attempt to right things, the cart itself rolling into the stand of Boston fern, which threatened to tip over except for Lizzie's quick thinking.

She settled the plant stand and with a wink at Bart, righted the teapot. "No harm done, Mr. Jameson," she assured him. "The teapot was empty. Just a tiny spill from your cup." She rang the bellpull that alerted the kitchen and rolled the cart out into the front hall.

He was halfway off his chair by then, and Lizzie marveled at the bulk of his back end. It was a wonder his horse could carry him.

It was a Noric, he'd explained, a workhorse particularly suited to work in the mountains, and strong enough to carry a mountain of a man. To Lizzie it just looked huge.

Jameson settled back down again and Lizzie saw sweat break out on his forehead. He swallowed hard, then gave her an appraising glance. "Would you like to use my jacket? Are you still cold?"

"Mr. Jameson, please. I'm not cold, but you're very kind to offer." She knew the patter now and engaged only one side of her mind with the conversation.

She would not invite him to her room. No matter how cow-eyed he looked at her, she could never let him climb on top of her, never let him smother her with his bulk.

"Very good, Miss. We'll just set here awhile then? I'm awful sorry about the dishes and such." His deep brown eyes went sorrowful, but she glanced away immediately.

She looked toward the piano, then just as quickly glanced away again. That way lay disaster. Out of sheer boredom last week, she'd mentioned she enjoyed the piano, but couldn't play.

"That's no problem, Miss. I'll play you a tune. I know a real pretty one." He lumbered over to the piano bench, which creaked and groaned under his massive size, and proceeded to pound out some horrible, raucous saloon ditty that had never been butchered more thoroughly.

No, no, she mustn't look at the piano. What then? Where could she take him for the next hour?

She sighed, tired of being the butt of jokes and him being a laughingstock. Even a lummox didn't deserve what some of the guests and girls said about him.

She cast about desperately for something to say or do to make him understand the impossibility of his attraction. "Mr. Jameson, could you please explain why you keep asking for me?" She kept her tone quietly reserved. Polite and cool, she thought.

"You're so small, your little hand would barely cover my palm."

Shocked with his nonsensical response, she touched his sleeve with the hand he held so dear. "Surely, you can see that would hold some difficulty for me. I'm not a . . . large woman." She looked around to see if anyone could overhear. He needed to see for himself that he should move on to one of the others.

A couple of the girls had even volunteered to take him off her hands. He was wealthier than a lot of the gentlemen and a taller, broader woman would be able to accommodate him more comfortably.

His lips pursed. "I know, but it's not like that." His face flushed crimson. "I don't expect you to..." He swallowed hard. "You know..." His voice trailed away, but the look on his face gave her pause.

He actually believed he meant it. "You don't?"

He shook his head.

She looked into his expressive eyes for longer than a glance. He was in earnest and, to be fair, in all these visits, he'd never once pressed her for more time or more attention.

Week after week, she'd expected impatience at least, but Bart had never been anything but grateful for the bit of company she'd given him.

Surely she could be generous this one time. "Shall we walk in the garden?" Maybe when they were away from the others, she could talk more openly without danger of him taking offense. She'd feel safe enough if they stayed within sight of the house.

"Oh, yes, Miss, I'd like to stroll with you." He stood quickly and reached to take her teacup and saucer at the same time she moved to put it down on the side table. Both pieces tumbled to the floor and shattered. "Oh, damn!" he said, then flushed to his ears. "Sorry for the curse, Miss. I'm just an ox."

He looked beseechingly at Belle, who stepped to the bellpull. "Why don't you two go for your walk in the garden?" she suggested breezily, patting Bart's arm.

He was an ox, but it irritated Lizzie that he kept trying to feel comfortable in a place he didn't belong. It was clear a front parlor with delicate tea things was the wrong place for Mr. Jameson.

The wrong place completely.

Once outside, Bart eased into a steady, rolling stroll that easily outpaced her. She tried to keep up, but it soon became clear it was useless. His long legs covered twice the distance in each stride.

Soon the distance between them was easily three yards.

"You go on up ahead if you'd like," she said. But instead, he reached into a tree branch to gather something close to his chest.

His hands, like shovels, held something delicate. She hurried up to see what he was going to break now.

She peered into his hands and caught her breath at what he'd found. "A nest. Oh, Bart, put it back before you drop it. The eggs are so tiny."

"I won't drop it. But I wonder where the mama's gone."

"The cat most likely scared it off. Poor things. No hope now."

His surprised glance shamed her. Rooted her to the spot.

He opened his jacket and placed the nest with a tenderness and gentleness she couldn't believe, next to his heart. "This'll keep 'em warm until I can tend to them properly."

"You think you can bring these eggs along to hatch?"

He pursed his lips. "Gotta try, now I found 'em."

She pursed her lips too, and tried not to feel a sense of wonder at his kindness. She failed.

"I suppose it's time for you to go, then," she said, impatient with herself.

"I'll let you know next week if there's any news with the nest."

"You do that," she said, distracted by the thought that time spent with him away from the stifling politeness inside the house wasn't horrible.

The next Friday, Lizzie opened her envelope without a word of complaint and strode from the office to the parlor.

"Mr. Jameson?"

"Yes, Miss?" He stood with a hesitant look in his eyes, cap

in hand, chest a mile wide and shoulders like a bull, ducking his head like a boy.

"Would you like coffee in the kitchen, rather than tea in the parlor?" Certain she was making a huge mistake, she kept her tone brisk.

He looked thunderstruck. "I can't think of anything I'd like more," he said with a grateful nod.

Once in the kitchen, with a heavy china mug in his hand and with a solid oak bench under him, Bart Jameson relaxed.

"Cookies, or a ham sandwich?" she offered.

His eyes lit with such joy, she couldn't help but smile up at him. "I'll take a sandwich if you've got one." He spoke with surprised gusto.

His sweet and honest confusion made her chuckle softly. She went to the counter and sliced a thick slab of ham, put it between two pieces of buttered bread and slid a couple of pickles onto a plate. She eyed him speculatively.

"Another pickle?"

His face broke into a smile that dulled the sun. His teeth shone bright white against the dark bristles of his heavy beard and his eyes glowed. His slash of a grin warmed her.

She slid the plate of food across the table and took a seat on the other side. He ate with full enjoyment, elbows on the table and sandwich gone in an instant. Now that he was no longer nervous of breaking the fine china used in the parlor, she saw the man underneath the bumbling giant.

"How's the nest doing?"

"They'd been cold too long, I reckon. Too little, too late," he answered.

She stretched her hand out to his and amazed herself by feeling a stab of sympathy. She patted his beefy knuckles to comfort him. He looked startled at the pat. She pulled her hand back before he took too much meaning from her gesture.

"You're not a front-parlor kind of man, Mr. Jameson. Why

come to Perdition House for feminine company? The house has worked hard to build a reputation for refinement." She settled and poured herself a mug of coffee.

"I'm looking for a wife," he said baldly.

"Oh my Lord! Here?"

Shock prevented her from saying more. She could hardly get her mind around his announcement.

He shrugged around a mouthful of cookies. He swallowed. "Yes. I want a woman, not a girl. I need a woman who's used to men and their ways."

She pictured an entire logging camp full of leering men and shuddered. "What do you mean, exactly?"

He reddened to his ear tips. "I mean to say, a woman who's not nervous around men, a woman I can leave in charge of my home."

"You want a partner in your life?"

His smile was breathtaking when he chose to reveal it.

"Yes, Miss. That's exactly right. I'm too busy to worry about leaving a girl to do a woman's job."

"And you see *me* as a potential wife?" She needed to get clear on what he was saying. It was too much to take in all at once.

"Yes, Miss, I do." He tipped his mug to drain it while she took a moment to gather herself.

She'd been faced with danger more than once in her life, but his matter-of-fact declarations unnerved her. Marriage.

He sought marriage in a whorehouse, filled with the most beautiful women Belle could find. Women for every taste. Tall ones, short ones, broad ones, full-figured ones. Ones far more suited to a big man like Bart.

She faced him squarely. "I should tell you I split my husband's head open with a frying pan and left him out cold on the kitchen floor. Garth Henderson was every bit as big as you." If that didn't send the man packing, nothing would.

19

One week later, Lizzie looked out the front parlor window and cursed under her breath. Bart Jameson rode his Noric, a heavy blue-black beauty, up the driveway.

The only difference this week was that he carried a bouquet of flowers and what appeared to be a box of candy under his arm.

"Damn." This time the curse was definitely not under her breath. After telling him about laying Garth Henderson out on the floor, she thought for sure he'd never come back.

An hour later, the ritual of the envelopes proved her wrong. He'd asked for her again. The man wasn't just an ox, he was stubborn as a mule, too.

She strode out to the hall, slapping the envelope against her palm, frustrated beyond all reason. Damn the repercussions, she needed to set him straight once and for all.

She nodded to him in the parlor but didn't take a seat.

"Let's go for a walk. It's such a lovely evening," she said, her voice just this side of tart.

He followed immediately and Lizzie took a jacket from the

front hall coat rack and let herself out onto the veranda. Music drifted from the gazebo side of the house and she worried he'd want to take her there.

He closed the door gently as he could, but the glass still rattled. Then he held out his arm for her to take.

"Thank you for the candy and flowers," she said, finally remembering her manners.

"I left them in the parlor. Should I go get 'em?"

"No, Belle will see the flowers are put in a vase of water and I'm sure Felicity will get into the candy. She'll save me some."

They walked in silence to the path that led to the other gardens. "After your announcement last week," she began, "and my less than gracious response, I doubted you would ask for me again." The man couldn't take a hint, so she decided to go straight to the point.

"One of the reasons I like you so much, Miss, is your spunk."

"My what?"

"You've got backbone and you're near as stubborn as me." His eyes twinkled with amusement and she caught the impression he was flirting! It seemed he responded better to straightforward talk than polite discourse in the parlor or kitchen.

The music rose louder in the quieting air. She knew he loved to dance and hoped Lizzie would teach him to waltz. At least, that was what he'd said weeks ago. Odd that she remembered so many of their conversations. They'd been pleasant enough as far as they went.

She wondered how long he'd keep up his pleasant façade. He'd done amazingly well so far.

If they went to the gazebo for a waltz lesson they could avoid conversation, especially conversation relating to marriage, but one lesson with him and she'd never walk again. He'd flatten her toes to dust with one misstep.

"Let's see how the vegetables are doing, shall we? We had a deer in the garden last week."

She finally accepted the arm he still held out for her. He promptly covered her hand with his. Warmth enveloped her hand, her wrist, and made its stealthy way to her elbow. Heat came off his body and burned like a furnace down one side of her.

Lizzie eased farther away, nervous in the shadow of the big man. He could crush her with a single blow.

The vegetable garden now seemed remote and too secluded for the conversation she was determined to have. The sounds from the gazebo faded as they rounded the corner of the house. Even the birds stopped their tittering as Lizzie and Bart approached the garden.

The sudden silence seemed ominous as clouds moved across the sun, chilling the air. The freshly turned earth of the garden smelled of decay rather than the life it usually signified.

She didn't know how Bart would react when she told him she wouldn't accept his company any more. His mind being on marriage was too much. She'd left one husband for dead.

She would never marry another large, rough man. Did he take her for a fool?

But not every man was like Garth Henderson. Not every man wanted to hurt and humiliate. Not every man deserved to be left on a kitchen floor with his head split open. Her stomach churned at the memory of her desperate act of self-defense.

In the two years since she'd left Garth, she'd never once wondered if he would find her, so secure had she felt hiding with Belle.

Never once had fear crawled through her belly at the touch of another man. Until she was faced with Bart Jameson.

It was his size, not his manner. In the past weeks, she'd come to accept that he thought highly of her and didn't mean to intimidate her. But she'd thought the same of Garth, too, and ended up with her farm stolen out from under her, her father dead from the heart-wrenching loss, and a vile man for a husband.

She shivered at her memories and glanced up at the man at her side. Clean-shaven, he might be presentable. He had even, straight teeth she saw more and more often in smiles. His humor was keen, but gentle. "Have you ever been clean shaven, Mr. Jameson?"

"Would you like me to be?"

She smiled and his eyes darted to her mouth. "Perhaps it would be nice to see more than your teeth when you smile. Did you know your lips are completely hidden? A woman can tell a lot from a man's lips."

"You can?"

Perhaps if she cleaned him up a bit, another of the girls would find his wife-hunt appealing. "Certainly. Some men have a cruel twist to their lips and smart women steer clear of them." If she'd known that before marrying Garth, she'd be a different woman today.

"I'll not have a whisker on my chin next time, you'll see." He bobbed his head and she chuckled.

"Don't shave for me, Mr. Jameson."

"I'd do anything for you, Miss, anything." The birds sang again, and the sun shoved the clouds away. The air warmed between them, as did his gaze, and she could delay the conversation no longer.

She took a deep breath, girded her loins for a lightning quick change in his demeanor and began. "I've tried to let you down gently, but—"

A deep, guttural cry came from the ring of trees that surrounded the grounds.

"What was that?" she asked.

"Sounded like a wounded animal," said Bart. "Stay here. I'll go see."

She couldn't. What if it were a wounded deer? She couldn't let him kill the creature, not if there was a chance it could be helped and turned loose a few miles away.

She followed right behind him as he moved into a crouch and quietly made his way through the bushes and shrubs that ringed the property. For such a big man, he moved with incredible stealth.

The cry came again, over from the right, deeper in the trees.

He halted dead in front of her so that she plowed into him from behind. "Oof!"

He held a hand back to hold her still and quiet.

But Lizzie wouldn't be held back, not for anything. She sidled up next to his shoulder to get a good look. He was stone still, focused on a small clearing.

"Oh," she said on a hushed breath. Felicity and her senator were naked in a bower of trees. Felicity's heavy breasts were rosy tipped and swayed with each movement; her auburn hair was loose and free. Her hair was darker below the waist, close to black. Her face looked gloriously alive and rapt. She obviously loved her work.

"Felicity," she whispered to Bart. "On one of her contraptions."

The man-mountain beside her was thunderstruck, but she noticed he didn't look away. His expression was red-blooded male.

She tracked his gaze back to Felicity and the senator. Heat rose inside as she realized she'd never seen people actually making love before. She wanted to turn away and especially wanted Bart to turn away with her, but she was held in thrall by the explicitness of the couple.

Felicity held nothing back. She was fully committed to the act, body and soul.

The joy in her friend's face shamed Lizzie for all the times she'd made a half-hearted effort. She wondered if the men knew how she allowed her mind to wander. Perhaps that was why they had all moved on so quickly.

The senator was a fine specimen of a man. Raven-haired and intelligent, he treated Felicity well and attended to her every need when he visited.

He sat naked on a low rocking chair that had no arms, his hands tied behind the back of the chair. The material at his wrists had the sheen of silk. The back rockers were shorter than usual. Truncated to half their usual length. How odd.

Felicity was rapturous as she slid up and down on her partner's lap. Her breasts moved and flowed across the senator's face while he tried in vain to catch a nipple in his open mouth. Felicity giggled and made a game of his seeking lips.

Bart's breathing changed and slowed and Lizzie recognized the intensity of arousal in his stance. Nerves jumping in his jaw, hands white-knuckled at his knees, he wanted to be the one Felicity serviced so saucily.

Sunlight slanted through the overhead canopy of leaves, highlighting the long, slim line of Felicity's naked leg. Suddenly rising to the top of his cock, she slid off the senator and rocked him backward to lie on the blanket. His legs were in the air, still draped over the seat of the chair.

Tied that way, he could do nothing while she walked on her knees to his face. Felicity squatted over the man's mouth and said, in a voice that brooked no argument, "Lick me!"

Lizzie felt a surge of desire rise up from her depths at the command in Felicity's tone. No wonder Felicity was so popular. She was inventive and adventurous.

Lizzie leaned forward to catch a better view.

The man obliged and set his mouth to work at Felicity's pussy. Felicity howled encouragement and they had their answer about the odd noise.

Bart started suddenly, apparently coming out of whatever trance he'd been in, and turned to her. "This is no place for us." But his eyes lit from a fire within and he silently begged for release.

"Wait, I want to see more," she said, without thinking what effect her words might have on him. She was always ready to learn more to pass along to the new girls, while Felicity usually kept her tricks to herself, so this was a treat to watch.

Felicity rode the man's mouth until her ankles could no longer hold her. She settled on her knees, the man's head buried between her thighs, and rode his face until she came with a cry that set the birds to flight.

Lizzie's own juices flowed at the delicious sounds of passion fulfilled. She particularly liked mouth music. She warmed and melted between her legs. She glanced at Bart and found him equally engaged by the show the other couple put on. His massive chest rose and fell as his breathing deepened.

His crotch looked full and ready.

Suddenly his beard seemed less intimidating and she wondered how it would feel pressed against her most delicate folds. Dare she ask?

His hands were on his knees as he crouched, still and silent. She traced the back of his right hand until he lifted it to caress hers, too.

She tugged at his fingers until he enclosed her hand in his own.

Holding hands, they watched in silence as Felicity wrung herself out over the senator's mouth.

Warmth and tension radiated from Bart. She leaned against him, heart pounding at the thoughts that ricocheted in her mind.

She hadn't ever watched anyone else in the act before. It was achingly beautiful, the soft murmurs and throaty sounds like music, the long, lean lines of the bodies healthy and wildly locked.

Lizzie's breath caught and held until she had to drag in a cooling draft of air.

None of the thin, languid men she'd had lately had satisfied her. She hadn't felt a stirring of need for even longer. Surprised by the surge she felt now, she decided to let it play out its natural course.

After her ride on the senator's face, Felicity stood and righted the rocker again, then untied her partner's hands. She lifted a breast to his mouth and let him suckle while he rubbed the blood back into his wrists. His penis rose, magnificently stiff in his lap.

She set the other breast to his mouth while her hand encircled his engorged cock. Pumping him like a piston, she brought forth a new bead of pre-come. She bent to lick it off and moaned at the taste.

He held her head to his lap and she laved and licked him, cupping his sac and moaning encouragement.

Lizzie could hardly stand it and slid her hand to Bart's crotch. The weight of him, the length and breadth of him, took her breath away, but still she explored. She hadn't held such a large man before and it made her wet just thinking of the stretch and pull a man like Bart could achieve inside her.

The senator reached for Felicity's waist, then pulled her to the blankets on the ground. Laughing like a girl, she raised her legs and opened them wide.

The senator clasped her knees and spread her wider as he speared his cock into her in one long plunge. The mutual groans signaled their complete enjoyment of each other. Sharp cries of ecstasy echoed through the trees.

Lizzie's channel opened and moisture gathered and slid. She caught her breath at the leap she felt under her hand. Bart's cock flexed when she squeezed lightly.

Rolling her fingers up and down on his thick shaft made him close his eyes and straighten to allow her better access. She stroked him through his pants. He turned as if to speak.

"No," she whispered, "watch them, not me. Let me touch you while you watch."

The beauty of the couple, long limbs entwined, bodies evenly matched, enticed Lizzie even more. Bart was as erect as a stallion, and breathing like he'd won a race. She wiggled two fingers between his fly buttons and felt the heat of his cock. She sought out the flesh and touched him delicately.

He groaned softly and she quickly opened his fly completely.

Settling her hand on his massive shaft, she played him up and down with light, seductive touches while her mouth watered to taste him.

He stood suddenly and backed against a tree, in shock at her boldness. The branches overhead shook. His eyes glazed with arousal, and Lizzie felt a spurt of pity.

"I can't do that to you," he said, referring to the spread-eagled way the senator took Felicity. "You're too small. I'd hurt you."

"Then I'll do this to you."

She dropped to her knees and used both hands to free him from his trousers. He sprang free, bulging and heavily veined, in excellent proportion to the rest of his heavily muscled size. Large head, thick trunk, purple and powerful, Bart was more man than any she'd seen before.

Lizzie tipped out her tongue to taste the very tip of him, sure he wouldn't take long to spill his seed. She just wondered if she could swallow it all.

His head slammed back against the tree and he stared straight ahead. His legs, like tree trunks themselves, were rock hard under her hands. She nuzzled his cock out of the way and searched out his sac with her mouth. Hot and bristly, he smelled of soap and clean clothes and arousal. The surprising scent of cleanliness drove her mad. So few men bothered.

A quiet rustling from the opening in the trees signaled that Felicity and her man were leaving.

She was alone in the woods with Bart. And she had not one iota of fear within her. He was a big man, bigger even than Garth had been, but he had a good and gentle heart, and for some unfathomable reason he'd shown it to her.

She set her cheek to the side of his cock and ran the head from one side of her face to the other. "So smooth and soft," she said, "like velvet on iron. You're so hot and hard."

"What are you going to do?"

She glanced up at him and saw sheer confusion on his face. "Kiss you, of course. Here." She kissed the side of his shaft in a gentle buss. "And here." She kissed the other side with open lips, giving him time to feel the wetness of her mouth.

He groaned.

"And then, I think I'll kiss you here, too." She shocked him senseless with a deep-throated, dripping slide into her mouth from tip to midway down the shaft. She could do better, but his sudden flex startled her as much as her mouth startled him.

She pulled back to the tip again and swirled her tongue around and around, gathering the delicious beads of pre-come into her mouth.

She plunged again and managed to take more of him this time.

His fingers felt gentle on her head as she played with him again and again.

With a ready flex, he spurted into her mouth and thrashed against the tree. His groans died away as she lapped his offering.

When she rose to her feet, Bart grasped her by her arms and hoisted her to his mouth for a voracious kiss. Her feet dangled, her breasts squished against his chest, his mouth plundered hers as his tongue swooped in to slide along her own.

"Oh, Miss, thank you. I've never . . ."

She thought not.

That was why he'd never pushed for more. He didn't know what he was missing and had probably gotten used to denying his need.

All that pent-up male energy called to her. For the first time in forever, she wanted a man's attention.

And she wanted it now.

20

Lizzie allowed Bart to lead her to the cozy nest of blankets left behind by Felicity and the senator. Heat rose from her slit to her chest and made her heart pound as if this were her first time.

Certainly it was the first time she'd ever wanted a man so much. Her husband had been perfunctorily quick and her memories of him were hazy and awkward. She remembered a sharp pain, the heavy feeling of a man covering her, and then it was over.

Until the next time and the next.

By the third night, she'd concluded her marital duties consisted of letting him raise her nightgown and stab into her a few times and then shoving his sleeping body off her when he was done.

It wasn't until she'd met Belle that she had any idea that sex could be different.

Different like this.

Anticipation wrapped around her heart with every caress of Bart's large hand. Each heated look from him sent her nerves clashing and clanging with desire.

Bart flapped the blankets out in the warm breeze and settled them into a fresh bed scented by the sharp sea air and pine that surrounded the quiet, sunlit opening in the trees.

Her blood rushed, pounding in her ears, so loud it drowned out the birds overhead.

"Bart?" she whispered. "This feels so—"

"Right? Beautiful?" he said in a rush. His eyes flashed concern.

She gentled her smile, although her heart thudded painfully. She cupped his bristly cheek in one palm. He closed his eyes as if to memorize the feel of her hand. "Are you afraid I'll say no?"

"I'm always afraid of that. Afraid I'll show up one Friday and you'll be sick of seeing me. My breakage alone costs a fortune in teacups. I can't imagine what you think of me here, now." He glanced down at his jutting cock, heavy with need already.

"I think it's beautiful that you want me again so soon." All fear had fled and urgency had flown away on the breeze.

She felt like a bride again. Nervous and wanting everything to be right.

From his fussing and preparations, he felt the same way. He focused intently on setting the blankets just so and bunching pillows to one side.

Then he stopped, no longer able to avoid looking at her.

"Bart, you don't have to fuss over me. I'm used to this." *Just not this wild flutter in my belly.*

He swallowed hard. "I'm not."

"I know," she said quietly to ease his mind.

"We can't do what they did. It'll hurt you that way."

"You won't hurt me." She smiled. "I won't let you." *Because you'll never touch me, not where it matters. Not in my heart.* That part of her was dead now, worn away by six weeks of being terrorized by a bully. She shook the memories out of her head and stepped close to the man in front of her. Settling her head on his chest, she wrapped her arms around him.

He tensed, but eventually held her close. "I want to pleasure you the way he did her, but I couldn't see exactly what he did when she was kneeling over his face."

"Just kiss me, Bart. That will please me for now."

"That much, I can do. With pleasure." He sat on the rocker and she settled sideways on his lap. Taking his cheeks in her palms, she touched her lips to his gently. He hesitated for half a breath, then took her mouth in the deepest way. His heart pounded beneath her palm, his lips sipped and coaxed and yearned over hers.

The rocking chair rolled beneath them, but it only served to increase the tempo of his deepening kisses. Bart tasted of peppermint and arousal and good clean man.

She sighed into his mouth and gave him full access. She teased his tongue with hers, traced his wonderfully strong teeth delicately, letting him see how she played with the kiss.

Tension built in her lower body and she shifted to signal her need. He responded by cupping her breast.

She quickly unbuttoned her blouse and freed herself for his exploration. His bristly beard tantalized the soft skin around her nipple as he suckled strongly on her. Each suck reverberated down to her womb and she lost her ability to think.

There was no more teaching, no more leading, as Bart took over. He might be an awkward man in a parlor, but out here, alone, with his mouth full of woman and his cock straining out of his trousers, he was in command.

The difference amazed her as he nuzzled each breast in turn, then set his teeth delicately to her collarbones and up to her neck and ear. He nipped and sucked and licked at her skin above her light corset, while his large, calloused hand slid ever so slowly up under her skirt.

Heat trails burned along her thigh as he traced the delicate flesh behind her knee. She shifted one foot to the ground so she could balance with her legs wide. Such a large hand needed a lot of room and she was ready to give him all he needed.

The trails of heat continued as he burned a path to her center. "Oh, yes, touch me there." She sighed against his ear.

"So soft—I might hurt—"

"Shh, no, you won't. I'm sure of it." She was as certain as the sunrise Bart Jameson was gentle of soul. "I trust you not to hurt me."

She guided his hand to her cradle and widened to give him enough room. He combed one finger through her hair, felt her moisture, and sighed. "You're wet."

"That's what you do to me. I want you so much. Touch me all over." No more guidance was needed as Bart took over once more.

He lowered her to the blankets and lifted her skirt to her waist. She raised her hips so he could remove her underthings. For a long moment he gazed at her, his intensity arousing.

Most men she was with were quicker, younger, and in need of training. While Bart was inexperienced, he was old enough to know not to rush.

"You're very pretty," he said, tracing a finger up her thigh. "So white and delicate here, but wet and dark pink in here." His fingertip grazed her folds in maddening circles. She bloomed for him and he gazed, rapt.

She closed her eyes with pleasure as his finger explored her more fully. He found her bud tucked under her hood and rubbed it gently. She moaned and thrashed with the sensations.

He grinned when he saw how much she enjoyed his delicate touches. He swirled her moisture from her slit to her bud. She crooned encouragement and he rubbed harder.

"Yes, yes! Do that, harder, faster." She rocked with explosions of tantalizing release. Crying out, she felt the gathering storm inside as it rose higher and higher. "Don't stop!" she pleaded.

She rose to her elbows to see what he was doing to create such a wonderful maelstrom of sensation. His tongue! Oh! His tongue came out to kiss and touch and lick her all over. His eyes focused intently, his forehead glistened between her thighs, and his hair caught the filtered sunlight.

She fell back, overcome with the storm he created. The sounds of him licking and kissing rang in her ears.

She exploded into a gushing come so fierce she cried out in abandon, "Fingers in, fingers in!"

When he plunged his fingers into her, her pussy gripped them in pulsating contractions as she came on his hand. His mouth tracked down to her slit as he licked her streaming pussy and his come-slick fingers plunged in and out.

She had no words for what had just happened. In all this time, with all these men, to find this now, with the one man she could never care for, was too much.

She waited for the pulsing release to ease, wiped her tear-streaked cheeks and murmured, "Oh, Bart, you make me explode."

"I'm glad." He dragged himself up to gather her close to his side, while she groped for his cock. She trembled in his arms.

He was already hugely aroused, while she felt played out. His satisfied smile made her see the joy she'd given him by opening herself to him.

Laying him out spread-eagled, she set to work on him again with her mouth. It was the least she could do for his most generous act.

She hadn't had an orgasm in all the time she'd been at Perdition, but there was something wildly appealing about enjoying a man's body without being invaded.

The push-pull of a man's heaviness on her chest usually caused near panic. But this, this, was fun and easy.

Bart's cock rose magnificently as she slid his boots, socks, and trousers off. Like the senator had with Felicity, she clasped Bart's knees and spread his legs wide, exposing his full sac and root.

He arched his back as she nuzzled beneath his root and took one of his balls into her mouth. She swirled her tongue around the bristly skin, then sucked on it gently. He groaned.

She moved onto the next and marveled at the texture and man-scent of him. She wrapped her fingers around the massive trunk of his shaft and slowly pumped and plunged, squeezing and releasing to bring him close to spurting.

"Not yet," she said as he flexed once. "Let me tease and play."

She felt her own arousal return as she enjoyed the power she wielded. Moisture pooled as she suckled and primed him, letting her mouth drip down his shaft. She took more of him into her mouth as she opened her throat. He pumped once, gently until she shifted over him.

Straddling his face, she settled her pussy on his mouth and let him lick and suck her clit while she plunged her mouth over his cock.

They came together in a glorious straining series of cries that echoed through the trees. She'd thought the first time was magic, but the second was volcanic.

That night, Lizzie couldn't settle to sleep, exhausted and sated though she was. Bart's soft snores reminded her of Garth's. The bulk beside her reminded her, too. Without trying, Bart's size alone commanded all the blankets. She'd had to get an extra sheet for herself.

She sat up, pulled the sheet around her and went to sit in her window seat to look out at the stars. She couldn't hear him breathe over here and it eased her to think she was alone.

How had she ended up with a giant in her bed again?

The soreness she felt between her legs gave her the answer.

Bart Jameson had seduced her in more ways than she cared to count. First, he'd doggedly persisted in asking for her, wearing away at her resistance in small ways every week. Then, he'd played on her sympathies by pretending not to hear the comments from all the others. He must have seen her softening each time one of the gentlemen sneered at his rough manner.

And then, to coddle the bird's eggs so gently. The man was a mastermind! But of what? Coercion? Trickery?

She didn't know. Perhaps she was completely wrongheaded and none of this had been an act. Maybe Bart Jameson was every bit as sweet, gentle, and caring as he seemed.

She tilted her head to the cool glass and searched the night sky for answers. He said he was looking for a wife, but the idea that he'd picked her terrified her.

After Garth, she'd vowed to never marry again. Not for love, and certainly she didn't have to worry about money or financial security living here. She saved most of her income and still thought about returning to buy her father's farm. Time had dulled that pain, though, and she didn't want to go back to that life.

A smart woman would stay and continue to save for life after Perdition. A smart woman would have a wonderful time enjoying Bart's enthusiasm and then pass him along to a more marriage-minded woman.

If Hope hadn't married Jed, Lizzie would pick her. She was a fine woman and a great friend. Yes, she could see handing off Bart to Hope.

She sighed and counted the stars in the Big Dipper.

"Lizzie?" Bart rolled to a sit, scrubbed his hair sleepily. "Why are you over there?"

"Can't sleep. But you need yours. Go back to it."

Instead, he rose and came over to stand beside her. His large hands cupped her shoulders. Completely covered them and she startled at the realization. He could crush her.

He tilted forward, crowding her against the window pane so he could look out at the sky. "Pretty night tonight. Real clear."

"Yes."

He sat across from her. The creak from the window seat sounded like timber breaking just before a fall.

"I can't marry you, Bart," she said sadly. "I think you should look to someone else. Maybe one of the other girls."

He pondered her comment for a moment. "I don't see as I want any of the other girls."

"Why not? They're every bit as pretty as I am, prettier even. And not a one of them is as scared as me. You could do much better." Worry crept through her chest at the expression she saw on his moonlit face.

"I scare you? What have I done?"

"You've done nothing." But he could, someday, and she'd never survive it, not like last time. "You just have to look at us to see we're not a match. I'm so small and you're so big."

"You think I'll hurt you? Even now, after everything we did together? I tried to be gentle." He frowned and considered. "I thought sure I didn't hurt you." He leaned in close and studied her face. "Did I?"

She smiled and patted his big, hairy cheek. "No. I've enjoyed every minute of our relations. You're quite a man. And such a fast learner! Gentle, sweet, and giving."

"Then come over here and let me keep you warm. You don't need that sheet." He lifted her without so much as a sigh of exertion and she landed with a plop on his lap. Heat enveloped her and she burrowed into his arms, seeking relief from the chilly night air.

He lifted her again and got her to straddle his lap. His shaft rose between their bodies, nearly as high as her sternum. The extra heat from his cock glowed through her belly. She slid across it, rolling and pressing her belly flesh against him. He caught his breath.

"I see how big I am. I see how I could hurt you, Lizzie."

He had it wrong, but it was better to let him think what he did. It was easier than admitting her real fear. Easier than admitting she was a coward, happier alone than trying to care again.

It was easier still to distract him with her mouth and tongue. She slid to the floor and lapped at his cock until his head went back against the window. The pane shook with his thrashing until he reached down to stop her with gentle hands.

He coaxed her to the bed, then straddled her chest, pressing his long, thick cock between her breasts. The warmth of his body pressed down until she felt the old panic rise, unbidden, to her mind.

Covered! She was covered by a mountain of flesh. She fought the panic and gasped for breath as she felt the bed shift under the weight of his knees. Knees that pressed into the mattress on either side of her.

Trapped, she heaved in a breath, held it to try to control her breathing, but it didn't help. The heaviness of him, the heat of him closing over her was too much. She couldn't get enough air in her lungs to scream.

He slid his cock up and down her chest, pressing against her, holding her immobile. She turned her head from side to side, seeking a breath of air. She found none.

Her fists pummeled at his arms, but he didn't feel her weak protests. Finally, he eased up enough so she could breathe and she gasped.

The nightmare of life with Garth Henderson flooded her senses.

"Garth! Get off, get off!" she yelled and thrashed against the overbearing weight of him. "Get off me!"

He rolled and she flailed in the coolness of relief.

"Lizzie!" Bart held her shoulders and called her name again. "It's all right, it's me. Bart. Not Garth!" He quieted and whispered next to her ear. "I'm not Garth."

"Oh," she said when the truth struck. "It felt so much like . . . him . . ." She couldn't think what to say to explain.

Her thoughts stopped whirling and she could see again. See Bart's concerned eyes, his sorrowful expression. Her panic eased, but her heart still pounded.

"My husband. He, he was big, too. Big like you and mean. He drank and, and . . ."

Bart dragged her close and crooned to her the way he might to a child. He made sure to let her sprawl on top of him so she felt more in control.

She lay her head over his heart and listened to the steady beat. He smelled of safety and comfort and warm man.

"I hit him, Bart. Brained him with a fry pan and left him for dead. I don't know whatever happened to him. Last I heard he was at death's door, senseless."

"When did this happen?"

"Over two years ago. I ran and hid with Belle. She took me in and found out Garth was in the hospital, still out cold. The police were looking for me everywhere, but since Garth was still alive, Belle agreed to keep me hidden."

He patted her shoulder and slid his palms down her back in gentle brushing motions.

"I haven't been with a big man since. Not 'til now. Not 'til you. I'm sorry. Do you want to try again? I'll do better this time. I swear."

"Jesus, girl! What do you take me for? A monster?" His voice rumbled through his chest, angry and harsh.

21

"I'm sorry, Bart," Lizzie stammered. "I got confused. I panicked when I couldn't catch my breath." She rolled to her back. "Look, see? We can try again." She pressed her breasts together to make cleavage he could use.

"No," he leaned over her, blocking out the light from the moonlit window. His face was in deep shadow, but she was certain his eyes glittered with anger.

She jiggled her breasts. "Put your cock there, Bart. It'll work this time, you'll see." Her stomach rolled, but she clamped down hard on her lips. She hated the pleading tone in her voice.

"I'm not doing anything until you understand." He dipped his head to her collarbone and kissed her lightly. "I'm not"—he kissed her throat—"going to"—he kissed the top slope of one breast—"hit you." He kissed her lips softly. "Not ever."

A single tear tracked from the corner of her eye down to her ear, where it cooled and felt clammy and wet. She nodded. "Okay. I believe you."

"Tell me how he hurt you. It's festering something awful in

here." He tapped her chest, then blessed the skin over her heart with a kiss.

"He slapped me around. Loosened a couple of teeth once, but they're all right now. Bloodied my nose and left bruises all over my ribs one time." Saying it out loud in a matter-of-fact tone took the sting out of the memories. It was as if all the hurt had been someone else's. Her breath eased, and her heart stopped working like a piston.

"Where was your pa?"

"Dead. He never saw anything, thank heavens. He was too sick to farm anymore when Garth came along full of promises. He only married me to get our farm. He made me so angry when he sold it that he figured I'd be trouble. He got worse after that. I couldn't do anything right."

"He was a bully." Bart hummed in his throat. "I know the kind. See it in the camp all the time. The younger men and boys soon learn to steer clear of 'em."

"I wanted to, believe me. I tried to cook what he liked, tried to keep house the way he liked, but it didn't seem to matter much what I tried."

"How'd you end up braining him?" Was that a chuckle she heard?

"I'm not right clear on it, to tell the truth. I meant to swing the fry pan to deflect his fist, but I used all my strength and swung. Hit him in the temple and he went down like a dead weight. I gathered my things and ran."

"Straight to Belle?"

"I figured he'd never think to look for me there. She was collecting women for this house she was planning to build. I never did care for what he did to me in bed, so I figured he would never think I'd go whoring."

"That was smart. So you've felt safe all this time."

"It's been wonderful. Until you, I've kept to smaller men, so

I haven't had the smothering feeling come over me. And I'm so far away from Butte that Garth would never think to look here."

"I hope not." But he went silent and kept his thoughts to himself.

Garth Henderson got off the train in Seattle and took a room in a hotel. He figured to track down Belle Grantham's place by nightfall.

No one easier to find than a stupid whore.

Maybe once he'd killed the bitch, the ringing in his head would stop.

Lizzie did her best to make Bart forget her midnight confession and for the rest of the weekend, they explored each other. Bart was gentle in every way. He learned where she was ticklish and where stroking her skin made her breath catch. He was a brilliant student.

She learned how many strokes it took to get him off quickly and exactly how much of his cock she could manage in her mouth.

Her need for him built under her skin, while his for her became insatiable.

Around the more public areas of the house, they were the epitome of restraint, but the moment they were alone, all bets were off.

Bart was inventive and clever with his newfound skills and by Sunday afternoon, developed a knack for arousing her with nothing more than the touch of one callused finger on the back of her hand.

When he left her to return to his logging operation, she missed his easygoing conversation and the wonderful appreciation he showed her for everything she did for him.

She hadn't been this happy since living on her farm. For

now, she was content. Bart seemed as happy with her as she was with him.

Maybe, just maybe, her life had taken another one of its turns. This time, for the better.

On the next Friday, Lizzie waited for Bart on the front steps, envelope in hand. At four o'clock, she heard the steady clip-clop of the heavy-footed Noric, right on time.

She smoothed her belly and patted her hair nervously. After last weekend, when she'd given herself to him, would he still want her? Foolish thoughts for a woman who earned her living on her back, but no one ever said a young girl's romantic heart couldn't still beat inside her.

Not that she wanted to marry again.

Especially not a man large as Bart.

But her mental protests sounded hollow and childish and she worried more than she had all week that perhaps her heart had been stolen, along with her good sense.

When the horse came into view she gasped. Bart had shaved all but his moustache and even that was neatly trimmed. He was more handsome under all that hair than she ever imagined. All his features were strong, honest, manly, and took her breath away.

He climbed off his mare, tethered her, and stood on the ground looking up at Lizzie. "I thought the gentlemen callers were supposed to pick," he said with a nod toward her hand. "What's that envelope?"

She flicked it with her finger, felt light, young, and silly. "Oh, this? This is from another gentleman," she teased. But underneath, where her fear lived, she wondered if he'd fall into a jealous fit.

"Is that so?" He cocked an eyebrow. "I'll go on in and ask about Miss Felicity, then."

"Like hell you will, Bart Jameson," she said. The last words were said on a whoop of exhaled breath as Bart reached up and swung her off the top step.

"Love me, Miss; I'm in powerful need."

"Me, too," she whispered. "But first we have to have tea."

He groaned and nuzzled at her neck, using his chin to slide her collar down. He licked the back of her ear, sending tracers of heat to her lowest belly.

"How about coffee in the kitchen?"

She grinned at his pained expression and the idea of putting him through the horrors of tea in the parlor lost its charm. "I've already got a platter of cookies for you," she whispered next to his ear.

"And a sandwich?"

"Two," she promised just before his lips claimed hers.

"Who put in for you?" he growled as soon as he'd kissed her thoroughly. "I want to know," he demanded with mock severity.

"No one. This week, I was allowed to put in for you." She'd been the butt of the other girls' jokes all week. She and her silly expression of secret joy.

An automobile arrived in a clatter of dust and noise, unsettling Bart's mare.

He patted the horse's neck and pulled her head down so he could whisper in her ear. "There, now, girl. You'll be fine." The mare gentled immediately.

"She doesn't much care for those things," he explained. "Can't say as I blame her."

Lizzie agreed, but all the men took joy in showing theirs off to the women. Most of the time she managed to look impressed.

Belle climbed down from the auto and untied her wide-brimmed hat. She'd been learning to drive for a week now. She dragged the hat off her head and let it dangle from the ties while she rummaged in the backseat.

"How did I do?" she asked Lizzie when she looked up.

"Fine. You looked like an expert to me." She grinned and helped take some of the packages Belle took from the car. Bart picked out the rest.

He held bags full of fruit and vegetables. The food staples like flour and sugar were delivered, but Belle insisted on picking out the fresh food herself, so every Friday afternoon she went shopping for the weekend guests.

"Let's head into the kitchen, Bart," Lizzie suggested. "We can visit there while I put these things away."

They settled in and Bart ate his first sandwich in three bites. "I didn't think Belle would allow you to put in for me," he said. "I thought it was gentleman's choice at Perdition House."

"She feels guilty about you having to wait so long for me to invite you to my room. She says to tell you this weekend's on the house."

He went red in the face. "You don't have to do that. I was more'n pleased with your company for those hours. I was happy and satisfied just sitting with you." The loving expression in his gaze twisted her heart.

"Just sitting with you was a great pleasure for me, too." And it was true. She'd felt no pressure, no impatience from Bart. What she had felt, in great measure, was acceptance.

She warmed to him all over again, and kissed him on the forehead in a gesture of pure affection. He was the kindest, most gentle man she'd ever met.

"Lizzie!" a man's voice screamed from the front hall. "I know you're here, you bitch!"

A roar rolled like thunder through her head and she couldn't make out the rest of the words. Bart looked worried and she could see him speaking, but couldn't hear him because the roar was so loud.

The room tilted, and her vision blurred as terror gripped her. She tried to hang on as the kitchen door slammed open. She tried to get a grip on her wild, spinning thoughts, but failed as fear split her in two. One side of her said to run; the other said stand and die.

Garth! He'd come to get her. Come to kill her.

She was dead.

Bart jumped to his feet and spun to face the man who came in.

Garth rushed toward her, teeth bared and hands up to grab her. If he got hold of her, she'd be gone with one snap of her neck. She ducked low and dived under the table, the roar in her head blocking out whatever her husband was shouting.

Bart roared with a rage she still couldn't hear. His expression said it all.

He lowered his head, charged straight into Garth's midsection, and took him down. They landed with a crash that shook the room.

She crawled out from under the table and looked for a weapon to use. A skillet hung from the wall over the stove. She went for it, but Garth saw her intent and struck out a foot as she tried to get past the rolling, grunting men.

She stumbled over Garth's foot, catching her ankle on his boot. She fell heavily and smashed her ribs against the edge of the stove on the way down. Pain shot through her shoulder and ribcage when she landed on the floor.

Winded, all she could do was roll to her side to see what else Garth had done.

Belle careened to a halt two steps into the kitchen. She stood still, quietly trying to take aim with a revolver she kept for emergencies.

Lizzie had never seen Belle actually use it, but she'd heard the sharp report of Belle's target practice at least twice a week. The roar in her head quieted as her faith in Belle restored her hope.

"He must have followed me, Lizzie! I'm sorry," Belle called

over the sounds of men pounding the hell out of each other. Skin smacked skin, and bones cracked and crunched under the blows.

"Don't shoot! You'll hit Bart!" The likelihood of that was enormous. Bart got on top of Garth and stayed there, pummeling her husband in the face.

Smashing blow after smashing blow turned Garth's face into pulp. Blood sprayed everywhere.

Red dripped from Bart's knuckles and splattered his face as the beating continued.

"You don't come here anymore!" Bart yelled. "Not ever again! I see you within a mile o' Lizzie, I'll kill you." The last was said on a vicious promise, quietly and firmly.

Finally tired, Bart lowered his fists and stopped throwing punches.

Garth spit out a couple of teeth. His eyes swelled into monstrous red lumps of skin and blood.

"I'll kill that bitch some other way, some other time—" The words cut off as Bart wrapped his hands around Garth's throat. He pressed his thumbs into Garth's Adam's apple until his eyes bulged.

Belle stepped over to the men while Lizzie tried to crawl to Bart. Pain made her dizzy but she had to stop him before things went too far.

Even more than the pain, fear for Bart consumed her. The room was filling with girls and men horrified at the scene. No one moved as Lizzie half crawled, half dragged herself to Bart's side.

She put a restraining hand on his wrist. "Stop!"

She wheezed in a breath, the pain in her side sharp enough to blind. It burned, oh God, it burned. But she had to get through his killing rage to the gentle man underneath. "Please, Bart, don't kill him."

She took another painful breath and tugged ineffectually on

Bart's wrist. The room, deathly silent, seemed large, cold in spite of all the spellbound people waiting. "Please," she wheezed.

She coughed, sending pain shooting through the top of her head. It hurt too much to moan.

"He . . . he's not worth it, Bart."

Bart looked at her, his eyes soft, but calm. "You are, Lizzie."

Garth slumped against the floorboards.

The tension in the room broke and noise filled the air. Women exclaimed and men moved toward Bart and Garth.

Belle held up her hand to keep everyone back, then bent over and touched the side of Garth's face. His head lolled toward Lizzie, eyes glazed.

Garth's lifeless, bloodied face was the last thing Lizzie saw before her world went black.

22

Voices, some near at hand, others more distant, confused her. The voices came and went as light faded in and out.

The bed dipped as someone sat beside her. Something cold and wet draped her face, then a hand smoothed across her closed eyes.

She opened them. Belle sat with her, while Bart hovered over Belle's shoulder. They stared down at her, Belle with detached assessment and Bart with worry-filled eyes.

Lizzie moved and Belle pressed a hand to her shoulder. "Don't try to get up. You're bandaged around the middle."

She was. She felt her ribs. Wrapped like the mummies they kept bringing out of Egypt. She reached up and grabbed Belle's blouse, tugged her close. "Where's the body?"

"Garth's?"

"Yes."

Belle sat up straight again. "Last I saw of him he was being thrown on the back of a wagon heading for jail. Man should know better than to trespass and start a brawl. He won't be back, Lizzie."

"You'll have no more to fear from him," said Bart, with a deep nod.

"You didn't kill him?"

"Hell, no!"

"But you would have," she whispered. "If you hadn't been stopped. You're every bit as violent as he is," she said, pain making her breath reedy and weak. She'd seen the stark rage in Bart's eyes. The killing rage. She hated it.

She shivered and closed her eyes. Turned her face into the pillow.

Belle murmured something to Bart Lizzie couldn't hear. The bedroom door opened and closed and she was left with Belle.

A Belle she barely recognized.

"You listen here, Miss High and Mighty," Belle snapped, eyes blazing fire. "That man's suffered enough without you turning on him. He's been worried sick about you."

Belle advanced on the bed. "I'm not going to put up with you mooning all over the house because you're too pigheaded to see the difference between a bully and a man defending the woman he loves."

She snatched the cool cloth off Lizzie's forehead.

So ended Belle's solicitous care.

For the next two weeks the only visitors she had were the other girls in the house.

Felicity read to her from her adventure novels and Hope came over with Lizzie's favorite pie, apple and raisin.

Annie insisted on rigging a bar to hang over the bed for Lizzie to pull herself upright without bending.

But no matter how often she asked, none of the girls had news from Bart.

Two weeks later, ribs nicely healed and skin a lovely shade of yellow she couldn't identify, Lizzie gathered her tattered courage and sent a letter to Bart inviting him to visit.

A friend of Belle's had stopped by and she wanted Bart to know about their conversation. He needed to know a lot of things.

She dressed in her prettiest gown and sat up straight. Her ribs felt pretty much healed, but still, it was easier not to bend or slump. Belle had finally forgiven her for what she'd said to Bart and instructed the others not to let her lift anything.

She was well past needing to be cosseted but she'd have to take drastic steps to prove it.

She had to get moving again and knew just who she wanted to do the moving with. Excitement bubbled under her skin as she thought of Bart's expert mouth and large, loving hands.

Judging by the light at the window it was late afternoon when Bart finally shambled in and stood inside her bedroom door, cap in hand. His beard had grown in thick and luxuriant and he looked a few pounds lighter.

She found it hard to breathe, she was so happy to see him. She sat on the side of her bed, smiling like a schoolgirl. "I had a lawyer come today."

"One of Belle's friends, I hear."

She patted the side of the bed in invitation, surprised he hadn't already joined her. "Belle has a lot of friends. Impossible friends, some of them. But powerful." She smiled tentatively.

He nodded but kept his lips firmed. He hadn't smiled at her yet and she began to worry she'd hurt him beyond repair. "Garth's agreed to divorce. I'll be free of him soon."

He nodded and stood away from the wall. "You're free of him now. And of me." He turned and put his hand on the doorknob. "I just came to see you're all right."

"Don't go! Bart, I'm sorry for what I said." She stood and walked over to him, raised her hand to touch him, but let it drop when he stayed with his back turned to her. "Belle told me how you took it. I was wrong. It was the pain talking. That's all."

He shook his head, lowered it. "No, it's all right. I understand now. You've got good reason to be frightened of me."

He still wouldn't turn to look at her. She stepped up even closer, nearly touching his back. Oh, she wanted so to lean her head between his shoulder blades and wrap her arms around his waist.

"I'm rough and big as an ox and, yes, violent sometimes," he admitted. "Bart's not the only man I've had to subdue. You learn a few tricks trying to ride herd on a logging camp full of young bucks. I know how to squeeze their necks til they black out. But they come around again after a minute or two." He cleared his throat. "I have to come down hard on 'em, Lizzie. I don't know no other way."

He looked at her over his shoulder, his gaze worn and sad. "But one thing I do know and that's I never shoulda laid a hand on you. I'll never get the taste of you off my tongue." He blinked and pressed his forehead to the door. "But that's my cross to bear and now that you're up and around again, I'll be on my way."

She could hardly make sense of his words. "You don't mean you're leaving me?"

"It pains me to stay and not have you. The way a man needs a wife." His shoulder rose and fell on a sigh. "I want a family, and you and me, we just can't fit. I thought it was just the physical parts, but you tried to tell me it's more'n that and I know it now."

He opened the door to leave.

"Bart Jameson, I don't want you to go." She softened her tone to a plead. "You're not like Garth, I know it in my soul and I don't care that you have to ride herd on a bunch of ruffians by being rougher and tougher than they are. You'll never bring that side of you to me. I know it in my heart." She thumped her chest, spoke louder. "Do you hear me? I *know* it!"

She slammed the open door shut with enough force to startle him. "You listen here, big man. I'm not done."

His sad voice and worn gaze convinced her more than his words that, if he walked out now, he'd never come back. Just as he had stubbornly clung to the hope she'd eventually take him to her bed, he would just as stubbornly ignore her pleas now if she let him.

"I will not let you ignore me. Not in this, Bart. It's too important for you to get stubborn about." Her fierce tone must have got through to him because he looked at her keenly.

"I love you," she said.

"Lizzie, it's not—"

"What? What did you call me?"

He looked confused.

"Say my name again, Bart. I love to hear you say it." She held his dear cheek in her palm, loving the soft, smooth feel of his fresh beard. "You make a plain name beautiful."

"Lizzie, oh, Lizzie," he whispered as he gathered her close. She could tell he wanted to squeeze and pick her up for a kiss, but he held her gingerly. She raised to her toes and kissed him slowly and thoroughly, letting him feel her desire.

Her desire became his and he heated quickly, his kiss deepening as his tongue sought hers.

He sighed and held her tighter. "I won't break, Bart. I promise."

His belly tightened when she ran her hands from his waistband to his pecs. She felt his cock stir to life and happily cupped him through his trousers.

He slid his hand between her legs and rubbed at her through too many layers of cloth. She widened her stance and raised her skirts in a desperate bid to feel his fingers on and in her.

He found her wet and ready and slid a fingertip into her deepest recesses. "Oh, Bart, I need more. Please, I need all of you."

The only way she could prove her feelings for him was to show him how they could fit together. He was a large man, but she was a ready woman.

She nibbled his neck, stretched up to pull the lobe of his ear into her mouth. He groaned and plunged a second finger into her. She melted over him and her heart threatened to break through her chest. "Take me, Bart, take me the way you want to."

He took his fingers from her pussy to his mouth and licked them clean. His eyes blazed heat and his chest heaved with each breath. "How?"

"Here, I brought us something in from the woods." She opened her closet and dragged out the rocking chair they'd used to such advantage.

She could manage him well enough this first time if she sat on his lap. "Sit here," she said with a coaxing nod.

He grinned and stripped off his clothes in no time flat. She did the same and knelt before him when he spread his legs.

Taking the tip of him into her mouth, she lapped at the pre-come she found so delicious and set to work on him. His massive, purple head wept more as she worked him into a neck-straining, head-thrown-back orgasm. He spewed and spurted across her mouth, chin, and neck.

When the last shudders and pulses eased she straddled him and stretched her toes to the floor. She set the rocker into motion and grinned into his beloved face. He held her head still and took her lips gently, letting his tongue mimic the motions they both craved.

"Are you sure, Lizzie?"

"I'm sure, Bart. This will work. I love you and I trust you down to my soul. And this will prove it."

"You don't have to prove anything. Just wanting me is enough."

She tipped her forehead to his. "I think I wanted you from the first time you climbed down off that huge horse. Before Garth messed up my thinking, I was partial to big men. You're so strong." She ran her hands up from his elbows to his wide, powerful neck, she cupped his jaw and kissed his lips with a feather-light touch. "You're so manly. But gentle and loving." Her palms cupped his granite-hard jaw.

She let her fingers play with his earlobes until he smiled more easily. "You should do that more. You don't smile enough, Bart Jameson."

He chuckled at that. Then he bent to kiss her bruised flesh. "Feeling better?"

"Much. The girls are fussing over me, but I've been doing for myself for a few days now. I wanted to get ready for you. For this . . ."

He nibbled at her neck and slid his thumb to her nub. He swirled into her dripping slit and spread her moisture all around her inner and outer lips.

She rolled on his lap as heat and passion joined forces to weaken her. "Oh yes, Bart. Take me there. I need you."

She widened her crotch to give him more room and he took full advantage, plunging two fingers into her while his thumb pressed and rubbed her clit. She rose on her toes and felt the full force of an orgasm rise up through her. She sobbed and cried out as she came, gushing and rolling on him.

His cock rose between them. She wrapped her fingers around the thick shaft, pumped it twice, and raised herself to take the tip.

Her inner walls, still pulsing with her come, opened at the first delicate probe. She arched and pressed down quarter inch by quarter inch, opening more fully with each movement of her hips.

He bit his lip as he watched. "Oh, Lizzie, take me inside." A muscle in his jaw jumped as he controlled his movements. Rock-hard and rock-still, he waited while she sank ever so slowly onto him.

Full.

Hot.

Stretched.

And oh so needy.

She rolled her hips on his full shaft, feeling the tap-tap of her sticky nub against the bristly hair on his pubis. She loved the feel of him, the man scent of him, the rock-hard stillness she'd created in him.

All this man's power was hers to command. The headiness of the thought emboldened her to move faster, harder, and daringly deeper.

Another orgasm rose from her depths as she clutched his face to her breasts. He sucked one deep into his mouth and worked the nipple hard as she crested and gushed on him.

As she went limp on his lap, he began to move.

Rising into her, his cock leapt to life as she felt the first flex of his come. Heat washed her inner walls as Bart's juices mingled with hers in a pulsating jet of sensation.

"Oh, Bart, marry me. Make me your wife."

"I love you, Lizzie. I love you more than life itself."

23

Faye woke with a sense of sadness. Lizzie would be gone. No more practical jokes in the garden. No more giggles coming from the ring of trees by the gazebo.

She rolled and stretched, considered telling Liam he wouldn't have to worry about hearing laughter in the trees any more. Not that he worried. Not only had he heard the giggles, he'd responded to the sexual stimulus Lizzie had invoked.

Now, he might even have a renegade spirit giving him dreams.

Poor man. Probably woke up as horny as she did.

Except this time.

She sat up, spine straight. "Hey! What gives? I usually need a little action after one of the dreams."

The only response was a tittering from outside her window.

Damn spirits! The least they could do was be consistent.

"Very funny, Lizzie. One last joke on me. Ha ha!" But she said it through a grin.

She flung off her duvet and rose for a stretch. Lizzie had finally joined Bart. Faye should be happy. It was selfish to want any of the girls to stay behind just to keep her company.

Still, the big old place would be lonely without them. The only ones left were Belle and Felicity.

Belle never spoke of affairs and Felicity had enjoyed too many to count. It didn't seem likely that either of them would be leaving Perdition with long-lost loves any time soon.

So, it would be Faye, Belle, and Felicity here. Manageable. Definitely. The other thing she needed to feel good about was how she had tamped down her desire when Grant Johnson had tried to hook up with her. She was developing more control all the time.

She turned on the hot water for a shower. When she stepped under the spray, Belle's face appeared in the tile. "Jeez! You startled me! What the hell are you doing?"

"Sorry to startle you. I'm happy you're learning more control, Faye."

Belle happy was probably not good news. "Why?"

"There are other girls here for you to meet."

"Others?" She spat out a mouthful of water.

"Dozens."

She slammed back against the shower wall in shock. "Shit!" She'd never be free. Never. She'd always be responsible for this place, these souls.

The water pummeled her as briskly as her thoughts did.

She collapsed against the wall. Turned her face from the spray. *Dozens.*

"Sometime soon, you'll meet them. I was concerned you might go into shock if you met everyone at once."

"Dozens?" She'd been sharing her orgasms with dozens of spirits, her thoughts with dozens of minds. She cringed inside. "How many?" She peeped one eye open. "Exactly?"

"I'd have to look up the numbers. The house operated for decades."

"Decades," Faye repeated. Belle had a nonchalant way with words sometimes. Big words. Seriously big words. Like *dozens* and *decades.*

Belle nodded. "Get a grip, Faye. You can handle this. You've already proven yourself capable."

"Oh, crap." She turned off the water. Skimmed her hand down her face to wipe away the remaining drops. Capable. Right. She didn't feel capable—she felt overwhelmed. "That's nice to know. Thank you." It was a perfunctory response because Faye was still reeling.

The phone beside the bed rang. She dashed for it, still dripping, because people didn't call this early unless it was an emergency.

She girded her loins and picked up. "Faye, I have to see you right away."

"Liam? What's wrong?" He sounded agitated. "It's not even seven a.m."

"I just woke up," he said.

The dreams could make sex urgent. Her fingers drifted delicately across her mons. "My place or yours, sugar?"

"I'll be right over."

Felicity materialized through the wall. "How I love an eager man."

For once, the morning was warm, dry, and sunny, so Faye took her coffee to the veranda to wait for Liam. She'd calmed down now that she'd had time to think.

There were more spirits, but she was gaining more control as time went on. Things would balance out. They had to, or she'd crack up.

She heard Liam's powerful Chevy rumble as it came up the drive. "You know what I like best of all your tricks, Belle?"

"No," she said from the ceiling.

"It's the way you make the cedar boughs part in front of the car. It's neat. I can keep the driveway covered by tree limbs so strangers won't bother me, but my car never gets a scratch on it."

"Neither does Liam's."

"Think he'll notice some day?"

"He already has."

Pleased, she watched him park and climb out of the car. Comfortable cords encased his long legs and a polo shirt covered his well-defined chest. She loved the lines at his eyes. His whole demeanor made her feel safe and secure. Her first impression of him had been correct. The man wore comfort like a superhero wore a cape.

Her heart would be secure with Liam. She was sure of it.

The light danced off the sun-tipped gold of his brown hair and his eyes lit at first sight of her. But would his heart be safe with her? The thought gave her pause.

"Is that smile for me or my coffee?" she asked.

"Depends—are you willing to share?" But he already had his hand outstretched. She passed him her mug.

He carefully turned it to cover the spot where her lips had been on the brim. She laughed at his sexy grin and obvious ploy.

"Come on into the kitchen," she said. "I seem to have lost my morning beverage." She wrapped her robe closed and turned.

His hand, hot and hard on her upper arm, stopped her. She turned and he untied the robe. "Might as well leave it open. I love the view."

She grinned and flashed him in a quick peek-a-boo dance, showing him one side of her naked body, then the other.

He held the door open for her and followed her through the front hall to the dining room. He stopped there, did a slow circle.

"You've been busy in here."

"Finally. I clean every day. An hour here and there makes a difference. My arms are actually getting some definition." She pulled up her sleeve and flashed her biceps. The wainscoting was the worst. Heavy with dust, the dark wood panels went almost to the ceiling, every inch in need of polishing.

"It's odd how you thought it was so clean and perfect the night you moved in."

"Yes, odd. Must have been a trick of the light," she said, heading through the swinging door to the kitchen. Heaven help her, she was every bit as vague as Belle. "As I clean, I'm finding damage on the wood. Some warping, that kind of thing. I'd like to get a restoration expert to take a look at the place."

In the kitchen, she sat on the counter to distract him. He needed to realize on his own that the mansion was haunted. She couldn't blurt it out. Besides, she had enough to worry about with dozens of spirits depending on her to keep the house going.

Her distraction worked. He poured himself a mug of coffee, then stood between her knees and sipped, his eyes watchful and hot. She felt a thrill of anticipation swirl through her belly. "You're here early. This is a first. Mind telling me what the rush is today?"

"I'm not sure you've considered how much money you could make on this place," Liam said, shocking the hell out of her.

"Excuse me?"

"It's millions of dollars, Faye. You'd be wealthy. Able to live anywhere."

"Anywhere but at Perdition House. The house would be bulldozed." The spirits homeless, left to wander. A chill skittered down her back. Belle's reaction, she supposed.

He turned his hand and brushed her cheek with his knuckles in a seductive stroke. She tilted into the caress, seeking more. The man was a genius at turning her mind to sex. She melted.

He lifted her chin with his fingertip and gently licked at her lips. She opened and he swept in with a voracious kiss.

They both set down their coffee mugs.

Liam tugged open her robe to expose her breasts. He cupped them with both hands, plucking and tugging the nipples into peaks.

"I love how you feel. Your breasts get me hot, and the skin of your neck's so soft I want to bite it," he murmured against her mouth.

"Yes, do that. Bite me, lick me, suck my nipples into your throat," she demanded, wrapping her legs around his back. She was wide open and ready.

She undid his belt and pants and reached for his burgeoning cock, hardly able to wait while he protected them. This morning wasn't about slow loving or sighs and deep breaths.

This morning was about fast and hard and rough.

Until he sat at her entrance, the head of his cock nudging at her lips, tantalizing her.

They tilted their heads, foreheads touching, to watch him slide inside. Slowly, millimeter by millimeter, they watched him press into her. Her lips opened as her body accepted his in the miracle neither of them took for granted. As her walls stretched to take him, he eased his thumb against her clit and rubbed in gentle swirls designed to make her tension rise.

He knew her needs, her body, so well.

Finally fully seated, he began the plunge and pull of their perfected mating dance. She knew his rhythm as he knew hers. Their bodies sang the same tune as they clung and moved against each other.

Liam's flesh was so hot, she felt singed, stretched, and on fire with need. "Oh! Yes."

He snugged her legs higher on his waist and plunged deeper, pressing hard and dragging her inner walls into ecstasy with him.

They came together, cries careening off the old cupboards

and walls, coffee sloshing in the pot beside them. Faye shook and trembled with the suddenness of her release.

"Oh, fuck, that was good," he said. "Just what I needed. You're so damn hot. I woke up and all I could think of was getting inside your deep, hot pussy."

A fine sheen of perspiration slicked her chest and she suspected a touch of audience participation had upped the heat considerably. She smiled. "Let me guess. You had a dream just before you woke up?"

"Yeah. Woke up with a raging hard-on."

She smiled. "Let's take a shower."

Thirty minutes later, she followed him to the front door, again wrapped in her robe, naked underneath.

The girls needed to leave the man alone. Faye wanted Liam to want her all on his own, without being tweaked by any of the spirits. "Was your dream about me?"

"Not exactly. But it was definitely about the house." He glanced toward the ceiling and walls, as if expecting to see someone or something looking back.

"A nightmare again," he explained. "I woke up with this insane urge to try to convince you to sell the house and land. It was like someone was pushing at me to understand something. I almost grasped it, but I woke up too soon."

"That must be frustrating," she said, thinking of the renegade. Whoever had Liam in their sights better back off. She didn't want to lose the man over some wacky dreams.

She didn't want to lose the man, period. She bussed his cheek.

"And now? How do you feel about me selling?"

"The urge is gone. But then, sex with you tends to scramble my brains anyway." He cupped her cheek in his palm and rubbed his thumb over her lips. The look in his gaze was deeply affectionate and warmed through her.

No, she didn't want to lose this man. Not over the house, not because of some renegade ghost. Her life was hers, damn it! He slid his hand to her crotch, gave her lips there a stroke and grinned. "Mm, I'll be back for some of that, later."

"Yes," was all she could say. A mere brush of his fingers was all it took to make her want more.

He bounded down the steps to the ground and went to his car. Door open, he looked up at her. "Still, you should think hard about what you're giving up just to stay in this rickety barn of a place."

Her spine went stiff with pique. Belle again. Faye mentally told her to calm down. To Liam's eyes, it *was* a rickety barn of a house.

"It'll look a hundred times better this time next year. A coat of paint, some fresh landscaping." She waved a hand at the empty veranda. "I plan to put some wicker furniture out here. White, I think."

He grinned. "I can see you've decided, then."

"I have."

"I want you tonight." His eyes flashed desire that rattled her to her depths. She wasn't the only one who couldn't get enough.

"I can't." She pouted around a grin. "Kim's moving in. We'll be getting her settled." And she had a phone date with Mark. They'd become a mainstay for nights without Liam.

"Right, she's going to manage the new store. When do you get the keys?"

"Friday. Then the work really begins."

He grinned and waved, then climbed into his car and took off for the office.

"He's a good man," Felicity said. "Delicious, actually."

"What do you think is going on? Is one of the other spirits giving him nightmares?"

"Probably. I'm sure whoever it is thinks they have a good reason."

"Can you find out for me?"

"I can try."

"I'd hate to have to let Liam go if he won't stop pestering me about selling. I like him so much."

"We all do," Felicity said. "But, I must say, your Mark is very inventive on the phone."

Faye warmed. Tonight she planned to be on the widow's walk while they talked. He would be on his deck so they could look at the sky together.

"When will he be back in Seattle?"

"He gets in the night before our grand opening date. He wanted to be here sooner, but it always takes longer to dot the i's and cross the t's than we think. Mark's not a patient man. Our phone conversations help keep the edge off."

"For both of you." Felicity chuckled.

Kim arrived on time, with all her possessions in a rental trailer that creaked, groaned, and sighed to a stop behind her ancient import. Faye was shocked at how little she brought with her.

She climbed out of her car and waved up at the house. At twenty-two, Kim was five years younger than Faye, but already looked world-weary and in need of a break.

"Wow! This place is wild. Did you ever notice the tree limbs covering the driveway seem to move out of your way?" She looked behind her, back along the driveway to the road, a quarter mile away.

"No, can't say as I have," Faye responded breezily as she strode toward the car. "Looks like rain. Let's get all this stuff inside right away." She walked to the four by six trailer and untied the ropes securing the pitifully small load of household goods.

"I'm glad you've got room to store my stuff for a few days. As soon as I find a place I can afford, I'll be out of here." Kim scooped her shoulder-length hair into a loose ponytail and wrapped an elastic band around it. She was also in need of proper hair care. The elastic she used looked like it had come off a celery stalk.

"Not to worry. I think we can manage to stay out of each other's way for the next few weeks." Faye said. "We'll need to focus on getting the new location launched and profitable before we worry about you moving out." She hoisted a rocking chair out of the trailer. "It's not as if Perdition isn't big enough for the both of us."

Four days later, key in hand, Faye stood with Kim in front of her new store. But her thoughts weren't on business. She'd been a wreck thinking about Kim's reaction to the house.

"How'd you sleep last night?" Faye asked Kim as she slipped the key into the lock.

"Like a baby again." She cocked an eyebrow at her. "Why?"

"The house is old. It creaks. We had a lot of wind last night."

If the spirits planned to go against Faye's wishes and harass Kim when she slept, they'd have started by now.

Even Faye had had four full, dreamless nights of sleep. She'd needed them, but she missed Liam.

Mark had called, stressed, and with the heavy work in the attic and store consuming her, their chats had been brief, focused more on work than pleasure.

She hadn't gone so long without sex since she'd lived at the house.

She pushed open the heavy wooden door. The glass panel in the middle had a decorative metal grate that was hardly noticeable from the outside. The lace curtain between the grate and the glass kept it neatly discreet.

"We need a new pressure arm for the door. It should be easier to open than this."

Kim whipped out a notebook to jot a reminder. "I'll take care of it."

She stepped inside to flip the switch on the lights. Built before 1950, the space was large enough, but still retained something of a mid-century feel.

"Wow," Kim said, "this place is cool. Willa picked a winner."

The display windows were deep enough for several mannequins, a specialty of Kim's. She loved dressing them and setting her displays against Hollywood backdrops and posters.

The lights were original and hung from the ceiling on heavy chains. No fluorescents to mess around with the true color of the materials. "We'll need to add recessed lighting around the edges. There's a lot of shadow by the walls," Faye said.

The floors looked like oak. Old scars and marks gave them character. "Carpet near the changing room would set the back area off nicely."

Kim had a good eye for the aesthetic. "I agree. Dark red?"

"Blood red, yes."

"We've got those old posters from the pirate movies. The swashbucklers that Errol Flynn starred in."

"The red in the posters! Yes! Great idea." Kim laughed.

"I'll call in an electrician for the lights and you go find some carpeting."

"Really?" Her surprise made Faye laugh.

"If you're going to manage this store, you've got to learn to take charge. I trust you. You need to trust yourself."

Kim nodded. "I haven't always made the best choices, Faye. Mistakes kind of knock a girl around."

"That's the truth." She thought of her ex and how easily he'd convinced her she was a bore in bed. "Especially the mistakes we make with men."

Kim walked toward the back of the store. "We'll probably just need a remnant. The space isn't very big." She pulled a tape measure out of her purse. "I'll measure before I leave for the carpet store." She grinned. "My father taught me to measure twice—"

"Cut once," finished Faye, taking the hint that Kim wasn't ready yet to confide in her about her newest break with her on-and off-again boyfriend, Jason.

Faye called Liam when they finished their inspection and she'd sent Kim next door to the café for take-out cappuccinos. "The space is perfect," she gushed when he came on the line.

"Great. How's the houseguest working out?" He'd been disappointed when they couldn't continue their quest to have sex in every room of the house until after Kim moved out.

"Super. She's been working like a dog with me, going through all the trunks in the attic. We'll have no problem filling the store. If we swap out some of our inventory with what we have in the other location, both stores will have a fresh and interesting new look." Everything was clicking into place. She'd told Mark the same thing last night. He'd been very impressed and offered a couple of suggestions she hadn't thought of.

"She having any dreams?"

"No." She wasn't surprised that he would ask. He grew more aware every day. "You still having nightmares?"

"Like clockwork. It's starting to get to me." He yawned.

"Poor man. I'll come over to stay with you tonight if you'd like. Four nights is too long not to have you. My inner bitch is rattling to get out."

He chuckled and the sound tantalized from her heart to her slit. "Glad I'm not the only one counting. I'm already rock hard. Your voice is very fuck-me today."

"And yours is making me wet."

He growled low and intimate into the phone, the sound

tracing heat trails down her spine. "We won't get *any* sleep tonight and it'll be the best night I've had in two weeks."

She melted.

"Meet me in the park for lunch."

"If I do that we'll have sex by the duck pond." She was tempted. "I'd like to, but I need to deal with things here. I'll see you tonight." She looked up when she smelled coffee. Kim must have heard the duck pond comment. "Kim's here," she said to Liam. "Gotta go!"

She hung up to the sound of his laughter.

"Thanks." She reached for her coffee.

"Sounds like you've got a hot one, there."

"I do. I won't be home tonight."

"Lucky girl."

She and Kim spent the rest of the day working at the store to prepare for the opening.

For Faye, the hours dragged in spite of the excitement the new location brought. She'd forgotten the high she'd had when she'd opened her first store. TimeStop had built a great clientele and, with Kim's expertise, a decent Internet presence.

So much was riding on the success of TimeStop 2. She had dozens more reasons to keep Perdition House going, so she need to make a decent profit.

In between her business concerns, she worried about meeting the new spirits. She couldn't deal with all of them at once. She'd have to trust Belle to keep them in line. Or figure out how to do that herself.

If Felicity had found out who the renegade was, Faye might be able to make him leave Liam alone. But for tonight, she wanted to set aside her worry and stress to focus on Liam. He'd been so patient lately, he deserved her undivided attention.

24

Faye placed her cheek next to the smooth pine planking of the wall and peered through a peephole set at eye level. The angle of the hole gave her a perfect view of the bed in the next room. Somehow she knew it would look exactly like this. The walls were in shadow, with the bed spotlighted.

All she could see was the bed and a couple standing beside it. Their faces were obscured. The woman wore her long blond hair in a fall of cascading white and cream. Faye couldn't make out her face behind the curtain of lustrous hair.

"She looks like you, but that's not me," Liam said beside her.

"If it's me, that must be you," she fired back. She glanced at him, felt the heat of his hand on her back as they both looked through spying holes into the bedroom. Two spy holes now, when there had been only one the last time.

"I've been here before," she said.

"Me, too." He looked at her. He was sweat-slicked, naked, and incredibly aroused, his cock strained full and heavy.

"But you weren't here with me," they said in tandem.

"I know it's a dream, but if I'm here, I can't be in there, too, can I?" she asked. He slowly rubbed his heated cock against her outer thigh, absentmindedly.

Arousal burned in his flesh, but not his face. It was as if he was on automatic, fully extended and ready for action, but unaware of it.

She too, felt moist and hot, needy and open, but couldn't move toward him, as if she was disconnected from her body.

As one, they turned to their peepholes again. Like the last time she'd been here, Faye saw only the bed spotlighted. The man and the blond woman stood beside it while the rest of the bedroom was in shadow.

It was eerie to watch this play out again. Eerie, but exciting, too. She moistened at the impassioned cries the couple made. She got a better look at the man's cock and nudged Liam's hip with hers. "I can see now it isn't you. You're much longer and wider."

His hand crept to her knee, then slid to her crotch, as they watched the other couple. "Mm," she said. "Yes, do that."

Finally her mind followed her body's response to the scene playing out in the next room. Like the last time she dreamed here, her nightie drifted off her shoulders on a breeze she couldn't feel.

She closed her eyes and let him play his fingers along her slit. "Shh," he quieted her when she moaned softly, "we can't alert them."

She doubted they'd care. The sighs and moans from the other couple rang through her ears, rebounding off the walls of the narrow passageway. Liam gave her a gentle stroke to get her off. Mid-come, she rolled so her back was against the wall, then rocked on his hand while he continued to stare through his peephole.

The scream came just as her inner pulses died away. "Who screamed?" she whispered. "What happened?"

"She screamed when she came, but then it turned frightened. She was on her knees, straddling him backwards."

"Facing the door?"

"Yes, she must have seen someone and screamed. Then the light went bright as day. Just like last time."

"You saw more than I did when I was here before."

He looked at her, his eyes focused and hard with lust. "Suck me, Faye. Right now. Suck me off."

Without moving, she was on her knees with his hot cock in her mouth. With flashes and blinks, the rest of the dream moved in fast forward as she sucked at him and took him deep into her throat. He came hard and deep, but she tasted nothing, felt nothing.

She rolled and woke.

Liam was awake and staring back at her, eyes wide but groggy. "What the hell was that?" he said.

"I don't know." She moved closer to take comfort from his reassuringly solid chest. "But I'm glad you were with me."

"And you were with me."

He pulled her hips into alignment with his.

"Was that your usual nightmare?"

"No, it was the lead-in." He frowned. "Normally, I'm at the peephole, jerk off, then she screams when I'm coming. When I open my eyes, the room's too bright to see what happened." He rose to an elbow. "Then I have the nightmare, which isn't nearly as clear. It's more emotional than visual. I don't see much. But I feel helpless, and by the end, I've lost hope. I think that's when I thrash around. Ever get nightmares like that?"

"Of course. I hate them. They're very disturbing. Mine usually come when I'm stressed and my life's out of control. I had a lot during my engagement." Oops, she didn't just say that, did she?

He went still. "You were engaged?"

"Yes." She kept her tone breezy and light.

"Until?"

"A few weeks ago."

"Before or after we met?"

"I walked in on him eating pussy, and it wasn't mine."

It was never hers.

"Ouch."

She clasped his cheek in her palm. "I don't want to talk about it."

"Fair enough." He settled back down, then snuggled her head between his chin and chest and held her. His warm chest rose and fell beneath her cheek, and his chest hair felt like silk. He wasn't furry all over, like Mark, but had a perfect V of hair down the middle of his chest. "My nightmare's about losing a lover. It hurts like hell. I wonder if there's a connection?"

"I doubt it. You didn't know about any of that when the nightmares started."

"Yeah. You said you've been at the peephole before. Very often?"

"Once, weeks ago, but it's bothered me ever since. If it's not me we're seeing through the peephole, then who is it?"

"Did you recognize the room?"

"I know the passageway we were in. The peephole exists."

"No shit?"

"It was put in place to keep tabs on some of the clients. Some men had violent tendencies," she explained. "But I couldn't make out enough to figure out who the blond is."

"Her hair's as fair as yours, but longer." He swept his fingers through hers from the scalp to the ends. "Yours is silky."

She yawned and felt the pull of sleep. "Think you'll slide into your nightmare now?"

"I hope not. Maybe with you here it won't come." He tilted his head to look at her. His cock, spent, warmed her thigh where it rested. "In the morning, we have some things to talk about."

* * *

When Faye woke, she slipped out of bed without disturbing him, gathered her clothes, and dressed in the adjacent bathroom. She still didn't want to talk about having a fiancé. Not with Liam. Something told her it wouldn't sit well with him to know she'd slept with other men while she was engaged.

He never knew her as the sexually repressed woman she used to be. Even she hardly remembered the old Faye. She wasn't ashamed of her decision to learn about her sexual needs, but Liam wouldn't understand. He wasn't as easygoing about relationships as Mark was.

She crept out of his bedroom, carefully quiet. In his tidy kitchen, which she doubted he ever cooked in, she scribbled a note to let him know she was thinking of him. She hadn't joined him in his second nightmare, but it was a doozy. He'd thrashed like a madman about half an hour after dropping back to sleep.

The sex immediately afterward had been some of the roughest and hardest between them. Wild and pounding, Liam had flattened her with his need.

She still felt bruised and his front hall mirror showed marks on her neck where he'd sucked the skin too hard. "Probably doesn't even remember," she muttered as she gathered her purse and slipped into her shoes by the front door. She raced home, mind buzzing with questions about the screaming woman.

As she pulled open the wrought iron gate, her fuzzy thinking cleared. Whether it was Belle's influence or not didn't bother her. "Wallpaper! Damn, I should have noticed right away," she said out loud, a habit she needed to break.

She had to drag the gate with all her strength. The first time she'd opened it, the hinges had been freshly oiled and moved smoothly. At least that's what she'd thought. Now, she knew it was Belle trying to make the mansion seem habitable after years of neglect.

She hurried to the house and up to the second floor. At the door to the bedroom, she halted and stared at the walls.

Pink roses bloomed on the walls. Cabbage roses. She walked over to the bed and gazed at the heavy wooden frame that camouflaged the peephole. Gauged the distance from the hole to the bed, then beyond to the opposite wall.

Pink roses that had been yellow buds in her dream.

She walked to the wall, found a thin line between sheets of wallpaper and started to pick with her index finger. It was old paper, brittle and dry. It was stubborn at first. She needed to be delicate.

Eventually, the paper pulled away in a strip about an inch wide. The paper underneath was creamy with age, but the flowers in the pattern were yellow rose buds. Not pink and not overblown.

"It's Auntie Mae, isn't it?" she said to the room in a voice that commanded attention. Damn that Belle.

Faye waited, her back against the wall, her arms folded. "That's who the blond woman is in my peephole dream."

Belle materialized, dressed in a deep purple velvet driving coat and wide-brimmed hat. She looked ready to drive off into the sunset. Too bad she couldn't leave the grounds.

Faye pursed her lips. "What happened to make Auntie Mae scream?" And why was she torturing Liam with dreams of lost love?

"You always were a smart child," Belle said. "But I have to say, it took you much longer to come to this conclusion than I'd have thought."

Belle avoided answering again. Faye wanted to scream with frustration.

She gathered her thoughts instead. "If I'm dreaming of her,

she must be in the mansion. Why hasn't she shown herself?" She tried another tack.

"Her lover's still alive. She's waiting for him, but in the meantime, she's making awkward contact."

"Awkward?"

"It takes time to become proficient."

Her own Auntie Mae, the sweet, happy woman she remembered, was the renegade. "I didn't think time meant anything to spirits."

"It doesn't. But everything takes practice."

"I'm not even going to ask who her lover was." Faye threw up her hands in surrender. "I won't get a straight answer anyway." She was the only member of the family who'd kept in touch with her auntie in recent years. She'd never forgotten the fun she'd had visiting the mansion as a child.

She was the only family member who'd mourned the old lady's passing.

"Oh, pooh! Don't be maudlin. Your great-aunt had a wonderful life. She loved you very much and we all agreed you'd be the best choice to replace her."

Faye sighed and rolled her eyes. "Yeah, thanks a bunch."

The yoke of responsibility tightened another notch.

A shadow passed by the doorway. Faye assumed it was Felicity until Kim peered into the room, sleepy-eyed and tousled. Her cheeks were flushed.

"Hi! Who're you talking to?" She yawned. "Didn't you stay at Liam's place last night?" She hitched at her flannel pj bottoms. Her breasts were pebbled and loose under her Daffy Duck tank top. "And man! What a dream I had!" She covered another yawn. "Got me all hot."

She turned serious. "When I get horny I have a bad habit of calling Jason. Don't let me do that, will you?"

"Promise." Faye crossed her heart.

"Thanks," she said. "He's really hot, but some men are just wrong for us and I need to find the right one this time."

Faye rolled so her shoulder covered the piece of wallpaper she'd torn off. "So do I." She meant it, too. Would she have to wait for eternity like Hope, Annie, and Lizzie did? "But hot's good for the meantime, right?" She thought Mark would agree.

Kim shrugged. "All I know is, Jason has never believed in me. He's in a band and all he ever talked about was his own ambition. There was never any room for mine."

"You mean running a store?"

"My art. He never supported me in my art." She finger-combed her hair. "We all need men who are there for us, right?"

"Right." Faye had seen paints and an easel among Kim's belongings, but when she'd asked about them, Kim had dismissed them as unimportant.

At least Kim had put the erotic dream she'd had down to lack of sex. She didn't seem to suspect anything more.

Faye would have to remember her promise about Jason.

25

Felicity arched her back, offering the senator her slit to tongue and lick. He was usually a wonderful and inventive lover and today was no exception. The swing had been his idea and she'd taken to it like a whore for money. She giggled at the thought.

But it wasn't the money that interested her, it was the men. And the thought of all she'd had, all she would have, brought her close to coming.

She held on to the silken ropes, tasting sweat on her upper lip as she swung her legs high enough to wrap her ankles around the ropes. The swing was like a hammock and the senator held her ass in both palms while he sucked and licked her pussy. She screamed with delight, unable to hold in her raging arousal.

She loved this! She loved the wildness of sex, the variety of men, the way they smelled and touched and coaxed her into coming.

Smacking sounds assailed her ears, while his tongue darted deep into her. He loved her taste and made the most of his mouth work. Her clit went rubbery under his attentions and he chuckled, letting the slight jiggling motion take her to the knife-edge of release. He held her there, balanced and open, eager to fall into oblivion. As she crooned her need, the bastard released the swing and set her free.

She swung away from his seeking mouth, heard him laugh at her outraged cry. Abandoned to the cooling evening air, clit exposed, channel open, the air stung like ice against her hot inner flesh. "Bastard," she said through a groan.

But just as quickly, the silk swing carried her back to him. Strong hands gripped her ass cheeks. He delved into her cradle once more as he licked and warmed her again.

"Keep your legs up this way. I fucked a dancer once who could keep her legs up for an hour."

"Oh! Do that, too," she begged, wild for the deep thrusts that would take her over the edge. He'd kept her close to orgasm for far too long.

He stood and teased her burgeoning nub and streaming wet slit with the velvety head of his cock. With her trussed up this way, he had all the control. She could do nothing but wait.

He reached for her ankles and pressed them closer together as his cock pressed against her lips. "Tight! Fuck! You're so tight and wet."

"Yes," she begged, "put it in. Inside me, please. Fuck me deep and hard."

His jaw flexed and he grimaced with his effort to hold on while he probed with his cock. Pushing through, he finally slid in to the hilt. Pushing and pulling on her legs, he moved Felicity up and down on his shaft.

Her nipples burned with the suction of the push-pull deep in her lowest belly. She took every thrust greedily, her inner walls clasping and releasing his thick, hot shaft, driven to an orgasm that made her cry echo off the trees. "Ahh, fuck . . . me. That's good." Oh, so delicious she wanted to weep.

Voices came to her ears as the senator continued to pound into her. He'd had three comes already so this one would take awhile. Already bored, Felicity looked to see who was walking through her private glen.

Captain Jackson and Faith, the new girl.

Of course. He asked for Faith these days. Before her, he'd asked for Lila. He was the one who'd reported Lila's growing belly to Belle. Concern for her, he'd said.

Worry he'd get the blame was more like it. But there was no blame in a whorehouse. There were only mistakes.

But Lila's mistake was made before she'd come to Perdition House. The foolish girl had loved unwisely, the way Felicity had. For that, Lila had always had Felicity's sympathy.

The captain halted when he saw Felicity on the swing with the senator buried in her pussy. With the senator pumping into her, it was hard to read the captain's expression.

Maybe if he saw the ecstasy she brought to her gentlemen, he'd finally want a taste of her himself.

His face may have been hard to read, but his actions weren't. He reached for Faith's hand and pulled her close to his side. He turned away. Piqued, Felicity cried out. "Oh, yes, big man. Do it, hard, fast."

The captain's back went gratifyingly stiff.

As the senator took her at her word, she imagined it was the captain whose cock was buried in her folds, pushing and pulling against her sticky clit.

She came again on a wild burst of moisture that slickened her even more. Her inner pulses squeezed and milked the senator for all he was worth and he spurted and spewed into her.

"Fuck me, Felicity, that was great!" he said as he slid her off his shriveling cock. He looked at her swollen pussy lips. "Poor thing, I've fucked you raw." He gave her a comforting lick.

He unhooked her ankles from the ropes, disposed of his rubber and set her on her knees in front of him. "Do it now," he demanded.

She cleaned his cock with her tongue, teasing to see if she

could get another rise out of him. They'd both come to enjoy the ritual in their time together. But her heart wasn't in it.

Her mind was on Captain Jackson and Faith.

One week later, Felicity stood at the kitchen door. Damn that man! Felicity fumed as Captain Jackson strode off toward the gazebo. He was handsome as sin and twice as manly as any of the other men she'd had in months! And would he give her the time of day? She smacked her hand against the kitchen door frame and watched him head across the sunlit lawn to meet Faith in the gazebo.

He cranked the Victrola and swung her into his arms to the sound of a waltz.

A damn fine dancer was Captain Nathaniel Jackson. Damn fine.

Faith, on the other hand, needed lessons. She tripped over her skirts and clutched at the captain as if he were a life-ring and she a passenger on the *Titanic*.

Felicity knew she shouldn't make light of those poor, frozen people, not even in her own mind, but oh! That man brought out the worst in her.

"Don't let him get to you, Felicity; he'll come around. They all do!" Belle soothed her from over her shoulder. The madam had the ability to glide through the house on silent shoes. No one ever heard her coming.

Not in ecstasy and not along the floorboards.

"He's not getting to me," she lied. He already had her. Her thoughts, her attention, her desire. And still, he refused to acknowledge her obvious charms. "It is I who will get to him."

She stopped, remembering something. "You've known him for years, haven't you? Have you ever . . . ?"

"No, the Captain's like a brother. We were neighbors as children. Neither of us has ever wanted to ruin a perfectly good comradeship with sex."

"So he knows your secrets?"

Belle chuckled. "Only some of them. And none of the more recent ones."

A movement out on the lawn caught Felicity's eye and she turned to see Faith stumble. The captain caught her and laughed, his face set in good-natured patience. Oh, that he'd look at Felicity that way. She glowered. "That Faith needs dance lessons. She's stepping all over her own feet." She snapped a glance at Belle and pointed out the window to show her.

"Can't you see the girl's unsuitable all around? Her diction's appalling. Her manners are atrocious at the dinner table, and she speaks—"

She stopped. Sounding like a jealous harpy was unbecoming and beneath her. "Excuse me," she said quietly.

She headed back to her needlepoint on the front veranda.

There, she picked up her hoop and needle and stabbed her finger as thoughts of Captain Jackson filled her mind.

When he bothered to look at her at all, she felt like a loathsome spider about to be tromped on. His infrequent stares infuriated her with their cool appraisal. Obviously, he found her lacking, but for the life of her she couldn't see where.

It had gotten so she tried to steer clear of him when everyone was in the parlor, or out at the gazebo for a party and a picnic. The wretched man was so full of command, with that severe, double-breasted peacoat and his captain's cap. All the other gentlemen seemed to want to engage him in conversation.

Which made it difficult to be attentive to whomever she was entertaining when they were determined to speak with the most arrogant man there.

She stabbed her flesh again and focused on sucking her injured thumb to keep from wondering what he could ever see in Faith. That gauche girl would not keep the interest of a man like Captain Jackson for long.

And then it would be Felicity's turn. Oh, how she would make him squirm.

She smiled around her thumb at the idea of having Captain Nathaniel Jackson in the palm of her hand.

Jackson slid into Faith's welcoming wetness and ground his pubis against hers. He held his position while her eyelids drooped in feverish response. "Move!" she demanded in a white-hot heat.

"Not until I'm ready."

She moved against him, her cunt gripping him through slippery juice. But her shudder and pleas did not break his control.

Faith was new at Perdition but she had a taste for being in charge. He had to break that habit.

His cock flexed inside her. He hitched her legs up higher on his back and he plunged again. With a deft thumb he opened her hood and exposed her clit so his pubis pressed and retreated with each buck and plunge.

She cried out and stiffened against him. His orgasm began at the back of his head and traveled down his spine to spurt out his cock in an explosion of relief.

When it was over, he slid out of her and rolled to his side, then sat on the side of the mattress. He couldn't remember when he'd enjoyed a woman less.

It wasn't Faith's fault. She was enthusiastic and pretty and had no idea she'd come up short.

He scrubbed his scalp. No, it wasn't Faith. It was some other piece of baggage.

A tart, smart-mouthed piece who was too bright for her own good. Immature and selfish. An attention-seeking snippet.

He smoothed a palm across his sweat-slick chest and shrugged off Faith's hand when she touched his back.

"You were great," she said. "Made me come so good."

He stood and walked to the wash basin to remove his rubber and clean himself off.

Then he dressed and let himself out of the room to the soft sound of feminine snores.

He found Belle at the bottom of the stairs, waiting for him. Whenever he was here for a few days, they shared a morning cup of coffee. It was a habit left over from childhood.

He would hop the fences between their houses and she'd be waiting at the kitchen door with a plate of breakfast for him. Her mother believed in children eating fruit and bread to start the day.

Her mother believed in a lot of things other mothers didn't.

It was early morning, but Belle looked fresh and revived from a night's sleep. Her wrapper draped her exquisite body, covering her from neck to toe, while still luring a man's eyes to wonder what treasures lay hidden. She was a magnificent woman at the peak of her beauty.

A magnificent woman who saw more than he wanted her to. The good thing about Belle, though, was she knew when to keep her mouth shut.

"You look like hell, Captain."

"And you look beautiful as always, Belle."

It was sad that to the best of his knowledge, she never took a lover. Made him wonder who had spoiled her for all others.

Sometime between their childhoods together and now, Belle had been hurt. She never spoke of it, but she wasn't the happy girl he remembered. Successful and accomplished, with a mind sharp as a buzz saw—but he still read loss deep in her eyes.

He'd tried to talk her out of leaving Galveston, but she'd been determined to see more of the country. Somewhere between there and here, she'd seen more than her share. Probably more than a good woman should.

The woman before him was sharper, harder than the girl he

used to know. He still liked her, but missed the wide-open smile she once had.

The scent of strong coffee steamed up from the china mug in her hand.

"Captain?" She used the nickname she'd given him since he'd confided his wish to sail and be the one to say where. He'd been twelve at the time and full of dreams. "Interest you in a cup?" She held up her mug.

"Surely. Thank you."

"Coffee's in the kitchen." She led him through the dining room and into the spacious kitchen.

Miranda was already up to her elbows in dough. She gave him a cursory glance as he passed her. The coffee sat on the stove in a pot large enough for a crew of ten. Water boiled in another pot on the stove while a young boy cut fresh fruit for breakfast. The youngster opened a can of pineapple and Jackson couldn't resist taking a look.

"I haven't seen canned before," he said, surprised at the uniformity of the rings of fruit. Amazing.

The cook walked over and now that she stood next to her helper, he recognized the resemblance.

"Some man in Hawaii just invented a machine that strips, cores, and cans them in their own juice. His machine can do one hundred in one minute," Miranda explained. "Can you believe it?"

"Think there's a market for that many pineapples?" He still stared into the can, marveling.

"I do, sir," said the youngster. "They're real hard to skin those prickles off of and these here taste just like fresh!"

"Go back to work, Henry," directed his mother. She was a pretty woman, full-bodied and soft where a man wanted soft. "My boy doesn't talk to the gentleman, sir." Her eyes went sharp with censure.

"You're a wise woman, Miranda."

She sniffed. "I don't talk with the gentlemen, either," she said with a quick retreat to her work. "I cook for a living."

He grinned. He appreciated women who were strong enough to speak their minds.

Belle passed him a mug with a quiet grin and let him pour his own coffee. Companionable friendliness surrounded them. The kind of companionship he'd always shared with Belle.

She pushed open the screen door and held it for him. "We need to talk and the morning's wasting."

"It's barely gone five-thirty. Give a man a chance to wake up."

Whatever she wanted was important to her or to her business. They rarely spoke of personal things these days.

Nathaniel's personal business was obvious here at Perdition, while Belle's was nonexistent. Except for the construction foreman, she'd managed to deflect every man who'd braved a second look at her. He wondered idly how long it would take for Ben Pratt to be cut off at the knees. He was exceedingly stubborn when it came to Belle. Jackson couldn't tell what she thought of Pratt because she refused to discuss the man.

He should lay a bet. She'd never have to know and he might make a fortune.

"How long do you think it'll take for Ben Pratt to figure out you're a lost cause?" he probed.

"You leave Ben Pratt to me. He'll get what's coming to him. After he's finished all the work that still needs to be done around here, of course. Annie up and left with Matthew so I need Ben to oversee the widow's walk Felicity's got it in her head to have."

She sat in one of the wicker wing chairs, motioning for him to take the other. "You wouldn't have any idea why Felicity has to have this widow's walk, would you?"

"No. I didn't know she wanted one."

"Oh, that's right. You never pay her any attention. Never seen you actually ignore a beautiful woman, Nathaniel." She cocked her head. "You couldn't even resist baiting Miranda, and yet you won't even look in Felicity's direction."

"She's flighty. Concerned only with her own pleasure, her own desires." He looked out over the lawn. "She's bright enough, but selfish and thoughtless."

"I didn't think men concerned themselves overmuch with the quality of a woman's mind."

"Any man who's known you for as long as I have can't help but judge all women against your mind, Belle. And Felicity comes up short."

"If you think she has no heart under all that fun, think again." She sipped her coffee and paused. When he didn't respond, she nodded prettily, point made. "And now to business, Nathaniel."

Thank God. "Good, I thought I might have to bring Ben Pratt back into the conversation."

Her eyes narrowed, then she chuckled. "I do believe he's good with his hands, so I may keep him around awhile."

She smiled behind her mug, and just for a moment, he caught a glimpse of the girl he grew up with.

Jackson bit his lip to keep from laughing.

If a discussion on business began among the house patrons, Belle pretended not to understand. But she listened to everything with a sharp ear.

Belle understood far more than she let on. Only a privileged few men ever saw the real power of her mind.

So if she wanted to talk business, he'd be the fool not to pay attention.

Jackson didn't consider himself a fool.

26

Jackson settled into his wicker wing chair and set his boots on a footstool. Songbirds twittered, but the crickets had gone silent with the dawn. Coffee steamed in his mug as he waited for Belle to speak her mind.

"One can only hope the clatter and clang of construction on the new locks won't destroy our peace," she commented.

"The dredgers are hard at work, but it'll be some time before they get as far as Shilshole Bay." It had been decided a series of locks from Lake Washington to the sea were needed. Construction would take years.

"Yes. The locks will bring changes to the area. Open business opportunity. Improve shipping."

He nodded. Sipped his coffee. "This is an unusual conversation for such a pretty morning and, like you said, the morning's wasting. Get to the point."

She smiled and laughed. "I've *been* getting to the point, if you'd only listen."

She'd always liked needling him. Like a sister, she took pleasure in making him twist in the wind. He refused to be baited.

"This construction project will take years, as you said."

"At least twenty at last reckoning. Maybe more if Europe falls to war."

"Construction materials may need to be brought in. Machines. Maybe even a labor force."

"Building another house? One that caters to the lower classes?"

"Not at all." She pursed her lips, to keep from laughing at him, he was sure. He rarely missed her point, but he'd been a mile off today. Mind too full of Felicity, he supposed. She was more distraction than he was used to.

"I'm thinking of shipping. Your area of expertise. I want to buy a ship and get the contracts to bring in the needed material. As you say, it would be a long-term investment with a great return."

"And you need my advice?"

"I need you." The smile she turned on him gave him pause. "Part of my stewardship here is to look out for my girls on a financial level. I take my stewardship seriously."

Shades of her mother's teachings. A radical thinker, Belle's mother had been a proponent of the Free Love Movement. Belle was the result, a fatherless child raised to think for herself, to be self-reliant, and especially, to be vigilant for less-fortunate women.

"You're the captain of your ship." He waved to encompass the house at his back and the grounds surrounding it.

She nodded. "In much the way you are."

She kept the women safe from harm, gave them their wages, the benefit of her advice.

"With you offering a home and benefits like good investments, it's no wonder the men who'd married Hope, Annie, and Lizzie went through hell." He shook his head in sad sympathy.

No woman was worth what those men went through.

"I want you to find me a ship, buy it, and deliver it. Then I want you to captain it for me."

"What about mine?"

"We'll sell yours. It's too small for what I want. I'm offering you a partnership, Nathaniel."

He was late. The man was six days late! When she was a child in Boston, six days was nothing, but today, with wireless radio transmitters, six days was an eternity for a ship to be out of touch.

Felicity walked to the edge of the cliff over Shilshole Bay and scanned every berth in the harbor to the south. His was empty. Still.

Damn that man! She'd heard reports all week about storms at sea. Ignoring them had done no good, because here she was, fretting and staring out at water that gave no answers.

Whitecaps formed and broke in the protected bay below.

Buttoning her coat against the sharp wind, she tried to judge how rough it would be on the open ocean. If his ship had been thrown against rocks or was taking on water, or—

She cut off the thought.

Damn Belle for going into business with him. If it weren't for her, he wouldn't be at sea in an unfamiliar ship with an untried crew.

She clasped her hands. Wrung her fingers. She hated that she cared. Hated, hated, hated it!

She lifted her face to the rain-darkened sky and cried out her frustration. The sound of her agonized wail whipped away on a suddenly cold gust. June in these parts could be colder than April sometimes. An oddity no one as yet had explained to her.

Summer did not come to the Pacific Northwest steadily. No, it lurched into the air in fits and starts, fell back into wintry gasps and spring rain through June. Sometime in July, it quietly settled as if April's heat was the beginning of a joke, with June the punch line. She hated that, too.

Dusk fell and still she stayed out on the cliff searching for sign of him and his blasted ship. There was nothing to see but distant pinpoints of light from the boats at harbor in the bay. Perhaps she'd created those dim points out of her own desperation.

Eventually, when the rain finally broke over her in a drenching downpour, she turned and strode back across the windswept, sodden lawn toward the house.

Damn that man again, causing this kind of worry when he wouldn't give a fig if she was lost over the edge of the cliff. He probably wouldn't so much as peer over to see her broken body on the rocks below.

Soaked through to the scalp, her hair hung in ropes across her face as she trudged through puddles and squishy spots on the lawn. Dinner had begun but she had no heart for merry-making.

No, she'd go upstairs, have a hot soak, and climb into bed.

Alone. As she'd been for two weeks. The senator had left for Washington and when he returned he would move on to another of the girls. That was how it worked for Felicity. She enjoyed a man for as long as it was mutual, but she was usually the first to see the signs of boredom. Letting go was easy for her.

And it was the only way to survive in this business.

She wove through the mad kitchen rush trying to stay out of Miranda's way. Henry was learning to serve in the dining room and the door swung open as he took a loaded platter in to the diners.

Not wanting anyone to glimpse her looking like a drowned kitten, she took the back stairs to the upper floor.

As Henry served, the door continually swung, allowing sounds of fun and laughter to echo up the stairs behind her. She had no stomach for frivolity, not while she fought the images of a deck awash in sea water and imagined the sounds of men praying.

It was wrong that not a word of concern had been uttered by anyone but her.

Not even Belle was worried and it was her money invested with the man and the ship.

But Felicity knew when concern was called for. Six days!

Fear of the sea was bred into her bones. She knew how many men died every year, how many ships could be lost in a season. The aching questions that haunted families haunted her now.

She straightened her spine. No! She was Massachusetts born and bred, and there would be no tears until she knew for sure that damn man was lost.

Annie! She'd promised time and again to get a widow's walk built, but it still wasn't done. Oh no! The one time Felicity had needed Annie's help, she'd up and gotten married. Even now she was on her honeymoon with Matthew.

She glared at her reflection in the mirror over her sink. Her eyes had dark circles beneath them, her hair was a matted, wet mess, and her skin looked half frozen. Her nail beds were blue with cold.

She filled her bathtub with hot water and threw in some Epsom salts and lavender to ease the chill from her flesh. She left her sodden, muddied clothes in a pile beside the tub.

She eased into the water, set her head on the rim to allow the heat to seep through to her muscles, and closed her eyes. Opened them again when her imagination took her to the deck of a floundering ship once more.

But she would not cry.

The door opened, bringing in the distant sound of music from the parlor.

"You!" She let go the side of the slippery tub and splashed into the water, head and all. She came up sputtering.

"How long have you been here?" the captain demanded. He

pulled out his pocket watch and checked it, waiting for her answer. He didn't bother to reach for her, letting her slip and slide around until she saved herself.

She spat out the salty bath water and gasped for air. The shock of seeing him had her heart racing. "What are you doing in here?"

"Trying to win a bet. Now how long have you been in the house?"

"A bet?" A horrible thought raced through her mind. "What were you betting on?"

"On how long you'd stand out there, of course. It was much longer than anyone thought." His smile lit up the room. He was delighted with winning. To Captain Nathaniel Jackson, life was a joke to be bet on. "I'm touched by your concern."

"You're touched all right. Touched in the head if you think I was out there worrying about your good-for-nothing hide!"

"Tsk, tsk, Felicity. Are you telling me it was the money Belle invested that kept you out in gale-force winds on the edge of a sheer cliff? If it was, then you're more mercenary than even I thought." He unbuttoned his dinner jacket and hung it on the hook on the back of the bathroom door.

"Where's the *Marie-Claire*? She wasn't in your usual berth." Her nipples peaked at the sight of his broad shoulders, outlined so nicely by his suspenders. He slid them down to dangle.

"She won't fit my usual berth. She's south, nearer Seattle."

"How long were you all making bets and laughing at me?"

He reached out a hand and cupped her chin in his fingers. He tilted her face up until her tear-filled eyes met his. "Tears, Felicity? Of humiliation or relief?"

She was not falling for that. She would not admit they were tears of relief at seeing him whole, safe and sound. Tears of relief that she could hear his damnable deep voice, see the gleam of arrogance in his smile, the heat of sex in his gaze.

So she closed her eyes.

Big mistake. She hadn't seen him aiming to kiss her until she felt the press of his lips on hers. Ambushed! Defenseless, she responded before she could stop herself.

Instantly, arrows of desire shot from her lips to her chest and down to her belly. She melted, so powerful was her response. His lips were more than she'd ever thought they could be. Hard, firm, ravaging.

She thanked the sea god who'd returned him safely to shore for this taste of him.

His tongue danced across her lips, coaxed her to open and receive. She accepted his tongue, allowed his deep exploration, all the while tugging him closer. A throaty sound rose between, them, but she couldn't be sure if he'd made it or if it was her own groan of need.

She raised her dripping arms and clung to his neck, soaking his open shirt, pulling him to her.

He broke the kiss, then tore off the rest of his clothes. She loved the sway of his heavy cock and balls as he opened his legs to climb into the tub with her. She raised her knees to give him room to sit.

He sat and looked surprised when he found himself in the lavender-scented water. Water droplets hung like jewels from his chest hair and Felicity wanted to gather them with her tongue.

"So why the tears, Felicity?" he asked as he settled himself.

"They were tears of anger, you damnable man. Why didn't you call Belle when you arrived? She was concerned."

His fingers played with one of her nipples, his thumb rotating around the full nub of flesh. "Why were you out on the cliff?"

"Because I, too, invested in this ship-owning venture and I wanted to know that I hadn't put my faith in a damn fool." She'd put her faith in the wrong man once before and learned a hard lesson. His callused thumb felt delicious on her nipple.

"Fool, am I?"

She had to force herself to hold on to the tart tone of her

voice. "Yes, I don't know why I ever agreed to put money on you. You're arrogant, difficult, and far too . . ." She sighed, completely dulling the sharp side of her tongue. "Austere."

The grin he slanted her was devilish. His other hand lingered by her knee, fingers tracing heated trails on the soft flesh underneath. She fought the urge to open her legs to give him more room to explore. The trails of heat were distracting enough.

He shrugged. "I thought you'd be happy to see me safe and sound, but now I find you upset that I'm here after all."

"I'm angry you didn't have enough consideration to let us know you'd arrived. I'm also upset at the idea of a roomful of people laughing at me and betting on my state of mind."

"Stop now, Felicity," he said on a stern note that grated. "I'm not here to fight with you."

"You're here to have me, though, and I'm not sure I want you!" She flounced in the water, setting her breasts to bob on the surface and the water to splash over the rim of the tub.

"Fine—when you do, let me know." He rose to his feet, water sluicing down his taut body. His erection jutted, proud and hard, and her mouth watered at the sight.

She clamped her mouth shut. No! As much as she yearned to take him into her wet mouth, she knew it would be a terrible mistake. Besides, she'd only carried on because she needed to teach him a lesson.

She'd pursued only one man in her life and it had been a painful mistake.

She would never offer herself to another man who didn't want her first.

"No, when you want me, you're going to beg!"

"Begging, is it? For what? A chance to see you strapped up in that swing of yours? To have you on that stupid rocking chair?"

Shocked by his vehemence, she straightened in the water and sat up, mouth open to speak, but she was so angry she couldn't form the words.

"Oh! You!"

His gaze raked her chest, anger burning in his eyes. Anger and desire. Captain Nathaniel Jackson would come to her again, she was sure of it. And when he did, she wasn't at all sure she'd have him.

"Did you win?" she asked coolly, sliding down so that only her head was above water. If he refused to behave properly, he wouldn't get any more peeks at the goods.

"What?" he said brusquely as he pulled up his trousers and grabbed his damp shirt off the floor.

"The bet? Did you win?"

One side of his mouth quirked up. "Yes, I did."

"What was the bet?"

"On when you'd come back inside. I bet you'd stay out there for longer than anyone else. But you fooled even me. I gave you an hour. You were out there three. I won four hundred dollars on that one. Which I need now go collect."

"One? That was only one of the bets?"

He laughed and grinned a grin the devil himself would be proud of. "The other was that you'd want to hide the fact that you'd been out there waiting for me. I knew you were."

Six days she'd worried, fretted and paced. "Bastard!" She threw a wet bathing sponge at him and missed, making her even angrier.

By rights, at least some of his winnings should come to her.

Two weeks later, Miranda bet Stella the midwife on the outcome between Felicity and her captain. Miranda said, "Felicity will get her man. And on her terms."

"No, the Captain will move on. There'll be an easier woman show up soon enough. That's the way the Captain works. That's the way all men work." Stella smiled quietly as she busied herself setting her medical bag to rights.

"Ain't that the truth," said Miranda. "Henry, don't you ever grow up," she said with an affectionate pat on her son's head.

Stella cleared her throat and gave Miranda a nod toward the boy. "Henry, go on out back to the root cellar and get me one of those nice turnips we got last fall."

"Yes, ma'am," he said and left.

"I've got the supplies Belle ordered, but she's not here. Let her know she can leave the money with you; I'll pick it up next time Lila needs me." She pulled a carton of rubbers out of her medicine bag. "I tell you, Miranda, I don't know where we'd be without these. Miracles, that's what they are."

Miranda took the carton under her arm and set it on a top shelf in the pantry with the other female supplies. "Too bad Lila didn't know about them before she got here."

She peered out the kitchen door window to check on Henry's progress, then she lowered her voice. He was still out of sight. "How is Lila? Any improvement?"

"Not good today, but she's young and strong. I've seen worse things turn around to a happy ending." She packed her stethoscope and swabs and closed the bag. "All set."

She walked to the door and opened it. "You have a good day, now, Miranda," she said and stepped out onto the back porch.

A man sat in one of Belle's wicker chairs, smoking a thin black cigar. The smell made Stella crave one.

"Hello," he said, with an appreciative glance down her chest.

"Down, boy," she said and lifted her bag to signal her occupation. "I'm not one of the girls."

He stood. "Sorry, ma'am. I expected to see Belle and when you appeared, looking so bright and sunny, I thought—"

"You thought wrong." She stepped down onto the brick path that led to the drive around front of the house, her mind already turning to her next patient. Ten children in twelve years. She'd try once more to convince Mrs. O'Malley to try the rubbers, but it was an uphill battle.

"I thought how lucky I was to be graced with the company of such a beautiful woman. And a redhead to boot."

The man was still talking! "Sorry, what was that?" The apology was absentminded. She had no real interest in further conversation.

But obviously the man did. She drew in her shoulders and hurried along.

He followed, eager as a pup. "Please excuse my confusion," he said. "It's rumored Belle has only the most lovely and gracious women working for her. You would obviously fit right in."

Appalled, she stopped and stared back at him before moving on, faster than before. "I'll ignore your comment, which I'm trying to believe is your idea of a compliment."

The man was obviously simple, or such a hedonist he couldn't control himself. Any woman, even one like her, worn out from half a dozen nighttime house calls and a full morning of work, looked good to some men. "Are you Irish?"

"And proud of it." He laughed deeply. The sound was infectious.

"You've kissed the Blarney Stone once too often. It's gone to your head."

He laughed again, deeper now. The silly man thought he'd charmed her.

He clasped the support beam with one hand and swung down to the brick path to walk with her. Damn, he'd taken her for a twit and thought she wanted his interest. She glared at him. "I've no time for flirtations. I've work to do and you're barking up the wrong tree."

She should have had some of Miranda's coffee. She still had Mrs. O'Malley to see and a drive ahead of her. She shrugged and some of the fatigue of her long night wore off, replaced with a welcome flash of pique.

Tossing her bag onto the passenger seat of her speedster,

Stella hiked her skirts to climb up. The man gallantly offered to crank for her, while she settled into the driver's seat.

At least he was good for something. "Thank you," she said as the engine putt-putt-putted to life. He stepped over to her and grinned. His eyes, sherry brown, brimmed with intelligence. How odd—she'd expected a vacant expression.

"Nice automobile." He admired the chassis.

"Thank you, again." She tapped her finger on the steering wheel, impatient to get moving, but he stood too close for her to pull away safely.

"New, isn't it?" His expression lit with admiration for the vehicle.

"Yes." She warmed a little.

"A speedster? I've heard tell of them."

This was safe. A conversation about a car was impersonal. "She's twenty-five percent lighter than the full Model T. Wire wheels in place of the wood ones and the monocle windshield means less weight, too." Modifications to the car had just been done. She was thrilled with the added speed. Her heart raced every time she accelerated.

"The panel between the running boards and body is gone," he said, with another discerning look at the chassis. "Impressive."

"I think so. It's one of the fastest cars on the road."

"As long as you stay out of the mud. These wheels will invite a mud pack."

She pursed her lips. "If you're going to keep me here any longer, it'll cost you a cigar. I have patients waiting."

The shock on his face when she asked for the smoke made her laugh as she released her brake and set off. The insufferable man jumped back out of her way and let her proceed around the circular drive.

"And the rain," he shouted after her. "Put the windshield back in before fall!"

She hadn't thought of that. The man was right. This monocle windshield would be useless in the rain. She waved at him and pretended not to hear when he shouted and asked for her name.

Felicity watched the exchange between Stella and Belle's visitor with an amusement she hadn't felt in weeks. The Captain had done everything he could to ignore her. Everything but find another woman. She only hoped he never set eyes on the midwife.

Stella was beautiful and competent. A woman who drove and smoked like a man, but with eyes that flashed humor. In a houseful of beautiful women, Stella would stand out.

The fact that she wasn't one of the regular women also made her desirable. More than one man had asked about her.

But not the Captain.

She pushed against the floor of the veranda and set the swing in motion. The novel she read couldn't hold her interest. Nothing did anymore. She used to love dime novels. She would read and dream of the adventures she could have in the Wild West.

She'd had more than her share of adventures now. None of them had lived up to her expectations.

Neither had the men.

She'd enjoyed her time at Belle's, but wondered every day if she should move on.

She had no idea where she'd go, but she knew it would have to be somewhere she'd never see Captain Jackson again.

The man who'd been so interested in Stella glanced up at her on the veranda, tipped his hat, and walked around the front of the house again, presumably to await Belle's return.

Once, she'd have smiled at him.

Once, she'd have cared that he smiled back.

27

Felicity sat across from Belle in her office at five minutes to seven on Friday evening. "There's no envelope for me?"

She couldn't quite grasp that no one had offered for her time this weekend. Not the senator's friend who'd come bearing flowers and candy just last week. Not the police chief, or the industrialist she'd spoken to last Sunday. The one who'd tried so hard to charm her.

Obviously, they were holding grudges because she'd refused all their offers.

But still it was a shock not to have even one request. Humiliation welled. "I don't know what to say."

Belle arched an eyebrow. "It's been three weeks since you offered yourself and last week you made it plain you were out of sorts and being difficult. I'm sure the gentlemen don't realize you've lifted your moratorium. They must be waiting for a signal from you that you're ready to entertain again. I'm sure that's all it is."

It was an explanation, certainly. An easy one she let her pride hang on to.

Periodically, she liked to take a break from taking partners. Especially when she'd been involved with one gentleman for a length of time. It was only proper there be a break between men. Once the senator had moved on, it seemed prudent to rest awhile.

Her decision had nothing whatsoever to do with the Captain.

But he should have been champing at the bit by now. It was clear they had a desire for each other. After his climb into her bathtub it seemed obvious he'd be her next lover.

"What miffs me most," she said to Belle, who listened with an amused half-smile Felicity wanted to wipe off her face, "is that the Captain knew I was concerned for his safety and he hasn't spoken to me since."

"So he's back to ignoring your existence, is he?"

She sank back into her chair. "Yes, drat the man!"

Belle shook her head in mock sadness. "You'd think I'd stop expecting business to go on as usual, since it never does."

Felicity huffed and ignored Belle's pained expression. "I'm at odds with myself every day. I'm even thinking of leaving the house. I could go to Europe."

Belle frowned. "Leaving?"

She shrugged. "Maybe I'll meet a count or a duke or something." She smiled as an idea struck. "If I married into a title, my parents would even welcome me home."

"Are you sure about this?" For the first time in their acquaintance, Belle looked shaken.

"No, I'm not sure of anything. But Europe is certainly an option. I've never been there, and I was desperately disappointed when plans changed with the senator." In truth, she hadn't cared a fig about missing out on a trip to the Continent with him. By the time it had come up for discussion they both knew it was a half-hearted attempt to bring back some of the spice of their early acquaintance. It was sweet of him to try.

"For now," said Belle, after a long moment of thought, "I think it sufficient for you to go in to dinner and drive Nathaniel mad. You know how."

But that was just it. She didn't know how to drive Nathaniel Jackson mad. He'd never responded to anything she'd done to catch his eye. He'd even been naked in a bathtub with her and managed to resist!

Something of her lack of confidence must have shown on her face, because Belle rose suddenly, then rounded her desk. "Come, we'll go in together. That way it'll look like we've been detained because of a business discussion."

"Thank you." Felicity had never had to save face this way before, and since no one took a seat at the dinner table until Belle arrived, she could nonchalantly enter the room and take her seat with the others. No one would notice that she had no escort.

She shoved her humiliation away and put on her bravest smile.

The meal was excruciatingly long, the conversation desultory. Felicity got through each course with quiet determination. Faith was blowing into the senator's ear directly across from her. Silly girl, she thought to make Felicity jealous, to let the table think she'd won the senator's affections.

Faith was too stupid to realize what she'd taken were simply Felicity's leftovers.

The girl waited for a lull in the conversation and gave Felicity a sly smile.

"And look at Miss Felicity there—not a man in the room wants to fuck her. How sad. Maybe if she learned to smile again, she'd have another go at some of the gentlemen."

Faith grinned and settled her elbows on the table, making sure to let her bodice droop. Like a slovenly tramp, she set her cleavage jiggling.

Felicity froze with her teacup halfway to her mouth. She paused, then continued on as if no insult hung in the air.

Unfortunately, Faith's voice carried like a fishwife's and she'd timed her comment perfectly. The conversation stopped as all eyes turned to Felicity. All eyes except Belle's.

Heat rose in her cheeks as she tilted her chin to its haughtiest point, while she set her teacup back down in its saucer.

"Faith," said Belle, "I'll have a word with you in my office. Now."

"But all I said was—"

"Now." Belle moved quickly around the table and out the dining room door. Faith followed with a dramatic flick of her skirts.

Felicity's vision narrowed to include nothing but the empty white square of linen directly in front her.

The senator cleared his throat, and in a move that would make Felicity ever grateful, asked the police chief about the crime rate. They started a lively discussion on criminals and punishment that most of the table joined.

Felicity closed her eyes and waited for two more heartbeats while she gathered her pride. But before she could rise from her seat, a commotion in the hall caught everyone's attention.

Faith was screeching and swearing a blue streak at Belle so loudly that the sound carried even through the heavy oak pocket doors.

Footsteps thudded up the staircase.

Felicity bit her lip. It seemed Faith's comment was the end of her stay at Perdition House. Since Belle made no bones about the gentlemen's conduct while here, she certainly wouldn't turn a blind eye to Faith's lack of manners any longer.

Henry slipped a dessert plate into the empty place in front of her, but Felicity ignored it. She had no stomach for more food, but she dreaded going upstairs while Faith was still slamming doors and stomping her feet. What the other girl had said was distasteful and rude, not to mention unkind, but Felicity had seen weeks ago that Faith allowed wine to loosen her tongue. Besides, the woman had been kicked out.

Nothing Felicity said could top that punishment.

All she wanted to do was escape, but with a howling wind outside and a storm of female anger upstairs, she could think of nowhere to go to find peace.

Instead of leaving the table, she allowed the conversation to rise around her while she settled back into her own thoughts.

The Captain hadn't looked her way once all through dinner. Until Faith's hateful comment, that is. Then, he boldly smirked across the table at her.

He was the one Felicity wanted to punish. He deserved whatever retribution she could come up with. He'd ruined her life in Perdition, made her the butt of a brazen girl's pitiless remarks. He'd even bet on her tender feelings for him.

Up 'til tonight, his ignoring her had burned to her bones, but it was anger that burned through her now.

She'd be happier if he showed active dislike rather than pretending she didn't exist. Her pride needed to know that at least he thought about her.

As it was, she doubted he ever gave her a passing thought, while her own mind was consumed by him. As was her heart.

Her heart! Oh! She'd sworn she'd never give her heart again. And to such a damnable man.

She peeped at him through her lashes. There he sat, like a large black cloud of censure. Thunderous anger stormed across his features as he reached for his wineglass. He drained it, but went back to staring morosely at his freshly delivered plate of apple pie.

Even Henry recognized the dangerously dour expression on the Captain's face and scurried on to the next diner.

She would not love a man like Nathaniel Jackson. She would not.

Silently, she rose and, for once, left a room with quiet dignity. She didn't even have heart enough to flounce.

A week later, at noon on Friday, Felicity packed the last of her things in her travel trunk and closed and locked the lid.

She'd said her good-byes, painful as they were. She only had time for one more glance around the room and one last look out the window to the sea before she headed out to catch the train to New York.

Europe was waiting.

She'd managed to pull some strings to get on a steam ship bound for England.

With some luck she could make a side trip to Boston to see if her mother and father would allow a visit. She doubted it, but perhaps enough time had passed for them to have forgiven her for running off with Blake, her father's factory manager.

In the time since, she'd also forgiven her mother for dallying with Blake. Her parents' marriage was cold, her father austere. Now that she knew the joys of male attention, she couldn't fault her mother for needing the same from Blake. The blame lay at Blake's feet for seducing mother and daughter.

He was more than a scoundrel and wastrel. What he'd done was vile and cruel. To play on a married woman's loneliness in a cold marriage while seducing the woman's daughter was unconscionable.

The burden of their shared guilt needed to be buried.

She would go to Europe. But before she left, she'd visit her home to make things right with her mother. She put on her hat and adjusted her pin to hold it tight for the ride to the train station.

An engine racing up the driveway called her attention to the window. She looked out to see Captain Jackson tear up the driveway and park on the lawn. Served him right if Belle caught him.

She wouldn't tolerate tire ruts anywhere on the manicured grounds.

Why did he have to be so dashing? So wild and free looking? He wore his hair longer than other men. Refused to cover his luscious mouth with a moustache and cut a fine figure in his peacoat. The navy blue brought out the brilliance of his blue eyes. And she hated that she noticed, but she couldn't tear her eyes away.

He shouted something up at her, but she couldn't hear, so she raised the window sash and poked her head outside.

"Were you addressing me?" she said, without raising her voice. She hated that. Women should sound like ladies, not fishwives.

He opened his arms up to her. "Yes, I am, Felicity Johnston."

"Gentlemen do not holler up at ladies. Keep your voice down."

He looked chastened, but only for a moment. A sly look crossed his features. "Is it true, then?"

"Is what true?"

"That you're leaving and giving up the life?" He removed his captain's hat and held it loosely in front of him, giving the sun a chance to glint off the glossy black curls on his head.

"Why do you care if I'm leaving? You never speak to me."

With that, he slid the hat back onto his head and strode with masculine determination toward the veranda. His boots thudded against the floorboards, then the door slammed open.

She dashed around her bed and through the adjoining bathroom into Hope's room, through there to Hope's bedroom door. She opened it a crack to the sounds of Jackson thudding up the stairs. She peeked out at him and saw him take the stairs two at a time in a grim-faced dash to the top landing. He pivoted out of her view and kicked in her bedroom door.

Stupid man, it wasn't even locked.

Whatever madness had gripped him, she wanted no part of it.

She stepped out into the hall and made for the stairs. She hiked her skirts to her thighs to make a dash to safety. She took two steps down when she was swept up into his strong arms from behind, legs dangling.

"Let me go!" She tried to kick him, but it was precarious behavior for the top of a long flight of stairs. His heaving breath caressed her ear.

"Stop struggling, or you'll kill us both," he said, sending a frisson of heat to her belly, then back up to her heart.

She did as she was told, only because he was right. The stairs were long, wide, and she'd much rather live than die on the second-floor landing sprawled in a heap.

He turned again, carried her through her bedroom door, and tossed her on the bed.

She bounced twice while he shut and locked the doors to the hall and to the bathroom. Trapped like a rat!

On the third bounce she went to climb off the bed, but he grabbed her arms and pulled her to him. She caught a blur of determined blue eyes as he pressed his lips to hers.

Instant desire swooshed through her body, claiming her mind and taking her to a dark, yearning place she hadn't been in years.

Her nipples peaked so quickly they hurt. Her legs melted, opened, and her lush spot between them moistened.

Heaven help her! She wanted *him*, Captain Nathaniel Jackson, and no one else.

"Stop! Please, Nathaniel, I can't." She pushed at his shoulders with a wild cry. "It'll hurt too much."

She couldn't control the deep sobs that rose from her throat as she rolled to her stomach and hid her face. This time, she'd been reduced to a quivering mass of crying female, too afraid to face her own heart.

If he made love to her now, she'd live with the memory forever and she couldn't face the fact that she'd wanted a man and lost. Again.

"Hurt? You? You're the girl with the rocking chair, the swing, and God knows what other nonsense you use to pleasure the men and yourself." His tone was bitter, lost, as if the words were torn from his throat.

She swiped at her cheeks, sniffed, and rolled to her back to look at him. "But this would be different. I . . ."

She raised her hand in supplication, but refused to say the words that beat at the back of her tongue. She'd said *I love you* to another man once, and he'd used the words, her feelings, against her. She'd had no idea of the power she'd given the wrong man.

She clapped her hands over her mouth.

"Felicity, you don't mean to leave without this, do you?"

His wicked hands traced slow, languorous circles on her ankles.

She tucked her skirts around her legs. He kept up the action, with a grin that lit his eyes.

"You're a devil," she said, and meant it. The cocked eyebrow, the slanted mouth, the hard jaw on the man made him look positively evil. And bad . . . very, very bad.

Without another thought, her ankles opened just enough to allow him to move up to her calves. He took full advantage and more as he palmed her calves gently. He weighed them, massaging and kneading as she allowed his fingers to seek the delicate flesh behind her knees.

"Felicity, I can't let you leave without having you. At least once, maybe more."

"More?" The question came out breathlessly, because he'd reached her sensitive inner thighs. Somehow, her thoughts had scattered and her legs, always easily opened by a handsome man, seemed to have forgotten that this man was important enough to hurt her. Deeply and forever.

Suddenly, he had her in a fast grip around her hips and tugged her close enough to drape her legs on either side of his thighs.

Her crotch was open to whatever lay in store.

She covered her face, suddenly ashamed of her need. Feelings of shyness enveloped her. She struggled to beat them back, knowing how ridiculous they were.

She needed his help. "I'm shy! I can't believe it, but I am. I'm afraid of this. I'm afraid of you and I don't understand."

"Don't you?"

She'd never been afraid of sex, not even the very first time in the barn with Blake. "Sex has always been an adventure. Romantic, even. I've been happy that way, Nathaniel. You've seen me with other men. You know I take joy in the act. I've been fulfilled and happy here."

"I've seen you give your body, Felicity. I've never seen you give your heart."

She had to deflect this thread of conversation. "You're a hurtful man, Nathaniel. You say things just to wound."

"If I've wounded you, I'm sorry. But if wounding you is what it takes to get through to you, I'll do it again and again."

She caught her breath at his determination. Where before he'd always been dismissive in his glances, this intensity made her feel worse. Frightened. Impaled by his focus. There was nowhere to run, nowhere to hide.

She had to at least try to save herself.

"Get through to me about what? The fact that you want to bed me? Fuck me? They all want that, Nathaniel. That's why Perdition House exists. So men can get fucked. We play house for a few weeks, make pretend love, and everyone moves on unscathed."

"But this is different, and you know it."

She couldn't look into his eyes. If she did, he'd look back and see the truth that was dawning. He'd see a truth too frightening to accept. So she looked to the ceiling, dropped her arms to her sides, and lay still.

"Do it, then. Fuck me and get it over with." Her limbs stiffened. Her heart hammered with fear that he'd arouse her, make her feel, take her those last steps into love. She felt herself falling, accepting, wanting more of him than any other man. She should have left the house yesterday, this morning, an hour ago.

If she, had she wouldn't be in this mess.

She would not be in love with a man who didn't love her back.

28

"You're an aggravating woman," Nathaniel said to Felicity, stretched out stiff as a board on the bed in front of him. "Offering yourself like you're nothing but a pair of hips for the taking."

He shook his head. She was stubborn, beautiful, and had a head full of fanciful nonsense. "And flouncing around when you don't get your own way is something I won't tolerate."

She went red in the face. At least he had her attention, in spite of the fact that her lips looked sealed shut. "We have to clear the air between us now, before you get another stupid idea into your head. If Belle hadn't telephoned me about your train reservation, you'd have been long gone."

"Belle?" Her look of outrage made him laugh. "Belle told you I'm leaving?" She went even stiffer under him.

"In spite of all your silly notions and flouncing, I felt your concern for me. It was a woman's concern, not a silly girl's. You've grown up, Felicity. You're a woman now, with a woman's heart to give."

"So what? Doesn't mean I'll give it to you." She still looked put out, but intrigued nonetheless.

"I should have let you know in the bathtub. I'm aware of you in a way I've never been aware of another woman. I know when you watch me, I know when you wait, I know you think of me even when another man's inside you."

Her pretty green eyes went wide. "Yes. Damn it, yes. Is that what you need to hear? That I'm lovestruck for you? It's plain enough. Even that hussy Faith saw it." Tears welled in her eyes as she fought for her pride.

"You're from Boston. You know how fickle the sea is. You understand how men are lost. You understand I live a precarious life, and still you waited for me."

She nodded stiffly. Her lips eased and she blinked.

He softened his tone. "You waited for me even though I've done my best to ignore you. No other woman has ever given me so much of herself as you have." And for no reason. He'd never encouraged her, afraid of falling for a faithless tart.

"Why? Why did you ignore me? I've wanted you for so long."

"You wanted me because I did ignore you. Like a child, you wanted what you couldn't have. So you made sure to flaunt yourself and your lovers every chance you could."

Which in itself had been hell. Ignore Felicity Johnston when all he ever heard, saw, and felt from her was wild enticement? Impossible.

There was that time she'd been swinging out in the garden with the senator between her legs. She'd cried out in pleasure over and over again, while the man had fucked her into wild ecstasy.

He'd have given anything to be that man, to slide into her time and again to the rhythm of the swing. He'd wanted to taste her juice, to lick her delicate flesh.

But he would not succumb to her charms unless he knew she was done with everyone else.

She'd looked directly at him while her pussy was impaled on the man's cock and she'd smiled. He'd had to turn away before rage had taken over. Her voice still rang in his ears as she cried out.

"Why are you leaving the house?" he asked.

She rolled her head to face the window. "I want to travel. I've craved adventure my whole life and I'm through here."

"You've had enough sexual adventure?"

She nodded, but still didn't look at him. He touched her chin and turned her to face him. "Then why are you offering yourself to me now?"

"It's what you want from me. It's all you want. I've decided you may have it."

"I want you, that's true. I want your body, I want your hands, I want your mouth. But there's more I want and you know it."

Her eyes widened. Then she blinked in understanding. "You mean?"

"I want you, body, heart, and soul, and I'll not have you if you're still craving the attentions of other men. I let you have all your fun without ever touching you. If you want what I want, we'll do fine. Otherwise, I'll let you go and we'll never see each other again."

"No, I don't want to never see you. I mean, I want you too, in a way—"

He cut her off with a kiss, aching for the taste of her. Sweet, hungry, his, her mouth welcomed him as he sank down on top of her.

Sweet Jesus, she was everything he'd dreamed of. More. Her mouth suckled at his bottom lip. Her arms held him close while her legs opened into a cradle he'd never want to leave again.

"Are you sure you want me, only me?" she asked when they could breathe again.

"Since the first day I saw you."

"But you never asked for me."

"You weren't ready. The rocking chair and swing held more interest. I would not be one of the lovers you took and discarded."

His hands roamed beneath her skirts, between their bodies and finally found her, sticky and open. "You're wet for me."

"Yes, always. Thoughts of you can make me drip and gush and—Oh! Yes, do that!"

He slid two fingers into her and pumped and circled, smearing more of her juices around her folds. Her eyes widened, then slid shut in pleasure as soon as he touched her bud of most tender sensation.

His cock, rock-hard, ached for her touch, her mouth, her dark, wet depths. He moved against her thigh as she kissed him again and again, writhing and surging up toward his seeking, plunging fingers.

She melted into his hand and her lips tasted of arousal and woman and heated things that went to his heart. She was his and would always be his.

Now and forever.

"You're mine, always," he said.

"Only yours, forever." She spoke with her heart in her eyes and he believed.

He pulled up and sat back on his haunches, tearing at his shirt, his pants, and finally shucking everything off to fall on the floor. Her hands ran across his chest, warm and clasping, then her lips followed when she rose to meet him. She licked his nipples like a cat and nipped them with teeth that shot sparks to his cock. "That's incredible."

"I'm still dressed. Help me!"

He tore open her blouse, exposing her glorious breasts to his view. He'd seen them before from a distance, but up close, they were fuller, whiter than he expected. Heavier, too, he found as he cupped one in each hand. He rolled the nipples with his thumbs, circling while she fussed with removing the rest of her clothing. He had to let go while she stripped off her skirt, but he was willing to make the sacrifice if it meant he could have her naked.

Finally undressed completely, they knelt on the bed and faced each other without touching.

"Miss Johnston, would you do me the honor?" He laughed when she shuddered at his question. From head to knees, her body quivered in need.

He cupped her mons, placed his mouth on a nipple and sucked deeply while one finger rolled her clit. Her quivers continued until she had to hold on to his shoulders to keep from tipping back onto the bed.

"I need to kiss you, to feel your beard on my neck, to know you're mine."

"Yes. I'm yours," he said, finally confessing to her and to himself what he wanted all along.

She settled on the bed, drew her knees up to her chest, tight. He watched, delighted when her ankles opened and he caught a glimpse of her dark curls for a split second.

Again she opened. Wider now, letting him see her pink slit, wet and dark. Before he could touch she closed again.

"Ah! Is this a game of hide and seek, Felicity?"

"Not at all."

But it was. He knew because she moved a hand to her center and the next time she exposed herself, her fingers revealed her pearl, dewy and purple and plump. He wanted to lick it, suck it, and send her wild.

He'd think she was a tease except her scent rose to him, aroused and womanly, exciting him beyond control. He snapped and cupped her knees.

"Oh, Captain! Whatever are you doing?" she asked in a singsong voice that made him laugh with her.

"Looking my fill, Miss Johnston. Looking my fill." He opened her knees, exposing her completely. Her hair parted, slightly matted from her wetness, then her folds revealed themselves and finally, the deepest pink of her inner channel.

He'd be inside there soon, driving in and up, pushing against her inner sanctum. His cock flexed in need.

Pulsing and straining, he slid his hand up and down his shaft to ease the release that threatened. She watched the movement, her eyes gleaming with desire and hot need. She licked her lips. "I want to lick you there," she said, nearly taking him over the edge.

He climbed up to her face, grasped the headboard, and looked down. Her dark hair lay glossy and shiny on the pillow. Her eager tongue tipped out and touched the head of his cock. He spasmed at the first fiery touch.

She put her lips into an O and took his cock inside up to the rim. Swirling and darting, her tongue drove him mad.

"You taste so good. Hot and spicy like mulled wine." She ran his cock across her cheeks, the softness of her beautiful skin a delicate caress. As his head passed over her mouth she opened her lips and let him feel the wetness of her mouth before moving to the other cheek.

"You're driving me mad." He bit back more because his mind had gone beyond thought.

She stopped, looked up at him. "This has to be slow, different. I need to love you, Nathaniel, not fuck you."

He nodded and clamped down on his control. She continued to play and explore him. Sucked each one of his balls into her mouth, licked at the skin behind them, slid his entire length down her throat. She took her time, let his flexes build until he couldn't hold on any longer.

With a cry that rose from his gut, he shot into her mouth, streaming and pulsing while she lapped and suckled at him, her eyes dancing with wicked delight.

"I wanted inside, but that was incredible," he said as he sank to the bed and tucked her close to his side. She fit, tits soft, nipples like hard buttons against his ribs.

"Thank you." Her voice threaded through him, hot and needful. "I had to take the edge off first because I need a long, slow fuck."

Her words stirred him to rise again.

Nathaniel's come tasted of hot spice and essence of virile man. The taste lingered even through his thorough kisses. It pleased Felicity that he'd kiss her afterward—some men wouldn't.

Her own need grew, so she did what he'd done and climbed to the head of the bed. She arched her back and presented her pussy in a plea for attention.

He attended.

Rubbing her ass cheeks, he molded them, then set his teeth to leave love marks of possession on the bottom of each one. The nip and buzz sent shocks of desire to her pussy and she moistened heavily.

He trailed his finger in the slippery stuff that rolled down her inner thigh, then plunged it into her up to the middle knuckle. Her lips opened, and her channel wept for more. He gave her another finger, then another and finally another. Stretched and wet, she felt the widening, the give of her flesh, the heat of his fingers reaching.

His wickedness continued as he used the pad of his thumb on her clit.

Tap. The stretch eased as he pulled back.

Tap, tap on her clit. Filling and stretching as he eased in again.

Tap, tap, tap. Her clit plumped and strained toward the enticing pad of his thumb.

Press.

Press.

Hold. Her clit surged against his wicked thumb, her pussy clasped at his wicked fingers, and she exploded into a kaleidoscope of sensation.

She came with a wild scream. Her breasts swayed heavily, increasing the tension in her buck and lunge for more fingers, more thumb, more Nathaniel.

Her legs quivered as her scream died away, but he showed her no mercy. Delicious.

He slid face-up under the triangle she still presented.

From there he gave her dripping pussy deep, deep tongue, lapping and sucking all the juice that flowed from her.

She squatted over his face, feet deep in the soft mattress. Reaching around her back she found his rod, stiff as iron.

She let him bring her to one more orgasm while she pumped his cock, then scuttled back to his magnificent erection and slowly, agonizingly eased down on him.

He arched his back, strained up into her as she rode him wildly. Her ass rose and dropped. She felt the tickle of his coarse hair on her plumping clit, his pubis against hers. The slap of flesh to flesh echoed in her ears before she stiffened on him and raised both arms to ride out the wildest come she'd ever felt.

He joined her and tightened his grip on her hips to hold her.

"This!" she cried. "*This* is making love."

Shudders ran through her, her breath caught, and she rocked on his lap, squeezing every drop of spew from him.

"And I've never done it before," she said in a whispered confession that rocked her.

He sat up and enveloped her, held her close, and she went into his arms like a gentled bride.

They tipped their foreheads together. "Captain Jackson, I do hope you make an honest woman of me."

"In my heart, I already have. I love you, Felicity. I love the woman you've become and the vixen you can be."

"And I love you, you damnable, stubborn, beautiful man."

29

Faye woke with Liam's cock slamming into her as she rode out an orgasm so intense it ricocheted up through her chest and out the top of her head. Felicity and the Captain could really rock!

"Oh, Liam! You're incredible." Spasms rolled on in an exquisite delayed release. She must have fed several of the spirits with that one!

The thought brought another orgasm to life, roaring right on top of the last. She cried out again as Liam pressed, stiff and hard and huge inside her.

Heart pounding, she shuddered and shook as the spasms eased.

Liam rolled to his back to let her ride him. He grabbed her hips and lifted her just enough so he could pump and plunge and bounce her up and down.

She clasped his shoulders so he could move her as he wanted. She had no strength to move herself. He lifted her up and down, grinding his pubic bone against hers with every buck.

"I'm coming again!" Unbelievably, deliciously, coming

again. She threw her head back and rode it out. Her heart wanted to pound through her chest. Her legs went slack as her head swam and her vision blurred.

"Fuck me," he demanded, pulling her back to him, "I thought you fainted."

"Never!" Her inner walls clasped his massive shaft one more time as she milked him.

He jerked and jutted, hard, into her. Pulsing, he shot into her. The heat of his spew filled her and she gloried in the sensation as another come roared to life.

She followed it to the end and sagged onto his chest when the last tremors eased.

A chill passed through her and she burrowed into his hot, slick chest, loving the feel of his arms around her.

"You're a good man to have around, Liam Watson."

He chuckled and ran his fingers through her sweat-damp hair.

"I'll race you to the bathtub."

"You go ahead." She rolled off him and chuckled, her arm tossed across her eyes to avoid the bright sunlight streaming in from the french doors. "I'll be there in a minute. I have to catch my breath."

"I've got court this morning, so I need to get moving." He rose and left her to stretch in front of the french doors. "Otherwise, I would spend all morning with you." He patted his flat, naked belly, then scrubbed at his bed-head hair.

He was more than good to have around. The man was perfect. "I have a lot to do today, anyway. So if you stayed, you'd be on your own."

He chuckled and walked into the bathroom.

She spoke in her mind. "Belle, I know you're here. I felt you being greedy during my come."

Belle's voice entered her head. "You would begrudge me the only sensation I can still feel?"

"Of course not. But I don't know how much of this can I take without having a heart attack."

"Your Auntie Mae lasted into her eighties."

She popped her eyes open and whispered, too shocked to keep this conversation silent. "She had sex in her eighties, and you fed off it?"

"Kept a spring in her step." Belle's voice came from inside the wall over the headboard.

Faye chuckled. "Yes, I guess it would." She sobered when she thought of her dream. "Felicity's gone now and I didn't get to ask her about what Auntie Mae was trying to communicate."

"Do you honestly think Felicity would forget something as important as that?"

More guessing games. She ran through the dream again, quickly. No, she couldn't remember anything significant in Felicity's story that would relate to something Auntie Mae would want to tell her. Except maybe that there was a difference between hot sex and making love. Something Felicity took a long time to learn.

Her inner vamp thought Felicity had had a hell of a lot of fun before she settled on her captain.

"Hey," Liam called from the bathroom. "Who filled the tub? There wasn't any water in it when I came in here."

Oh shit. "Who was it?" she whispered harshly.

"Sorry, Faye, it was me," responded a feminine voice she didn't recognize.

"Who are you?"

"Stella. I was the midwife here." A tall redhead smoking a thin brown cigarette perched on the heavily carved fireplace mantel.

"You're one of the others?" She remembered now. Stella was the midwife who showed up in Felicity's story. She drove some kind of speedster and supplied Perdition House with cartons of rubbers. Just what every whorehouse needed.

"Yes, sorry about the bath water. I just wanted to help."

Liam strolled into the room, naked and gorgeous.

Belle and Stella winked out.

He hooked his thumb over his shoulder to indicate the steam drifting from the bathroom behind him. "It's time we had a talk."

Past time.

She'd often wondered how she would explain. A welcome flash came to her. "You thought you heard laughter in the trees that first time we jumped each other in the gazebo. Remember?"

He nodded.

"This is kind of the same thing." She bit her lip while he considered.

His eyes widened. "This place is haunted. There's too much weird shit going on for any other explanation."

She let her expression confirm it.

"Okay," he said. Then he turned and went back into the bathroom. He popped his head back in the doorway. "Does this have anything to do with my nightmares?"

"Probably."

He grinned. "Thought it might. Sooner or later, I'm going to figure them out." He went back to his morning routine.

Belle's chuckle distracted her. "Not only is Watson the Younger hung like a bull, he's also got a pretty fine backside," she commented with a smile of admiration. She hovered near the dresser, only visible from the waist up. "Not to mention his mind. The man's quite a catch."

"Could you fill out, please?" She moved her hand to show she needed to see Belle full size. When Belle obliged, Faye asked, "Why would he take this so calmly?"

Belle gave her a wide-eyed look of innocence. "For one thing, you handled him perfectly. By allowing him to think things through, you made each step to acceptance easier for him. I'm proud of you, Faye."

Nothing was ever this simple with Belle. "And?"

"The Watsons have a long history with Perdition." Belle faded to see-through.

"And?" She refused to let Belle off that easily.

"His grandfather was one of Mae's lovers."

A week later, Faye slid her printer into position under the cash desk. She took a moment to admire the completed window displays, the polished floors, and the new carpet by the fitting rooms, and enjoyed a comforting sense of accomplishment.

"Have you called the printers to see if the catalogues are ready?" she called to Kim at the back of the store. She wanted a stack for opening day.

"They'll be done by four." Kim responded from the changing rooms where she was checking the freshly installed lighting and making eyes at the electrician.

It seemed Kim enjoyed her erotic dreams. She'd taken to them with gusto. From mousy, quiet, and tentative, she'd gone to confident, sexy, and decisive in seven days. "I'm glad you went with full color glossy, Faye. We've got to catch people's eyes," Kim added, her voice fading.

The husky note Faye recognized as "come get me" said the electrician was going to be a happy man. She grinned, remembering how hot she'd been when the sexual tweaking was brand-new. Kim was going to enjoy these next few days.

Things had gone quiet in the changing room.

She turned to look. The curtain was closed but Kim's sneakers were snugged up tight between the electrician's work boots. She grinned. One of Kim's shoes lifted out of sight as she wrapped her leg around the man's hips.

She sighed. At least one of them was gettin' it on. She'd been so busy for the past week, Liam had taken her at her word when she said she needed to work twenty-four seven. Which was true. She'd hardly left the store.

But she missed him. Missed *that*, she thought with another quick glance at the booth. Her pussy twitched at the idea of the hunky electrician hip-deep inside Kim.

Kim had good taste—the man was built. There was something hot about a good-looking man in a tool belt.

Mark was due to arrive from Denver tonight, so at least she had a little something coming her way. The phone sex had been a fun stopgap measure but it didn't come close to the real man. Keeping Mark and Liam apart was going to be a problem. They were both excited about her store opening. She would have to think on her feet to stay ahead of them.

She was reaching for her purse so she could get a cappuccino next door when the shop door opened. In came a massive display of roses and lilies. Beneath the spectacular bouquet walked a pair of long, lean legs dressed in tan cords. "Liam! How sweet! Welcome to TimeStop 2."

He set the flowers on the counter and swept her into a hard embrace. His embrace wasn't the only hard thing she felt. She moistened immediately and pressed her soft parts against his hard.

"Oh! I'm happy to see you, too," she gasped as his hands crept to her ass and anchored her to his hips. "Your timing's incredible." She stretched up to whisper in his ear. "I'm so horny, I could bite you."

He answered with a kiss. Long, deep, and tantalizing, the kiss moved from *Hi, I've missed you* to *fuck me* in record time.

"Where can we go?" he asked, skimming her ass and the top of her thighs. Her legs opened, begging for more. Just a touch, a skim of fingers . . . anything would do.

She turned to lead him by the hand toward a fitting room.

"Oh, sorry, I think Kim's back there," she whispered. Damn, she was so hot she'd forgotten.

"Send her on an errand," he said and strode to the back booth before she could stop him. He lifted the curtain.

She bit her lip to keep from laughing.

The electrician had his head braced against the back wall, his eyes closed. His slack expression told of his pleasure. Kim squatted in front of his crotch, head bobbing. Licking, sucking sounds and quiet moans filled the booth. The muskiness of sex and need swirled around the pair, heightening Faye's need to desperation.

Liam dropped the curtain and nodded toward the store front.

They quietly edged away, grinning at the enthusiastic moans that emanated from behind the curtain.

At the front counter again, Liam hooked his thumb toward the changing room. "Known each other long?" His other hand smoothed her nipples into taut peaks.

"No." She grinned back at him and shrugged, patting his hard crotch. "Probably just a one-time thing." She lowered her voice. "Kim's dealing with a nasty break-up."

"She having dreams?"

"They started about a week ago. She wakes up flushed and pretty every morning. Her confidence has improved, especially in the store." She nodded toward the booth. A steady thudding from the back wall told them matters had progressed.

The bouquet caught her eye. A perfect distraction. "Thank you for the flowers. They're beautiful."

He cocked an eyebrow, but allowed the change of topic. "You're welcome."

She moved the vase off to the side of the counter under a display light to show off the gorgeous blooms to best advantage. The scent from the roses went to her head. "I love roses. Thank you."

"They'll need a few more minutes," he said. He opened the door for her. "And since we're not going to get any privacy, let me treat you to a coffee next door."

Settling in at an outside table, coffees in hand, he said, "You've been busy and the store's fantastic, but I've missed you like hell."

She slid her hand up his thigh. "You've missed this," she said lightly.

"More than you know, but it's beyond sex, Faye. I've missed your face." He tucked a stray strand of hair behind her ear. "Missed your laugh, your smile, knowing you don't think I'm a nut job for having these nightmares."

"I'd never think that. Besides"—she leaned in close so no one could overhear—"you're the one who's accepted my, ah, friends in the house." She patted his hand. She wanted to tell him Auntie Mae was probably the one giving him his nightmares, but she could be wrong. So far, letting him figure things out for himself had worked well, so why stop now? "Are the nightmares getting worse?"

"Not exactly." He ran his hand through his hair, took a sip of his coffee. "Today I woke up and understood what they mean. And who's giving them to me."

Their conversations lately had centered around the store opening and had left too little time for him. She'd been selfishly involved in the store. "Is it Auntie Mae?"

"Yes. She's tried to give me clues, but I couldn't make sense of them. They were disjointed, out of order. But once I understood that she loved my grandfather, the nightmares made sense."

She held her breath, suddenly afraid. She had no idea what message her Aunt would have for Liam. "Why didn't Auntie Mae come to me?"

"I think she realized Belle would get to you first. Your auntie wanted the house destroyed."

Aghast, she demanded, "Why?"

"She wanted to prevent something from happening. Now, I think she understands she has to let us figure it out for ourselves."

"What? What do we need to figure out? What do I need to do?"

"You need to choose."

"What do you mean?"

Liam studied her, his expression harder than she'd ever seen. "Faye, it's clear to me now. We've been having a great time: fun, fast sex whenever and wherever we wanted. But the dreams have shown me it's time we move on."

"You're tired," she said, feeling a constriction near her heart. "The nightmares have left you exhausted. When the store's up and running, we'll get away for a while. Get some perspective."

She didn't want him to move on. She wanted to keep what they had. She clasped his hand where it rested on the bistro table. "I don't understand," she said.

"I think you do." His serious gaze made her wary.

Faye helped Kim load the last of the inventory from the wardrobes in the attic into the little trailer she'd used to haul her belongings to Perdition.

"That girl must move a lot if she owns her own trailer," Belle whispered inside Faye's head.

Faye shrugged. "I'm glad we had use of your trailer, Kim. It's been useful to haul things to the store in batches."

Kim grinned. "I move a lot. Can't seem to settle down." She climbed into the driver's seat. "Hop in!"

Faye shook her head. "You go on. I'll be along shortly." She tossed her the keys to the store.

"But it's our grand opening!"

Faye grinned. "I trust you. You're the manager. Manage." She turned and headed back into Perdition.

She had a phone call to make.

She'd taken Liam for granted. His supportive phone calls, his helpful advice had simply been part of her life every day. Not only did Liam wear comfort, he *was* comfort.

With Mark in Denver, it had been easy to keep the men separate in her mind. In her heart. But it was wrong to string them along. She thought she could be blithe about her sexual needs and keep two lovers, but she couldn't. Not now.

Auntie Mae had made her point, awkward as it was.

"You haven't spoken to Liam since yesterday," Belle said.

"I know, I had to think," Faye said. "I called Mark's hotel last night and left a message for him to come here this morning. He'll be here in a while."

"I didn't know."

Faye turned to see her face. Searched it for any sign of a lie. "Are you saying I managed to keep my thoughts private?"

"I told you things take practice."

"But that was about Auntie Mae trying to make contact, not about me shielding my thoughts." All she'd done was focus inwardly.

Belle grinned like Belinda the Good Witch. "And that focus provided all the shield you needed."

She had her mind back. Her thoughts were her own again. Relieved tears threatened. She closed her eyes to savor the moment.

To have her private thoughts private, to control her own body, to know she was alone inside her own head. Oh! Heaven! "Does this mean what I hope it means?" She opened her eyes again.

"That we won't be able to share in your orgasms?"

"Or tweak my sex drive?" She'd miss that.

Belle smiled like a teacher on a favored pupil. "You're in control now, Faye. If you like the extra sex, why stop? If you like the dreams we give you, they'll continue." Belle patted her arm, sending a chill to her shoulder. "All you have to do is choose. We can be with you or not."

Choose. Mark or Liam?
Choose. Spirits or no spirits?
Choose, Faye, all you have to do is choose.

Faye sat on the window seat in the bedroom that used to be Annie's and watched the driveway. She tilted her head to the glass. Mark would be here soon and she still hadn't decided. The clock over the fireplace ticked away the seconds as she sat in quiet contemplation.

Choose.

Life could be like this forever. No one reading her thoughts, filling her tub with hot water, making her want sex to the point of rapacious need.

If she chose to end the dreams, all of the spirits would be on hold, while she lived out her life in peace.

So many of the women had sat watching the driveway, waiting. Annie for Matthew, Lizzie for Bart, Hope for Jed, and finally, Felicity for her captain.

And now, Faye waited for Mark. The agony of indecision tore at her. So much to think about.

Mark and Liam. Two great men any woman would want to keep.

The sun warmed the window seat and, for once, Faye knew no spirit would dare to enter her space and send a chill along her arms.

But they waited too.

The dozens of souls she was now responsible for.

It got so quiet she heard her lungs work and heart beat as she considered. Souls waited, lovers waited.

Auntie Mae had chosen to stop the dreams. That decision

had forced Hope, Annie, Lizzie, and Felicity to wait to join their men. But had that choice made Auntie Mae's life better?

She looked at the clock, saw the time had come and rose to head down to the veranda.

As she opened the front door, she heard a car come up the drive.

Mark.

Choose.

She felt the pressure from the spirits at her back, hovering, waiting. But these thoughts were hers to know, and she refused to share them with anyone but Mark.

An elegant Lincoln Town Car pulled up and Mark climbed out of the driver's seat. Tall, handsome, scowling.

"You need to trim back those cedar boughs. Scratched the paint." He looked at the front bumper. "Looks like shit now."

"You won't have to worry about it, Mark. We need to talk," she said.

A collective sigh of relief exploded out the door behind her and a sense of lightness and celebration lifted her heart.

"Is Faye at the store?" Stella settled into a wicker chair beside Belle on the side porch.

"Yes."

"Think it'll be enough to keep the house going?"

"Not according to that woman Willa."

"What will Faye do if Willa's right?"

"I've given that some thought." Belle smiled at her friend. "I think hosting parties could prove profitable."

"What kind of parties?" Stella's eyes went wide.

"The house was built for entertaining. Why not put Perdition to good use?"

"Oh! Those kinds of parties." Stella laughed. "Works for me."

"Before we go ahead, though, the house needs repair. Faye's

found problems with the wainscoting. I refuse to let the house look shabby when we invite guests."

Stella smiled in agreement. "I'm sure Faye will find the money for restoration somewhere. She's very resourceful."

Belle grinned slyly. "And I know just the man we need to call. He has a certain touch with restoration."

"Oh, sounds like fun."

"Yes, it will be."

"Explain," Faye demanded, afraid to hear Belle's idea. Then, Belle had been a successful businesswoman for decades. It was smart to tap into her experience.

Faye leaned her hip against the dresser and crossed her arms, feigning calm. Liam would be here soon and she was eager to see him.

Belle still hadn't explained, so Faye took a stab at it. "You mean sex parties. Like swinging couples, that kind of thing?"

She wouldn't know where to start to find enough people to make it pay. It wasn't like she could search the Internet with an ad that read: "Wanted: Couples to pay to come to my rickety old mansion for wild sex parties with the ghosts of prostitutes."

"No, that wouldn't do at all, although from what I gather, you'd get lots of response from this Internet you always think of," Belle said drily. "I want something more"—she tapped her chin while she groped for the word—"exclusive."

Exclusive meant expensive, expensive meant people with a lot to lose. People with a lot to lose meant the secret would be kept. "In the way you kept the house exclusive in the beginning."

"Oh! The quality of men we got was excellent. Politicians, police chiefs, captains of industry!" Her eyes shone with delight at her memories.

Faye had met some in her dreams. "I remember Felicity's senator."

Belle sat on the windowsill like a bird decked out in full plumage. A flush of excitement brought some pink to her cheeks. "This time out, our client base should be women. Wealthy women." She paused while Faye considered. "It's a grand idea, don't you think?"

"How did you come up with it?"

"I caught wind of bachelor auctions some time ago. Charities use them to great advantage. Marvelous idea, really."

"A bachelor auction!" Faye gasped. A babble of ideas flew at her from every direction. She closed herself off and her mind stilled. Now she could think.

"If we get the word out that our bachelors do more than go on dates," Faye said, we would attract major interest. "A lot of women are in high-powered positions with no time for romance." Faye knew some.

"We would, of course, need to restore the house to an appropriate level of opulence. Perhaps even do something with the grounds," Belle suggested.

"That'll take some time, but I agree." The new location looked to be a winner if opening day had been any indication. Interest was incredible.

"Any suggestions where to find these women?" Belle was a great idea woman, but her experience came from before instant communication.

Faye grinned. "In Hollywood, that's where. I already have tons of contacts through TimeStop. And there are a lot of lonely, wealthy movie stars who would appreciate discretion." She'd had an instinct about holding on to the acres of trees. Privacy at Perdition had always been important. Even more so now, with the paparazzi aiming telephoto lenses into celebrities' business. ·

Fresh ideas threaded through her mind. Giddy with excitement for the new plan, she was surprised when she heard a whistle from the driveway.

Liam!

She ran through to a front bedroom and opened the window. "Hey, big fella, looking for some action?" she called.

"You bet!" Liam laughed, his arms open wide.

"Meet me in the gazebo."

"A picnic! What fun," said Belle.

"Just like old times," Stella agreed. Miranda came and stood beside her.

Belle looked at Miranda's flour-covered apron. "This is a celebration, Miranda. Can't you dress for it?"

"It's not enough that I cooked all the food?"

Liam stood in the gazebo, hands on his hips, relaxed and laughing at the array of tables, chairs, and candelabra on the lawn. She needn't have worried—he looked delighted.

She crossed the lawn as her heart soared. He was so perfectly at ease amid the linen-covered tables and chairs.

A breeze lifted his hair, and set the linen to fluttering like swirling ball gowns.

He turned when he heard her approach and she walked into his open arms. His warm gaze heated her. "Mr. Watson, welcome to Perdition House. May we offer our hospitality?"

He hugged her close, then released her to walk to the Victrola set up on a stand. He cranked it and the tinny strains of a waltz rose through the air.

"May I have this dance, Miss Grantham?" He bowed and held out his hand to her.

She stepped into his arms and joined the other couples as they twirled and danced. The love they shared filled the gazebo and skipped through the trees that ringed the gardens.

From the corner of her eye she caught glimpses of Felicity, Hope, Annie, and Lizzie, as caught up in their men as she was.

"Do you see what I see?" Liam whispered, his voice throaty and hot next to her ear.

"I see love."

"Forever love. Like mine for you. That's what your auntie wanted to tell me."

"I know. She loved your grandfather but took another lover. He caught her with the other man, and couldn't forgive her." She didn't want Faye to make the same mistake she had. Faye blinked away tears of gratitude.

"You've chosen, then." Liam's eyes glowed so deeply she wanted to lose herself in them and never find her way out again.

"I love you, Liam Watson, and I will to the end of time."

Sample "A Taste of Honey,"
by Delilah Devlin, from WILD, WILD WOMEN
OF THE WEST.
On sale now!

Prologue

1880, West Texas

The wind whispered softly through the short, scrubby oak trees lining the creek, arriving at last at Honey Cafferty's back door where it tousled the hollow wooden chimes she'd hung above the stoop of the only home she'd ever known.

The sound, like half a dozen reed flutes, rose and fell with each stirring of the air, rousing her from her restless slumber. She'd opened the shutters of her windows in hopes of catching a breeze after the stifling white-hot heat of the day. As the warm air drifted over her moist skin, she sighed with relief and let herself drift back to sleep.

Then a scrape, like a footstep on sand, came from the side of her wagon. Honey jerked fully awake and snuck her fingers beneath her goose down pillow for the revolver that was never far from reach.

She eased up from her mattress, making sure she stayed away from the pools of silver moonlight that shone through her small windows, and peered around one casing, her pistol cocked and loaded, ready for whatever trouble awaited her outside.

She worried for the horses she'd tied to trees next to the shallow creek and wondered why they'd remained quiet. Someone was out there. She could feel it—and she never ignored the intuition her father had said was as much a part of her Irish heritage as her red hair, green eyes, and the touch of fey that kept her hitching her wagon to follow the stars.

A shadow passed in front of the window and another scuff sounded next to the door. She drew back, not wanting to act too quickly. The advantage would come when the intruder slammed through the back door expecting to find her groggy from sleep and unprepared.

Her eyes narrowed on the door and her arm descended, the butt of the pistol resting in one hand, a finger sliding around the trigger.

"I bring the plants you want," a raspy voice said from beside her, a round face resting on the windowsill like a disembodied head.

Honey stifled a shriek and lowered her weapon. "Señora Garza! Why didn't you call out to me? You scared me half to death."

"Girl like you shouldn't live in a wagon," the old woman groused. "You need ground beneath your feet, not wheels."

Ignoring the familiar complaint from her old friend, Honey grumbled, "I came by to see you today."

"I been walking in the hills. Found somethin' special for you."

Honey set down her pistol on the built-in dresser. "You didn't have to come all this way. You know I wouldn't leave without restocking my supplies and visiting a while."

The old woman's index finger appeared above the windowsill. "This is magic plant. Have to pluck at midnight on a full moon."

Honey tried one more time—she really did need the sleep. "It can't keep until tomorrow?"

"Gotta brew tonight. Fresh. Make very special medicine."

Honey groaned inwardly. The heat had sucked the energy right out of her, but she knew the *curandera* meant well. She believed in the magical properties of the plants she harvested. If brewing her potion by the light of the full moon kept the old woman happy, she wasn't going to complain. Señora Garza's "magic" kept them both fed and clothed.

"I build fire—you get dressed."

The *curandera* squatted in her brightly colored cotton skirt and busied herself uncovering the smoldering embers of Honey's campfire. While she blew on the coals and slowly added kindling to raise a flame, Honey slipped on a wash-softened pair of blue jeans, tucking in her shift, and tied back her hair. Although she would have liked to go barefoot to the fire, she slid on slippers, knowing scorpions might be about.

Stepping down the folding steps of her stoop, she shivered slightly at the hint of chill in the breeze—a reminder summer waned and soon she'd have to find a place to ride out the winter. Somewhere . . . needy. A quiet little town ready for a little shaking up and whole lot of her healing potions.

"So, what's so special about this medicine?" Honey asked as she drew near the crackling fire. "What will it cure?"

Señora Garza muttered a low incantation in an incomprehensible mix of Spanish and Comanche, her graying black braids swaying as she chanted. Honey's iron stew pot sat in the middle of the flames, filled with water that slowly burped as it started to boil. When she'd finished her "spell," Señora Garza smiled a wide toothless grin and dropped gnarled bits of roots into the water. "It no cure illness. It gives *fuerza* to a man's parts."

Honey shook her head, not understanding.

The old woman rolled her eyes. "His *cojones, mija*. Makes his *pinga* strong and virile."

Honey was glad the darkness masked the heat blooming on her cheeks. "What am I supposed to do with something like that?" She whispered fiercely, although no one else was around to hear their scandalous conversation. "Won't it cure a headache or settle a stomach, too? I can't tell decent folks it makes a man's . . ." She cupped her hand and made a gesture at the juncture of her thighs that indicated a lengthening cock. ". . . His . . . thing hard!" she sputtered. " 'Sides, who needs something like that?"

The old woman's shaggy eyebrows waggled and she laughed. "You tell the women what you have. They will buy."

Honey wasn't done with her tirade—the heat in her cheeks fueled a spirited anger that ripped right through her and settled as always on her tongue. "What the hell am I gonna call it?" Images of bottles labeled "Miracle Manhood Enhancer" and "Poker Potion" came to mind. *Jesus, Mary and Joseph!* She'd be run out of the next town—tarred and feathered for her licentious product.

"Easy, *mija*. Call it . . ." Señora glanced back with a wicked grin. ". . . Elixir of Love."

Honey sucked in a deep breath. It had a ring to it all right. "Elixir of Love," she repeated, liking the soft, romantic sound of it even more, now. She lifted her arms and practiced her slogan. "Cleopatra's secret weapon that captured the undying love and devotion of Caesar and Marc Antony."

The *bruja* snorted and started to cackle. "It no makes a man fall in love. Nothin' to do with the heart. Makes a man *horny*."

"Horny?"

"Builds his juices. Makes him feel like he will die if don't find a woman to—" She clapped her hands three times in rapid succession.

With a mortified blush heating her cheeks, Honey got

Señora Garza's meaning. However, "Elixir of Virility" was just too crass. "Elixir of Love" it would remain.

Nothing excited her like playing with her slogans. When her imagination was engaged, it seemed the sky was the limit for her ambitions. And she had big, brass-band-and-Fourth-of-July kinds of dreams. Someday, she'd have enough money saved up to build a house and get the kind of life she'd only seen from the top of her wagon seat as she rolled past the towns.

Her eyes widened with excitement. "I've got it!" She tilted back her head and raised her hands for dramatic flair. "Straight from the bazaars of Zanzibar—" That had a nice ring to it. She hoped like hell Zanzibar was somewhere near Egypt. "I bring you the very potion Cleopatra used to conquer Caesar." A very nice ring indeed!

Señora Garza's excited cackle rose like the twittering of a hoarse bird. "Only you be careful or you be the one who gets conquered, *mija*."

1

"Sheriff, you've gotta do somethin' about that woman!"

The note of exasperation in Curly Hicks' voice was one Joe Tanner had heard often in the past couple of days—at least from the unmarried men of the town. He didn't need to ask which woman he was talking about—he already knew who was responsible for Curly's agitation. Her name was on everybody's lips, although the tones with which her name was spoken varied widely.

He was curious what the normally reticent shopkeeper had to say about the lady in question. "Just what do you want me to do about her, Curly?"

"Send her packin'! She's up to somethin'. Cain't tell you 'xactly what, but ever since she came, nothin's been the same."

So, he wasn't the only one to notice. Since the day Honey Cafferty's fancy painted wagon had rolled into town, the mood around One Mule had seemed . . . expectant, like the town itself was wakening from a long slumber and suddenly discovering it was every joyful holiday all wrapped inside one bright, shining moment.

Which posed a dilemma for Joe. One Mule had elected him to keep the peace and things had been riding smooth like a Conestoga over flat land—no bumps, no bone-jarring thuds. So far, the townfolk had been pretty satisfied with their lives. It was a quiet place—the right kind of town to set down deep roots—and he intended to keep it that way.

However, Honey Cafferty had a way about her that was anything but quiet. She radiated a shimmering sensuality, from her vibrant red hair and cat-like green eyes to her lushly curved lips and body. Everything about her shouted like Fourth of July fireworks and crazily spinning whirligigs, eliciting a restless hunger in him that had no place in his tidy little life.

Just looking at the woman made his teeth ache, made him want to touch the fire he sensed smoldered just below the surface of her sweet-smelling peaches 'n' cream skin.

"Whatcha gonna do, Sheriff?"

Not what he really wanted to, that was for damn sure. "Has she committed a crime?"

Curly's cheeks reddened. "You're not list'nin' to me. Amos Handy didn't open his smithy shop 'til half past noon, yesterday. That ain't never happened before."

"Why do you think Miss Cafferty had something to do with that?"

"Amos's wife bought a bottle of her special ee-lixir the day before."

"So, you think Miss Cafferty poisoned Amos?"

"I'm not sayin' she did it on purpose, but Letty was sure lookin' happy when I came to see what was wrong. And you know that woman has the sourest disposition of any female this side of the Mississippi."

"What about Amos? Did he look like he was sickening?"

"Well, no. But he's mighty tired, he says. Said he was gonna close his shop for a couple of days—take a vacation. You ever heard such a load of horseshit in all yer born days?"

"Still don't see where Miss Cafferty fits in with all this."

"Sheriff, you need to open your eyes," Curly said, his own eyes bugging wide. "Look at all the married folk. The men are lookin' glassy-eyed and the women are hummin' like mosquitoes. I tell you, it's that woman's fault!"

"What about you, Curly? Do you have any complaints?"

"I'm plain tuckered out keepin' one step ahead of Sally. She's been tryin' to get me to stop by for her apple pie, but she has that look in her eye, again."

"Which one's that?"

"That marryin' look. The one what's got me too sceert to step outside her mama's parlor for a kiss. It might be all over for me," he said dolefully.

Joe suppressed a smile. Not that he blamed Curly for his skittishness. Despite his longing to set down roots, the thought of marriage made him itch, too. "Do you know anything about this special elixir the Cafferty woman's selling?"

"Nope. Soon as she sold her dyspepsia cures, she shooed the menfolk away for a private chat with the ladies. They sure as hell aren't talkin' about what she give 'em."

"Have you asked her straight out what she's been selling to the womenfolk?"

Curly's cheeks grew a fiery red. "I cain't do that, Sheriff," he said, his tone mournful. "I open my mouth to have my say, and all she has to do is aim those pretty green eyes my way and I'm meltin' like ice cream on a hot summer day. Before you know it, she's done sold me somethin' else I don't need!"

Joe pressed his lips into a straight line to keep from laughing. Yes siree! Looking into the woman's eyes did test the mettle of a man. If a man wasn't on guard against her charm, she'd tie his tongue in knots and swell his . . .

Best not let his mind head down that dusty trail. "Tell you what, Curly. I'll pay a visit to Miss Cafferty. See if there's anything to your story."

"Don't have to go out to her campsite. She's in the saloon, right now. That was the other thing I was gonna mention. No righteous woman like she claims to be oughta be rollin' on the floor of a saloon with Paddy Mulligan! It's just not seemly."

Joe stiffened. "She's in the saloon?" At Curly's solemn nod, he grabbed his hat and stomped out of his office onto the planked walkway, making a beeline for the Rusty Bucket. Miss Cafferty had seemed so coy, so modest, when he'd sold her the permit to solicit. She'd dressed in an outfit any Eastern-raised schoolmarm would have given the nod. He should have listened to his gut in the first place. No decent woman had ever made him so damn out of control. She was just like the rest of those independent-minded women who thought society's rules somehow didn't apply to them.

The red hair had been a bright glaring clue to her true nature—no matter that it was always neatly styled and pinned. She'd snookered him just like she had the rest of the townsfolk.

He slammed his palms against the swinging doors leading into the saloon and came to a halt. A ring of men filled the center of the room. Those on the outer perimeter stood on tiptoe to peer over the shoulders of the men standing at the center of the circle.

He elbowed his way inside and sucked a slow breath between his teeth to calm the anger that burned hot and fast as a match to gunpowder.

The sight that greeted him only raised the pressure pounding in his head another notch. The "shy and modest" Miss Cafferty straddled the barrel chest of the town drunk, her petticoats rising above her knees. Her woolen stockings hugged an expanse of ankle and calf that drew every male eye watching her wrestle the behemoth.

Paddy Mulligan groaned beneath her, sounding like a cross between a drunken bear and a man in the last throes of lust. Given his sorry state, Joe suspected his moans were due more to the heat from the woman's open legs rubbing his wide belly and her bottom bumping his private parts than the wicked set of shiny pliers she had shoved inside his mouth.

Joe's own body reacted swiftly, urgently. That was the last damn straw! "Woman, what the hell do you think you're doing?"

Honey Cafferty blew an errant curl of flaming-red hair from her eyes. "Not now," she said, not looking away from Paddy's tonsils. "Now Paddy, if you'd let me give you my special painkiller first—"

"Smelled like skunk fart," one of the men in the circle said. "Don't blame him for refusin'."

"Shoulda just let him get drunk first," another said.

"Drinking spirits makes a man bleed faster." Honey muttered and twisted her wrist, eliciting a strangled groan from Paddy.

"Yeah, but then he wouldn't give a damn," said the bartender, who stood with his arms folded over his chest, a glower darkening his usually jovial face.

"Someone's standing in my light," Honey said and looked over her shoulder. When she caught sight of Joe, her eyes blinked and she gave him a weak smile. "If you'd just shift to your left, Sheriff, I'll be done with this extraction in just a minute."

Joe's eyes narrowed, but he moved sideways, taking a deep breath to calm the fury building inside him. He'd bide his time for now, but he and the little "lady" were gonna have a talk.

Her hand twisted again, and Paddy's eyes rolled back in his head.

"Thank the Lord, he passed right out," said the bartender, looking as pale as a ghost.

Both Honey's hands wrapped around the pliers and she leaned back. Everybody drew a deep breath and more than one man's face winced as she yanked a blackened tooth out of Paddy's mouth.

"Got it!" She raised it high for everyone to see. "When he wakes up, he'll feel so much better."

She plucked the tooth off the end of her pliers and tucked it inside Paddy's shirt pocket. Then she reached for a tapestry carpet bag lying on the floor beside her. She pulled out a small folded paper and poured a rough yellow-brown powder into her palm, then packed the powder into the bleeding hole she'd left in Paddy's gum. "That should stop the bleeding and help him some with the pain."

She wiped her hands on a bar towel, and then clambered off his chest and smoothed down her skirts, pulling her cuffs back down her forearms, cool as a cucumber, while the crowd of fascinated men watched her put herself to rights.

Joe had no doubt that every man there was reversing the process in his mind. His cock surged again against the placket of his trousers, which only made him madder.

When she finished, she flashed a bright smile. "Now, if anyone else has trouble with an aching tooth, you know who to come to."

There were a lot of heads shaking and low mutters among the men. However reluctant they might be for a visit from her plier-wielding hands, half a dozen men still reached down to pick up her bag.

"Thank you, gentlemen. I'll leave you to your business."

The crowd parted like the Red Sea for Moses, and she sailed right through, brushing past Joe with a ladylike nod.

He clamped his jaw tight and turned to follow her out the doors. On the planked sidewalk, he caught her arm. "Now, wait a minute there. You and I are gonna have us a little talk."

"Oh? Do you need a tooth pulled, too?" she said, a smile tugging the corners of her lips.

He narrowed his eyes. She wasn't wriggling her way out of this with charm. A quick glance behind them, and he realized the swinging doors were open and the men had spilled onto the walkway to watch them.

All he needed now was for a few of that beer guzzling crowd to decide a rescue was in order. "You're coming to my office."

"Anything you say," she said, her voice soft and a little breathless.

Her feminine tone had his loins tightening again, and he dropped her arm like he'd touched a red-hot poker. Hectic color rose on her cheeks and her gaze widened as she stared up at him. She was starting to look worried, which suited him just fine.

Extending his hand in front of him, he let her precede him down the walkway. She took a deep breath, lifted her chin, and glided down the sidewalk like she owned it.

A breeze caught her light rosewater scent and wafted it right under his nose. Without her gaze keeping his appropriately engaged, he was free to look his fill—and he did, his glance sliding down the slim straight line of her back to the flare of the womanly hips that twitched from side to side. It was all he could do not to reach down and adjust the front of his trousers.

They passed the front of Curly Hicks' store and several interested gazes followed. At the doorway, Mrs. Sessions, the preacher's wife, gave Honey a wide, beaming smile.

Honey shook her head and murmured, "Not now, Daisy. The sheriff wants a word with me."

Daisy Sessions' gaze landed on him and two round spots of color rose on her cheeks. "Later then, my dear."

Odd, but the woman looked flustered, almost guilty.

Finally, they reached his office and Honey breezed inside. He closed the door behind him and turned to find more faces peering through the window. He cursed under his breath and pointed to the inner room where the jailhouse was.

Her back stiffened, but she didn't demur and stepped inside. When he had her out of sight and hearing of all the interested folk of One Mule, he lifted a foot and nudged the door closed behind them.

Honey had her back to him and her slim hand lifted to smooth back her hair.

He stayed silent, deciding to let her stew for a minute. When a body got nervous, she tended to talk and Joe wanted to hear everything the little lady had to say.

At last, she cleared her throat and turned, a small, tight smile pasted on her lips. "Am I under arrest, Sheriff?"

"Should you be?"

Her breath gasped, lifting her gently rounded chest against her staid gray shirtwaist jacket. "You're angry with me."

He crossed his arms across his chest and leaned his back against the door and tried not to think too hard about the fact they were completely alone. A tantalizing prospect he'd imagined often the past couple of days.

As he watched her standing in the narrow, darkly lit room with the bars of the cell block behind her, his imaginings became disturbingly carnal. He cleared his throat and forced his mind back to business. "I sold you a license to solicit your medicines," he said, keeping his voice even although the memory of her straddling Paddy Mulligan still burned hot. "Yet I found you rolling on the floor of a saloon performing surgery."

She gave a short, strained laugh. "I wasn't rolling on the floor—Paddy's a large man and I couldn't see into his mouth when he was seated. Besides, I only pulled a tooth. I do have some expertise—"

"I'm getting complaints about possible poisonings—"

"Poison!" Her finely arched brows rose. "I don't deal in poisons, sir."

"Then explain why all the married men in town have taken to their beds."

She opened her mouth, but quickly clamped it shut. Her back straightened.

"You don't deny you're responsible?"

A blush the color of the pink roses his mama used to grow spread quickly across her cheeks and down her neck to disappear beneath her collar. "It's not what you think, Sheriff."

He wondered if the blush extended to her breasts, but didn't dare let his gaze fall below her rounded chin. "Then tell me exactly what it is."

She lifted that stubborn chin high. "I can't. That information is privileged. Meant to remain private between me and the persons I sold the medicine to, like a priest receiving confessions or a doctor—"

"You're no doctor. Those rules don't apply."

"Have you talked to these men? Have any of them made complaints against me?"

"No, but you're up to something, and I don't want any trouble." And she was trouble with a capital T. "I'm thinking you should hitch up your wagon and head on down the road."

She blinked and, for a moment, her expression faltered. "I had hoped to winter here. Mrs. Sessions—"

"—is an innocent lady. She's not wise to your ways."

Her stillness cut him, and he felt heat warm the back of his neck and the tips of his ears. He'd crossed the line between being professional and being cruel.

Then her chin jutted higher, and her hands fisted on her hips. "You're implying I'm not . . . innocent?"

His gaze swept over her, from the tip of her red-haired head to her toes. Another insult. He couldn't seem to help himself where she was concerned. Something about her had him firing with both barrels blazing. "You travel alone—without chaperone. What's a man supposed to think about that?"

She took a step closer, her eyebrows drawing together in a fierce scowl. "Being alone in the world means I'm a whore?" she said, her voice rising.

"A decent woman," he bit out, "would set roots in a community—seek help and protection from a husband or her neighbor."

"I don't need any man to protect me or my virtue, sir."

"I'll grant you had me and most of the town fooled. But your charm's a little too practiced, and you've got a slick tongue—"

Her mouth gaped and her cheeks went from pink to a dark red that clashed with her bright hair. "A slick tongue?"

Her anger goaded him on like a burr under a saddle. "You're a snake oil salesman, a charlatan—"

She stepped so close her chest nearly touched his, and she glared up into his face. "Now, you look here, buster!" she said, pointing a finger at his chest and giving him a nudge. "I'm a business woman. I sell cures people need. I haven't broken any laws, and I sure as hell haven't poisoned one damn person in this town." She paused to catch her breath . . . and that's when it happened.

Her breasts brushed his chest, and he felt a spark arc between their bodies, igniting a fire as fierce as lightning striking dry prairie grass. It filled his loins with a heavy, pulsating heat and drew his balls tight and close to his groin. His hands shot out and grasped her shoulders to pull her flush against his body, but he halted, holding her an inch away. What he wanted of her wasn't very civilized. Best not cross that line.

"Sheriff!" Her plump pink lips gasped, but her head tilted back.

Invitation enough. He slammed his mouth down onto hers even while he damned himself for being a fool.